Louise Fuller was once a t[...] pink and always wanted to [...] Princess! Now she enjoys creating heroines who aren't pretty push-overs but strong, believable women. Before writing for Mills & Boon she studied literature and philosophy at university, and then worked as a reporter on her local newspaper. She lives in Tunbridge Wells with her impossibly handsome husband, Patrick, and their six children.

Clare Connelly was raised in small-town Australia among a family of avid readers. She spent much of her childhood up a tree, Mills & Boon book in hand. Clare is married to her own real-life hero, and they live in a bungalow near the sea with their two children. She is frequently found staring into space—a surefire sign that she's in the world of her characters. She has a penchant for French food and ice-cold champagne, and Mills & Boon novels continue to be her favourite ever books. Writing for Modern is a long-held dream. Clare can be contacted via clareconnelly.com or at her Facebook page.

A CONSEQUENCE CLAIMED

LOUISE FULLER

CLARE CONNELLY

MILLS & BOON

First published in Great Britain 2025
by Mills & Boon, an imprint of HarperCollins*Publishers* Ltd,
1 London Bridge Street, London, SE1 9GF

www.harpercollins.co.uk

HarperCollins*Publishers*, Macken House, 39/40 Mayor Street Upper,
Dublin 1, D01 C9W8, Ireland

ISBN: 978-0-263-34459-2

04/25

This book contains FSC™ certified paper
and other controlled sources to ensure responsible forest management.

For more information visit www.harpercollins.co.uk/green.

Printed and Bound in the UK using 100% Renewable Electricity
at CPI Group (UK) Ltd, Croydon, CR0 4YY

NINE-MONTH CONTRACT

LOUISE FULLER

MILLS & BOON

CHAPTER ONE

HARRIS CARVER STARED down at his phone, his stomach clenching around a knot of frustration and disbelief. The voice message from Sydney Truitt, the hacker he'd employed to find his intellectual property on Tiger McIntyre's server, was short and to the point.

'Sorry. *I failed.*'

Her voice sounded as tense as he felt but then she had just waved goodbye to a life-changing amount of money. But that had been the deal. No IP, no fee.

His IP. The schematics for a drill bit that Tiger had stolen from him to make his own prototype. He felt his shoulders and spine tense, his frustration giving way to an old, familiar anger that accompanied any mention of his greatest rival.

Tiger McIntyre.

They could have been allies. They had been best friends at university.

Growing up with half-siblings who had both their parents on site, he'd always felt like an inconvenience, a burden. An outsider. But he and Tiger had the same interests, the same determination to succeed. They'd been like brothers.

Or so he'd thought until he'd caught Tiger with *his* girlfriend.

He'd been nineteen, raw with jealousy, drunk on the pain of their betrayal, so of course he'd hit him. Tiger wasn't called

Tiger for no reason so naturally he'd hit Harris back and the whole thing had escalated. The dean had got involved, and Tiger had kicked off again and then been kicked out.

Since then, everything they had planned had come true. They were business rivals now and like two apex predators they circled one another, keeping their distance but always aware of the other's movements. That had been bearable until Tiger stole from him. He always had people keeping a close eye on his biggest rivals and the drill-bit prototype sounded near identical.

His hand tightened around the phone. He had been livid, a mindless fury that blunted all reason or calm. On some pretext of wanting to upgrade his security systems, he had got his people to reach out to a hacker: Sydney.

But in reality, he was looking for revenge. Sydney, or rather her feckless brothers, needed money and so he'd offered her a temptingly large enough sum to hack Tiger's system and find his IP.

He'd planned to ruin Tiger by revealing the theft but now he had nothing. No proof. No means of revenge.

Outside, a quarter moon seemed to sneer down at him, and he stared at it furiously, reminded as always of his father's blank, uncomprehending face when he looked at Harris. As if he were talking to a stranger rather than his son.

At the time, his degree and subsequent career path hadn't felt like a conscious choice, but he could admit now, to himself at least, that it had been partly driven by a hope that it would bring him closer to his astronaut father.

It hadn't.

His father had been interested in the science and the engineering but not proud or happy that his son had chosen to follow obliquely in his footsteps.

He stared across the room at where the rain was running

down the windows. It made him feel as if he were drowning and, abruptly, he got to his feet.

What he needed was to get out of this apartment, out of Manhattan and go find a woman who, like him, was looking to lose herself in the white heat of an anonymous one-night stand.

It took ten minutes for him to pull on some jeans and a T-shirt and a battered leather jacket that he'd loved the hell out of five years ago right before his business had taken off into the big time.

He caught the subway downtown. By the time he emerged back at street level the rain had slowed to a light drizzle. As he slipped out of the side entrance to his building, he started walking. He had no idea where he was going but it felt good striding down the sidewalk without the shadow of his security detail. It would mean a ticking-off later, but he was the boss and, for what he had in mind, two was company, anything more would be a crowd. Besides, the risks of anyone recognising him were low. It wasn't as if he were a movie star.

Not that he didn't get his fair share of female attention.

More than fair, he thought, as he sidestepped past a couple of women who both glanced over at him in unison like synchronised swimmers, their eyes narrowing approvingly, mouths curving into smiles that made his pulse beat harder.

They were beautiful, but it was too easy, he thought as he carried on walking. What he wanted was friction. Something that would chafe and burn a little, just enough to give him something to focus on other than the pain and frustration in his chest.

His footsteps faltered.

In the weeks that followed he would wonder what made him stop.

From the outside, the bar wasn't promising. Or visible, in

fact. The door was down a flight of stairs and there was no name above it, which was why he had almost walked straight past. But then he'd heard it, a faint but steady bassline pulsing in time to his heartbeat.

He doubled back and ran lightly down the stairs. As he pulled open the door, the sound and heat hit him like a wall.

The bar was rammed.

At one end of the room a hen party wearing sashes and devil horns were shrieking and giggling around one of those old-fashioned jukeboxes. There was a huge TV screen on the other side of the bar, and a large group of mostly men were gazing up at the two boxers slugging it out. Of course, it was the heavyweight title fight tonight. No wonder it was so packed in here.

It was perfect. All of it. The noise, the smell of hot, excited bodies and cheap alcohol, and, best of all, nobody knew him. Here in this downtown bar without a name, there were no pasts or futures, just a present filled with possibility.

He hesitated for a moment and then he joined the swaying, sweaty throng of people waiting for a drink. At this point in his life, that was a novelty. He couldn't remember the last time he'd waited for anything. When you were as rich as he was, there was never any waiting. Doors opened; tables magically un-booked themselves. There was always a car or a jet on standby.

'Excuse me—'

He moved aside automatically to let the woman pass, his brain carrying out a silent but thorough inventory. Petite. Brunette. Smokey eyeshadow and nude-coloured lips. Small, heeled boots and a sleeveless floral dress that made him think of the last days of summer, and last, but registering loudly in his mind, a tiny tattoo on her shoulder of an apple with a bite taken out.

She turned. 'So, what do you want to drink?'

Her voice was light and husky and at first he didn't realise she was talking to him. He was too busy trying to place her accent—she was American but there was a hint of something else, English maybe?

But then he felt the pull of her gaze, and the pounding music seemed to skip a beat as their eyes connected.

Hers were green and narrowed like a cat's, and impatient, he realised with a jolt as his gaze snagged on her soft pink mouth or, more specifically, on that kissable, full lower lip, which was curved up questioningly in his direction.

He felt it jerk him forward like a fisherman's hook. *You*, he thought, *I want you*. His pulse was vibrating violently, and his breath felt hot and dry as if his chest were a furnace. His first thought was outrage that she could do this to him, and so effortlessly. And he almost wanted to punish her for making him feel so out of control and unlike himself.

Only wasn't that exactly who he wanted to be tonight?

Yes. But in his head, he'd thought it would be more transactional. More you scratch my itch and I'll scratch yours. Sex as a balm. An analgesic to soothe the chaos inside his head. But this woman was already kicking up sparks and overturning tables.

He cleared his throat. 'You want to buy me a drink?'

She shrugged. 'You look thirsty, and I'll get served before you do so I thought I'd offer but if you're happy to wait—'

Good luck with that, he thought as she ducked under his arm. She only came up to his shoulder so the chances of her attracting the barman's attention were zero whereas he—

'A San Alvaro. And a shot of Coughlan.'

She didn't raise her voice, but he felt the huskiness in all the right places. The barman seemed to as well, stopping in his tracks as if he'd been shot with a stun gun.

The woman glanced back at him. 'Last chance.'

His fingers twitched as something charged shimmered in the air between them.

'I'll have what you're having,' he said.

She rocked back on her heels, that green gaze skimming over him assessingly—critically, he realised. And that was not so much a novelty as it was a challenge.

'Make that two of those.' She had turned back to the bar, and he took the opportunity to admire the mass of dark silky hair that clung damply to her shoulders. And to imagine what she would look like wearing nothing but those boots.

His skin felt hot and taut and, blanking his mind, he shifted his stance. 'Are you celebrating?'

Her face stilled a fraction. 'No, I just need to cut loose.'

From what? Or who? As if he had spoken those questions out loud, she turned. Her mouth pursed in a way that made him lose his bearings momentarily, as if it were him who had been cut loose.

'It's been one of those weeks, you know?'

He did. Rarely had things gone so off-piste for him. 'Will next week be better?'

She seemed surprised by the question or his interest, and he was surprised too because he wanted to hear her answer. Wanted to keep her talking.

'Yes.' She nodded, but there was a vulnerable slant to her gaze that pulled at something inside him because he understood the need to hide weakness or doubt.

'Let me get them.' He leaned forward but she was already holding out her phone to pay.

'It's done.' Her eyes met his and he felt the challenge there like a lick of flame. 'Here.' She handed him the bottle and the shot glass. She had small, slim fingers and her hair wasn't uniformly dark but threaded through with reds and golds.

Her skin was gold too and so smooth it looked as if it had been poured over those curving cheekbones.

'Then let me get the next round,' he said, his body moving closer to her of its own accord.

Her lips parted to show small, white even teeth and she stared at him for a moment, her chin tilted up. 'You don't need to do that. I'm not keeping a tally.'

'Maybe you should.'

Her eyes were very green then and his pulse jumped for no reason as she held his gaze.

'Fine, I'll keep a tally and when I've made up my mind what I want, I'll let you know,' she said in that husky way of hers that made his body feel loose and restless and yet tenser than he had ever felt.

'See you around,' she said abruptly and before he could respond, she had melted into the crowd. After a moment, he shrugged mentally and made his way over to the group of men gazing up at the screen.

An hour later he was still gazing at it. He liked sport, but his mind wasn't really on the match. It was stuck, like a stylus skipping in a groove, endlessly replaying that moment when the petite brunette with the dare in her green eyes had spun on her heels and left him standing there.

See you around, she'd said. But where was around? His eyes scanned the bar again as they'd been doing roughly every five minutes since she'd walked away from him.

But there was no sign of her.

His fingers tightened around the bottle. He could have settled for another woman. More than half a dozen had brushed against him as they'd walked past. Others had stood nearby with their friends, laughing in that way women did when they wanted you to look at them.

Only he didn't want what they were offering. Without his

permission, everything inside him seemed to be interested in just one woman.

One of the boxers, the reigning champion, lunged forward, and there was a roar of approval from the spectators as the contender stumbled backwards. Watching the boxer crumple, he felt a surge of animalistic satisfaction, gratification almost, but it wasn't enough.

And then he felt it.

Cool, concentrated, intent. Seeking him out. A tractor beam, except they didn't exist outside science fiction. No, this was like the gravitational pull of the moon on the sea. Or perhaps it wasn't, he thought as he turned around. Perhaps it was something that had less to do with physics and more to do with biology.

She was standing by the door, her green eyes fixed on his face. Not just standing. She was watching. Waiting. For him.

He felt suddenly untethered. Unbalanced.

Earlier, he'd thought he wanted a distraction. Not any more. Now he wanted to focus. On her. To feel her body against his, beneath his. He wanted the frenzy and release that touching her, kissing her, possessing her, would bring.

His breath floundered in his throat, hot and heavy like the blood stumbling in his veins, and the noise in the room faded as it all gave way to the pounding of his heart.

For a moment, he couldn't move, and then he was shouldering his way through the crowd, stopping just far enough away from her to make it impossible for him to give into that wild, nearly ungovernable urge to pull her against his body and take what he wanted from her mouth.

'I've made up my mind,' she said slowly, and there was a hoarseness to her voice that he felt everywhere. 'I know what I want now.'

His mouth was suddenly dry. She was talking about a

drink, obviously. Except that he knew she wasn't. Only he needed to hear her say it.

He met her eyes. 'Same as before?'

For a moment, she didn't reply, and he felt a flicker of panic that he had misunderstood, but then she took a step backwards and pushed open the door.

'Let's get a room.'

It was an invitation or a dare. Maybe both. Either way it didn't matter, because the answer was yes, and, heart thudding against his ribs, he reached for her hand.

Eden felt the floor shudder sideways beneath her feet as he took her hand. His fingers were warm, his grip firm and the calloused skin on the palm made her blood race through her limbs as they left the bar.

Outside it was raining hard. People were running for the subway, sidestepping puddles and clinging to their hoods. But she barely registered it.

Since walking into the bar earlier, she had barely registered anything.

Except him.

She had noticed him straight off. Wanted him too. Who wouldn't?

He looked older than her, early thirties maybe, and he was tall and broad and blond. Not the Nordic kind of blond. His hair was the colour of ripe wheat and early morning sunlight and the palest acacia honey.

But it wasn't just his blondness or his height or the breadth of his shoulders. He had been scanning the bar, and there was something about his intense concentration and his stillness and the latent power beneath that stillness which reminded her of some gorgeous, sleek predator.

Because obviously, he was also immoderately and shockingly gorgeous.

His face was a masterclass in scale and symmetry. And there was something about the shape of his skull.

She wasn't an artist, but she had watched her mother and grandmother sketch and paint most days and she knew what beautiful bone structure looked like. And this man had beautiful bones. *Beautiful everything*, she thought. He turned to look at her, his slate-coloured eyes fixing on her face as he pulled her underneath a shop awning, pressing her body up against his and fitting his mouth to hers.

Her belly clenched as he parted her lips and deepened the kiss and it stunned her, the rawness of his desire, his hunger. And hers.

It was hot and mindless, and she forgot they were in the street and that it was raining and she didn't know his name because, whatever it was he was doing with his mouth and hands, it felt as if he was claiming her. Reminding her that she was his.

He drew back and stared down at her for so long she couldn't breathe. And then he took her hand and began leading her back the way they had come.

She felt a rush of panic. Had he changed his mind? Her fingers tightened around his, pulling down hard—

He stopped and turned.

'What are you doing?' she asked.

He frowned. 'I need to go to the drugstore. I don't have any condoms.'

'That's fine. I have some.' She opened her purse and their eyes met as she thrust one into his hand.

'There's a hotel back there on the corner. I saw it when I walked by. They might have a room,' he said finally and the hunger in his voice made her breath go shallow.

She stared at him, shivers of anticipation dancing over her skin. She had walked into the bar to get out of the storm. But there was a storm in his eyes that she wanted to hurl herself into.

It had been such a difficult week, and it was a good thing that people saw only the face she chose to present to the world. None of the emotion she was feeling had been visible, which was lucky because inside everything had been a howl of chaos. Like a tornado in a jar. They had made one once at school and for a short while she had been fascinated and excited by the power she'd had to turn the still, clear liquid into a swirling maelstrom.

Only it felt different when someone else held that power in their hands. A power to turn your life upside down. What made it worse was that she was supposed to be over Liam. And she was. Even if he offered her the moon, she wouldn't take him back, but there was a part that felt connected to him still. To what they'd had.

What she had lost.

He shouldn't have texted her.

She shouldn't have read the text. Or looked at the accompanying photo. Had he no heart?

Stupid question, she thought, remembering Liam's handsome face and the confident gaze that had seemed to rest on her so approvingly back then. He had no heart. He was like the Tin Man, except he didn't want to change. Which was why he could send a photo of his new baby to the woman he'd lied to. The woman who had loved him and miscarried his child shortly before he'd broken up with her.

It was too late for regrets. Except apparently it wasn't, so for days now, she had been teetering on a ledge, swamped by a need that she couldn't control.

Her eyes moved to the man staring down at her.

But he could.

He could quiet this chaos beneath her skin.

She reached up and touched his shirt, too scared to touch his skin in case it lit the touchpaper beneath hers, but still needing to feel him.

'Yes,' she said, and he took her hand and they started to run.

The hotel did have rooms. The receptionist on the front desk seemed unfazed by their lack of luggage but then this was New York in the fall. Probably loved-up couples were constantly tumbling through the doors like autumn leaves.

Not that they were in love. This was purely about sex and that was exactly what she needed it to be about.

She watched as he pressed the keycard against the lock, on the door to their room. *Their* room.

As if *they* were a couple.

The weird thing was that it did feel as if they were. The moment their eyes had met back in the bar; it had felt as though he could see through her armour. See past the small, taunting smile and the glitter of her green eyes. It felt as if he saw her, knew her. Or maybe it was that he wanted to know her, know everything about her, and she had a sudden, ludicrous urge to lay out all her secrets before him.

Even just thinking that might happen should have sent her running back down the stairs and through the hotel foyer and out into the street because she had never felt this way. Normally, she was clear in the moment. Her motives were simple. It was just sex for the sake of pleasure and to feed that human need for intimacy in bite-sized portions.

Her hand moved to touch the apple on her shoulder.

A bite, that was what she wanted, all she could contemplate.

But this felt different.

'Have you changed your mind?' His voice snapped her thoughts in two and she turned to look up at him. In the half-light of the hallway, his beauty should have been lost to her, but it wasn't. If anything, the shadows seemed to highlight the flawless contours of his face.

'No.' She shook her head, and he pushed open the door for her to step into the room.

It was small but clean with just three pieces of furniture. A mirrored dressing table, a chair and a bed. But that was all they needed.

She heard the door close, and turned to face him. For a moment or three, they just stared at one another. Then he took a step forward, his arm sliding smoothly round her waist, and, tipping her face up to his, he kissed her.

It was like the Fourth of July.

She moaned against his mouth, her hunger for him beating hard in her blood. His taste was making her dizzy. Nothing to do with the whisky. She could taste his need for her, and it was intoxicating. He felt incredible. Hard and smooth, and she wanted to feel more. He clearly did too because his hands were moving over her urgently, taking a path that was as tortuous as it was potent.

Shivery pleasure danced across her skin, and she arched helplessly against his body, her hips meeting his, nipples hardening as they grazed his chest.

She began pulling at the waist of his jeans, clumsily, her fingers urgent but ineffectual, and he made a noise in his throat. Wrenching his mouth away, he yanked his T-shirt over his head, then unbuttoned his jeans and pushed them down his thighs in one smooth movement.

There was a beat of silence, pure and stunned like a ray of moonlight hitting glass.

She felt her face still, knew that he must be able to see her reaction and tried to turn her head to compensate, but she couldn't look away. She didn't want to because he looked even better than he felt.

Heat, liquid and electric with currents that moved in sharp, expansive ripples, was pooling between her legs, and she could feel a pulse leaping erratically in the hollow on the left side of her throat.

Better was an understatement.

She breathed out unsteadily, her gaze pulling with magnetic force to where the thick swell of his erection was pressing against the fabric of his boxer briefs, and then her heartbeat shuddered sideways as he tugged them down too, letting them fall to the floor.

Yes.

Yes.

Yes.

The word blinked inside her head three times like the lights on a fruit machine. *Jackpot.*

He was definitely a prize, she thought, stepping forward and running her hands over his chest, drunk on the feel of the hard, smooth muscles. And for one night only, he was hers.

All of him, every glorious, *naked* inch.

She licked her lips.

He had the most incredible body. It made her feel… Actually she had no idea how to describe what she was feeling, but it wasn't just his body. It was the way he was looking at her. The intensity of his eyes.

'I want to see you naked,' he said hoarsely, his breath hot against her mouth, his fingers pulling at the buttons of her dress. Which was what she wanted too, and yet—

Her body gave a silent yowl of protest as she pulled back. 'No, not like this. I want you to watch me undress.'

His pupils flared and a muscle jumped in his jaw. *Better,*

she thought. She wanted him to watch, to wait, to want her as much as she wanted him.

He stared at her in silence as she stepped backwards, small, slow, steady steps, *impressively steady*, she thought, given that she knew how it felt to have his mouth and body fitted against hers.

It felt as if his dark grey gaze had already stripped her naked. His expression was hard and unfathomable but his eyes, they were molten heat, and she felt a corresponding heat bloom low in her pelvis.

Head spinning, she pulled at the buttons of her dress, feeling his gaze, his intense focus and the flutter of the fabric against her bare thighs as it slithered to the floor.

He said nothing, did nothing, just stared at her, but that muscle was pulsing in his jaw again and there was a dark flush along his cheekbones that made her belly clench.

No one had ever made her feel like this, helpless and out of her comfort zone but also hungry and strong and demanding. It was so confusing, without precedent, but it felt right, she felt right. With him, she was the woman she wanted to be, the woman she had lost somewhere along the way.

Her fingers reached behind her back to unhook her bra and that soon joined her dress. Now he moved, walking slowly but purposefully towards her, his eyes not leaving hers, all smoke and shadow, so that it felt as though they were puncturing her skin, and yet it also didn't feel real. It was as if she were dreaming...

He stopped in front of her.

'I've got it from here,' he said then and she jolted back to him, feeling the authority in his voice like flames licking her body. His mouth found hers again, his hands were on her waist, and his body was hot and hard against her. Blood roared in her ears, and she felt her belly flip as he lifted her hair away from her neck and kissed a path down her throat, then lower to the swell of her breasts. His lips closed around first one, then the other nipple and she arched against him, lost in the sensation of his open mouth and his tongue and his warm breath and the heat of his body.

He moved closer again, close enough for her to feel the insistent press of his erection against her stomach, and she felt an answering wetness between her thighs.

As if he could feel it too, one hand slid down her body, over the curve of her waist, and her breath fluttered in her throat as his fingers pushed under the waistband of her panties, inching down—

They stilled and she almost cried out in her frustration and then he moved his hand to part her thighs, pushing gently into the slick heat. His thumb grazed the hardened bud of her clitoris and she leaned into him blindly, her mouth seeking his, her hand reaching for the thick length of his erection to steady herself.

Her fingers tightened infinitesimally around him. He felt amazing. Hard and solid, with a life force that beat through the palm of her hand in time to the stampeding of her heart.

He grunted, and she felt his breath catch and then he was gently batting her hand away and rolling a condom on. She gasped as he pulled down her panties and then spun her round so that she was facing away from him, towards the mirror.

The blood roared in her ears as she stared at their reflections.

His eyes were dark like hammered pewter. 'It's your turn to watch,' he whispered against her throat. 'Touch yourself, baby.' He nudged her fingers towards the triangle of curls between her thighs, his hand covering hers as she did what he asked, his other hand clutching her hip, pressing the curve of her bottom against his groin. Dazedly she pushed backwards.

He felt so hard and with every passing second she was softening, becoming liquid, turning inside out, her whole body expanding, shrinking and tightening around an ache that she could taste in her mouth, a need that only he could satisfy.

He was nipping her throat, not biting, just letting his teeth graze the soft skin, watching her intently as if she were the most fascinating thing he'd ever seen and that almost sent her over the edge.

'Wait,' he said in that way of his that was both commanding and soothing. 'Just a little longer. Let it build.'

He touched her breasts, pulling gently on the nipples, and she gripped the dressing table, whimpering, wanting more.

'Now—' she said hoarsely. 'I need you now.'

She felt the change in him as his control snapped. He parted her legs and then suddenly he was thrusting into her, moving rhythmically, his body lifting and rocking her like a strong current at sea, his hand gripping her shoulder, his fingers stroking her clitoris so that she wanted to climb out of her skin and fuse with his.

A noise rose in her chest, involuntary, burning her throat as it burst from her lips. She writhed closer, desperate for him as something hot and wet and impatient swelled inside her, humming and quivering and stretching and contracting and—

The jolt of pleasure hit her with such force that for a moment it was impossible to do anything but hang there tautly, straining, outside her body and yet so much a part of his that she could feel his heart thundering beneath her ribs.

And then it burst inside her, leaving her breathless and panting and stunned. This was more than pleasure, it was sublimation and she let it roll through her as he jerked against her, his big body thrusting upwards. Now she was being pulled out on his tide, buffeted by his waves, rising and dropping back down again and again and again and again.

* * *

Eden woke in the darkness to a car alarm. Thinking it was a different type of alarm, she reached for her phone only to realise her mistake. For a cluster of seconds she had no idea where she was or how she had got there. But then she sensed the man sleeping beside her and she remembered everything.

Every glorious second.

She pressed her hand against her mouth to stifle the moan that rose to her lips, to stifle the hunger that seemed almost ill-mannered after her greed earlier. And also, to stop herself from reaching out and waking him. She couldn't ask for more, and not because it would be rude to do so but because if she let herself touch him, she honestly didn't know if she would be able to stop.

She couldn't go there again. She couldn't ever allow herself to need someone like that, not even for sex. Not after what happened with Liam. Her chest tightened around the imperfectly healed wound beneath her ribs. Even though things had ended between them so long ago, it had been such a shock to find out that he was a father. Despite the small screen on her phone, she'd been able to see the likeness between him and the baby. He had looked happy, and she knew it made her a smaller person, but she'd hated him for that.

Hated that he now had what she'd unknowingly lost.

Hated him for proving to her that she was not genetically programmed for intimacy and permanence.

Which was why she wasn't going to wake him now. This beautiful stranger who had opened her up with his soft mouth, bored into her with his hard gaze and even harder body. His touch had been so urgent, so precise, and powerful, possessive and devastating. Staring into the darkness, she could still feel the imprint of his hands on her belly, her hips and between her thighs.

She stared down at him, watching his chest rise and fall, trying to memorise the details of him—the curve of his jaw, those ridiculously long eyelashes, the contoured muscles of his arm—wanting to remember everything, to hold on to him for as long as she could in her mind at least.

Surely that was allowed.

But then how did she know?

She had been raised by her mother and grandmother, two single moms with big hearts and bad taste in men. The kind who weren't looking for love or anything like it. They would be there for a couple of days or weeks, maybe even months, but then they left because, '*You can't catch what don't want to be caught.*' That was what her grandma used to say when her mother was weeping on the porch again, watching the tail lights of yet another car disappearing down the street.

Growing up, watching from the sidelines, she had been sure in the way that children could be about things they didn't fully understand that the stable, loving, respectful relationships that had eluded her mother and grandmother would not be out of reach to her.

She had been wrong. Because now she knew love was a game that you couldn't win unless you knew the rules. Which she didn't.

But now she had new rules. Better rules.

Liam's betrayal coupled with the heartbreaking loss of her baby weren't things she could survive again. Better to face reality, which was that Fennell women didn't attract the kind of men who wanted marriage or long-term relationships or exclusivity.

These days intimacy for Eden meant sex, not love and certainly not marriage, and as far as settling down went, well, she had an office space in London and had just opened up another in New York and she was building a roster of wealthy, international clients who kept her constantly moving around the globe. Plus, she had an arrangement for regular short term lets in the same apart hotels, which felt like a kind of semi-permanence.

Truthfully it was all she could manage. A deeper commitment would simply highlight the lack of it elsewhere in her life. And it was enough for her.

Or it had been until last night.

She had never suspected that two bodies fusing together could produce such fire. Or such honesty. Of course, he hadn't known that she was opening herself to him not just physically, but emotionally, releasing all the confusion and tension and turmoil of the last few days.

That was what she'd done, but only because there was this barrier of anonymity between them. Now, though, she had to leave. Because it felt as though she had given away too much of herself and the last time that had happened, her world had turned to dust.

She dressed quietly and forced herself to leave without looking back.

Downstairs, she approached the concierge's desk. It was a different receptionist, which made it slightly easier to do what she needed to rebuild the barriers she had let fall, and then she was pushing open the doors and stepping into the cool dawn air.

Outside the roads were silent. It had stopped raining, but the sky was a mottled purple, streaked with gold like the cover of one of her mom's old glam-rock albums.

Normally, she liked waking at dawn. At home, her mom and grandma almost never closed the curtains, and she found the serenity of those hours comfortingly familiar. But not today. For some reason, the first pale rays of sunlight that were creeping down the buildings made everything feel abandoned and desolate.

She felt abandoned and desolate, which was ridiculous because she had abandoned him. Her nameless lover. Picturing him on the bed, his head in the crook of his arm, she felt a pang under her ribs that was so intense and sharp that she had to reach out and steady herself against a lamp post.

He was a stranger. She didn't even know his name. He didn't know hers either, but he'd touched her as if he knew her. As if she were his. And she had wanted to be his. Wanted to burn in the wildfire he had unleashed.

Her heart was banging inside her chest. It made no sense for her to feel like this.

It was just sex. Only she'd had 'just sex' before and it hadn't felt like that. Before, with other men, it had been instant gratification and been as instantly forgotten. And last night should have been no different.

But even though she would never see him again, she knew she wouldn't forget him.

Don't think about it. Don't think about him, she told herself. *Just do what you always do. Don't look back. Just keep moving—*

It had started to rain again, and she felt a pang of relief, and something like regret. But if that wasn't a sign to keep moving, she didn't know what was, and, flicking up the collar of her jacket, she began to walk quickly down the street, keeping her gaze focused on the cracks in the sidewalk.

CHAPTER TWO

THERE WAS A cracking sound like a bone breaking as a Y-shaped branch of light flickered across the bruise-coloured sky above New York. The fierce storms that had been predicted by weather forecasters all week had hit the city that afternoon.

But nature's most powerful pyrotechnic display was like a damp squib in comparison to the tension in the HCI boardroom.

Lounging back in his chair, Harris scanned the faces of the people sitting around the table, a slight narrowing of his eyes the only sign that he was even listening to the debate taking place.

'Enough.'

He spoke softly, because he could. Because everyone in the room was paid to listen to him. Then again, they would still listen even if no money were involved. Wealth was not a prerequisite of leadership.

It was one of the few things his father had taught him and maybe that was why he had always remembered it, because evidence of the father-son bond they nominally shared was scant and mostly negative.

But that had stuck, and so he had trained himself to speak with intention and conviction, to always be prepared and to get to the point. And not to shout. Speaking calmly and quietly made people stop and listen and being heard gave you power.

His father had taught him that as well. His mother too. Growing up, he had felt neither seen nor heard.

Or wanted?

His spine stiffened against the leather upholstery, and he pushed the question away, reluctant to even acknowledge it within the privacy of his head. The past was unassailable. Fixed. It was history. There was no point in wasting time and energy on it. What mattered was the present and here he was respected, and for good reason. He had built a business from the ground up and he was taking it to the stars. Metaphorically and literally.

HCI was currently in the process of finessing a remote AI-powered lunar module, which, if things went according to plan, would be searching for minerals on the moon's surface roughly this time next year.

Unfortunately, due to his impetuous and ill-judged attempt to expose Tiger McIntyre, things were no longer going to plan. Not only was his reputation under scrutiny but his shareholders were rattled. Enough for him to call his C suite into the boardroom for this unscheduled meeting.

There was no direct evidence linking him personally to the hacking of Tiger's server and plenty of people would think it was just one billionaire throwing shade at another, but shareholders hated conflict and scandal.

The irony was that he hated it too, but Tiger pressed all his buttons. Which was why he'd gone and hired Sydney and it had seemed to make perfect sense at the time. Tiger was known to cut corners and blur lines. All he'd had to do was prove it. The idea that he would end up in the firing line simply hadn't ever occurred to him.

'This is getting us nowhere.'

A drumroll of frustration, irritation too, because he wasn't the bad guy here, vibrated against his ribs as he stared down at his laptop, his eyes fixing on the headline that played on his name: *What a Carve-Up!*

It had started small. Just a couple of carefully worded paragraphs about rumours of IP theft and industrial espionage on a blog online.

Naturally, he hadn't been named as the perpetrator, but his was a niche industry. There were only so many people it could be. Then again, the Internet was a rumour mill. Surely no rational person would be swayed by something so random and half-baked and, having run it past his legal team and his head of Comms, he had taken their advice and decided to simply ignore it. To do otherwise would be to give it credence, to fan the flames that would shrivel and die of their own accord if deprived of the oxygen of publicity.

And that was what had happened. Everything had gone quiet.

Job done. Problem solved.

Until today at five o'clock, Eastern Standard Time, when everything had come crashing down around his ears.

Because of course it wasn't just any blog. The Bit Bucket might have started out as a nervy, acerbic column by MIT dropout, Chase Fordham, but it was now the go-to destination for anyone looking to take the pulse of big business.

In other words, those two paragraphs were actually a baited hook. And someone had taken the bait. A much bigger fish, big enough to name names.

His name.

He scrolled slowly down the two-page article in the *New York Chronicle*. It was good journalism. Punchy, and unfortunately true. Deniably so, but the damage was done.

Which was why he was here in the boardroom instead of

heading off to Monaco to look at his latest yacht. Another twinge of irritation.

Stifling it, he glanced up, the pen in his hand tapping out a clear message to the people sitting round the table even before he spoke. 'I'm struggling to understand what it is that I'm looking at.'

Outside the storm was raging but nobody inside the room was watching the clashing clouds and flashing thunderbolts.

They were watching their boss.

'Isn't this story supposed to be dead?' He spun the laptop round to face the table. 'Because from where I'm sitting, it appears to be not just alive but in excellent health.'

His lawyer cleared his throat. 'Obviously, the source is anonymous, but we have our people looking into—'

'I am way past worrying about who the source is,' he said firmly. Obviously, his team knew nothing about his ill-advised meeting with that hacker but even if she hadn't signed an NDA, he knew this 'leak' had nothing to do with Sydney Truitt. This was Tiger McIntyre. It had his paw prints all over it. 'I want this story shut down.'

'And we can do that, sir,' his head of Comms, Avery Williams, said. 'But if we want to deny it—'

'I do,' he said coolly.

She nodded. 'Then first off, we need to issue a statement denying any allegations of wrongdoing. And then we need to focus on reminding everyone exactly who you are and what you stand for. We need to set the record straight and give you the opportunity to be the man the world thinks you are.'

Her words echoed inside his head. She made it sound so simple and in theory it was. He had a reputation as a meticulous, straight-talking, cool-headed businessman that was fully justified. Except when it came to Tiger. Even hearing his name made him feel awash with a rage that he knew was both excessive and irrational.

A rage that had momentarily blocked out all logic and good sense so that he had momentarily 'gone rogue', acting on impulse, driven by a need to take down the man who had so casually betrayed his trust and treated their friendship as something disposable.

It had been an uncharacteristic act of recklessness, and the worst part was that he still hadn't managed to punish Tiger. Instead, he was the one being made to jump through hoops.

Lifting an eyebrow, he stared steadily at Avery. 'And how exactly are you planning to do that?'

She hesitated. 'I know you like to handle most media matters in house but, on this occasion, I think it would be better to involve a reputation management agency with specialised experience in mitigating these kinds of negative incidents.'

He nodded. 'So, you want to start interviewing people?'

Avery smiled at him. 'I've already hired someone. All you have to do is meet them.'

Avery's words were still echoing inside his head as he took one of the nutritionally balanced meals from the fridge at his triplex penthouse that his chef prepared every day and dropped down onto one of his huge cream-coloured sofas. It was still raining heavily, and he stared out of the window at the blurred New York skyline, mechanically forking up edamame beans and smashed avocado.

His body still felt so on edge, and he could feel the tension humming beneath his skin as if the storm were trapped there. It was Tiger's fault he was feeling like this.

And he hated him for it. Not that he could hate him any more than he already did, and that would never change.

But other things were going to have to, he thought irritably. Unlike Tiger, he was not of the opinion that all publicity was good publicity. His PR people worked hard to keep his name out of the headlines so that he could ensure that his life ran like clockwork. Now, though, he was going to have to do whatever it was people in his situation did when they messed up.

He tossed his half-empty plate onto the sofa, his hand moving automatically to reach for his wallet.

Gazing down at the photos in his hand, he leaned forward greedily.

The one on top was an ultrasound scan. It looked like one of those weather maps on TV of an incoming storm, all indecipherable curves and lines at first. Then your eyes adjusted, and you could detect the shape of a baby lying on her back, her nose distinct, arm waving up as if to say, here I am.

Now he held the two photos side by side and looked at the second.

After nine months in the warm, watery gloom of the womb, his newborn daughter's small face was scrunched up against the light, grey eyes, *his eyes*, wide and still stunned after the shock of birth, her tiny, flawless fingers curled like petals against some kind of shawl. She had been perfect. Unreal. Miraculous. Only he hadn't realised the miracle of her until after she was born and was living on the other side of the world from him.

By then it was too late. She was gone.

He'd found her again, but it had taken years and money that he didn't have back then. By the time he'd been able to pay someone to find her so much had changed. Jasmine had a new father. Not new to her, because he was the only one she'd ever known. Which meant that Harris was not only absent but superfluous as well.

Obviously, he had a legitimate biological claim and these

days he had unlimited wealth with which to demand his paternal rights. Only it wasn't that simple. He knew from personal experience that after food, shelter, warmth and comfort, what every child needed was stability and him barging back into her life all these years later felt like self-indulgence, not a right.

He flinched as a snap of lightning illuminated the room, momentarily blinded, just as he had been earlier when the photographers had swarmed towards him. He'd been lucky today. The tumultuous weather had been on his side, but it wasn't going to rain for ever. The press would come back and in greater force. So, as much as he wanted to pretend this wasn't happening, that wasn't going to work.

Decisions and actions, both had consequences. He was still living with his from twelve years ago. He stared down at the photo, his heart swelling to fill his chest.

It had been taken in the hospital just after Jasmine was born. Taken by the man who had stepped up in his place. A man, not a boy.

That's what Jessie had needed when she'd told him she was pregnant.

They'd done the paternity test and he'd been supposed to go with her for the scan but had bottled it. He'd been so young and hadn't been ready to be a father. Hadn't been in love with Jessie. And his parents' marriage had shown him what happened when you forced people into a lifetime commitment under those exact same circumstances.

So he'd made a bad choice, never thinking that it would have such absolute and irreversible consequences.

But it had.

He hadn't understood it at the time but that one small decision had been the last straw for Jessie.

She'd needed a man who was willing to support her, not a

teenager hoping it was all a bad dream and that he was going to wake up real soon.

That was why he'd skipped the scan. He'd done the paternity test, but the scan would make it scarily real. When he hadn't shown up, Jessie had reacted accordingly. Within days she was gone, back to Australia and out of his life. Had he realised that would happen? Had he understood the full, lifelong consequences of that moment of panic and cowardice? Had he imagined another man becoming Jasmine's father so quickly? No, he hadn't.

But even if he had, would he have done anything differently? Would he have fought to change Jessie's mind or tried to make it work between them? Probably not, because deep down a part of him had thought she'd be better off with someone less damaged. Someone who could be the father his daughter deserved.

That was part of his reasoning then, swimming in the slipstream of his panic and shock, the need to not repeat the mistakes his parents had made. They'd been two square pegs forced into a round hole because he'd been conceived by accident. Was it any wonder their marriage had failed? And failure came with fallout.

They'd remarried other people and had more children. Half-siblings, who, through no fault of their own, were a constant reminder that he was on the outside. They were the focus of their parents' love and attention, and he was always an afterthought, a reminder for ever of a past everyone wanted to forget. A visitor who stayed in the guest bedroom.

His beautiful daughter must never experience the pendulum swing of two homes, because it was a lie. In reality, two homes meant no home. Just a temporary address with a pull-out bed surrounded by boxes of books and old sports equipment, and an angry, confused boy lumped in with all the other unwanted, unnecessary detritus of life.

He breathed out shakily. Thankfully, he could afford to give his daughter an entire suite of rooms, decorated just as she wanted. Money was no object.

His shoulders tensed. It was an empty phrase and also misleading because money was just an object, a thing. But it also had the power to change lives and it would be disingenuous to pretend that his money didn't matter to him or other people.

And yet, it had limitations. Jasmine lived in a world where she felt safe and seen. He had hired a very expensive investigator to make discreet inquiries and she'd reported that his daughter was happy and stable, so his money could only offer her material things. Better things? Possibly, and more of them. But did that really matter? Arguing that it did made him feel shallow and he didn't believe it anyway.

This whole Tiger McIntyre mess was doing his head in. To get it sorted, he needed to be the man the world thought he was, but right now he just wanted to lose sight of that man. To break free of him. To be a stranger to himself.

What he needed was a distraction. Could he call Rebecca?

They had ended things two months ago. Not because he didn't like her. He did. She was smart, driven and beautiful, but she had started dropping the odd hint about the future. Their future.

That wasn't what he wanted. Not now, maybe not ever. Or maybe it wasn't about wanting or not wanting it, but instead not knowing how it worked.

As a kid, he'd always been fascinated with the inner workings of machinery. That was another thing he and his father had in common, that need to open up the hood and see the mechanism, to understand the nuts and bolts, the cogs, the pistons.

That need to know was the engine of his success.

But he didn't know how to make a relationship work. How could he when he'd only ever seen them failing?

He got to his feet and stared out at the city below. The rain had stopped again and at street level the lights flashed as they changed colour, beckoning him as they had the other night.

Heart throbbing against his ribs, he watched them blink, red then green—

Green eyes and a tattoo of a bitten apple on her shoulder.

A pulse of heat beat across his skin as he replayed what had happened when he'd met her two weeks ago.

His hand splayed against the glass as he scanned the city skyline.

Who was she? And where was she now?

If only he could snap his fingers and summon her here.

If only…

'Excuse me, Mr Carver.'

Harris looked up at his PA and frowned. 'What is it, Sean?'

'Ms Williams just called. She sends her apologies but says she's going to be another fifteen minutes.'

Fifteen minutes was nothing in the scheme of things, but he didn't like waiting at the best of times, and this was far from the best of times. But that's what this meeting with the reputation manager was all about. Putting the worst behind him and regaining control of his narrative.

Then, finally, things would go back to normal.

Tapping his fingers on the armrest, he stared around the room. He could have had this meeting at the office, but he preferred using the club for anything more sensitive.

The last meeting he'd had here was with Sydney Truitt. Same room, same chairs. The difference was he'd been on his own and that should have been a red flag because he should have had his people there. Except he hadn't been able to because what he'd done was fundamentally, legally wrong. Not that there was any hard evidence to connect him with the rumours. His lawyers had been very clear about that.

Unfortunately, there was always that lingering sense of no smoke without fire. Rumours could and did do enormous damage.

It was too late for regrets, though. Yes, if he'd told his team what he was planning the meeting would never have taken place. But he'd been so furious with Tiger, he would have ignored every flag including the skull and crossbones.

And the rest, as they said, was history.

Or rather he'd like it to be. Currently it was very much in the present, but, shutting down the memory of what had been far from his finest hour, he glanced at his watch. 'Fifteen minutes, you say?'

'Yes, sir. But the reputation manager is already here. Would you prefer to wait for Ms Williams? I can take some coffee—'

'No, send her in. Let's keep things moving. Ms Williams can join us when she gets here.'

As was usual with an outside hire, he'd been sent a short biography and résumé of the person, which ordinarily he would have read.

Ordinarily.

But for some reason, he'd barely skimmed the report. He couldn't seem to concentrate. His mind had been all over the place.

Instead, time and time again he had thought about that hotel off Bowery.

His eyes narrowed as if he had X-ray vision and could see through brick and plaster into the hotel room where he had spent six hours at most.

Six hours. It wasn't even the length of a working day, but if he closed his eyes, he could replay almost every minute right up until the moment he fell asleep.

Then the screen went blank.

Because she'd left without waking him. Without saying goodbye or leaving so much as a note. Oh, but she had paid for the room.

He knew he should open his laptop and read the report through quickly, but his gaze kept being pulled towards the windows. The staff hadn't closed the drapes and something about the arrangement of the fabric nudged forward a memory of waking alone in that hotel room. Feeling alone, and wronged. As if something had been stolen from him.

He'd hated that feeling.

He gritted his teeth. Hated too that she had paid for the room. He knew that it was ridiculous, but he did.

But why? No doubt she earned a wage so why shouldn't she pay for the room?

And yet, still it rankled.

Which was no doubt why his brain remained so fixated on her.

Now, though, he needed to focus on the matter at hand. He picked through his memory for anything he could remember about this woman from the conversation he'd had with Avery when she'd told him they'd found someone.

'She's a bit of a wild card,' Avery had said. *'Not in ability. She comes highly recommended, even though Aletheia One is a small agency. She's just opened a second office in New York, but she started out as a one-woman band. She's young and very media savvy and there's a creativity and a freshness in her thinking that I think could work very well for us.'*

We'll see, he thought. This interview was a formality really, a nod to his authority and an opportunity for him to meet the successful candidate, but he was always wary about outside hires. They might lack loyalty, and this IP theft accusation was such a sensitive issue.

Of course, his team had done everything by the book. No details of what had happened would have been released until the NDA was signed. And yet, despite that caution, Avery had still hired someone who was, in her own words, a 'bit of a wild card'.

He heard the door open.

'Mr Carver. This is Eden Fennell.'

He felt it first in the air.

A shift of something, a tightening, so that momentarily he was distracted enough to get to his feet on autopilot, holding out his hand to the woman standing in front of him.

And then his brain caught up with what his eyes were seeing, and he froze.

Petite. Brunette. No smokey eyeshadow this time and the tattoo on her shoulder was just a blur beneath the sleeve of her cream silk blouse, but the green eyes were the same and once again they were narrowed on his face.

It was the woman from the bar.

And this time she had a name.

Eden.

CHAPTER THREE

EDEN STARED UP at the man standing in front of her, her fingers clamped around the handle of her purse, her heartbeat silenced, shock and disbelief flooding her veins. And then a shiver that had nothing to do with shock or disbelief scampered over her skin because it was him. It was the guy from the bar.

Only in some ways seeing him again shouldn't have been a shock. For the last couple of weeks, she had been thinking about him continuously. And not just thinking. She had found herself looking for him too.

And she had finally found him. Or maybe he had found her?

Waking that morning in the hotel, she had greedily watched him sleep, wanting, needing to remember him. But now he was here and the sheer randomness and impossibility of that was making her feel as if she were floating outside her body. She almost reached out to grip his arm to see if he was real. Behind her, she was aware of his PA's slightly stunned gaze, probably because nobody in history had left his boss standing there with his arm frozen in mid-air, but she couldn't move or speak.

Harris Carver recovered first.

'Ms Fennell. Thank you for meeting me,' he said, his voice sending a hard shiver down her spine.

I wasn't meeting you, she wanted to say. I was supposed to be meeting a billionaire CEO with a reputational crisis.

She knew the name, of course, and him by reputation or should that be reputations? Because he had two now. The first was low-key and immaculate, a bit like that expensive suit he was wearing.

Her eyes flicked over the dark fabric. Sleek lapels, trouser hems hitting the tops of his shoes, the jacket moulding to those broad shoulders and chest. Subtle details that elevated what were essentially the by-products of sheep and silkworms into the perfect example of quietly luxurious amour for a business titan who preferred to stay out of the limelight.

A frontrunner in the field of space exploration, Harris Carver was known to be hardworking, detail-driven and discreet. He never spoke out of turn, never made waves, except in the financial markets where shares in his company kept rising as if they too wanted to reach the stars.

In other words, he was not supposed to be potential client material for her.

But that had all changed a couple of days ago.

Now he was being linked, not openly, but the clues were there, to claims of IP theft and industrial espionage; only the brief she had been given was so carefully worded it was impossible to identify him as the client.

And even when she'd signed the NDA, she still hadn't connected his name with the man who had unravelled her so completely.

Beneath her feet, the floor started to shake as she felt the memory of that night swirl inside her, warm and dark and honeyed. But she couldn't leave him standing there any longer and, stiffening her shoulders, she reached out and shook his hand. 'Mr Carver.'

His grip was warm, and firm, and she could feel the hard calluses on his fingers. It was all too easy to remember them sliding over her naked belly as he stared down at her with hot, hungry eyes…

She felt his hand tighten around hers and her breath jerked in her throat as she met his gaze head-on. There was nothing warm in his eyes now. Instead, there was a cool anger and the fading aftershocks of a surprise that made no sense because, unlike her, he must have known who he was going to meet today.

She knew how these things worked. His people would have given him some kind of synopsis of her career to date, and all the pertinent facts would be accompanied by a photo. Which meant that either he hadn't been curious enough about who he'd hired to check them out or he hadn't recognised her from the other night.

Given his earlier reputation as a meticulous, detail-driven workaholic, the former seemed unlikely. But thinking that she had slipped his mind stung. Not that she would ever admit that to anyone, him most of all.

She pulled her hand loose. Working as a reputation manager at this level had taught her a lot about herself. She knew she was resilient. Smart. Adaptable and ambitious. But it had also taught her a lot about wealthy, powerful people. What she'd learned was that showing weakness was a taboo.

And they didn't get much more wealthy or powerful than this man.

'I think we'll take that coffee after all, Sean,' he said, but his eyes stayed on her because it was simply an excuse to get his PA out of the room, she realised a moment later, her stomach somersaulting as Sean retreated. She heard the door click behind him. Harris Carver did too because his pupils swelled, the black eclipsing the grey of his irises, and she felt the effects of it stampede through her body.

They were alone.

The air stretched around them and, for a fraction of a second, she thought he was going to lean forward and fit his mouth to hers as he had done in the street.

But this was reality, not some fantasy.

He took a step towards her. 'What is this? What are you doing here?' The tension in his voice rippled through her.

She frowned. 'You know what I'm doing here. You hired me.'

He shook his head. 'Right, so I'm supposed to believe that this is all just one big coincidence, you and me in that bar and now you here.'

Her eyes clashed with his. 'Is that a question?'

'I'm asking you if that was a coincidence?'

His voice was all serrated-edge consonants and clipped vowels. Did he think she had somehow engineered their hook-up? That she'd slept with him because she thought it might give her an edge over her rivals?

No, that was ridiculous. He couldn't think that. For starters, the timings were all wrong, and, anyway, his people had reached out to her.

'I don't go hunting for clients in bars, if that's what you're implying. Sorry to dent your ego but I didn't recognise you that night, and it's not as if we exchanged names and contact details.'

When you worked with a high-profile, high-net-worth individual, discretion was mandatory. Potential clients often used a go-between in the first instance who would outline a 'theoretical' reputation crisis event and request a strategy, but client anonymity was common practice up until an NDA was signed. Today was no exception.

Sure, Harris Carver's name had been in the news over the last few days, but he was one of a number of notable people currently facing down a reputational crisis. And as she'd just told him, she'd had no idea who he was that night.

She did now.

It was still making her head spin that this man and the man who had been stalking through her dreams every night were the same person.

Her pulse twitched as she thought back to the moment they'd met. He'd been wearing jeans and a T-shirt and that battered leather jacket and she'd *assumed* he was just an ordinary guy meeting up with mates to watch the big fight. And when he'd taken her hand, his skin hadn't been smooth and soft like the hands of some pampered billionaire. She'd *assumed* he was a mechanic or a carpenter.

Wrong assumptions.

'And that's my fault?' His voice was an explosive mix of anger and frustration, and he was staring at her as if she were an intruder he'd caught opening his safe.

Which was not only deeply unnerving but unjust.

'It's not mine. None of this is my fault. I didn't even get told who I was meeting today until your PA came and got me. But you knew who I was. If you had a problem with that, why didn't you—'

'I'm so sorry I'm late.'

They both turned as a middle-aged woman in a pale grey trouser suit hurried into the room, accompanied by the PA carrying a tray of coffee.

'There was an accident out on—'

'It's fine, Avery.' Harris Carver cut across her explanation. 'We've literally just started.'

He turned back to Eden, his expression flat and unreadable. 'Ms Fennell, this is my head of Comms, Avery Williams. You have her to thank for your being here today. She championed you from the start.'

In other words, had he played a part in the selection process, he wouldn't have chosen her, she thought. But he didn't have to say it out loud. The taut twist to his mouth did that for him.

She held out her hand to the head of Comms. 'It's lovely to meet you, Ms Williams.'

The older woman smiled as they shook hands. 'So, where are we up to? Obviously, you've been introduced.'

Eden nodded. 'I was just saying how surprised I was that Mr Carver agreed to hire me given what he knew about me.'

The other woman's face froze momentarily. 'Why? Have you met before?'

'*No.*'

They both spoke at once, Harris's deeper voice overlapping hers in a way that felt oddly intimate and exposing.

Eden smiled stiffly. 'I just meant that I'm a bit of a new kid on the block.'

'But you do remind me of someone,' he said after a moment.

Obviously, he wasn't expecting her to tell the truth. Quite the opposite in fact. He was treading quietly but heavily on her toes. Which of course made her want to shout it from the rooftops because after Liam she had sworn never to be any man's dirty little secret.

In the months after their split, she had wondered why she hadn't realised the truth.

With hindsight it all seemed so glaringly obvious. For starters, he'd always been having to rush off. But she hadn't understood then that it wasn't just teenagers who had curfews. Married men had them too.

Then there were the other glaringly red flags like the fact

that he'd never invited her back to his place. He'd always had an excuse. The boiler was broken. The neighbours were having work done and the builders were just so loud. And despite dating him for a year she had never met any of his friends or family.

She felt it beneath her ribs. Not anger, but a cool slippery shame, squatting there like a toad. Liam had always had excuses for that too. And for why all his calls went to voicemail.

The truth had been there in huge letters that would have been visible from space to anyone else on the planet. But she had been young, straight out of college and desperate to prove that she was immune to the same curse as all the other women in her family. That she would be able to attract that most mythical of men: the one that didn't want to get away.

Which was why nobody from her family had known about their 'relationship' either. She hadn't wanted to jinx it by telling her mom and grandmother. She had wanted to hold it close, to keep it precious and unsullied because she'd been so convinced that she was different from them, so determined that she would be the exception and not the rule.

'I have that kind of face,' she said coolly. 'People are always thinking I look like somebody they know. It can be a bit confusing sometimes.'

Those mesmerising grey irises were steady on her face. 'That must be it, then.'

But it was she who'd got confused. Back in the bar, she had sensed something raw about this man, something intensely male, primitive almost. And it was still there, that same compelling sensual masculinity. Only now it was sheathed, not just in a suit that flattered every hard contour of muscle but with the indisputable authority of someone who was used to getting what he wanted. And no doubt casting it aside when it no longer served a purpose.

Her eyes darted around the quiet luxury of the lounge. This was his natural habitat. This exclusive private members' club with its deferential staff and expensive furnishings. Because he wasn't anything like the other men who'd been in the bar.

They were all interchangeable. Easy to read.

Easy to forget.

She felt a cool, silvery shiver like liquid mercury tremble down her spine as his eyes met hers.

Even without a name Harris Carver was not someone you could ever forget.

'Take a seat.'

The command in his voice whipped at her senses and she sat down in one of the leather club chairs, wishing she had worn trousers instead of a skirt as his eyes grazed her legs. She had dithered over what to wear but ended up going for a navy pinstripe pencil skirt because coupled with the heels it made her look like one of the grown-ups.

Sometimes she was so jaded with life and people and all the stupid, mean stuff they did that she felt as old as the Sphinx. But she knew that, to clients, she looked young, and they equated youth with inexperience.

It didn't help that like all the women in her family she was petite. Unfortunately, and unjustly, taller people were perceived as more authoritative, which was why she'd picked her highest heels for today's meeting.

Also, she liked the silhouette of the skirt. All that time in the gym had given her quads and glutes. Yes, it was a cliché, but at the time, when she had been reeling and wounded from Liam's betrayal, a revenge body had felt like a kind of win.

It still did. Walking into the club today, she had flexed her muscles on purpose because it reminded her that she was a survivor. That power was always there for the taking and that she was a powerful woman who had walked through fire and survived.

Looking up, she shivered inside as her eyes clashed again with his molten silver gaze. But some fires burned brighter and hotter than others.

She watched, her nerves twitching as he opened his laptop and scrolled slowly down the screen, taking his time, flexing his will as she had flexed her muscles. 'You come highly recommended, Ms Fennell.' Now he lounged back in the chair, his eyes roaming over her face, then stopping abruptly to pin her gaze just as he had in the bar.

And in the bedroom.

And in the mirror as he'd held her shoulder and watched her shudder to a climax as he'd thrust powerfully inside her.

Her skin felt hot and tingly, and she glanced away. Did he remember it too? Was she imprinted on his brain in the same way? Had he spent the last two weeks chasing shadows across the city trying to assuage that sharp, relentless ache that wouldn't soften and fade by itself?

It was impossible to tell just by looking. His face was as impenetrable as a brick wall.

'Thank you.'

He smiled but it was a smile that remained on his lips. His eyes stayed cool and hard. 'It wasn't a compliment, Ms Fennell. Just an observation.'

Her chin jerked up. Right, so that was how this was going to go.

She glanced over to where he was seated, his long legs stretched out casually. But she knew he was still furious because her turning up here had taken away his control. Here with his staff, he was the big boss. A rich, powerful, smooth-shaven, hard-talking CEO lounging like an emperor in his handmade suit and shoes. Why would he ever want them to know that there was another hungry-eyed version of him who had anonymous sex with strangers?

Was that what he usually did?

It hurt more than it should, thinking that she was just one in a long line of nameless women he'd hooked up with. It hadn't felt like that at the time. They might not have known each other's names, but there had been something there, an ease and a friction that was both contradictory and yet true. She shivered inside. That was dangerous thinking. But he had been so tempting, and she had been so tempted.

Which was why she'd left without waking him. She hadn't been sure she could resist him, and she couldn't be that needy even for a moment. Not any more.

Only it was hard, because just like every other woman in her family she craved security and certainty above all else. It was that craving that had driven her into Liam's arms, and, like moths to a flickering flame, they got burned every single time.

Her brain hiccupped as a new thought suddenly occurred to her, one that might explain why Harris was radiating such intense displeasure at her presence. Because she had left him sleeping in that hotel room, which she was pretty sure didn't happen to him very often, possibly never.

Tough! She wasn't here to manage his male pride.

Sitting up straighter, she leaned forward slightly. 'For me it's a compliment to be recommended by any of my clients,' she countered. 'Why wouldn't it be? They're all demanding, successful people with high standards.'

She felt the atmosphere in the room quiver to attention as his fingers tightened on the arm of his chair and she remembered again how they'd gripped her hip. That moment of need and recognition—

'Your client list is impressive,' he admitted begrudgingly

as if he regretted admitting it. He glanced down at the screen. 'Given your age.'

She blinked.

Wow, that was condescending, and it was so tempting to tell him that. But she was too ambitious to get mouthy with clients, even one as vexing as Harris Carver. She couldn't afford to be labelled as stroppy or difficult or thin-skinned, because all it would take was one or two stray remarks and suddenly she would have a reputation and there would be no new clients coming in.

That was the thing about human beings. They all had opinions about one another, but if enough people thought the same thing, then those opinions became your reputation.

Take her family. With her short shorts and flirty smile and paint-splattered tank tops, her mum was nothing like her friends' mothers, and her grandmother was definitely not some apple-cheeked little old lady sitting in a rocker on the porch.

But just because they ran life-drawing classes and drank beer and laughed and dated unsuitable men didn't mean they deserved to be called names.

Even as a child, when she hadn't fully understood the meaning of those names, she had wanted to make it stop. Maybe that was why she'd ended up in this job and why it felt less like a job and more a way of life.

She caught a glimpse of silver and steel and, looking up, she found Harris Carver watching her. Holding his gaze, she nodded. 'Almost as impressive as the fact that most of my clients have come to me through word-of-mouth recommendations, including those in Europe.'

Her pulse dipped as his eyes dropped to hers.

'I saw that you started out in London. An odd decision to quit the States so early in your career. Was the pond too big for you to get noticed here? Or were the other fish just that much bigger than you that you couldn't compete for food?'

Screw you, she thought, resentment surging through her.

'First off, I didn't quit, Mr Carver, and secondly, even in a capitalist economy, bigger doesn't always mean better. Sometimes "bigger" can be a disadvantage. It can encourage complacency, which in turn can lead to a stifling of imagination. That's not a criticism,' she added coolly, holding his gaze. 'It's just an observation.'

Okay, that was pretty mouthy, but he was pushing her hard, too hard.

His head of Comms smiled minutely and nodded.

Harris Carver didn't smile or nod. He just stared at her and for so long it felt as though they were in some kind of staring competition.

'You didn't answer my question.'

She lifted her chin. 'I moved to London before I started the business. My father is English, so I have dual nationality. I wanted a change and also a chance to connect with that side of my heritage.'

It was more than that. Still raw from Liam's rejection and from losing their baby, she had needed to put an ocean between herself and her memories. Moving to England had been a chance to put some literal distance between herself and her past mistakes and the pain that kept catching her unawares whenever she saw a couple with a baby. When she was surrounded by strangers her pain and shame were invisible, and that was what she'd wanted.

'Hence the accent.'

He had noticed. Not many people did. It wasn't that pronounced but that was the difference between him and those other guys in that bar. He didn't just hear, he listened. Bluff and bluster, charm, good looks and luck, they all got you so far. But sustaining success, preserving power, only happened if you paid attention.

Which he did, she thought, her insides tightening as she remembered the soft meditative trace of his fingers. He had known instinctively where to touch her to make her squirm because he had been listening to her body, to the stagger of her breath and the noises she'd tried and failed to hold back. But he must also have taken his eye off the ball at some point otherwise she wouldn't be sitting here.

In short, he was that most compelling of all men. A contradiction, an enigma, a puzzle, and she loved solving puzzles.

Jigsaws. Crosswords. Sudoku. Whodunnits.

But complicated men had complicated lives. Sometimes they even had a whole other life with a wife in it.

Which was why she met men in bars. Why she didn't learn their names. Why she left before they could leave her. And why she was going to keep ignoring the strange, shimmering thread between her and Harris that pulled taut every time she met his glittering grey gaze.

'I do have an accent, particularly when I've been over in London for a while. There are certain words I mix up. Some spellings too. I forget where I am sometimes.'

Avery Williams smiled.

Harris Carver didn't. He didn't so much as move a muscle. Because she was watching so closely, she could see the rise and fall of his chest, but she felt something in his gaze narrow on her.

'Does that happen often? You forgetting where you are?'

The hairs on the nape of her neck shivered to attention.

She thought back to her confusion when she'd woken up in the hotel room. But that hadn't been forgetting. It was him. He had made all of it slide out of her head. Her past. Her fears. Her failures. His touch had opened her up and everything had spilled out until nothing remained except her hunger and a need for him to keep touching her.

Her heart thudded as his eyes met hers. 'Not often, no.'

She tried to pretend that the silence that followed her reply didn't get to her, but it was hard when he was watching her so closely. 'To recap, then,' he said finally. 'Your agency is small, smaller than your rivals, and you have less experience and outreach than they have. So, what exactly is it that you are bringing to the table, Ms Fennell? Other than an occasional episode of amnesia and some poor spelling.'

That grated. As it was meant to. He was needling her, trying to get a rise. To get her to trip up on her anger.

Because he wanted her gone, wanted her to walk away from this job.

But she wasn't going anywhere. This was her life. She wasn't just piggybacking on someone else's, and she wasn't going to give it up for anyone.

'I know you considered other candidates,' she said crisply. 'I'm guessing you were looking at the heavyweights.' Her mind flashed to the boxing match. His did too. She could see it in his eyes.

'And I can't compete with them.'

'Then why are you here?' he said in that clipped, economical way of his, reminding her again, as if she needed reminding, that he was a man who was used to his opinions being treated not simply as commentary but as protocol.

'If you don't have what it takes to compete with your rivals, Ms Fennell, then I would suggest you leave now because I need someone exceptional to fight my corner.'

There was a short, sticky silence as his head of Comms stared into the middle distance. Eden felt her face grow warm.

She held her breath. Counted to ten. Then ten more.

'You misunderstand me, Mr Carver. What I was trying

to explain is that I can't compete with those other agencies. Then again, I'm not trying to. I'm not criticising them. They are strategic and well connected and expert.'

She inclined her head towards Avery Williams. 'But I think it's worth pointing out that your people considered and discounted them. As they should have done, in my opinion. You see, those agencies have a reputation too. And that can be an advantage. Sometimes in situations like these just hiring the right firm can shut down the rumour mill—'

'But not in this case?' He eyed her across the room, his slate-coloured gaze as demanding as his question.

She paused. 'No. Not unless you're looking for a hard-charge, high-profile litigation—'

'I'm not.'

'Again, because you understand that it can backfire. Fan the flames of something you want extinguished.'

His gaze had sharpened, that fascinating mouth of his pursing in a facsimile of a kiss. The memory of that kiss in the rain immediately slid into her head, unprompted and intrusive, and it took a moment of concentrated effort to recover her train of thought.

'And because, like I said before, bigger is not always better. In this instance, it could actually be damaging. You're a very wealthy, powerful man but those big-name agencies have better brand recognition and that will make you look small and subservient. Never a good look, particularly when it comes to defending one's reputation,' she added, giving in once again to that childish urge to goad him as he had been goading her.

His nostrils flared, eyes locking with hers, narrowing above his uptilted chin.

'So, you're saying you'll be subservient to me.'

There was a rough edge to his voice that made her body

loosen and heat bloomed low in her pelvis as she replayed the moment when he had caught her wrists and held her captive.

'I'm saying that I won't be the story here. And by the time I've finished, you won't be a story either. You talked earlier about having someone in your corner. I will be that someone. I will always be that someone because, unlike those other agencies, I only work with one client at a time. My attention will be entirely on you, twenty-four hours a day.'

She tilted her chin, mirroring his stance.

'As for all this talk of fighting—it's just a distraction. It's noise. My success will be measured by the absence of events, the absence of headlines and chatter. So, in answer to your question, what I'm offering is the quiet elevation of your reputation.'

For a moment he didn't react but then he nodded slowly and her heart lurched. To cover her reaction, she reached for her laptop.

'Out of interest, is the timing of this story in any way significant?'

'Significant in what way?' he asked, grey eyes boring into her face.

'Someone has targeted you. I just wonder why and why now. What are they getting out of it?'

He shrugged. 'I don't know. Does there need to be a reason? I'm in the public eye. Isn't this just what happens sometimes?'

'Yes, it is. Only it doesn't happen in a vacuum, and, more importantly, it has never happened to you before.' Holding his gaze, she turned her laptop. 'I've just typed in your name and nothing controversial or contentious comes up except this one story. Which is odd, don't you think?'

'What I think is that it's one of those distractions you say I don't need in my life.'

'So, you have no opinion as to who might have started these rumours? Because, for example, if it's a disgruntled employee we can—'

He held her gaze. 'It's not a disgruntled employee.'

'A rival, then? Someone who stands to gain in business terms.'

'There is Tiger McIntyre,' Avery Williams said quietly. 'He's HCI's closest competitor.'

'What difference does it make who's behind the story?' He was still staring at her, and she had to stiffen her neck to stop from turning her head just to escape his gaze.

'It tells us if this is a warning shot or just a stray bullet.' She cleared her throat. 'Look, I understand that it's hard for someone in your position, Mr Carver, to lose control of their narrative but, if I am going to help you, I need you to commit, and that means being honest with me. I'm not your priest, I don't need to hear your confession, but if there is anything that could impact on your character, anything that might come to light which is pertinent, then I need you to tell me asap because further down the line it will be a far greater challenge to make it go away.'

There was a silence that made her feel as though she'd been jettisoned into space.

'There's nothing to tell.' His pupils flared as he spoke and, too late, she realised that he'd thought she was talking about what had happened between them in the hotel.

Her heart squeezed as he got to his feet abruptly.

'Thank you for coming in, Ms Fennell.' He held out his hand again and she took it reluctantly, but this time his fingers barely grazed hers before he was pulling away. He waited, impatience pulsing from every pore as she shook hands with Avery Williams, then— 'Sean, take Ms Fennell next door and arrange her security clearance.'

She watched him turn away, feeling oddly flattened.

But his PA was already on his feet, and, collecting her things, she turned and followed him out of the room. It felt like a minor triumph that she managed to do so without glancing back once. Although, really, she had more to celebrate than that. She had survived what was probably the trickiest meeting of her career. The contract was signed. All the i's had been dotted and the t's crossed.

Why, then, did everything still feel so unfinished between her and her new boss?

CHAPTER FOUR

HARRIS FELT RATHER than saw Eden Fennell leave.

He wanted to pinch himself to make absolutely sure that he wasn't in the middle of some elaborate dream but he'd already acted out of character this evening. And it was because of her. From the moment Eden had walked in, he'd felt as if everything solid and real were turning to sand.

Of course, if he'd bothered to read the report that his staff had compiled, none of this would be happening. He would have seen her photo, and he would have made an excuse to his team. Or perhaps he wouldn't. He was the boss and that was one of the perks. Never having to explain or apologise.

Either way, he would have vetoed her appointment.

Or would he?

His mind returned to the moment she had sashayed into the room in that skirt and those heels. The last time he'd seen her she was naked on the bed, her arms stretched above her head, that tempting curve of a body arching up as she offered her breasts to the heat of his mouth, so understandably it had been a shock to see her again. And even now it was almost impossible to believe that the petite, cool-eyed brunette in the pinstripe skirt and sky-high heels was the same woman who had come apart beneath him two weeks ago.

She had been shocked to see him too.

Not openly. She hadn't gasped or pressed her hand against

that mouth of hers, but her eyes had widened fractionally as she'd recognised him.

He knew exactly how she'd felt, finally putting a name to a face.

To a body.

To a pulse.

He knew because he was feeling it too. That pinprick of shock like an inoculating jab and then the slow, numbing spread of disbelief.

Beside him, Avery was putting her laptop into her bag, and he could sense her confusion. He couldn't blame her. Today was supposed to have been a friendly meet and greet, and normally in these meetings, he was happy to let his team ask the questions. He preferred to watch...

His body tensed, groin hardening as he remembered watching Eden in the mirror and he had to blank his mind quickly to the image of her body shuddering against his.

'I'm sure you must be wondering why I took the lead.' He waved away Avery's protests. 'I just wanted to know she can do the job.'

Which was true, but what was truer was that the shock of Eden being there had left him feeling tricked and exposed, and he'd needed to own the room.

Own the room or own her?

Gritting his teeth, he glanced at his watch. 'I have to go. I have a dinner this evening. I'll see you tomorrow.'

'But you liked her. Ms Fennell. You think she's a good fit?'

He nodded. 'Yes, I do. You chose well.'

As he strode through the club towards the doors, he saw that his car was already idling outside, sleek and dark, the tinted windows only partially concealing his driver. Beside it, his bodyguard stood, solid and imposing.

But he wasn't looking at them, instead his gaze was fixed

on the limo behind his. The one that would take Eden Fennell back to wherever she wanted to go.

Eden. He rolled the name on his tongue. Another woman, most women in fact, would find it impossible to carry off. But it suited her and not just because she was beautiful. In those few febrile hours they'd shared together there had been a wildness to her and a lack of inhibition that had transformed that simple hotel room into a paradise of pleasure.

Today though she was poised and aloof, and that aloofness had wound him up. That was why he'd been so hard on her. He had wanted to see that flare of passion again, so he'd pushed her on every point. But she'd held her ground. Pushed back, he thought, remembering the snippy remark she'd made about him being small and subservient.

He gritted his teeth. This was the second time Eden Fennell had knocked him off balance and left him scrambling to make sense of his world.

But things had changed.

She was working for him now and the sooner she realised what that meant, the better it would be for both of them. Waving away his bodyguard, he stalked over to the second limo. She wasn't in it, so she was probably still sorting out her security clearance.

By the time Eden appeared through the doors, he was back in control, lounging against his car, his eyes ostensibly on his phone but he knew exactly when she caught sight of him because he saw her falter.

'Ms Fennell—'

'Mr Carver—'

She was walking towards him now, her eyes steady on his face and he felt another tiny jolt of admiration and a curiosity that rarely troubled him when it came to women. But there was usually nothing to be curious about. Women liked him because he was rich and good-looking, and he liked them because they were beautiful, willing and endlessly available.

His jaw clenched and he had a sudden vivid memory of waking alone in that bed, and of reaching across the mattress to find nothing. He couldn't think of one woman who would even have contemplated walking away from him.

Except this one. Who wasn't even looking at him, he realised with a flicker of irritation. Instead, she was turning slightly, frowning at the tail lights of the departing limo.

'Was that—'

'Your car? Yes.' He nodded. 'I told the driver to leave. No point taking two cars when mine is heading in the same direction.'

She didn't like that. Even before she spun round towards him, he could feel the annoyance snap down her spine.

'I doubt that. I don't live in the Upper East Side.'

'Then it's lucky for you that I'm not going to the Upper East Side.' He held her gaze. 'Look, it'll be a small diversion for my driver, and it's good for the environment too. Besides, we need to talk,' he added.

'You just spent an hour grilling me. I think that's enough talking, don't you?' She reached into her bag and pulled out a phone. 'You go ahead. I'll call a cab.'

'Just get in the car, Ms Fennell. It's a ten-minute drive. I mean, what are you scared of?'

'Not much. Spiders. Snakes. The occasional very big beetle.' Angling her chin, she looked up at him in that cool, taunting way of hers. 'You know, if fear is how you motivate your staff, Mr Carver, I'm surprised that this is your first reputational crisis.'

'And I'm surprised you need any motivation to have a brief conversation with your boss. What was it you said about being in my corner? Something about my having your attention twenty-four hours a day? Yet here you are quibbling over giving me ten minutes of your time.'

Her green eyes flashed, and she glanced away because he was right, and she hated that. He loved that he could read her reaction so easily now, because she had spent the last hour keeping her emotions in check—keeping him in check.

'Perhaps I didn't make myself clear. I'm very happy to have a conversation of any length with you. But only if it doesn't involve you making accusations about why we ended up in bed.'

He swore under his breath. 'And *that* is exactly why we need to talk.'

She held his gaze as he took a step forward and he felt another reluctant flicker of admiration. He was six foot three. She barely reached his shoulders yet here she was staring him down.

'Fine,' she said coolly. 'You can take me to Cooper Square. I have a hotel room just off there.'

She did?

Then why had they rented another one that night?

But she was already sidestepping past him, opening the door on the passenger side, slamming it after herself before that thought had finished formulating, and he laughed. It was either that or pull her back out of the car and kiss her until she accepted that they were doing things his way—

'Mr Carver?'

His driver's voice snapped him back into his body and, feeling exposed and annoyed that Eden could make him feel that way, he turned and said curtly, 'Change of plan, Owen. We're taking Ms Fennell back to her hotel first.'

Yanking open the other door, he slid onto the seat beside Eden and, having stretched out his legs, he turned to where she was sitting stiffly.

She spoke first. 'So that's what this is about? You think I'm going to go and tell everyone what happened?'

Their gazes collided. No, she wouldn't do that, he thought, without missing a beat. Inside the club just now, she had been eloquent—but that was business.

How many words had she spoken to him before they'd left the bar? Thirty maybe. Less than that in the hotel. But by then, they'd had other things on their minds aside from conversation.

He shrugged. 'It crossed my mind,' he lied.

She glanced away. 'Well, uncross it. I'm not a fan of blabbing about my private life to anyone and I don't expect you to do it either.' Her head turned slightly, enough for her green eyes to pierce him, steady, determined, proud. 'What happened that night was between us.'

Us. The word vibrated inside him. He had never managed to be a 'we' or an 'us' with any woman. How could you be something that you fundamentally didn't understand?

Sex was different. There was nothing to understand. It was hormones, pheromones, biology. You didn't need to learn it; it was a primal urge, an instinct. And some relationships were instinctive too, or they were supposed to be. Parents were programmed to love their children, to want to protect and nurture and indulge them.

Not in his family.

His chest tightened with the old, familiar mix of fury and bafflement and pain. Logically, he could see why it had been like that. His parents had nothing in common with each other except one night of cheap beer and careless sex. They hadn't wanted to marry. They certainly hadn't wanted a baby. But that was what they'd got. And maybe in the beginning, they had thought that against all odds they could make it work. Or maybe they had simply been marking time until they could get divorced. Either way, despite being man and wife they'd not been a couple except in name only.

Yet, the strange thing was that even though he and Eden had spent only six hours together at most, they had felt like an 'us'. And he'd felt at one with himself, and with her, in a way that was absent from any other relationship he could remember.

Which was probably why his daughter was being raised by another man on the other side of the world.

'Is that why you wanted to talk to me? Because I meant what I said. My private life is private.'

He nodded. 'But you can understand why I would have concerns. I don't need any more bad publicity.'

There was a lengthy pause.

'As your reputation manager, I can only concur.' Another pause. 'I just didn't know that's what I was.'

He shook his head. 'You misunderstand me—'

She shrugged. 'What's to understand? You like to pick up women in bars for sex.'

Her directness surprised him enough to tell the truth. 'I usually don't, and you picked me up.'

He felt his body respond to the sudden heat in her eyes. 'Whatever.' She shrugged. 'It doesn't matter either way.'

'Is that why you left before I woke up?' He spoke unthinkingly, her absence still a raw wound, but as her chin jerked up, he felt a tiny stab of satisfaction that he had got beneath her skin even if it came at the cost of her having got beneath his.

'I had something to do.' Her voice was fierce, and he felt a sudden compulsion to ask her what could have been more important than their feverish need for each other.

'And you paid for the room—'

'Why does that matter?'

Good question, he thought, only it was one that he couldn't easily answer even though he was feeling the same sense of shock and outrage as before, the same irritation with himself for minding so much about something so trivial. But any answer he gave would make him look like some Neanderthal throwback. She would think it was his ego.

And it was, but not because he needed to pick up the bill to feel like a man.

It cut deeper than that. He had felt that same sense of being surplus to requirements. Maybe if they'd had a conversation about it, he would have let her pay if that was what she wanted, although that in itself was mind-boggling. He couldn't remember the last time a woman had offered to pay for anything.

But she hadn't talked to him. She had simply paid and left.

Just like Jessie. Only she had bought an air ticket back home to Australia.

Aged eighteen, he had been relieved. Relieved? It shouldn't hurt that much when something was true, but he felt a hot wave of shame and anger rise up inside him and although his voice was quiet when he finally answered her, it cost him.

'I'd already given them my credit card details.'

'I know, but I wanted to pay.' She frowned. 'I don't see what your problem is. Surely, you're not so old-fashioned that you can't let a woman pay for a hotel room.'

'I'm not old-fashioned—'

'Then what's the big deal? Yes, I paid, but before that you left your credit-card details so how is that any different?'

'Because you were there. You saw me do it. You had a chance then to say how you wanted things to be.'

Unlike him. He had been sidelined his entire life, first by his parents and then by the mother of his child. Not that Eden Fennell needed to know about any of that.

'I'd have preferred to be consulted.'

Yet another pause.

'Would you have hired me if you had been?'

He felt a pang as he remembered the remark he'd made when he'd introduced her to Avery.

'I mean, if you had realised who I was?'

He glanced over to where she was sitting. In the sub-dued lighting of the car, she looked defiant and young. She was young, he reminded himself, remembering her date of birth from the résumé Avery had sent him. The same age he'd been when he'd finally had the money to start trying to track down Jasmine. By then, he'd felt so old, as if he'd lived a hundred lives.

'Probably not,' he admitted. 'But I trust Avery. She has good instincts and you presented well today.'

'I know it must feel like you're taking a risk but I'm very good at my job.'

'I hope you're better than good. In fact, I expect the best and by that I mean I want this process to feel organic, not staged in any way.'

'Of course.' She nodded. 'Don't worry. I won't have you judging best in show at the county fair or kissing babies—'

It was instantly and shockingly, piercingly painful, just as if she'd leaned over and punched him in the face. Because it didn't matter how many years had passed. In fact, with every year that passed, it was getting harder and harder to not think about his daughter because she was always in his heart.

Beside him, Eden shifted forward. 'I will do a good job for you. I'm not a quitter.' There was a different note to her voice now, a certainty and a confidence that made her seem older than twenty-five.

'I'll hold you to that.'

Outside the car, the city was changing tempo. The rhythm of the night was starting to overlap the end of the working day.

He felt the memory of that night lap up against his skin and, even though she was sitting on the other side of the limo, he felt crowded by his need for her. His fingers twitched as she looked over at him, her pupils huge and dark, holding him steady, and he felt the combative tension between them dissolving like salt in warm water.

Glancing away, she cleared her throat. 'This is fine for me.'

He tapped on the privacy screen and the limo pulled smoothly alongside the kerb.

'I'll send a car to pick you up in the morning. Be ready for eight.'

'No need. I know where your office is, Mr Carver.'

He shook his head. 'The paparazzi are already sniffing around the building.'

'I can take care of myself.'

His chest tightened sharply as he pictured her trying to push her way through a baying pack of photographers and journalists. 'Take the car, Eden, and that's an order.' It was the first time he had spoken her name out loud, and he felt something loosen in him as her chin jerked up and their gazes locked momentarily, her green eyes clear and startled. Then she was opening the door and stepping onto the pavement.

She didn't look back and after a few seconds she was swallowed up by the crowds. As the car began to move, he found his gaze pulling towards the window. But that was understandable, he told himself. He was still coming to terms with her sudden reappearance. It was frustrating that just when he needed to be most stable, he was feeling so unfettered, so like a stranger to himself.

Tomorrow would be different.

By then he would no longer be in shock, and if they spent more time together then Eden would become a woman like any other and stop feeling like some fantasy who had sprung unexpectedly and distractingly to life.

Leaning back against the headrest, he deliberately closed his eyes. Everything was under control, and he fully expected that in a matter of weeks his reputation would be, if not fully restored, then well on the way to it. Finally, he would be able to put this whole disastrous episode behind him.

And that night in the hotel would be nothing more than a half-remembered dream.

His expectations had proved correct, he thought a week later as he stepped out of the elevator on the executive level. Except on one account. His mouth formed around a four-letter word.

Eden.

It had been a promising theory, thinking that proximity and familiarity could dull the senses, and with every other woman of his acquaintance it had swiftly and effortlessly become reality. But not with her.

It was almost the end of the working day and most of his staff were picking up their coats and bags. A few were chatting. Others were heading towards the elevator.

Soon the office would be empty and quiet. He liked it like that. Liked watching the sun set from his office. Some days, most days if he was being truthful, it felt more like home than his glittering, echoing triplex. Particularly at the moment. He seemed drawn here, coming in earlier, staying later than usual, returning when there was really no reason to do so.

The lie fizzed inside his head. There was a reason. He was looking at her now.

His stride faltered infinitesimally as his gaze narrowed in on Eden, and that was annoying in itself. There were any number of brunettes currently working at HCI and yet without exception every time he walked into the open-plan office, his eyes seemed to find their way to her unerringly like a heat-seeking missile.

Although he couldn't put his finger on why.

It wasn't as if she dressed outlandishly.

Take today. She was wearing another of those silky blouses and a pair of slim-fitting trousers, and that his brain had even registered that blew his mind. He wasn't remotely interested in women's clothing and usually had no opinion on what they wore. But he could pretty much remember every single outfit Eden had worn this week and all of them seemed to have been designed with the express purpose of hinting at what they appeared to hide.

He watched her leaning forward to look at something on Avery's laptop, her hair falling to cover her profile, and he felt a flash of regret that he could no longer see the curve of her jaw.

The two women were talking intently and then Avery's assistant, Aaron, came over and said something and Eden nodded and smiled, and he felt his insides clench. She had a sweet smile, natural and warming like spring sunshine. Not that he'd experienced it first-hand. The smiles she reserved for him were polite and perfectly calibrated to reveal nothing and he suddenly found himself willing her to look over and smile at him like that.

Harris Carver was back.

Eden didn't look up, but she didn't need to see him to know he was there. Her body had already quivered to attention like a dog hearing its owner's car in the drive and as she felt him walk towards her, the noises in the office seemed to fade away and she was aware of nothing beyond the pounding of her heart.

And his eyes.

When finally she could no longer bear it, she looked up. Her throat tightened. He was staring down at her, those grey eyes of his boring into her like the drills he was designing for the moon.

'Mr Carver—'

'Ms Fennell.'

He inclined his head slightly and she gave him one of her specially patented you're-the-boss smiles that she had been pinning to her face for the last five days.

'You seem very focused on something. What are you thinking about?'

You, she thought, her eyes zigzagging down over his body. Every mesmerising inch of him. Ever since he'd dropped her off in Cooper Square, she had spent too many hours to bill researching him, and usually that was the part she enjoyed the most. Not just because it gave her the foundation stones to build a strategy. There was something relaxing about research. It was like doing a jigsaw puzzle.

Except in Harris's case, it felt as though there were multiple missing pieces and others that simply didn't fit into any of the holes.

His media footprint up until the *Chronicle* story was incredibly light. There were no puff pieces, hardly any interviews and the biography his Comms teams had given her could be best described as minimalist.

She had other ways of researching her clients. Eavesdropping on staff as they congregated around the water cooler or waited for the elevators or even in the restrooms. None of which had revealed much that she didn't already know.

The data from the social listening company had hinted at a rivalry between Harris and Tiger McIntyre, which tied in with what Avery had said at that first meeting, but it was mostly uncredited fragments of supposition.

Still, she found herself poring over every detail like some teenager reading fan fiction about her favourite character so that even when her laptop powered down in exhaustion, he was there inside her head. Worse, when she finally made it to bed, as she fell asleep, Harris would still be there beside her, his arm pressing her tightly against him, his heat spreading through her limbs.

So that was relaxing.

She cleared her throat. 'This is the mentoring website. It's not completely finished but I'm really pleased with it.'

'Come into my office and I'll take a look,' he said, picking up her laptop and snapping it shut as he walked off. She stared after him for a moment, then followed him reluctantly as he must have known she would, not least because she needed her laptop back.

'So, when does it go live?'

'The morning you visit the school. We're letting them manage all the publicity so it will be quite basic and amateurish but that's what we want. And it won't stop the story getting picked up by the mainstream media outlets.'

'Isn't that a bit risky? What if it doesn't?'

'It will. Your name guarantees that, but we want it to look authentic. It has to feel organic and speak to your character. Otherwise, I might as well have you jumping out of a cake in swim shorts waving fistfuls of dollars and pledging your support for orphans and widows.'

'You don't see me doing that?' His gaze had risen to meet hers, sharper than before, as if he wanted to watch her reply, and then his mouth pulled minutely at the corners, and she had to press her feet into the polished concrete floor to stop from turning and running out of his office. Because that ghost of a smile made her feel blurred at the edges as if she were melting...

She shook her head partly to answer his question but mostly because she hoped it would hide her reaction from his all-seeing gaze. 'Funnily enough, no.'

His eyes drifted down to where the pulse in her throat was beating in time to an invisible pair of castanets and in desperation she spun round slowly.

'This is a beautiful space.'

It wasn't the first time she had been in this office but before there had been other people and there hadn't been much time to take in her surroundings. It was predictably and impressively large. What was less predictable was the artwork.

She stared up at the pictures on the wall. She had been in other offices of wealthy, successful business leaders. There was a definite decor among the superrich. They liked clean lines and high ceilings and tall windows. And they loved art.

Old Masters. Impressionists. Picasso. Pollock. Rothko. Hirst.

But this man had drawings. Not the Michelangelo kind. Technical drawings of machinery. Blueprints for the future of humanity. She peered forward.

'It's a motor driver. For the lunar rover we designed.'

Harris's voice made her jump inside her skin. Steadying her breathing, she said over her shoulder, 'Are you included in that "we"?'

'I understand the components and the engineering, and I probably could design something fairly basic, but nothing like that. Not any more. And I don't have to. HCI have teams of designers who will do it for me. But I like to be involved.'

'And consulted,' she said softly.

He had moved closer while she was looking at the pictures and, glancing up, she felt his intent gaze and the latent power of his body envelop her.

'That too.'

She licked her lips and forced her attention back to the drawings. 'Are they special in some way? Is that why you have them in your office?'

'Some are. That one.' He pointed to the print on her left. 'That one was the first of our designs to make it up to the International Space Station. It's a safety tether, which is a basic piece of kit for astronauts. Essential, really, if they don't want to join all the other space junk orbiting the Earth. Others, I just like the look of them because there's something pleasing about the ratio of straight lines to curves.'

'Like this one.' She pointed to a different print. 'That's probably my favourite.'

'Mine too,' he said quietly. 'It's a pistol grip drill.'

She glanced at the scale at the bottom of the drawing. 'It must be quite big in real life.'

'It is. It has to be, because of the gloves the astronauts wear. But it's made of glass-coated plastic covered in aluminium so it's light.'

'Do you ever get to see the finished product?'

He nodded. 'I do. I see all the various prototypes before they go into production. And we get sent footage of them in situ.'

She frowned. 'You mean on the moon?'

He shook his head. 'Not currently, but in the future. Right now, we have around thirty products in operational use on the space station.'

There was an odd note to his voice, guarded almost, and she was suddenly desperate to ask him why, but then she came to her senses and moved over to the window, her gaze tilting automatically up to the darkening sky. 'Is it visible from here? The space station, I mean. Or do you need a telescope?'

He shook his head. 'No telescope required. It's a bright

white pinpoint of light. Typically, it's the brightest object in the sky aside from the moon. In fact, we might even be able to see it now.'

'How do you know that?'

'I get alerts about its location, and I noticed that it was passing over New York tonight.' He stared up through the glass. 'It's there. No, lower.' She felt his hand touch her shoulder, his touch light but emphatic, guiding her forward, closer to the glass so that she had to tip back her head. 'Look along my arm.'

The fabric of his sleeve was smooth against her cheek, and she could feel the press of his biceps and her heart twitched as she breathed in his scent. He smelled so good—

'I can see it.' Smiling triumphantly, she turned, and he smiled too, and she was about to turn away again, but her hand had somehow ended up pressed against his chest, and his hand was in her hair, and it was suddenly an effort to stay standing. His grey gaze was about an inch away from her, pressing into her like hot steel. Except it wasn't grey because his eyes were all pupils. Soft and dark and as fathomless as a black hole.

She could feel their gravitational pull. Or maybe that was his scent. Or the heat of his body.

Either way, she could feel herself leaning in, and she knew it was dangerous because she wasn't wearing a safety tether. If she got close enough there would be no pulling back—

'Sorry, Mr Carver—'

They both jumped apart as the light flicked on, blinding white, the intimacy dissolving like a broken spell. It was one of the security guards. 'I'm sorry, sir, I didn't know anyone was in here.'

'It's fine, Ted. I was showing Ms Fennell the Space Station, but she was just leaving—'

Eden blinked up at him. She felt like Titania waking from her enchanted sleep. 'Yes, I should be going.'

'Have a good weekend,' he said, and there was a trace of impatience in his voice along with a roughness that scraped over her skin, making her feel hot and flustered and unsteady on her feet.

'You too.'

He nodded, but he was already staring back up at the night sky, and she walked quickly towards the door before she did something stupid and regrettable. Even worse than standing in the dark alone with this incomparably beautiful man whose presence kicked up dangerous sparks in her.

Sparks that should remind her that it was dangerous to play with fire. As if she needed reminding.

CHAPTER FIVE

'IF YOU WOULD follow me, Mr Carver, Ms Fennell.'

Eden turned away from the line of lockers and smiled at Principal Evans. 'Sorry, being back at high school is giving me flashbacks.'

The principal smiled. 'I'm sure you were the model pupil, Ms Fennell.'

That was true academically. She had studied hard and been a high achiever. But outside class, things were a little trickier. She hadn't been a troublemaker as such, but you couldn't have a mother like hers and not end up with a target on your back so there had been quite a few altercations with the 'mean girls' at her school.

A few with some of the boys too. Boys who saw her mother's long legs in their short shorts and thought 'like mother like daughter'. It was one of the things that had first attracted her to Liam. He hadn't been interested in her family or her background; he'd told her that it was just her and him and it had been exactly what she'd wanted to hear.

Of course, he had only said that to justify keeping his own life secret for the very obvious reason that he was married.

Her stupidity made her squirm and, pushing away the memory, she shook her head. 'I wish. What about you, Mr Carver? How were your schooldays?'

Probably he'd been valedictorian, and quarterback for the

school team, she thought, picturing his broad shoulders in a football shirt. No doubt he'd dated a cheerleader. Most likely, all of them.

Beside her, Harris's smooth stride stuttered for perhaps a tenth of a second. Not enough to draw the attention of Principal Evans or his security detail, who were keeping pace discreetly alongside them.

But she'd noticed even though she didn't want to. Her eyes were drawn to him, always, and not just her eyes. Whenever he was present, it was as if each of her five senses was tuned to the way he moved and to the shifting tones in his voice and when he left the room, everything seemed to go staticky inside her head so that she had to really concentrate on even simple tasks.

His grey eyes were cool and clear as he shrugged. 'I don't really have any strong memories either way. Once something is over, I prefer to look forward.'

She heard the warning in his words, but he really didn't need to bother. Since that moment in his office when they'd almost kissed, he had been stiffly formal and careful to keep his distance. It was stupid to feel hurt. They'd had sex once, and it wasn't as if she wanted anything from him, like a relationship or a future. Which was lucky, because today was the final day of her contract.

She should be pleased, and proud. Everything had, not just gone as she'd hoped, but exceeded her expectations. Quietly and by stealth, Harris Carver's name had disappeared from the news headlines.

Today was his chance to reclaim his narrative.

'We're set up in the gym.' The principal smiled apologetically. 'I know that the scheme is for the senior school, but there's been so much excitement about you coming in to talk, so I hope you don't mind, Mr Carver, but we decided to let the lower years join us.'

The gym was packed. As well as the pupils, the entire staff appeared to be there too, but then it wasn't often that you got up close to a real life, self-made billionaire. And Harris Carver was worth the entrance fee. He not only looked the part, but also had that aura of power and confidence that shrank the huge hall so that it felt like an average-sized room.

He was a good speaker too, despite not having received any coaching. She had checked that with him beforehand, but it seemed that he instinctively understood how to connect with an audience, speaking to the back of the room, fluently and without a script.

'Do you think Mr Carver might take some questions?' Principal Evans was looking at her hopefully when Harris finished.

She had anticipated this, and prepped Harris. Private schools might frequently get speakers like Harris Carver but for a public school, particularly one in a deprived neighbourhood like the Wendell Wells Academy High School, this was the rarest of opportunities.

Glancing at her watch, she nodded. 'Fifteen minutes, and then we really will have to go.'

The questions were the typical kind of random, unfiltered ones that teens asked.

'Do you have a private jet?'

'Are you going to run for president?'

'What's the most expensive thing you've ever bought?'

Above the roof of the gymnasium, she could hear the tell-tale thwapping sound of a helicopter hovering. She tilted her head slightly. Several helicopters, in fact. Which meant the news of Harris's presence had leaked out as she'd known it would. She felt his gaze seek her out, so he had heard them too. After a moment, his mouth pulled up ever so slightly at the corners and she felt his approval shiver through her like a light summer breeze and she had to actively stop herself from just grinning like a fool.

'Hi, Mr Carver. My name is Alyssa and I wanted to ask you if you ever wanted to be an astronaut.'

There was a pause. 'No, I never wanted to do that,' Harris said slowly.

'But why not?' Alyssa frowned. She looked baffled and Eden could understand why. Even without the spacesuit, with his carved bone structure and cropped blond hair, he looked exactly like a Hollywood version of an astronaut. 'I think going into space would be so cool.'

'It is cool, Alyssa, but astronauts have to be a very specific kind of person. I'm not sure I'm that person. In some ways, I hope I'm not.'

There was a tension in his shoulders, as if he were carrying some invisible weight, but then it had been a long three weeks. She glanced at her watch. The helicopters would have got here first but it would be the news crews on the ground next and she didn't want this to turn into a circus. Tapping the principal on the arm, she said quietly, 'Let's make that the last question.'

'That went well.'

'It did.' Harris turned and nodded. The tension in his shoulders seemed to have lifted.

'Three of the news channels have already covered the visit and it's extremely positive. I have the links. I'll send them over to you.'

'Thank you. And thank you for all your hard work.' He hesitated. 'As you know, I had my doubts about whether this was a good idea, you working for me—'

'Working *with* you,' she said firmly but without any heat.

His eyebrow lifted. 'I was concerned that you might have overpromised but you've more than delivered.'

'You were easier to work with than I thought you'd be,' she said after a moment.

'You sound surprised.'

'Not surprised, but it can be hard to speak truth to power.'

'I didn't notice you struggling.' He smiled in a way that made her feel grateful she was sitting down.

'I did tell you that we needed to be honest with each other if this relationship was going to work,' she said.

'You did. But it seems a little one-sided. I mean, I know next to nothing about you.'

He was being polite or passing the time. It meant nothing, but she felt panic ripple through her like quicksilver and she couldn't tell if it was because she wanted to keep herself hidden from him or, more confusingly, to tell him the truth.

'Not much to know. I grew up in San Antonio. Went to school, college. Graduated, went to—'

'Went to England,' he finished her sentence. 'Started the business. Do you want me to list your clients? Because I can. It's all on your résumé, which I've read.'

'The trailer is the best way to sell a film,' she said, keeping her voice light and casual. 'I don't want to bore you with the four-hour director's cut.'

He waited, and she held her breath, hoping he'd move on.

Damn, he was good at waiting.

She sighed theatrically because it gave her a chance to adjust her breathing. 'Okay, I'll trade you. You ask me one thing that's not on my résumé and I get to ask you one thing.'

'I've already told you so much—'

'Yeah, stuff I can read on the Internet.'

'Fine.' He made a surrendering movement with his hands. 'We each get one question.'

She should have tacked on some conditions, she realised as he leaned back, his grey gaze lingering on her face as if the answer were already there even though he hadn't asked his question yet.

'So, what made you go into this business?'

Was that it? She had half expected him to ask her something more personal than that. She knew she could have lied or dissembled about the things that made her feel exposed and stupid, but Harris had a way of looking at her that pulled memories and feelings to the surface. If one had come loose, she'd been scared the rest would come tumbling out like water pushing through a breaking dam.

'I don't know. I suppose I don't like injustice.'

'Meaning?'

'That's two questions.'

Her breath caught as he leaned back into the upholstery and stretched out his long legs. And waited.

She shrugged. 'I don't like people name-calling and lying and getting away with it. It's not fair, or right.' Her stomach knotted as she remembered how people had spoken about her sweet, hopeless mother and grandmother.

'Why not be a lawyer? A litigator?'

'That's four questions.'

His mouth curved up infinitesimally. 'Three. I was just qualifying what kind of lawyer.'

'It takes twenty years to build a reputation, and five minutes to lose it. But it takes something in between to get a case to court and I don't want to get bogged down in weeks and months of he said/she said. I want to make a difference in real time. No.' She held up her hand like a police officer stopping traffic. 'It's my turn now, okay?'

Looking over to where he sat lounging casually, her stomach fluttered with nerves and anticipation. There were so many things she wanted to ask him. Quite a few were un-askable out loud, like *what did you think of me when you saw me in that bar*? Or *do you still dream about that night*?

And then suddenly she thought back to the moment in the gym when he'd hesitated. 'Did you really never want to be an astronaut?'

For a moment he said nothing, just stared past her, but he didn't need to say anything for her to know that his mood had changed. His features looked granite hard, and the easy warmth of moments earlier had faded from his eyes.

'I'm not in the habit of lying to schoolchildren,' he said slowly.

'I wasn't accusing you of lying. I was just surprised that it wasn't a dream of yours.'

'A dream?'

His anger caught her off guard but, in the light streaming through the windows of the limo, his grey eyes were shad-ows that offered no explanation for his sudden flash of rage. 'Why would you think that choosing a dark, lifeless vacuum over everything on Earth would be a dream of mine?' His skin was taut across his cheekbones. 'It shouldn't be any-one's dream.'

She thought back to how they'd looked up at the night sky together, his body hard and hot against hers. It was stupid, but it felt as though he'd lied to her. 'But you get alerts from the space station—'

'I track it because a lot of our equipment is up there.'

That was probably true, but she knew instinctively that he wasn't telling her the whole truth. Only what was there to lie about?

'You just seemed to know a lot about space, and usually when people are that informed it's because they're inter-ested. So—'

'So, you presumed to think you know me.' Abruptly he leaned forward. 'Three weeks. That's how much time we've spent together. Do you think that's long enough to know someone?'

'Three weeks and one night,' she said coolly. 'And yes, I do think that's long enough. Three weeks is pretty much all I ever have to get to know clients. I can't do my job if I don't know them because I don't have a one-size-fits-all strategy, not even in a niche industry like yours. Or do you think I would use the same strategy for you as I would for Tiger McIntyre?'

She hadn't picked that name by chance. The two men were in direct competition, and they were like chalk and cheese. There were also those rumours of a long-standing rivalry. It felt like an unsurprising choice, so she was shocked by the stunned expression on Harris's face. Actually, he looked more shaken than stunned.

'What has Tiger McIntyre got to do with any of this?'

'He's your biggest competitor.'

'He is *nothing* like me.'

'That's not what I said—'

'Then perhaps you should say what you mean.'

'Oh, I don't think you want me to do that, Mr Carver,' she said stiffly, after a taut, electric moment that left her feeling shaky and singed. 'You might not like what I say.'

His eyes narrowed. 'Then it's fortunate our time together is at an end and that our lives were only briefly, and out of necessity, connected.' Shrugging up his shirt sleeve, he glanced at his watch. 'I have a conference call at four, but we can meet afterwards for the review.'

The review meeting was short and without incident. Avery gushed over her approach and her insight. Harris Carver thanked her politely for her work and she thanked him just as politely for giving her the chance to prove herself, and then they shook hands and she left.

It wasn't as if she'd expected flowers. Most of her clients were grateful and relieved in equal measure when she started working with them but, by the end, their relief typically outweighed their gratitude because they had regained control of their lives.

'He's got a lot on today but he's very pleased with you,' Avery said as they made their way back to the office Eden had been using during her time at HCI. 'I'm just going to freshen up and then we can head down to the lounge.'

Eden blinked. 'To do what?'

'There's a party. Not for you,' she added, laughing as she caught sight of Eden's no doubt appalled expression. 'Cathy's going on maternity leave on Monday so we're just giving her a little send-off.'

'That's very kind of you to invite me, Avery, but I'm not—'

'Nonsense,' Avery said firmly. 'You've been like one of the team, and, besides, Cathy asked specifically if you would come. I know you wouldn't want to disappoint a heavily pregnant woman—'

Growing up in a house full of women, she had always felt part of a sisterhood, but after losing her baby it had been hard at first to celebrate other women's pregnancies. Sometimes she'd had to physically look away from their bumps. It was still hard, but she liked Cathy a lot and she wouldn't be happy with herself if she didn't go.

'Okay, then, you've twisted my arm.'

She was still getting used to being part of a team. At school she had been a bit of a loner. University was better in terms of feeling that people had accepted her for herself but by then she had already been so guarded. Liam's deceit and abandonment had left her warier, and wearier, than ever. But she had enjoyed working here.

The party was in full flow by the time they arrived.

'Wow, there's waitstaff.'

'HCI isn't a family business, but we try and take care of our staff,' Avery said proudly. 'Mr Carver has always been very clear about that. And generous too.'

'Would you like some champagne?' One of the waiters was leaning in with a tray of glasses. 'Or we have a non-alcoholic elderflower fizz?'

'Actually, what I'd really like is a cup of tea. Milk, no sugar.' She smiled sheepishly at Avery. 'I know, but I always miss it when I first come back to the States.'

Avery smiled. 'If that's how you want to celebrate. And you should be celebrating, Eden. You did an amazing job.'

She smiled at Avery. She liked the head of Comms. Avery was a role model from an older generation, but she had championed a younger woman, which was inspiring.

'I would say I'd love to work for you again, but I think that's the last thing either of us would want.'

Avery shook her head, serious suddenly. 'You're a good fit for HCI. If I had a staff job, I'd be offering it to you now.'

'Thank you, I'd love to work for you. You have a great team.'

'Well, Harris is a great boss.'

Eden felt her smile stiffen. Avery was not alone. Everyone at HCI thought the same. But then look at Liam. Presumably his wife and friends all thought he was one of the good guys too. Or maybe they didn't, and she was the only mug to think he was perfect. Either was a depressing thought. Maybe that was why she felt so deflated, and the party felt less like a celebration and more like a marking of the end of things.

But then, after three weeks of working long into the evenings, it was the end. No wonder she felt so shattered.

Her eyes flicked to the door as she caught a glimpse of broad shoulders, her stomach flipping, but it wasn't Harris. She knew he wasn't going to appear. That weird conversation in his office with Avery standing there like a chaperone was going to be the outro to this strange, shimmering episode in her life. And it was for the best, she told herself firmly. But just the same her gaze jerked over to the door as it opened again.

Not him.

'Shall we grab something to eat?' Avery was looking at her curiously and, pulling her gaze away from the door, Eden shook her head. 'I think I might skip the food. I'm catching a flight in a couple of hours.'

'To London?'

'San Antonio. To see my family. It's a surprise.'

That was another consequence of Liam getting back in touch like that. It had reminded her of the secrecy surrounding their relationship, the lies she'd told her family, and she had felt all that remembered guilt on top of her new guilt for not confiding in them. She wanted to make amends now that the shock and pain of his revelation were no longer visible on her face.

She took a sip of her tea and frowned. It tasted weird.

The milk at home had been off too. Maybe it was the weather. She'd read somewhere that thunderstorms could curdle milk and there had certainly been plenty of those over the last few weeks.

Like the one the night she and Harris had run to the hotel.

Pushing aside the memory, she walked over to Cathy.

'You look incredible,' she said as they hugged. Cathy looked just like one of those women who modelled for pregnancy stores online. Her hair was lustrous, and her skin had a kind of luminous quality to it as if it were being lit from the inside.

Cathy smiled. 'You should have seen me seven months ago. I had all these breakouts, and my hair was greasy. I was so tired all the time and everything tasted weird. I kept throwing away stuff because I thought it had gone off.'

The door opened again, but this time, Eden didn't turn to look. Instead, she stared at Cathy, a cool, clammy panic trickling down her spine.

'Would you excuse me a moment?' She smiled. 'I'm just going to nip to the cloakroom.'

She managed to keep the smile in place right up until she shut the cubicle door. Pulling out her phone, she checked her period tracker. Everything had been so crazy since she'd arrived in New York and she'd lost track of time.

Even using her longest cycle, she was still two weeks late. Two weeks.

Don't panic, she told herself quickly, pushing back against the memory of Harris. His hand gripping her shoulder. Breath hard and hot against her throat. A dark flush along his cheekbones and that storm of passion in his eyes.

But they had used a condom.

Trying to steady her breathing, she leaned against the wall, wishing the cool bricks could soothe her fevered brain enough to think straight. Ever since she'd opened the office in New York her cycle had been all over the place. Her friend, Lauren, who was a doctor, had told her that flying long haul could sometimes do that.

She ran her tongue over her teeth, trying to shift that metallic taste. Trying not to remember the last time she'd tasted it, trying to stem the panicky thoughts swelling up and filling her chest.

So do a test. There was no harm in checking. In fact, it would put her mind at rest, she thought as she returned to the party, and picked up her bag.

'You're not leaving, are you?' It was Cathy.

'Sorry, yes.' She held out her phone. 'It's a bit of a family emergency,' she lied. 'But I've got your socials, so I'll keep an eye open for any announcements—'

She glanced across the room and froze. Harris Carver was talking to Avery, but he was watching her. Her heart began to beat like a jackhammer. Earlier when she was talking to Avery, she had been scanning the room for him because she was stupid enough to want to see him again just one last time, but now the idea of talking to him, being in his orbit, made her feel hot and dizzy, and cornered.

'Are you okay?' Cathy was staring at her anxiously. 'You look really pale. Do you want to sit down?'

'I'm fine,' she lied. 'It's just been a long day. I have to go, but take care—'

She broke off. Harris Carver was moving purposefully across the room, and, snatching up her bag, she turned and made her way to the door.

'Eden—'

She darted out of the room and narrowly caught the elevator. But as the doors closed, she caught a glimpse of his narrowed grey, questioning gaze.

She stopped off at a drugstore on her way back to her apartment. Twenty minutes and one test later she was standing in the bathroom in just her blouse and bra, staring dazedly at the stick on the edge of the bath. Or more specifically at the word in the window.

Pregnant

That couldn't be right. It must be faulty. Thankfully, she had another two back up tests sitting on the kitchen counter.

But she couldn't make her legs move. There was no point. The test was right. She knew it was because she could remember how it had felt the last time. Only that time she hadn't known what it was she was feeling. It had been winter, cold and damp. She'd thought she was coming down with the flu and that was why she felt so heavy and exhausted.

She and Liam had gone to Chicago to see a band they loved, and it had been snowy. Liam had almost slipped over in the street, and she'd grabbed his arm. He had pulled away and she'd thought it was because he was embarrassed.

It wasn't that. Much later, when she had been torturing herself by replaying their relationship over and over again, she had realised that he hadn't wanted her to think that he needed her for anything. And she'd wished she could go back in time and let him fall on his backside. Or, better still, push him in front of a snow plough.

He had broken up with her by text, and even then he had lied to her.

I've met someone.

As if it had just happened when, in fact, he'd been married for two years. Was it any wonder then that when the cramps started, she had thought it was just her body going into shock?

They'd told her at the hospital. That she was pregnant but she was losing her baby. So, she had never done this part. This testing and watching the future emerge in a small white rectangle.

Back then, with Liam, she would have been thrilled. They'd talked about getting a place together. He'd sometimes teasingly called her 'wife'. They would have celebrated, cried, talked about names. Of course, none of that had meant anything. All of it, the talking about the future, the joking about marriage, had been lies designed to keep her hooked and stop her realising that he wasn't as invested in their relationship as she was. In reality, she'd always been on her own.

Just like now.

Only now she wasn't celebrating. She was terrified. Terrified at the thought of being a single mom. Terrified that this baby would be snatched away from her because she wasn't ready or happy or capable of being good enough. And she knew that she wasn't good enough. Just look at how unthinkingly she had got pregnant.

Worse than that, she'd done what she'd always striven to avoid doing. She had got pregnant by a man who didn't want her. The curse had come true. She was going to be another Fennell woman raising a baby alone.

Her body tensed as the buzzer to her apartment vibrated through the apartment, cutting across her panic. It was probably some food delivery guy dropping yet another pizza to her neighbour. But he'd work it out.

It buzzed again, loud and insistent. Whoever was pressing that buzzer was not going to give up, and, darting into her bedroom, she snatched up a pair of pyjama bottoms and pulled them on.

'Whatever it is, I didn't order it,' she snapped, yanking open the door. 'So, could you stop—'

Her voice died in her throat.

It wasn't a pizza delivery guy. It was Harris Carver.

She stared at him, her legs suddenly unsteady. Her lungs felt as if they were bruised on the inside. He couldn't know. Of course, he didn't. But what was he doing here? The panic she had been working so hard to stifle rose to her head in a rush and she stared at him mutely.

'You left your jacket at the office.'

He held it up, and after a moment she took it from his out-stretched hand.

'Thank you. You didn't need to bring it round.'

'I wanted to check if you were all right. You left in a bit of a hurry and Cathy was worried about you. She said you'd had some kind of family emergency.'

Had she said that?

'Everything's fine.' She lifted her chin, smiled stiffly. She felt as if she were made of glass, that her skin was transparent and that she was open to him, just as she had been in that hotel room. Only that had been sex, and this was—

What was this?

The many, all equally unsettling answers to that question made her grip the edge of the door as if it were a cliff edge. 'I'm fine.'

Try telling that to your face, she thought as his gaze moved over her silk blouse and down to her striped pyjamas. She must look like a crazy person.

'It's nothing I can't handle.'

'You don't look like you're handling it.' Before she could stop him, he had taken her elbow and was gently guiding her back into the apartment.

'Sit down,' he ordered.

She sat, but then almost immediately got to her feet again as he turned and began striding away from her.

'What are you doing?'

'I'm getting you a glass of water.'

'I don't need one—' She reached out to grab his arm, but it was too late. He was already in the kitchen. There was still a chance he might not notice the boxes of spare tests—

But then she felt his sudden stillness. And it was how she imagined it would feel when a star collapsed in on itself in some giant, epic implosion. She knew without even needing to open her eyes that he had seen them, so she opened them anyway because choosing not to see something didn't stop it happening.

He was holding one of the boxes in his hand. His beautiful carved face looked like a bronze Emesa battle mask, and she felt her ribs snap tight as his grey gaze locked onto hers. She knew that she had gone pale, and that there was no way to hide that.

'You can't be pregnant. We used a condom.' There was a short, stifling silence as his gaze switched to the other boxes on the counter, then back to her face.

'Are you pregnant?' he said hoarsely. 'Have you done a test?'

She licked her lips, the directness of his questions making her sway a little as if his words were a series of jabs to her body. 'I've only done one and it could be wrong—'

Her voice faded, but then the look on his face was enough to rob anyone of speech.

'How pregnant are you?'

'I don't know. Six, maybe seven weeks.'

She could see him doing the maths. 'So, it could be mine?'

It? She swayed slightly as a rush of fury that was as fierce as it was unfair surged through her, but she didn't feel like being fair. She felt like weeping and hiding from this man who had already disassembled her poise and steadiness and was now barking questions at her like an inquisitor.

'If you mean *my* baby, that's none of your business.'

Which was a lie. It was very much his business. But earlier on today he had pretty much told her that she had nothing to do with his life. Obviously, she knew that was not a reason to hide the truth from him, and she would have told him at some point. But right now, she had hardly processed it herself and he was here wanting to call the shots just as if she were still working for him. But this baby wasn't some proposal that needed his signature.

'None of my business,' he repeated slowly and the tension in the room ratcheted up several notches.

'What?' She stared at him coolly, but given that she was dressed for work and sleep at the same time it seemed unlikely that she was pulling it off.

'We had sex once. We weren't exclusive,' she lied.

'You were sleeping with other people?' He seemed stunned.

'Oh, and you weren't.' Just thinking about him with some other woman made her feel wronged. Which sounded insane even in the privacy of her own head.

'Don't judge people by your own standards, Eden.'

'Maybe, don't judge, period, Harris,' she snapped back. His name fizzed on her tongue like sherbet. 'What gives you the right to—'

'Fathers have rights too.'

Was that true? Panic stabbed her stomach. His voice was hard, all menace and that authority he wielded so casually in the office, but which felt terrifyingly out of place in this small apartment.

'Being there at the moment of conception doesn't make you a father except in the biological sense.'

'So, I am the father.' He moved then, leaning in, his hands pressing against the wall on either side of her.

'I didn't say that.' Being here with him was making her brain malfunction. She wanted him gone. Wanted to be alone so that she could process. But she also didn't want him to leave. There was something solid and reassuring about his presence and after last time—

She could remember it as easily as if it had happened yesterday. She hadn't understood what was happening. She had been alone and so scared—

She was still scared now, but at least she wasn't alone. Only she wasn't ready to deal with his reaction when she hadn't even come to terms with her own. And it wasn't fair of him to make this about himself. This was happening to her.

'You need to leave,' she said finally. 'I have a flight booked for San Antonio this evening, so I need to pack.'

He was looking at her as if she had grown a set of horns.

'I'm not going anywhere, and neither are you.'

'You're not my boss anymore. You can't tell me what to do.'

His face was harsh beneath the kitchen spotlights. 'I can tell you this, I'm not going to be letting you out of my sight until I know for certain if that baby is mine or not.'

'What are you going to do? Put me under house arrest?'

He took a step back, but his hands were still on either side of her face, his arms and chest crowding her back against the wall.

'That's not a bad idea.'

'I was joking.' She felt a rush of panic. Could he make that happen? The whole thing was too ludicrous to contemplate but there was a tension to his body that made her think that, from his perspective, it was a definite possibility. 'You can't keep me locked up here for the next seven or eight months.'

'I won't need to. You can do a paternity test at seven weeks.'

She felt her stomach twist. A paternity test. This was all moving way too fast.

'But I just told you I'm only about six weeks pregnant.'

'Exactly.' His eyes snapped up to meet hers and he lifted his hands from the wall. 'Which means I need you to come with me and stay with me for at least a week.'

'No—' She was shaking her head, but he didn't even notice or most likely he had noticed but he didn't care.

'I'm not going to stay with you. I don't need to. I have an apartment. You're standing in it.'

'I'm not talking about staying in New York. You won't relax here, and you need to relax, and rest.' He assessed her face. 'You've been working flat out for weeks now and don't bother trying to tell me otherwise. I know how many hours you've put in, and that would take a toll on anyone. But you're pregnant. You need to take extra good care of yourself, and the baby.'

'I can take care of myself and my baby,' she began but he cut her off.

'But it would be much easier if you didn't have to think about anything else. I can make that happen. I have a villa in St Barth's. It's fully staffed, so you won't have to lift a finger. You can just lie by the pool for a week and then we can take the test.'

They didn't need to do one but, given that she had pretty much told him that she had slept with other people, he was hardly likely to believe that.

As for resting and relaxing, with Harris living under the same roof as her that seemed unlikely.

Her hands balled at her sides. He was glancing impatiently at his watch, and she desperately tried to think of an alternative to his crazy suggestion.

But then she remembered his knock on the door earlier. This was not a man who would give up or be open to persuasion. She would have to fight him, only she couldn't fight the way he did, as if it was all or nothing. Not even on a good day, and she was so tired and strung out right now.

How could that be good for the baby? Her lungs sucked inwards, scrabbling for breath. She felt not just tired now but sick with panic. She couldn't lose this baby too. Harris was right about her needing rest. Only that wouldn't happen here in New York. Or in San Antonio.

There would be too many questions to answer at home.

Maybe a week away in the sun might give her the space she needed and make him back off a little. It would be worth going if both those things happened.

'Fine,' she said stiffly. 'I'll come to St Barth's with you. For a week. Now, if you wouldn't mind, I need to shower and pack, so why don't you go sit in that nice, air-conditioned limo of yours and I'll be down when I'm ready?'

Without giving him a chance to respond, she turned and walked back into her bedroom, slamming the door behind her.

CHAPTER SIX

EDEN HAD KNOWN Harris was rich, but there was something about a private jet that made that fact screamingly obvious, and now she was more uncertain than ever that she was doing the right thing. Although it was a little late to worry about that, given that she was currently midway between New York and the Caribbean island of Saint Barthélemy.

She still wasn't entirely sure why she'd agreed to come with him other than she had simply run out of fight in the moment, and there was no obvious alternative. Getting him to leave would have been like trying to move a mountain.

She had been suddenly, brutally tired of it all. Not just the unreasonableness of his demands but the simple, ground-shaking shock of finding out that she was pregnant, because the last time that happened, she had already been losing the baby she hadn't even realised she was carrying.

The memory of those excruciating, agonising hours in the hospital made her fingers dig into the leather armrest. Through all of it she had been on her own.

Only she hadn't been alone earlier. And maybe that was the real reason she had agreed to go with Harris.

She glanced across the cabin to where he was working on his laptop. After she had reluctantly agreed to his plan, he hadn't left her apartment as she'd asked. Instead, he'd stood outside her bedroom like some watchdog while she'd jerkily packed a bag in silence. Then he had part guided, part escorted her downstairs to his car, which had sped them through the city to some private airfield and his waiting jet.

And that was that.

Maybe if she closed her eyes for a moment, everything would stop spinning long enough for her to be able to plan her next move.

'There's a bed.'

Her eyelashes snapped up like a roller blind. Harris was standing next to her, his grey gaze narrowed critically on her face as if she were a piece of modern art he wanted to understand.

'I hope you're not suggesting we use it.' It was a pointless, provocative thing to say but she had wanted to knock him off balance. Only now she felt off balance because she was thinking about the last time they'd shared a bed.

He ignored that, but a muscle twitched in his jaw, so he was likely thinking the same as her, which was something. 'You look exhausted. Instead of trying to sleep in your seat, you might like to lie down.'

She stared up at him warily. 'And where are you going to sleep?'

'I have some projects to sign off, so I'll be working for a couple of hours, and then I'll just sleep in my seat. But I'm not pregnant.'

His fingers pressed against the edge of her seat. 'Just go and lie down, Eden.' He turned his head and one of the stewards appeared to accompany her to the other end of the cabin.

The bedroom was quiet, and the bed was surprisingly comfortable.

Stifling a yawn, she lay down, tucking her hand under the pillow.

'Oh, could you leave them open please?' she said as the steward started to draw the curtains.

'Of course, Ms Fennell. Is there anything else I can get you?'

'No, thank you.'

The night sky was different up here. There seemed to be fewer stars, but she wasn't looking for stars. She was looking for a single, bright white pinprick of light, and she was still looking when her eyelids closed five minutes later.

Tilting his head slightly to the left, Harris let his gaze track a yacht that was cutting a crisp white line through the brilliant blue sea. If that angle also allowed him to take in Eden's downturned face it was a coincidence, he told himself firmly.

They were eating a late breakfast out on the villa's deck. They had arrived in darkness and to lashing rain that was the tail end of a hurricane that was now heading to the mainland.

But this morning the sun was a brilliant Meyer lemon yellow, and the faded-denim-blue sky was cloudless. Better still, the forecast was for unseasonably placid weather so he would be able to make good on his promise to Eden of rest and relaxation beneath the Caribbean sun.

Although, truthfully, he didn't give a damn about the weather. All that mattered was that she was here. Not so much a prisoner as a hostage. As soon as he knew whether she was carrying his baby, she could leave. It wasn't exactly a chore, spending a week in the Caribbean. Most women would be delighted.

Eden was not.

He glanced over to where she was now staring pointedly out at the ocean. She was angry with him. But what gave her the right to be angry?

She wasn't the one who'd been left in the dark, because when exactly had she been planning on telling him she was pregnant? He had wanted to ask her that question multiple times already and he would if it turned out the baby was his.

And if it was?

He had asked himself that question multiple times too, and the answer changed each time. Except in one way. He would be a *major* part of his son or daughter's life. He would make sure of that, but he was getting ahead of himself. There was no point in spooking Eden by giving her advance warning of what he had in mind.

The last thing he needed was for her to disappear into the night as Jessie had, even though he fully understood why she had gone. Not turning up for the scan had sent her a clear message, or it must have seemed like that to Jessie, anyway. The truth was nothing had been clear. He had been floundering and scared and there had been nobody to ask what to do. He had felt so alone and ashamed and somehow responsible for having no one to go to. How could he be a father when he hadn't managed to be the son anyone wanted?

Pushing back against the tangled mess of emotions that thought provoked, he moved his plate to one side.

'Did you sleep well?'

Her eyes flashed to him then, the green of her irises vivid in the sunlight. 'Yes, it was very comfortable.' She hesitated. 'It's a very beautiful house.'

'I think so.' He had no reason to feel as pleased as he did by her somewhat reluctant approval. Maybe it was because she had offered it up uninvited, unlike the news about her pregnancy. 'I knew the previous owner and I asked him to let me know if he was in the market to sell and he called me two years ago.'

'Why this house in particular?' She had momentarily forgotten her anger and he wanted to keep her talking. Keep her looking at him like that as if she were genuinely interested in his answer, even though he knew it was just a hangover from their working relationship.

Relationship. The word jangled inside his head, and he

was back to wondering about what would happen if he was the baby's father.

It would be different this time because *he* was different. When Jesse had told him she was pregnant, her assumption that he would marry her had made him feel as though he were drowning. She had been pretty and confident, and he had desired her in the moment, but he hadn't loved her, and she hadn't loved him. Just like his mom and dad hadn't loved each other. That mirroring of his parents' unhappiness had loomed large. So large that he hadn't been able to see past it.

By the time he'd realised what he'd done, she was gone, and his daughter was growing up with another man as her father. Picturing Jasmine's small, soft, trusting face, he felt his stomach knot. He had lost one child. He wasn't going to lose another.

He felt Eden's gaze on his face and, turning, he shrugged. 'Location, really. Saint Barthélemy is a beautiful island.' A true paradise on earth.

That wasn't the only reason.

Here in the Caribbean, the sky had the thinnest atmosphere, which meant the stars and planets were brighter and clearer. Explaining why that was important to him would reveal more than he was willing to share with anyone, but particularly the woman who might be pregnant with his child.

'And the villa is right at the tip of the island so the beach can't be accessed by anyone not staying at the villa. It's just you and me, and the staff, of course. I'll show you around. That way you'll know where everything is.'

'That's very kind of you but I'm sure I can get my bearings on my own. In fact, I might do that now.'

He waited until she was almost out of sight and then he got to his feet. He caught up with her easily, his longer legs making up the distance of her shorter strides. She turned, annoyed.

'I'm not going anywhere except the beach. So, unless there's some portal I can step through to get to London, you don't have to follow me around.'

'I was bringing you this.' He held out a sunhat and a tube of sunscreen. 'It's too hot for you to go bare-headed, and you need to protect your skin. Or I can do it for you,' he added as she stared at him in silence.

She snatched the hat and the suncream from his hand.

'I can do it myself.'

'Pity,' he said softly.

Her eyes fluttered up to his, looking startled.

'Why did you lie about where you were going?' he asked.

'I didn't. I am going to the beach.' She frowned, two lines creasing her forehead above her nose, and he felt a sudden almost unbearable urge to reach out and press his thumb into the grooves, then cup her cheek and pull her closer.

'I don't mean now. When I came to the apartment. I thought you said you were going to San Antonio so why did you say just now you'd go to London if you could?'

Her face stilled as if she'd just admitted to having a fake passport at border control, but then she recovered. 'London is further away from you.'

He sighed. 'This is going to be a long week if you keep on fighting me at every opportunity.'

'I didn't fight you. I gave in,' she said flatly. 'But if my being here bothers you that much, I'll happily leave.'

His jaw tightened. *Not happening*, he thought. Not until he knew for sure, and then—

He swore silently as his thoughts came full circle and he was back at the unanswerable question. Ignoring both it and her last remark, he took a step closer, holding her captive with his eyes, wishing he could do the same with his hands. Wishing he could touch her, hold her, press her close—

'Don't swim in the sea if you're on your own. You can paddle but if you want to swim, use the pool,' he said softly. 'Don't even think about climbing on the rocks. Put the hat on and use the sunscreen.'

'Don't you think that's a lot of rules for a twenty-five-year-old woman?'

'It's only four. For now.'

He turned and stalked away. 'Just don't break any of them, Eden,' he called over his shoulder. But only because he didn't trust himself not to stalk right back and kiss that disdainful curl of her mouth if he turned to look at her.

Eden.

She hated it when he called her that. But only because she loved how her name sounded in his mouth. He said it the way it was meant to sound, two soft vowels around a hard consonant. Hard and soft. Him and her.

As Harris's tall, muscular body disappeared from view, she turned and walked determinedly in the opposite direction.

Except there was no him and her. There was one night of amazing sex and a baby that was currently the size of a pomegranate seed.

Oh, wow—

Her footsteps faltered.

She was in paradise or at least the earthly version. Turning slowly on the spot, she let her gaze drift slowly over a perfect coalescence of the palest pink sand, brilliant blue sea and swaying green palm trees.

Without even realising she had done so, she had slipped off her sandals and scrunched up her toes in the warm, powder-soft sand, and some of the tension she had been carrying in her bones since walking into the club and seeing Harris waiting to interview her faded a little.

Actually, she had been tense before that. More than tense. She had been rigid with misery and self-loathing and envy.

It was the week before she'd met Harris in that bar. She'd been getting ready to go out when Liam had got back in touch, and she had been shaking so much it looked as if the mirror were breaking apart. Or maybe that was her. It had certainly hurt that much. Hurt to move, to be alive.

She knew it wasn't just the shock of finding out that he had had a baby. That was a slap in the face but seeing Liam holding his son had stung for another reason, one that she had fought so long and hard to deny. Looking at a photo of her ex with his child was the closest she would get to having the family unit she coveted.

No wonder she'd still been spinning out when she'd walked into the bar. It was such a crushing reminder of who she was, who she had always been and could only ever be. To fight against that family curse would be a fruitless exercise, which was why she lived as she did. Why she had set up two offices on two different continents. Why she never met a man for a second date. Why she had taken Harris's hand but not asked his name.

Only then they had gone to that hotel room, and all the pain, shame and envy she had been feeling had melted away.

It was supposed to be just a night of passion with a stranger. Love, commitment, parenthood were not options. Except now they were. Somehow, that moment of ultimate pleasure had led her here to this beach.

She gazed out at the sea she couldn't swim in because she was alone.

He was right, she thought, glowering at the cool blue water, resentment simmering inside her. This was going to be a long week.

But first she had to get through today.

Harris might have wanted her to be under his watchful eye, but he was perfectly happy to delegate the watching to someone else. One of the maids came to find her on the beach with a jug of chilled cucumber water, and every now and then as she wandered down the beach picking up shells, she would catch a glimpse of one of the security detail.

Harris did join her for lunch, briefly. But then, having reminded her that she needed to wear her hat and sunblock and adding in a new rule about staying hydrated, he murmured something about a conference call and disappeared.

After lunch, she was tempted to go for a long hatless walk, but the glaring heat of the afternoon sun defeated her, and she retreated into the villa.

Which was how she ended up standing in silence, staring at his shut office door.

He would never say it to her face, so he had let his door do the talking and the message was clear. She was useful as an employee and he was happy to share a bed with her for a night but other than that he had no interest in her.

That thought made her want to hammer loudly on the wood, and she was just lifting her hand when she heard his voice, followed by a deep laugh.

Her pulse accelerated sharply. She had never heard him laugh. But then their interactions to date had held few comic moments. Just raw, uncontrollable passion, angry accusations and some mutual cold-shouldering.

What would it take to make him laugh like that?

Nothing she had to offer, that was for sure. Even with Liam, when she had thought that theirs was an actual relationship rather than a side dish to one, they hadn't laughed much. Hadn't talked much either. Or argued. And at the time, she'd been so proud of herself, so convinced that it meant she'd found the yin to her yang.

Her fingers clenched at her sides. It was only later when she'd realised he didn't need to laugh or talk or argue with her because he could do all those things with his wife.

For Liam, she'd only ever been a thrill, a diversion.

And for the man on the other side of this door, she was just a baby carrier.

Inching backwards, she turned and walked softly away to continue her exploration of the villa. It was a lot more relaxing doing it on her own and without Harris's edgy, silvery gaze fixing on her face when she was least expecting it.

An hour later, she was hunched over a book she wasn't reading, trying not to watch him as he powered up and down the pool.

After New York's autumnal dampness, the blast of heat had knocked her out and she had decided to lie by the pool on what looked like a four-poster bed complete with sheer curtains that quivered in the whisper of a sea breeze.

She had been almost on the edge of dozing off and then Harris had emerged from the villa looking cool and composed.

And semi naked.

Okay, he was wearing swim shorts and flip-flops, but his chest and shoulders were bare and unadorned except for the flickering rays of sunlight that seemed to want to caress him as much as she did. She was still a woman, albeit a thwarted, pregnant one, and for a moment she let herself drink in his beauty.

Her breath stuttered in her throat as he pulled himself out of the pool, picked up his phone and began walking towards her. He stopped and squinted up at the sky, and she stared at the contoured muscles of his thighs and tried not to remember what it had felt like when they'd pressed against her bottom.

'What happened to the hat and suncream rule?' she said coolly, dragging her gaze away from his smooth, golden body.

He sat down beside her, and she had to snatch her feet back and tuck them under her legs to stop them from touching him.

'I'm used to it. And besides, I'm the boss. The rules don't apply to me.'

She glared at him. 'Let's just get one thing clear. You're not my boss. And I'm only following your rules because I choose to do so.'

'Or you like me giving you orders.' He turned his head slightly, staring at her steadily, his gaze soft but unyielding, and she felt suddenly unanchored.

'Do you mind?' She pushed his leg. 'You're getting water all over me.'

'Speaking of water, you don't seem to have any,' he said calmly as if she hadn't spoken.

'Then maybe you'd like to get me some. Please,' she added, handing him her empty glass.

He eyed her, then got to his feet, holding up his hand to stop the maid rushing forwards as he walked over to where a refreshing array of chilled water and juices and fresh fruit was laid out on a table.

Leaning back against the cushions, Eden tried to breathe normally but it was hard when Harris was still in view. Thankfully, his phone buzzed then, giving her a reason to look away. It was probably a notification about the space station. Did that mean you could see it from here? Would she be able to find it without his help? As much to distract herself from the sight of his back muscles as because she was curious, she picked up his phone.

She frowned.

It was a notification about Tiger McIntyre.

That was weird. Okay, McIntyre was a competitor, but that seemed a little obsessive, particularly as Harris played down their rivalry at every opportunity.

'Are you reading my messages?'

She glanced up. He was standing beside her, his grey eyes harsh in the sunlight.

'No. Well, yes, but only because I thought it was from the space station. Why are you getting notifications about Tiger McIntyre?'

'Because he's in the same industry as me and I want to know what he's doing.'

'But you have lots of competitors. Why follow him?'

'He's my biggest competitor, and I don't follow him.' But she got to her feet and chased Harris as he turned and walked inside.

'What is your problem with McIntyre? And don't play dumb because I know you know what I'm talking about.'

The tension in the room clicked up several notches. He was doing that staring thing he did so well.

'Okay. Don't tell me. But you know what, Harris, whatever he did, I'm starting to think you deserved it.'

'Then you'd be wrong. You don't know Tiger McIntyre. You don't know what he did. What he's capable of.' He stopped abruptly as if he'd said too much.

'So, tell me? What did he do?'

'What does it matter to you? You're not saving my reputation now, Eden.'

Her breath stumbled as it always did whenever he used her first name. Which was why he'd done it, she realised a moment later. He was trying to knock her off her stride.

'It matters because, weirdly, I'd like to be able to think that the father of my child could be open and honest with me.'

'You want to talk to me about being open and honest?' The flare of incredulity in his voice made a shiver run down her spine. 'That's rich coming from you. I mean, when exactly were you planning on telling me you might be pregnant with my child?'

She hesitated. 'I don't know—'

He shook his head. 'In other words, you weren't going to. But given your lack of exclusivity, I suppose you thought the chances of my being the father of your baby were pretty remote.'

'That's not why I didn't tell you. I wasn't not going to.' That was too many negatives, wasn't it? 'I wasn't ready. I'd only just found out I was pregnant, and last time—'

Last time.

The words were out of her mouth before she even realised what she was saying and she felt all the air leave her lungs as she saw the look on his face—

She stepped past him, walking swiftly, blindly, back through the house and up the stairs into her bedroom. Darting into the bathroom, she crouched over the toilet bowl, a visceral, twisting panic slopping heavily in her stomach like wet concrete, her fingers splaying protectively against her flat belly.

A flash of memory. Of a dull, throbbing pain doubling her up and blood, enough to scare her into a taxi to the nearest ER. The doctors and the nurses had been kind but brusque. But then it was an ER, and they'd been dealing with multiple casualties from a six-car pile-up on the freeway, so she had felt as though she were standing in the eye of a hurricane. They had asked questions she could barely answer and given her answers she hadn't been able to process and all the time she had been losing her baby.

Last time...

How could she have said that out loud? Might Harris not have heard her? Stupid question. She knew that he had. She had seen the expression on his face. Confusion. Shock, then understanding.

But he didn't really understand.

And she didn't want him to. She didn't need him to pretend that he cared. That he was interested in her. Yet it hurt to admit that. Just as it had hurt to admit that there was something off-key about her relationship with Liam.

The queasiness in her stomach was subsiding and she got to her feet and ran her hands under the tap to cool her wrists.

'Are you okay?'

Looking up, she flinched.

Harris.

Hovering outside the door, dressed now, looking not entirely sure of his reception.

'I'm fine.' He stepped back as she pushed past him. 'You don't need to check up on me.'

'But I do,' he said simply, and it sounded so genuine that for a moment she thought she might start crying.

'I don't want to fight you,' she said flatly.

'And I don't want you to give in.' He rubbed his jaw as if trying to erase something. 'I shouldn't have said what I did. I spoke out of turn—'

'Isn't that the point of being the boss? That it's always your turn—'

'But I'm not your boss. I didn't mean to upset you.' His jaw tensed. 'It's always like that. With him. With Tiger.' He stared past her, and she sensed that he was looking inside himself, seeing something there.

'So, you do know him.' A statement of fact, not a question.

He nodded. 'We were mates at college. For a time I was

probably closer to him than anyone else on the planet. But then he slept with my girlfriend.'

She winced. No wonder he hadn't wanted to highlight his feud with McIntyre.

'How did you find out?'

His grey eyes snapped back to her, and he gave her a small, bitter smile. 'I wanted to talk to him about something and I saw her leaving his room. If they'd told me they wanted to hook up I would have been upset but finding out like that… I was so angry I wanted to hurt him.'

'What happened?'

'I punched him, he punched me back and we rolled around for a bit. It would probably have been okay, but Tiger mouthed off to the dean and got kicked out. That was the last time I spoke to him. We see each other at industry events, and we go to the same parties, but we don't talk. I guess people notice that kind of thing and that's how the rumours started.'

He rubbed his jaw again.

'It was a stupid ego thing, which is why I've never talked about it. But I should have told you.'

'I understand why you didn't.' It wasn't fair that telling the truth made him look so solid and dependable then. Or that there was a softness to his eyes or maybe it was his mouth. Either way he was too close to her for it to be safe for him to look at her like that.

'I think I might have a nap,' she said, glancing pointedly at the door.

For a moment, she thought it had worked because he turned fractionally, his big body moving with that mix of precision and easy, masculine grace that had a gravitational pull all of its own. But then he stopped, and she fought down the desperation that was swelling inside her because she knew what he was going to say even before he said quietly, 'What did you mean, downstairs? About the last time?'

Harris watched her face stiffen. He knew what he'd heard, even though it was just two words. Last time.

Before he'd had a chance to fully absorb their implication, she was gone.

He'd stared after her, feeling every kind of terrible because he had hurt her. No, he corrected himself. He'd added hurt to her hurt.

Which was why he began moving, walking swiftly first to his room to change clothes and then to Eden's room.

The door had been open, which had spooked him as at first glance he'd thought it was empty, but then he'd seen her huddled over the toilet and he'd retreated, thinking she would rather him not see her like that. Only he hadn't been able to leave. His legs had simply ignored the messages from his brain.

Last time.

'Eden—' he said softly.

Her green eyes were wide like a child's. 'It doesn't matter.'

'It feels like it does,' he said carefully.

'It was a long time ago.'

He nodded as if he knew when it had happened, and what had happened.

'I've never been that regular with my periods so I didn't know.'

'You were pregnant.'

She nodded. 'Ten weeks. It was winter. I'd thought I was coming down with a virus and then I started getting these cramps. There was so much blood… I was on the way to the hospital, and I tried to call Liam, my boyfriend, but he didn't pick up and I didn't want to leave a message. I didn't want to panic him.' She made a noise like a laugh except it didn't sound as if she found it funny. He certainly didn't.

'I was scared, and I wanted him to be there, but then he texted me back.' Her voice was thick. 'He said that he'd met someone and that it was over.'

He stared at her in disbelief. 'Did you tell him what was happening?'

'I couldn't. He'd switched off his phone. I think he was scared how I'd react.' She pressed her hand against her mouth, and he wanted to find Liam and scare him as much or more than Eden had been scared.

'He texted me a couple of days after and I told him about the baby. He said…he said—' she breathed in sharply '—he said it was probably for the best. And it was for him because I found out later that he hadn't just met someone else. He was married.'

He could feel her shock and shame even now.

'I should have known.' Her voice was taut, as if she was having to break off each word to say it. 'It was so obvious, but I wanted to be different from my mom and all the other women in my family who pick lying, cheating losers. I wanted to prove that I had the good judgement they lacked, and that I could make a relationship work, so I just ignored all the signs. I didn't see anything, not even the fact that I was pregnant.'

She bit into her lip, hard. 'It was my fault. If I'd realised that I was pregnant—'

He reached out and pulled her against him. 'Miscarriages don't work like that, Eden. There's usually a reason they happen that is beyond our control.'

Her eyes found his, and he felt her fingers curl around his arm. 'I did want to tell you. That I was pregnant.'

'But you thought I'd react like he did.' He flattened his

voice to make sure it didn't sound like an accusation, but she was already shaking her head.

'No, I didn't think that.' Her mouth quivered and there was a brightness to her eyes that made his throat burn with anger, and something softer, an urge to protect her and keep her safe from the men in the world who took and broke and wrecked without impunity.

'I was just scared of saying it out loud. Scared that something would happen to the baby.'

He pulled her closer. 'But nothing has.'

'It still might—' Her fingers tightened around his arm. He felt her fast breathing and he hated that she was so scared and that he had cornered her when she was so fragile but having to hide it.

It won't. He almost spoke the words out loud, but something in her face stopped him. The truth was that he couldn't say for sure that it would be all right, and she had been lied to enough by that bastard of an ex. Maybe he hadn't told her the whole truth about Tiger, but he couldn't lie to her about this. After being so bravely honest with him, she deserved honesty in return, and he wanted to give her that.

'It might,' he agreed finally. He spoke gently but firmly, projecting the calm neutrality that Eden needed right now. And that was the thing: even though they'd known one another only a matter of weeks and nothing between them was straightforward, he badly wanted to give her what she needed so that she would trust him and know that he was no Liam.

'But believe me when I say that I'll make every effort to ensure that doesn't happen.' Her grip loosened a fraction and he let his hand move to cup her head, feeling her soften against him. Despite the difference in their height, they fitted together easily, her curves accommodating his lines.

And on a purely selfish level it felt so good to hold her close.

His heart was pounding in his throat. Maybe she felt the same way, he thought as Eden looked up at him, and he allowed himself to let his hand slide through her hair and press her closer.

To let his lips brush against hers and taste her sweetness…

His breath hitched.

Her mouth was soft and warm, and he parted her lips, tasting her with his tongue, his stomach balling into a knot of heat as she leaned into him, deepening the kiss.

It would be so easy for his hands to roam over her skin, to nudge her back onto the bed.

He felt his body ripple to life. Easy and wrong.

He was not going to exploit her need for closeness and comfort to satisfy his needs, his desire. If it stung a little, so be it. He deserved it.

Gently, he loosened his grip. 'Why don't you get into bed and have that nap? If you want, I can stay up here. I have some more work to do.'

He hadn't planned to say that, but he was glad he did. She seemed to relax a little and five minutes after she slid under the covers, she was asleep. He could have left then, or he could have worked. But he did neither. Instead, he sat by her bed and watched her sleep.

It was something he'd never done. Something he'd never wanted to do. It was intimate on a different level and opened up a chasm of vulnerability he had never wanted to mine. But he couldn't leave. More accurately, he didn't want to. It felt right being here with her. There was nowhere else he could imagine being.

Not just then, but ever.

CHAPTER SEVEN

SHIFTING BACK ON his elbows against the sand, Harris tipped back his head and stared up at the black velvet of the sky, his gaze tracking the disappearing lights of a plane.

It was nearly one o'clock in the morning and it was a calm, cloudless night. Perfect for stargazing and he had already done a quick scan of the sky, ticking off the various stars and planets that were currently visible in this hemisphere. There was the Crux and Centaurus, and that was the Carina Nebula, a beautiful interstellar cloud that couldn't be seen in New York.

But he always came back to that bright speck of light.

Perhaps because of his navy training, or maybe it was just his natural reticence, but his father had never talked much about his working life. He had an office with the usual certificates and photos that men like him accumulated over their careers and even the odd souvenir of his time in space, but he'd never talked about his life up there.

Not with his son anyway. But then, out of all those photos, there was not one of his family.

Maybe that was why when his father had bothered to sit down one crisp winter evening and show Harris the light from the space station, it had stayed with him. Most days, when it was visible he would look up at least once during the evening to stare at it just as he had done when he was a kid.

Back then, those few minutes of gazing at that small but luminous pinprick of light had often felt like his only connection with his father.

It still did.

But there was another reason now that he kept up with his old habit. He liked to think that somewhere on the other side of the world, his daughter might be looking up at the brightest star in her sky and that her gaze and his would somehow meet in the middle.

Maybe she was looking right now. Looking for him.

Except he knew that she wasn't. Why would she be looking? She had a father.

It was a physical pain.

But at least she was alive.

He thought back to the moment when Eden had told him about her miscarriage and the pain in his chest made it hard to swallow. She had looked like a wounded animal, not just stricken but stunned, as if she were still there in the hospital losing her baby.

She had been so scared and alone and up in her bedroom it had been clear that she still felt that way now. He didn't know how to make it happen, but he knew he wanted that to change. He needed to do something so that she would feel safe, and know that she wasn't alone, that he would be there for her.

His pulse slowed as he remembered holding her close. She had felt right in his arms, so familiar, which made no sense because they hadn't even met six weeks ago.

Maybe it was because so much had happened in such a short time that it felt longer. It wasn't just the baby, it was the mess he'd made of his life trying to cage Tiger, and beneath it all an emptiness that seemed to mock his diary of prestigious invitations.

He had all this wealth and power. People hounded him to

attend their events and yet he felt alone, just as if he were standing on the moon and gazing down at the Earth. But then he'd always felt alone even when he was theoretically part of a family. After his parents' divorce the feeling had been exacerbated but school had helped him lose sight of it. There you were rarely alone for long or given enough free time to dwell on how you were feeling.

By the time Jessie was pregnant and he'd found out he was going to be a father, he hadn't known how to let anyone get close.

And yet with Eden, it had been easy. Obviously, they'd had sex, so intimacy was a given.

Only it wasn't just about the sex. He'd felt a connection with her that went beyond bodies and damp skin and hands gripping each other tightly. Like in his office when he had shown her how to find the space station like some science geek. He'd wanted to see her reaction, to watch the way her green eyes danced with excitement when she spotted the light.

He had almost kissed her then. If Ted hadn't blundered in, he would have done.

He had wanted to kiss her yesterday after she'd told him about the miscarriage even though he'd known it would be reckless to do so. Kicking up the sparks from what had happened in New York would only complicate things and he hadn't wanted Eden thinking that was why he'd brought her here, because it wasn't.

Don't lie, he thought, his body loosening and tightening all at once. *You can lie to everyone else but not yourself.* Which was maybe why he had gone ahead and kissed her.

But she was here because until he knew if that was his baby she was carrying, she had to be.

His eyes lifted once more to the glittering stars. He wasn't going to lose another child. And to make sure that didn't happen he needed Eden to feel that her trust in him was not misplaced.

The following morning, she came down slightly late for breakfast.

He had expected… Actually, he didn't know what he'd expected, and perhaps that was a good thing. He'd made assumptions about Eden before and been wrong.

She met his gaze politely as she sat down opposite him and began to eat some of her fruit and home-made granola.

'About last—'

'I wanted to—'

They both spoke at once.

'You go first.'

She hesitated a moment. 'I just wanted to thank you for last night. I didn't mean to dump all that on you.'

'You didn't dump anything on me and there's nothing to thank me for,' he said slowly. 'I don't know how you've held it all together. Finding out you were pregnant and then me barging in on you when you were still stunned, press-gang-ing you into coming here.'

Remembering how he had frogmarched her to the waiting limo, he felt a hot wave of shame spill over him.

'It wasn't ideal. But if you hadn't turned up, I think I would have just stayed stunned. I needed to talk about what happened before.' Her green eyes were suddenly naked in a way that made him feel unhinged. 'That's why I got so upset yesterday. Saying it out loud for the first time. It was a bit of a shock.'

She'd never told anyone. But she'd told him. He stared down at her at the exact same moment she looked up at him and for a moment he could see himself reflected in the depths of her pupils. He knew that she must be seeing herself reflected in his and it felt so intimate and all-consuming that it took him an almost ludicrously long time to simply say, 'I can see that.'

'I know it must have been a shock to you too, but I wanted to tell you that you were very sweet, and kind.'

She hesitated then, and he waited, not wanting to probe or push; after all, he'd done enough of that already. Was that it? Was she including their kiss in his sweetness and kindness? Or did she not want to talk about that? His eyes flicked over her face, looking for clues.

Or maybe she just wanted to pretend it had never happened or almost not quite happened.

The latter, he thought, as she picked up her herbal tea and sipped it cautiously. She didn't say as much but he wasn't so lacking in empathy that he couldn't sense how little she wanted to have that particular conversation with him.

To distract himself from how intensely he wanted to know why that should be the case, he glanced over to where she was still sipping her tea.

'Is there something wrong?'

'No, it's just some things taste a bit odd at the moment, like coffee and regular tea, but this is fine.'

'Good.' He hesitated, feeling suddenly almost nervous. 'Look, I don't know how to put this, so I'm just going to come straight out and say it. I've arranged for us to see a doctor in St Martin this morning.'

'I don't understand.' Eden was staring at Harris in confusion.

'It's an island just a little further south from St Barth's. You might have seen it when we flew in,' he added. 'There's a private medical clinic there that I'm confident will be able to help us.'

'But it's too early. They can't tell yet—'

Frowning, he shook his head. 'It's not to do the paternity test.' He reached across the table and took her hand.

'I know you're worried about the baby, and I did some research and found out there's an early scan that can be done.'

The clinic in St Martin had a scanner that would be able to tell them what Eden needed to know right now. He would have preferred to use his own medical clinic in New York, and he had considered flying back, but it was the difference between a ten-minute hop in a helicopter and a four-hour flight and Eden was already stressed about the pregnancy. He didn't want to add to that stress.

'If you don't want to go,' he said quickly, 'that's fine. I just thought it might help.'

He felt a flicker of self-loathing because what had he done to help her so far?

Nothing.

His actions had been entirely self-serving, but he had justified his behaviour in the moment because of what had happened in the past.

Except it was his past, not hers. Hers had been unknown, irrelevant. He had looked at her pale, stunned face and seen fear but assumed that she was scared of his reaction, never once thinking that she was terrified she might lose her baby.

He had put his own needs before hers.

But then what did he know about the needs of a pregnant woman? When Jessie had told him she was pregnant, his initial reaction had been a white-out of panic and disbelief followed by a string of swear words and a pinch of blame.

Unsurprisingly Jessie had seen him as another responsibility after that, rather than the support and confidant he could have been. He had never seen her again. She had left for Australia two days later and so, in answer to his own question, he knew nothing about the needs of a pregnant woman.

His jaw tightened. Out of all the many things he'd said and hadn't said that day, that pinch of blame was what he regretted the most. Thankfully, he hadn't done that with Eden, which was something at least. But he had coerced and chivvied her into doing what he wanted.

And he was going to have to live with that, as he was living with the consequences of letting Jessie down. But Eden didn't have to live with her fear. He could at least do something about that.

'It's called a reassurance scan. It's carried out between six to ten weeks. They can see the heartbeat and whether the pregnancy is the right size according to the date of your last period.'

Eden was still staring at him across the table.

'You did that for me?'

'The first proper scan isn't for another few weeks, but I know you're worried and the waiting is probably making it worse. I thought seeing the baby on screen might make you worry less.'

She smiled shakily. 'I think it will.'

It was already making her feel calmer, Eden thought as she walked back downstairs thirty minutes later to look for Harris. But it wasn't just the appointment. It was the fact that he had arranged it. That he wanted to help.

Which was astonishing given everything she had thrown at him yesterday. Most men would have been blindsided by what she had told him.

She had certainly blindsided herself.

Yesterday was the first time that she had properly allowed herself to go back there. To start at the beginning and push through to the end. At the start it had felt so real, not like a memory at all but as if it were happening all over again.

She'd felt that gut-wrenching panic and desolation of losing the baby she hadn't had time to acknowledge.

Until Harris had pulled her close and she'd felt his warmth and strength seep through her, and her fear had subsided. Then it had felt real in a new way, a way she hadn't anticipated.

Finally, she had felt able to admit her grief out loud for the baby she had never met but whose absence she still felt so keenly. Harris had made that happen. Made the invisible visible. He had given shape to her loss, and she had never felt so complete, so seen.

And held.

Not shouldered like a burden that someone was waiting to put down, which was how Liam had made her feel. Harris had made her feel precious and necessary.

If she closed her eyes even a fraction, she could feel his body next to hers when he'd kissed her.

Her fingers twitched by her side as she remembered how his hand had splayed against her back for a second or two and how he'd inhaled deeply, breathing her in as if she were oxygen.

Standing there in his arms, she'd been lost in his heartbeat, completely at one with him to the point where she hadn't been able to feel where he ended, and she began.

And everything in the room, in the villa, on the island, on the planet had felt as if it had shrunk to the size of a pinprick, distant stars in the vast expanse of space.

There was just him.

Harris.

His mouth.

His pulse.

His breath.

The taste of him, and the heat of him.

The feel of his body tensing with pleasure as she'd leaned into him, deepening the kiss.

Her senses had exploded, body blooming, opening like a flower with the strength of her desire. She could have kept kissing him like that till the end of time. And she would have prised herself open or, better still, let him shuck her like an oyster.

But he had stopped it before they'd even got that far, and she should have been relieved. Things were already complicated enough between them. They didn't need to add another sexual encounter into the mix.

She knew that and yet she had felt hugely conflicted. More than conflicted, she had felt torn in two, and when he'd stepped away from her his absence had been like a physical ache.

'Ready?'

Harris was waiting for her at the bottom of the stairs. He looked casual and relaxed in cream chinos and a dark green polo shirt that emphasised the stretch of his biceps. Day-old stubble added to the whole 'billionaire on vacation' vibe, although there couldn't be many billionaires on the planet who were quite as temptingly louche and sexy...

'Yes.' She nodded firmly to try and shake her thoughts about Harris being sexy out of her head. 'Are we going by boat?'

He shook his head. 'We could take the boat, but it's quicker to fly. Not the jet, obviously. We'll take the helicopter. It's only around a twelve-minute flight.'

Of course he owned a helicopter. And there it was, squatting on a square of concrete like an oversized housefly. Except it was white, not black.

'Very chic,' she said quietly.

'Have you flown in a helicopter before?' he asked as he

opened up the passenger door for her. 'Are you okay with this?' he added as she shook her head in answer to his first question.

'Yes, I'll be fine.' She frowned. 'Don't you want to sit in the front?'

'I will be.'

Her eyes moved over to the pilot's seat and then back to where she was sitting. 'How? There's only two seats and the pilot's going to be sitting in that one.'

Harris nodded. 'He is. I am.'

Before she could react, he had closed the door. She watched him walk around the front of the helicopter and then he was climbing in beside her.

'You're the pilot?'

His mouth did that curving thing, which made the interior of the cockpit fade. 'I seem destined to constantly underwhelm you. Yes, today I am the pilot. Getting my licence was one of the first things I did after I had money to spare. I've been flying for about five years now.'

'I see.' Except she didn't. She just about managed to go to the gym twice a week. How on earth did anyone as busy as Harris have the time to learn how to fly a helicopter?

'You don't sound convinced.' He pressed a switch on the instrument panel.

'It's just I was remembering what you said about people not finding it easy to speak truth to power.'

He laughed. 'I wasn't talking about my helicopter instructor.'

She nodded but as soon as he'd laughed her brain had seemed to lose all functionality. All she could do was stare at him because she had got her wish. She had made him laugh and it felt undeniably good and a whole lot of other things that she couldn't give a name to.

Clearing her throat, she gave what she hoped was a casual, offhand shrug. 'Okay, then. But I think it's fair enough to have my doubts. I mean, I've watched enough movies where the hero has to fly something, and it all goes horribly wrong, and they have to use an inflatable dinghy for a parachute. What?' He was shaking his head. 'Is this where you tell me that helicopters are safer than cars?'

'Not right now. I'm too busy enjoying the fact that you see me as a hero.'

Her mouth felt suddenly dry. 'I didn't say that,' she protested.

He glanced over, his grey gaze resting steadily on her face, which felt hot and was probably tomato coloured.

'I was just…never mind…now could you please stop looking at me and watch the road or the sea or whatever it is that you have to watch?'

She had nothing to base her assessment on, given that she had never flown in a helicopter before, but Harris seemed to be as expert as he'd suggested. Occasionally, he would lean forward and press some button on the instrument panel. Once he pointed out a school of dolphins in the sea below and she had pressed her face against the glass, enchanted by the perfect synchronicity of their gleaming bodies as they leapt out of the water. Other than that, he was quiet and focused and exactly twelve minutes later the helicopter touched down on a different square of concrete.

A car was waiting for them, because that was how it worked in his world, and ten minutes later she was sitting on a couch in a pleasant, south-facing room at the Concordia Medical Centre.

Samantha, the sonographer, was very smiley and friendly but Eden could feel her body tensing as she waited. The last time she'd had a scan was after losing the baby. It had been a transvaginal scan with a probe that hadn't been painful but nor had it been particularly enjoyable.

'Do I need to undress?'

Samantha shook her head. 'No, not for this kind of scan. But if you could just pull up your top, Ms Fennell.'

She felt Harris shift forward in his seat. 'I don't have to stay if you—'

'I want you to,' she said quickly. 'If you want to stay.'

Their eyes met and he nodded, and the softness of his grey gaze and the size and solidity of his body made it easier to reach down and pull up her top.

'That's perfect, thank you.' Samantha smiled. 'Now, have either of you done this before?' As they both shook their heads, she gestured towards the window. 'Then you might be wondering why the blinds are closed. That's because it helps us to see the images more clearly. Now I'm going to put some gel on your skin and then I'm going to pass this probe over your tummy and a picture is going to appear on the screen.'

Eden glanced up at the monitor, her chest tightening. Please, she prayed silently. Please let everything be okay.

'And there is the baby.'

She breathed out shakily, relief churning inside her stomach. Harris's hand covered hers and she turned towards him and saw that he looked relieved too. Which made her feel guilty and yet oddly happy.

Samantha tapped the screen.

'So, everything looks good. First things first. I can see one baby. Heart is beating at around one hundred and forty per minute.'

Eden swallowed. 'That seems very fast.'

'Babies' hearts beat faster than ours.' Harris's deep voice seemed to fill the room as he spoke.

Samantha beamed at him. 'That's correct, Mr Carver. The

foetal heartbeat is around twice as fast as an adult heart rate, so Baby Fennell is well within the normal range.' She moved the probe, then pointed at the screen. 'That's the umbilical cord, and I can see that the placenta is nice and high. As far as a due date is concerned, I could give you a rough estimate or if you're happy to wait then the twelve-week scan will be far more accurate.'

'I don't mind waiting.' Eden turned to him. 'Do you?'

He shook his head and she felt him squeeze her hand. 'I'm happy to wait.'

Samantha turned to type something into her notes. 'Obviously this scan is just showing us the baby's development at this time, but I hope you're both feeling reassured by what you've seen today.'

Eden nodded. 'I am, thank you.'

But it wasn't only the scan that had reassured her, it was Harris. The more she got to know him, the more she felt that she could trust him. That cool-eyed man with a list of demands who had pushed his way into her apartment was a hangover from the working day. Here, beneath the Caribbean sun, she was seeing a completely different side to him.

Softer. More approachable. A good man, a kind, decent man who would make a great father.

Which was more than she could have hoped for her baby, and that was all that mattered, wasn't it?

Yes, she told herself firmly. Okay, so there was something else between them other than the pregnancy. A heated shimmer that clung to the air around them, pressing in on them, pushing them closer, but that was just something left over from that night at the hotel. It would fade.

Samantha handed her some paper towels to wipe away the gel.

'I've asked Dr Krantz to step in, just to look over my

notes, and if you have any questions, she'll be happy to answer them.'

Dr Krantz was older than Samantha but equally reassuring. 'I can see nothing of concern. Everything looks completely normal. So, keep doing what you're doing. Get plenty of rest. Keep active. Stay hydrated. I'm sure you're already following the guidelines when it comes to avoiding certain foods. If you're unsure, this booklet is very helpful.'

She handed it to Eden.

'I find that after experiencing a loss in pregnancy, many of my clients are often concerned about sex.' She glanced at each of them in turn. 'But unless there's been bleeding in the current pregnancy, which there hasn't, there's no reason to not have sex. Although you might be more comfortable trying out different positions. Now, any other questions? No? Then, I think we're all done. Except, would you like a photo of your scan? You can pick them up in Reception. There's just a small charge.'

On the flight home, neither of them spoke much. She was too busy looking at the photos of the baby, and Harris's attention was focused on the instrument panel. But as they walked back into the villa, she wondered whether he had been as focused as she thought because he still seemed oddly quiet and distracted.

She would give her right arm to know what he was thinking and feeling.

Her heart bumped against her ribs jerkily. Would he be feeling something different if he knew for sure that the baby was his? She felt a quiver of guilt that she had robbed him of that knowledge, and layered through that guilt was regret at her stupidity.

Why had she lied to him about having other partners?

But it was too late to do anything about that now. Once

the paternity test had been confirmed then he would know exactly where he stood.

And then what?

It wasn't the first time she had asked herself that question, and she had assumed, hoped really, that time would bring greater clarity, but with every passing day she felt less sure of everything.

Other than that she liked him. A lot.

Best not to think about it too much, she thought, for the umpteenth time.

It was strange being back at the villa. She felt relieved, and then confused because it felt as if she had come home. But then it had been an oddly intimate morning.

What she needed was some time alone.

They had reached the top of the stairs, and she turned to face him. 'Thank you for arranging that. I feel a lot calmer now, but tired, so I might have a lie-down on my bed.'

'I might do the same. On my bed,' he added quickly. 'And I'm glad you feel easier about it now.'

As she made to move past him, their hands brushed, and his eyes locked with hers and she felt her stomach twist and tighten. They had been touching more today than any other day. In the clinic, he had taken her hand and then helped her off the couch and somehow, they had kept holding hands until Harris had broken his grip to shake hands with Dr Krantz.

This felt different though.

It felt charged. Expectant.

Harris was still staring at her, and then he looked down and seemed to remember that he could move his hand and he reached up to oh-so-casually rub the nape of his neck.

'Get some rest.'

He turned and walked away and she watched him for a couple of seconds before turning and walking in the other direction. The blinds had been left half down and her bedroom felt pleasantly cool. She sat down on the bed.

Rest.

She had told Harris she wanted to lie down, had thought she wanted to have some space, but his absence felt tangible and she had to curl her hands into the bedspread to stop them from trembling.

Restless.

That was what she was. Her skin felt twitchy and too tight and just as it had when she'd walked into that bar all those weeks ago and seen Harris.

He'd scratched that itch in the way it'd needed to be scratched and then some.

She stood up and was moving out of the room before her brain caught up with her legs. Harris's door wasn't quite shut. Maybe if it had been, things might have turned out differently but, with her pulse racing and her mind clearly offline, it didn't seem like a big deal to just push it open a little further and walk straight in—

The room was empty.

Her stomach plummeted with disbelief and a disappointment that knocked the wind out of her so that she had to grab hold of the door frame.

'Eden—'

She blinked. Harris was standing in the doorway to what was probably his dressing room or bathroom. Or some other place where you might get undressed, because he had taken his shirt off.

He was staring at her, his expression pitched somewhere between shock and panic.

'Are you okay? Has something happened?'

Her heart folded in on itself because she loved that he cared. Loved that he cared enough not to hide his concern.

'Yes…no, I mean yes, I am okay and no, nothing's happened.'

Yet.

The word reverberated loudly inside her head, so loudly that she was surprised he didn't hear it. But maybe he did because now he was looking at her intently as if he might have misheard.

'You're not wearing a shirt.' Her gaze moved over his bare, muscled chest. The blinds were down lower in his room, but the sunlight loved touching him as much as she did and so a few stray rays were licking the curves and lines of his torso, gilding and illuminating them so that he looked like a painting by Caravaggio.

'I was getting changed. I thought I might go for a run.'

'In this heat?'

He cleared his throat. 'I can't seem to settle so I thought it might help.'

'I can't settle either. But I can't go for a run—'

He cleared his throat again, but his voice was still hoarse as he spoke. 'Perhaps something else might help.'

'Yes, I think it would.' She hesitated. 'I was thinking about what Dr Krantz said.'

His pupils widened and she knew that he wanted what she wanted, needed her as much as she needed him, and knowing that almost knocked the air out of her lungs. There was a moment of silence, a kind of charged stillness pulsing with possibilities. But really there was only one.

There had only ever been one.

They moved at the same time. He reached her first, pulling her against him with one hand and pushing the door shut with the other as he fitted his mouth to hers. Her fingers curled over his shoulders, scrabbling at the smooth, warm skin with relief and a hunger that was both rampant and infinite.

CHAPTER EIGHT

HARRIS COULD FEEL his pulse jerking in his throat. It was a clumsy kiss, urgent and inexpert, but it was all the more arousing for that.

She tasted so sweet, so hungry, and he was almost out of his mind with his need for her.

He pressed a kiss against her cheekbone, then her throat, then he opened her mouth with his tongue, deepening the kiss, tasting her, savouring her flavour—

His breath hitched as he thought about all the places he was going to kiss her. And lick her. He was going to lick that soft, pale skin until it gleamed like freshly poured cream and then he would lick inside her too.

He shuddered inside.

But first he needed to strip her, and, with his mouth still fused to hers, he reached for the hem of her T-shirt.

Eden moaned against his mouth, pulling away enough to make him growl an objection until he realised that she was tugging her top over her head.

He watched, his blood throbbing heavily through his limbs as she slid the straps of her bra down over her shoulders and he leaned in to lick her nipples.

Her hand fluttered against his arm, and he widened his mouth, sucking the swollen tip. She was gripping his arm now, fingers tightening as he licked and nipped and tongued first one then the other nipple.

A trembling warmth was creeping over his skin. He was so hard already—

Pulling back, he stared down at her, his heart raging in his chest, and then he found her mouth and parted her lips, kissing her hard, nudging her back towards the bed until she had no option but to teeter backwards and he had no option but to follow because their mouths were still fused.

They kissed hungrily and then he jerked backwards and pulled off her shorts and then dropped to his knees and pushed his face between her thighs, breathing in her scent, sensing the wetness beneath, stretching the cotton panties with his thumbs so that he could see the outline of her damp curls.

It felt indecent. Exquisite.

For a moment, he just stayed there, his hand gripping the bedspread, trying to steady himself, wanting to live in that moment, on the cusp for ever—

She arched then, pushing forward impatiently, and he hooked his thumbs under the waistband and slid her panties over her legs.

Now she was bare to him.

Soft. Wet. Warm. His.

He placed open-mouthed kisses up either thigh, feeling her tremble against his tongue, and then he parted her thighs gently with his hands, sliding the palms beneath the curves of her bottom, lifting her fractionally like an artist arranging a model, and then he lowered his mouth and licked.

She was slick, and blood-hot and so soft except her clitoris, which was as taut and swollen as her nipples, and he wanted to keep tasting her for ever.

Her fingers were tight in his hair now, biting into the roots, the pain overlapping the pleasure he was feeling vicariously through her moans as she lifted herself against his mouth, rolling back and forth chasing the tip of his tongue.

He moved then, placing one hand on her hip bone just as he had done in the hotel all those weeks ago, anchoring her to him as he found her clitoris, grazing it with his incisors, sucking it fiercely into his mouth, then nipping it gently, then a little harder—

She swore then, breathing out the one-syllable word as if it had five syllables, and then she thrust forwards, body flexing against his mouth—

'Harris, Harris…' Her fingers twisted his hair as she pulled him onto the bed beside her.

Her fingers groped for his groin, clutching the front of his jeans as she felt the size of his erection.

'I want you inside me,' she breathed.

'Are you sure that—'

'Dr Krantz said it would be okay.' She was panting, pushing him back against the bed, reaching for his zip.

'Eden—' His voice was ragged, her name becoming a groan as she managed to free him, her fingers moving lightly, almost reverentially to trace the veins beneath the velvet-smooth skin. Exhaling sharply, he snatched her wrist as she straddled him.

'I can control the depth this way…'

Good, he thought, because he couldn't control anything.

She was lowering herself down onto the tip of his erection, and it was her turn to set the pace, dipping back and forth, curving herself in a way that he felt everywhere.

'Like that, like that,' he chanted, swearing under his breath as she dipped again because this time she stayed low, then pushed lower still and stopped. The feel of her stretching around him was almost enough to tip him over the edge and now he was panting too, his breath scraping up through his throat in time to the rocking motion of her hips.

His hands moved to clamp her waist and he rocked against where she was so warm and pliant, lifting her slightly so that he could withdraw and brush the blunt head against her clitoris, and he could hardly breathe through what was undoubtedly the most potent pleasure he'd ever experienced.

She made a choking sound as she slid down onto him again and he came, quicker than expected, hotter and harder than he'd ever come before, his body spilling inside her, his mind wiped clean of everything except the rightness of it all.

She was shaking, he was too, or at least his arms were and, gently, he lifted her up and instantly had to stifle the yelp that rose in his throat because it felt as though he'd been cut adrift like an astronaut floating off into space. He tipped her gently to one side and she slithered onto the mattress, her warm breath shuddering on his chest as he scooped her against him.

'Eden...'

He pulled her closer, sliding his leg between her thighs so that he could feel her wetness and his combined.

She was his, he thought, pulling her closer, his mouth seeking hers, then dropping to the pulse raging in her throat and licking a line back to her mouth, his hand sliding over to where their sweat was pooling on her still-flat belly.

Always his.

Eden woke with a jerk to darkness. Every day since that first time with Harris she had woken abruptly, feeling lost, displaced, confused. Not today. Today she knew exactly where she was even though this was a strange bed.

She knew because Harris was here too, lying beside her, breathing softly, his arm draped across her waist, tethering her to him. They could never be strangers. Had never been strangers, she thought, remembering how she had felt the morning after in the hotel. It had been so hard to leave him because it was like trying to separate herself from her shadow.

Or her soul.

Unnerved by the unfamiliar poetry of her thinking, she shifted position, turning away from the beautiful man who had dominated her thoughts ever since that night in the bar and now felt like a fixed presence in her life.

Like the moon.

She stared up at where it sat in the inky night sky, pale and serene and unchanged from when she had stared up at it as a little girl who dreamed of finding, not a prince, but a man with integrity and stamina and strength of character.

Liam had acted like that man. But he was a charlatan. A snake oil salesman.

Harris was everything that Liam was not.

Her cheeks stung suddenly.

What must the villa staff have thought? They had spent the rest of the day in bed. Although Harris must have got up at one point and gone downstairs because when she'd woken up in the early afternoon, there had been a tray of food waiting for her.

He had brought cutlery and napkins too, but they had been like survivors of a storm. She hadn't even bothered to thank him. She had just started to eat, picking up pieces of fried chicken with her fingers. And he'd watched her, making sure she had some of everything before he'd started to eat. Looking out for her. Taking care of her.

She felt blissfully relaxed, as if every piece of tension had been smoothed flat by a hot iron. Unsurprisingly, given that the first time she'd ridden him to a shuddering climax had been just the beginning. And after each subsequent time, he would pull her close, and she would collapse against him, her body spent and limp and her muscles inside fluttering like a kaleidoscope of butterflies.

That was a good description, she thought, her hand moving lightly over the muscles of his chest. She had read about people who experienced life in colours—synaesthesia, that was what it was called. It was when two senses merged into one. Sex with Harris was like being at the centre of an opal. It was not just a physical act but a metaphysical one.

An act of love.

She stiffened against the mattress, panic stealing the breath from her lungs.

No, she wasn't looking for love. In fact, she was actively avoiding it. Avoiding anything that might lead her down that self-destructive path. Liam had cured her of thinking that was ever an option for her and, even if a part of her dreaded becoming yet another Fennell woman raising a baby on her own, it would be different with Harris.

They might not be together, but she wouldn't be on her own. He was already more involved than her father had been at this stage. Look at how quickly he had arranged the scan, and earlier he had made sure she ate.

She felt a pang of guilt, remembering his expression of relief when he'd seen the baby alive and well on the screen. Had he known for sure it was his, then he would have been able to fully express his excitement. They could have been excited together.

If only she hadn't panicked when he'd turned up at her apartment. But if she had told him that he was the father, would he have taken her word for it? It seemed unlikely. The paternity test would give him the certainty he needed, and, for the first time since she had found out she was pregnant, she wished she could bring the date forward.

'Eden—'

She blinked as Harris's voice cut across her thoughts. Moments earlier, his eyes had been closed, but now he was rolling onto his elbow and looking down at her, his grey eyes silver in the moonlight.

'Are you okay?'

'I was looking at the moon.' But it was forgotten now; its gravitational pull had nothing on Harris, and, clutching blindly at his muscled arm, she leaned into him, feeling her body soften and open for him once more.

'I thought we might go down to the beach this morning. We can take a swim and then I could show you the rock pools.'

Eden glanced over at Harris. They had spent almost every minute of the last few days together, so it was easy for her to press her hands to her mouth and mime shock. 'I thought the sea and the rocks were off-limits. Aren't you breaking your own rules, Mr Carver?'

He caught her ankle and tugged her towards him gently beneath the table so that her chair scraped against the decking. 'I prefer to see it as unmaking them.'

She raised an eyebrow, her green eyes dancing in the sunlight. 'In other words, there's one rule for you and one rule for everyone else.'

'I'm the boss, remember? There are no rules for me.'

'But you haven't always been the boss,' she said after a moment, still teasing him.

Not as a child, no. Then he'd been powerless to change anything in his life. He'd been as small and irrelevant as a pawn on a chessboard. And that feeling had got worse after the divorce, because both his mother and his father had been so eager to pursue the life they'd each wanted without the other that he had been forgotten in the rush to move on.

Which was probably why becoming wealthy and powerful had felt so good, feeling stronger and more authoritative than everyone around him. He hadn't misused his power. He wasn't a bully but for the first time in his life he was in control. He felt safe being the boss, and staying safe meant keeping his life free of anything random or spontaneous.

His thumb twitched against the skin of Eden's ankle.

Like picking up a beautiful stranger in a bar and renting a hotel room for a night.

And yet he couldn't regret that night. He didn't regret it.

He couldn't even completely regret turning up at her apartment because it had brought them both to this island. Brought Eden into his bed.

If he had a regret, it was that he'd not woken first that morning at the hotel. Had he done so, he would have made it clear to her that he wanted it to be exclusive between them.

The idea of another man being with Eden, doing what he had done, touching her, caressing her, opening her body to his, made him want to smash things. He had never felt that way about any woman before. So possessive, so proprietorial. So jealous. Not even with Franny, his ex, the woman he'd got into a physical fight over with Tiger.

But then, despite what he'd said at the time, that fight had been as much about Tiger's betrayal as hers.

More, in fact, because he hadn't loved Franny.

And yet when he thought about it now, it all seemed so long ago, and it was hard to see why it had felt so important.

Why did it matter if Tiger had hooked up with one of his exes a decade ago? As for Franny, maybe she had sensed that his heart wasn't in it. Which, he could see now, was a betrayal of a different kind.

He glanced across the table. Eden had been hurt a lot, and betrayed too in the most devastating way, but she hadn't gone after Liam with the sole, precise purpose of ruining his life. Nor had she risked everything she'd worked so hard to build simply to prove to the world once and for all that she was the bigger and better person.

Even though she was.

She was certainly a far better person than him. He thought back to the moment when she'd thanked him for taking her to the scan. How would she feel about him if she knew he had a daughter living on the other side of the world? A daughter whose scan he hadn't attended. He hadn't been there for her birth. Or her first steps. Or her first day at school.

'I haven't always been the boss, no. And I'm not your boss, Eden,' he said softly. He gave her ankle one last caress, then released her. 'In fact, I'm in awe of you.'

Her eyes found his. 'I thought you wanted me to be subservient to you.'

His body tensed, and it took a second, several actually, before he could speak. 'Two things can be true at once.'

'Schrödinger's cat, you mean.' She held his gaze and then abruptly got to her feet. 'I think they can. But maybe we should test that theory. And keep testing it until we know for sure.'

They made it down to the beach after lunch for the promised expedition to the rock pools. From a distance they looked empty but up close they were home to a surprising amount of sea creatures.

'It's even more crowded than New York,' she said, leaning over to peer at the underside of a rock that was covered in spiny sea urchins. 'Although it's a lot quieter.'

'Do you mind the quiet?' he asked curiously.

'Of course not. Quiet is how I measure my success, remember?'

His heart stumbled as she smiled. 'Or perhaps you were too busy gunning for me to listen to what I was saying.'

'Gunning for you?'

'That first interview. With Avery. You were so furious with me—'

'It was more the situation.' He stopped as she rolled her eyes. 'Okay, yes, I was furious with you. And with myself for not reading up on who I was meeting.' *Because I was too busy thinking about you*, he thought. Busy and bereft too. As if he had misplaced something precious. 'For a moment I thought I was dreaming and that any moment I was going to start falling out of an airplane—'

She laughed. 'In my dreams I feel like my teeth have fallen out. Or that I'm naked.'

'I wish I was in your dreams,' he said softly and as her eyes met his, he thought he had never felt more rooted in the reality of his body, and his need for her.

Ducking her chin, she lowered her gaze back to the water. 'Why do you think they're called urchins? It seems such an odd name. I thought it meant some scruffy child.'

'It comes from an old Latin word that means hedgehog, which was what they used to be called, I believe.'

'Sea hedgehogs.'

'Exactly.' He nodded. 'What?'

'Nothing.' She was staring at him, curious and a little confused and perhaps also with something that bizarrely felt like delight. 'I thought you were an engineer, not a biologist.'

He pulled her closer. 'I'm very interested in biology.'

It was a beautiful afternoon. The sky was cloudless and there was a light breeze that made the water dance and shimmer. Not that he cared. Frankly he could have been standing in the middle of a desert. He only had eyes for Eden. The sight of her in a bikini made it almost impossible to keep his hands off her. So, he didn't.

And she was as eager to touch him.

'I think it must be my hormones.'

'Are you saying I could be any man?' Sweeping aside the swathe of dark, glossy hair, he leaned in and kissed her throat, licking the salt of her skin, his body hardening as he felt shivers of anticipation ripple through her body.

'Well, any billionaire with a villa on a Caribbean island and a private jet and a helicopter— Ouch!'

She twisted out of his arms as he nipped the apple tattoo on her shoulder, but then leaned back into him almost immediately, pressing the curve of her bottom against his already hardening erection.

'He doesn't exist. I'm the only one.'

'My one and only.' She fluttered her eyelashes at him, biting into the smile curving her mouth.

Yes, he thought, gazing down at her mutely, except looking wasn't enough. It rarely was, he found, and he pulled her closer, wrapping his arms around her waist. Fitting his mouth to hers, he kissed her fiercely.

He'd never been one for love bites or tattoos, but he wished there were some way he could mark Eden as his.

'If you keep touching me like that we're going to have to go back to the villa,' she said, her voice husky, her hand curling over his to flatten it against her body in a way that knocked the air out of his lungs.

'Why? It's a private beach.'

'Not that private.' Shielding her eyes, she tilted her head back and he followed her gaze across the water to where a yacht had dropped anchor. She cut a glance in his direction. 'Do you have one of those too?'

'Yes. Mine's a lot bigger.'

'Is that what you say to all the women you bring here?'

She was teasing him, but he shook his head. 'I've never brought anyone here,' he said, surprising them both because he could never be accused of oversharing. But Eden had told him so much about herself and her life and all he had given her in return were some half-truths about his relationship with Tiger.

'This place is just for me. And you,' he added softly.

For a split second, her eyes were naked to him, and he watched a series of emotions flicker in the green irises.

'As for the yacht, I mostly use it for business meetings.' He grimaced. 'I know that must sound crazy, but it makes a lot of sense for people like me who work in sensitive industries. It means we can talk freely away from prying eyes.'

'I can understand that. At least they're not photographers.' She turned to him, biting her lip. 'Or could they be?'

He shook his head. 'No, they'd be snapping away by now. They don't hold back. Particularly if there's a beautiful woman in a bikini on show.'

A flush of pink seeped into her cheeks. 'I think they prefer their women in bikinis to be more glossy and less unkempt.'

'Glossy is fake. Your beauty is natural. Untouched. Except by me,' he said, leaning in to brush his cheek against hers. He meant every word. Without make-up and with her hair loose and grains of sand sticking to her skin, Eden looked like some Girl Friday and her beauty was all the purer for it.

He had kept his hand around her waist, but his thumb was stroking the smooth skin there as if she were a piece of fruit he was testing for ripeness.

He could think of other, better tests only they would involve nudity and more privacy than the beach was currently offering, and he glared at the yacht, tamping down his irritation at not being able to take Eden in his arms again. 'I suppose you're right. Al fresco sex on a beach in front of a bunch of day trippers might not be the most sensible course of action for someone with a reputation crisis.'

She frowned at him. 'Former reputation crisis, you mean— which reminds me... I might just have a quick browse online. Can I borrow your phone? What? It'll take two minutes and it will help me relax.'

'Fine. Two minutes and then we go back to the villa.'

Rolling over, he grabbed his phone. He felt weirdly jealous and annoyed that he was having to compete with himself for Eden's attention.

'Here.'

He watched her type in his name.

'What the—'

She was staring at the phone as if it had turned into a snake.

'What is it?' His hand stiffened against the sand. 'What are they saying?'

'It's not about you. It's Tiger McIntyre. He's engaged!'

He waited for anger to swell against his ribs, but he felt nothing, except curiosity.

'Really? I never had him down as the marrying type. Who is she? I hope she's smart enough to keep him interested—'

'She's a white hat hacker, whatever that is, so I guess she'll keep him on his toes.'

There was a knot in his throat that made it hard to breathe.

'A hacker?'

Eden nodded. 'Her name's Sydney Truitt— What is it? What's the matter?'

She was looking at him, her face still, frozen with something that was on the way to confusion, and he knew why, knew that the shock, the utter disbelief, maybe even the panic he was feeling must be completely visible on his face. But he didn't know how to hide it, because she had made him soften, made him open a crack, and he was angry with her for doing that to him, and angry with himself for letting her, and so when he replied, his voice was taut and defensive.

'Nothing.' The lie stung. He didn't want to lie, and he couldn't look at her while he did so he glanced away, fixing his gaze on the yacht. 'I'm just surprised Tiger's settling down.'

Eden was still staring at him, and, slowly, she shook her head. 'But you weren't.' Her green eyes roamed over his face. 'Not really. Not when I first told you. You were just interested—'

'So, I had a delayed reaction.'

'But that's my point. You didn't react. Not until I told you about Sydney.'

This time he managed to keep his voice level when he heard the name. 'You don't need to monitor my responses any more, Eden. Your contract ended days ago.'

'Do you know her?' The bluntness of her question made him blink. But the answer would be too exposing.

'No.' He shook his head, the lie vibrating inside him and there was nowhere to look where it wouldn't still be a lie. 'I've never met her.'

At the shoreline, tiny waves were rippling over the sand, then withdrawing to leave it spotless. If only he could rewrite his past as easily. Beside him, Eden shifted position, and his palms itched to touch her again but there was something brittle about her posture, as if touching her might cause her to break apart.

'That's a little baffling,' she said flatly. 'You see, this article has a quote from Sydney Truitt saying that it was you who introduced her to Tiger.'

'Eden—'

'How do you know her?' She cut him off. 'And don't tell me she's lying.'

'She's not lying. But she's certainly twisting things.'

'Why would she do that?' She breathed in sharply as if he'd upended a bucket of cold water over her. 'Did you sleep with her?'

'No.' He shook his head vehemently. 'She worked for me, okay? Just briefly. I only met her once—'

'Then why is she saying you introduced her to Tiger Mc-Intyre? Why would you even do that? You hate him. You told me you hadn't spoken to him for years.'

'I haven't and I didn't introduce them.' He hesitated, because in a way he had. 'Not directly—'

'Then why…why would she—'

Her voice faltered and he saw it first in her beautiful green eyes, her brain stumbling over the truth, the dawning realisation of what she was looking at, of what he had done.

'She's the hacker, isn't she? She's the one you paid to hack McIntyre's server.'

He stared down at her, watching an overlapping slideshow of emotions cross her face it, and the incongruity of their swimsuits seemed to highlight the cruelty of his simple, 'Yes.'

But he couldn't lie to her when she was looking at him like that. As though she was struggling to breathe.

She flinched, her green eyes widening, and abruptly the slideshow stopped, settling on anguish. His heart felt as if it were splitting in two. He had never felt so wretched or so alone.

'Eden—'

'Don't.' She was getting jerkily to her feet. 'Whatever it is you're going to say, don't bother.'

'I can explain—' He was standing now, moving closer,

holding up his hands because he needed her to stay, to listen, to understand.

'I'm sure you can.' She was inching back from him as if he were a rattlesnake. 'Men like you always have an explanation for everything, and it's always so believable, so eloquent. But I don't need to hear any more lies.'

'I'm not going to lie to you.'

She was moving now, her stride clumsy and uneven as she walked.

'You know, funnily enough, that doesn't carry much weight right now, Harris. Because you are a liar. A compulsive liar. You don't even know you're doing it, or maybe you do, and you just don't care—'

'I do care. But you have to understand, he stole from me, and I was trying to prove that.'

'What about Avery? Does she know?'

'No, she doesn't know anything about it. None of the C suite do. I met Sydney on my own. I know, it was stupid, but when I heard about the prototype of the drill that was exactly like ours, I was so furious with him.'

'So, you lied to Avery too.'

'I didn't lie, I just didn't tell her about it because—'

'Because you knew it was wrong. And they would have stopped you.'

'Yes. But they didn't need to find out.' He hated how she was looking at him. As if she was seeing him for who he really was. 'Look, Tiger plays dirty. If he wanted to shaft me, he wouldn't do it obliquely. He's warning me off, but that's all it is, a warning. It doesn't matter.'

He reached for her wrist, but she didn't seem to notice.

'It does matter. It matters to me.' Her green eyes slammed into him. 'You know, weeks ago I asked you if there was anything I should know, anything that might come out, and you never said a word. Not then, not afterwards. And I stood beside you. But what if this comes out?'

They were back at the villa and now she seemed to notice his hand on her wrist, and she began to tug at it. 'I'll look like a fool. My career will be over.'

He tried to pull her closer.

'That's not going to happen. I would never let that happen to you.'

Eden hadn't felt nauseous for days but now she felt sick again. He made everything sound so plausible. Made her believe in him. Because, just like the last time, she had wanted to believe.

'Forgive me if I don't take your word at face value, Mr Carver.' She glanced up the beach. 'I can't do this. I can't be here. With you. With someone who lies and thinks that it doesn't matter.' Her hand moved protectively over her stomach. 'I thought you were a good person. I thought you were different, but you're not. You're a liar. But guess what?' She gave a mirthless laugh. 'So am I. I didn't sleep with anyone else. I said that because I was angry with you, and scared. But I wish I had.'

'Don't say that—'

'Why not? It's true. You don't deserve to be a father.'

His face stilled. She had wanted to hurt him like he was hurting her, but she had assumed he would react, deny her words or tell her that she was a hypocrite as well as a liar. But he said nothing. He just stared at her, an expression on his face that she didn't understand because it didn't make sense. He looked stricken.

Haunted.

'Yes, you're right. I don't. I'm just grateful it took you this long to work that out,' he said slowly. 'If you want to leave, I won't stop you. Use the jet.' There was a strange brightness to his eyes now and, for a moment, he hesitated as if he was going to say something else, but then he sidestepped past her and walked back down the beach.

CHAPTER NINE

SHE STARED AFTER HIM, a stone sinking heavily in her stomach.

He was in the wrong.

He had lied to her.

To Avery.

To the world.

He had jeopardised his reputation, again. And hers.

He was bad news. Literally.

But none of that seemed to matter. All she could think about was that look on his face.

Thanks to its proximity to the equator, the sun was already starting to sink. The first few days in St Barth's it had surprised her that the evening light disappeared sooner than in New York.

Now it filled her with panic. Not like in the apartment when she'd found out she was pregnant. This was the wordless, slippery kind that made thinking impossible. She'd felt it at the hospital when her world had expanded and then devastatingly contracted in front of her eyes.

There was nothing she could have done differently to keep the baby. She knew that now. Or rather, thanks to Harris, she had accepted it.

And in accepting it, she understood the difference between having a say in the outcome of something and having no choice. Here, now, she had a choice, and she was choosing to go after him. She had left a linen shirt of his that she was using as a cover-up by the pool, and she slipped it over her bikini, and then ran lightly down the steps to the beach.

She walked swiftly along the shoreline using the reflection of the moonlight on the water to find her way. She had expected to find him quite quickly, but it was a good ten minutes before she saw him sitting on the sand, his gaze fixed on the stars.

She felt suddenly fragile and untested. In his room, on his bed, she felt strong and sexy and insightful. She knew instinctively how he liked to be touched. Knew that if she caressed the flat of his stomach, his breath would go shallow, and he would grab her wrist as if he wasn't quite in control of his body's responses.

She loved the power he let her take in those moments. Loved giving power to him too. Being subservient to each other's needs was not just an aphrodisiac, it was a shared moment of vulnerability, and responsibility when they revealed and unlocked themselves.

Only looking at him now, she felt that confidence falter. He looked barricaded and yet desolate and, until recently, she'd had so little experience of addressing her own demons, was it likely she would be able to help him face his?

But she had to try. It was as simple as that.

So, in the spirit of that simplicity, she walked up and sat down beside him. He didn't react. Didn't acknowledge her in any way but she felt his body tighten.

'When I went to the hospital, they were kind about it but when they told me that I was…' she frowned '…that I had been pregnant, I could tell they were surprised I didn't know. Because I was a college graduate with a job and a partner. I felt so stupid. Not just about the baby, but about Liam, and I felt like I was being punished for my stupidity. I felt like the worst person in the world. The worst mother,' she said slowly. 'But I wasn't to blame. I didn't deserve to lose my baby—'

'Of course not.'

He spoke now as she'd hoped he would, his arm brushing against her leg as he twisted towards her. 'You didn't deserve that lying jerk of a boyfriend either.' Against the pale sand, his profile looked bleak suddenly. 'But then I'm no better.'

He turned away, or tried to, but she reached for his arm, curling her fingers around his elbow.

'I can assure you, you are. And I'm not the only person to think so. Avery thinks you walk on water. All your staff do. And no, I didn't ask them. I eavesdropped in the restroom and in the elevator and I didn't hear one bad word about you. You're a good person who did a bad thing but you're not a bad person.'

Hunching his shoulders, he shook his head. 'You only think that because you don't know what else I did.'

'You mean the details?'

'I'm not talking about the hacking.' He ran his hands over his face, pressing the palms hard against the temples as if he wanted to crush his head to a pulp.

'Harris, don't.' She moved to kneel in front of him, reaching for his hands.

'It's not just the baby I don't deserve,' he said tiredly. 'I don't deserve you. I don't even know why you're here.'

'I'm here because you're not the only one who lied, remember? I did, back in New York. I told you I'd had other partners. But I didn't. There was only you.'

My one and only, she thought, replaying the moment when they had been teasing each other earlier.

'Which makes you the father of this baby.'

'Which is the reason you should leave.' His voice was

barely a whisper now. 'I don't have what it takes to be a father. If you don't believe me, ask Jasmine.'

The silence that followed that statement seemed at home with the darkening sky and the stars. But Harris was staring at them as if they were a judge and jury combined.

'Who's Jasmine?' she said softly.

He didn't answer immediately but she could feel him sifting words inside his head, stacking up sentences then abandoning them just as she had done so many times when she'd tried telling someone about her miscarriage. Which was why she let the silence stretch because this had to be on his terms. If he wanted to go through every word in the dictionary she would wait.

'She's my daughter.'

A daughter. Her head snapped up.

Harris had a daughter.

He was still gazing up at the sky but there was a tightening around his mouth, and she knew that all of his senses were tuned into her reaction. She was shocked and yet part of her wasn't. A part of her felt as if she had always known. Maybe it was the way he'd reacted to her pregnancy. He had been so focused and yet also on edge. Not because she might be pregnant with his child but because she might not be.

Harris was silent again, and again she waited, because that sentence and all that it implied deserved to be absorbed and acknowledged without some rushed and intrusive questioning on her part.

'She could tell you exactly what kind of father I am because she's never met me. Never spoken to me. I don't even know if she knows what I look like.'

'How old is she?'

'She's eleven.'

'Where is she?'

'Tasmania. She lives there with her mother.' A pause. 'And her stepfather.'

His voice was calmer now, but there was an ache beneath the calm when he said 'stepfather'.

'Were you married?' She wanted him to say 'no' so badly it made her teeth hurt and she felt a mix of guilt and shame, but mostly relief when he shook his head, his expression bleak.

'When Jessie found out she was pregnant, I think she thought we'd get married, but I didn't want to do that. Not at first.'

His hands were clenching beneath hers, the whites of his knuckles visible through her open fingers.

'But you did want to marry her later?'

She phrased it as a question because again she wanted him to say no, but instead he nodded, and she felt that jerk of his head skewer her heart. 'I didn't love her. But I wanted to give her security. To prove that I could commit. But it was too late. She'd already left the country and gone home.'

His mouth curved into a smile that made her eyes burn.

'Maybe she would have stayed in the States if I'd stepped up immediately like I should have done. But I didn't. So, she left and I never saw her again. Never talked to her again.'

There was a harshness to his voice now, an anger that she knew was preferable to pain. 'I'm sorry,' she said softly. Beneath her palms, his hands tightened a fraction.

'How did you meet her?'

'She was trying to parallel park her car and she reversed into mine. I'm not sure that she would ever have talked to me otherwise. I was eighteen when we met, and she was older than me. Twenty-two, I think. She didn't do any damage, but she took my number anyway. I didn't think she'd call but she did, and she was easy to talk to and cool about stuff that the girls my age weren't.'

She felt a pang of jealousy. 'You mean sex?'

He nodded slowly. 'Yeah. That was pretty much the sum of it. I mean, I liked her, but it was the summer before I went to college. I didn't want anything that serious. I never did, and she didn't either. But then she got pregnant.'

'And you're sure that—'

'She's mine?' He finished the end of her sentence for her. 'I did a paternity test. That's when Jessie talked about getting married. She arranged a scan, but I didn't go. I couldn't. I mean, I knew it was my baby except I didn't really believe it, and I think I knew that seeing it on screen would make it impossible to deny,' he said hoarsely. She thought back to the scan on St Martin and the way Harris had gripped her hand with emotion churning in his eyes.

'And you wanted to deny it?'

She thought of her own baby, slipping from its moorings like a beautiful gemstone disappearing into a crack between the floorboards.

He nodded again. 'Yes. I just wanted it all to go away. And then it did. Jessie left and I got what I thought I wanted.' His voice was flattened of emotion, which only seemed to emphasise the misery burning in his grey eyes. 'I went off to college and I told myself that I'd had a lucky escape. Because I knew, you see, that I couldn't be a husband or a father.'

'Why not?'

'You know why. You told me. Some people just aren't cut out for those kinds of commitments. You have to have luck or good judgement or both. My parents didn't have either of those things. They met at college, got drunk and had sex at some party and she got pregnant. They had nothing in common. Not even me.'

He stared past her at the moonlit water.

'They never said so, but I think I always knew that I'd

messed up the lives they'd had planned. My mum was going to be a lawyer, but the pregnancy was really hard on her, and she had to drop out of college. They got married but I honestly can't remember them ever being happy. She was quietly angry all the time and my dad was in the navy flying jets when I was really small, so he was away quite a bit. And then he became an astronaut, and he wasn't even on the planet.'

'Why would you think that choosing a dark, lifeless vacuum over everything on Earth would be a dream of mine?' he'd asked her in the limo after they'd left the school, and she could still hear the anger in his voice. But now she could hear the pain layered beneath it. Understand it too.

'I was so lonely growing up,' he said then, and the stark honesty of his words caught her off balance. 'My family wasn't obviously damaged from the outside, so nobody really understood what it was like for me at home.'

'And you didn't want them to know anyway,' she said quietly.

His eyes found hers. 'No, I didn't. I guess I felt ashamed. Like it was my fault that they were together and so unhappy. And that's what I thought about when Jessie told me she was pregnant. The unhappiness and the loneliness. I couldn't see past it, couldn't see past the similarities between my parents' situation with me and my situation with Jessie and the baby and I panicked.'

'You were only eighteen, Harris, of course you panicked.'

'I know it must sound crazy, but I was so desperate not to repeat my parents' mistakes.'

It didn't sound crazy to her. She had spent years chasing after a life that had eluded generations of the women in her family solely to prove that she was different from them. And like Harris she had gone and repeated exactly the same mistakes.

Except being pregnant with his child didn't feel like a mistake. It felt like the most wonderful prize.

'I did nothing. I just acted like it wasn't anything to do with me. Only as soon as I got to college, all I could think about was Jessie and the baby, so I called her, but she didn't pick up. And I left messages, but she didn't reply and then her number changed so I came home from college and went to her apartment. That's when I found out she'd left the country almost straight after the scan.'

He tilted his head, gazing back up at the stars. 'Her flatmate told me. She'd given Jessie a lift to the airport. All she knew was that Jessie was going back to Australia for good. And then when I was walking out to the car, she ran after me. Said she'd forgotten to give me something. That Jessie had left it for me. She handed me an envelope and inside it was a photo. From the scan. The one I didn't go to.'

His mouth twisted into a shape that made something cold and serrated slice through her.

'There wasn't anything I could do. She was gone. I went back to college and that's when I met Tiger. Right from the start there was this rivalry between us but also an understanding that we both wanted the same things. It made me work hard and that was good because I didn't have time to think about Jessie or the baby.'

He hesitated then, and breathed in sharply as though he needed more air to say what he had to say next.

'And then about seven months later, out of the blue, she sent me a photo of the baby just after she was born and that's when I realised what I'd done. What I'd given up. Who I'd given up. My daughter. Jasmine.'

Eden remembered her own devastation when Liam had sent her the photo of his child. How she hadn't been able to eat, to sleep, to even get out of bed for days. She'd been dehydrated, her head had felt as if it were splitting in two, but that was nothing compared to the agony in her heart.

'Did she want to get back with you?'

He shook his head. 'No. She'd already met Eric by then.' The name sounded painful in his mouth, as if just saying it was giving him ulcers. 'I guess she thought I had a right to see the daughter I'd abandoned.' His hands tightened again so that she could almost picture the nails puncturing the skin on his palms. 'I think I had some kind of panic attack. I couldn't breathe, I felt like I was going to throw up and I wanted to talk to someone—'

Fragments of an earlier conversation vibrated through her body and suddenly it all made sense. That random act of aggression from a man who was strong and domineering and passionate but never violent. She hadn't understood it before but now she knew why it had happened.

'Tiger. You wanted to talk to Tiger. That's when you saw him with your girlfriend.'

He nodded slowly.

'What did you do?'

'Apart from punching him, you mean. Nothing. I wanted to do something, I guess I tried but there was nothing much to go on. All I knew was Jessie's name and that she'd worked in a bar in town.'

He shivered.

'I tried to find her for years. I even saved up some money and flew out to Australia, but it was only when the business took off that I was able to hire a private detective to look for her.'

'And you found her. And Jasmine.'

'It doesn't change anything.' He sounded exhausted and she knew without him even having to say so that, while this might be the first time he'd had this conversation with another person, he'd had it many times inside his head. 'Jasmine is settled now. She has a life. A father.'

'You're her father,' she said gently.

'Biologically maybe, but there's more to being a father than just getting someone pregnant.'

'There is. But parenting doesn't have a sell-by date. You still have time to be a dad to Jasmine. I know because I never spoke to my father until I was older than she is now.'

'He wasn't in your life at all?'

She shook her head. 'He didn't hang around when he found out my mum was pregnant with me. But then he turned up one day at the coffee shop where I worked after school. My mum had told him where to find me. I was so furious with her. And then he said he just wanted to talk and I lost it.'

In the event, she had done all the talking in a short, blistering monologue.

'I told him where to go. But he didn't give up. He sent me birthday cards and Christmas presents and postcards, and when I split with Liam and lost the baby he was the person I called. Not because I don't love my mum or my gran. But my dad has different strengths. He can put his own feelings to one side and that's what I needed. He made it bearable even though he didn't know what had happened. He was there for me, and one day you'll be there for Jasmine, and you will matter to her as much as she matters to you.'

Harris's eyes fluttered shut just for a few seconds, as if the possibility of that being true was too painful to look at head-on.

'What if Jessie doesn't want me in her daughter's life?'

'She doesn't have that choice. Any more than my mum did, because one day Jasmine is going to want to know who you are. But if Jessie's anything like my mum she'll want you to be in Jasmine's life. Because there's room for you in her life, and in her heart.'

The stars above blurred and there was a roaring in her ears that sounded like the sea. He wouldn't be in just Jasmine's heart, she realised, her stomach twisting with something that felt like pain only there was a sweetness beneath the sting.

Harris was in her heart too because she loved him. That was why she had gone looking for him, and probably in all honesty why she had agreed to come with him to St Barth's. Yet it was terrifying. Too terrifying to even think, much less admit to the man sitting in front of her. The man who had become as necessary to her as the moon was to the ocean.

'You're a good person, Eden,' he said quietly.

'So are you. But most importantly you're you. And the mistakes you make will be yours. Not your parents'. It's the same for me.' Only she hadn't realised that before. After Liam, she had simply assumed that she was fated to tread in her mother's and grandmother's footsteps. But there was no curse. She was her own person, and most women had a Liam in their life, especially when they were young.

She thought back to Harris flying her to the scan in his helicopter. It was true that he had wanted to check the baby was okay, but he had also wanted to take care of her. To make her feel safe and certain, and she did feel certain now, and not just about the baby. She felt confident in her judgement too.

'Both of us need to remember that, and if we do that and we keep talking then things will work out.' She gave him a small, swift smile. 'We're a good team.'

She had been going to say partnership but that had 'couply' overtones. Team was a business word that she could say without revealing the hope in her heart.

'We are.' He held her gaze, and she saw surprise and acknowledgement and something else she didn't recognise in his dark grey eyes.

'Although I probably deserve most of the credit,' she said, making a joke to cover up the way she was feeling. The way he made her feel.

'I've never met anyone like you.' His eyes were fixed on her face, and she felt something hot and liquid and electric skate across her skin as he reached up to brush his thumb across her cheek.

When he let his hand drop, she almost cried out in disappointment but instead she said quickly, 'We should probably get back.'

Her disappointment multiplied exponentially as he nodded, but then he reached out and caught her arm, his warm fingers curling round her wrist, and the sound of the waves seemed to swell and double in volume, or maybe that was the beat of her blood.

'Eden,' he said softly, stretching out the first syllable as if he never wanted to finish saying her name, and then he pulled her forward, his grip firm even though his hands were trembling slightly, and he fitted his mouth to hers.

His mouth was gentle and yet she could tell how much he needed to kiss her, and she breathed him in, tasting him, her love mingling with her hunger in what had to be the most delicious, intoxicating cocktail ever invented.

She moved his hand to her waist. Her breath was hot against his mouth as his fingers moved over her bare skin in tiny concentric circles, and she had no idea how something so light and imprecise could feel so good. Now they moved up to cup her breasts then back to her waist, making her skin tingle with a pleasure that she knew he was feeling too. He was taking his time, and she knew that this was about more than sex and bodies and that feverish need they had felt before. It was about closeness and two hearts beating the same rhythm, merging into one.

'I want you so badly,' he whispered.

'I want you too.' She buried her face against his throat, breathing in his scent. She could feel his pulse twitching against her cheek and then his fingers pulled at the string on her bikini, sliding over her thigh to where she was already soft and swollen.

'Then tell me what you want from me.'

The roughness in his voice sent a charge of electricity down her spine that she felt everywhere, and she was suddenly so ready for him. She wriggled forward, clumsy, and uncaring of her clumsiness, pressing her body against the hard, straining shape of his erection.

'I want this,' she gasped.

'Then take it. Take everything. I'm yours.'

His knuckles brushed against her labia just once, but it was enough and she pushed down the waistband of his swim shorts, freeing him into her hot hand and then guiding herself down onto him.

She moaned softly as she pushed against him. Her muscles clenched, and she started to shake with a pleasure that had no equal, and then seconds later Harris angled his hips and thrust up inside her, shuddering until finally he stilled against her. And they stayed like that for a long time, mindless and unravelled, clinging to one another beneath the moonlight.

The next day, their final day on the island, they both woke early for the first time in days. They made love slowly, taking their time, changing positions, their pleasure rising and tumbling them over like the waves outside their bedroom window. But his need for her never changed tempo and he found that thrilling and terrifying in equal measure.

'What time are we leaving to go back to New York?'

Harris glanced over to where Eden sat in one of his shirts that she'd somehow appropriated as her own.

'Whenever you want,' he said, leaning across the mattress to pour out some juice. He handed her a glass.

'Whenever I want? I thought the appointment for the paternity test was first thing tomorrow morning.' She gave him one of those teasing smiles that showed her small white teeth.

'It is. But we have a certain amount of flexibility, so you choose.'

She bit into her lip, and he felt a flicker of envy because her lips, her mouth, her body felt as if they belonged to him. 'Aren't you the boss?'

'I'm into power sharing at the moment,' he said, more to see her reaction than because he meant it. But maybe it was true, he thought, a moment later. With her, he was happy to give up control. Sometimes. *Under the right circumstances*, he thought, replaying the moment when she had straddled him on the beach.

Was it happiness he was feeling? He'd felt triumphant before when he'd won a big contract and obviously there was that calm that followed sex, although he'd never felt as sated as he did with Eden. But this feeling wasn't so much to do with sex. It was about wholeness and certainty—or at least that was the closest he could come to describing it.

And it was because of her. She'd made him feel whole and certain and lighter today than he had for years, and hopeful in a way that he had never felt before. But then a burden had been lifted from his shoulders. By Eden.

He had felt that he'd given up any right to being in Jasmine's life before she was born and that had felt unalterable. But Eden's relationship with her father had given a kind of shape to how that might change. He hadn't lost his daughter, just lost his way at the start of the journey to being her father. And no matter how many diversions or obstacles he met enroute, he wasn't going to give up the chance to find his place in his daughter's heart.

But he also wasn't ready yet to stop this thing with Eden.

Her eyes held his for a long beat of silence and his pulse twitched as she sat back on her haunches and began to unbutton her shirt, because of course she knew what he was thinking, and what he wanted.

'Then let's go this evening.'

They spent the rest of the day moving easily between the bedroom, the pool and the beach.

It felt natural, this rhythm between them. Domestic almost, except this was a holiday and like all holidays it had little to do with real life.

And when they got back to real life in New York, what then?

Leaving the city, he'd been entirely focused on not letting her out of his sight until he could do a paternity test. Arriving in the Caribbean, he'd had a different question spinning inside his head. What if I'm the father, what then? This was the more nuanced version of that because he had, privately at least, accepted that Eden was carrying his baby so there was no longer a 'what if'.

Which meant that their lives were going to be intertwined. But how?

On the flight back to New York they talked through how he could get back in touch with Jessie, and he realised once again how much he valued Eden's opinion. And that he had got used to having her around.

'Excuse me, Mr Carver, Ms Fennell.' John, the air steward, was smiling down at him. 'The pilot asked me to tell you that we'll be touching down in New York in around twenty minutes so if you could buckle up, please.'

'I was thinking we can drop by your apartment and pick up whatever you need and then go back to mine.'

Eden glanced over at him, her green eyes widening a fraction. 'We don't need to do that. I can just wing it until tomorrow morning.'

'You're right. You don't need to worry about any of that. If you give me the keys, I can get someone to pack up your things—'

'Pack them up?' He saw her jolt of surprise, but he was distracted by the light flush of colour along the curve of her cheeks and that sprinkling of freckles that came from spending a week in the sun. She had never looked more beautiful and, impulsively, he leaned forward and kissed her, his body hardening as he felt her mouth soften. There was a bedroom at the other end of the cabin. Could they—

'There's not enough time,' she whispered against his mouth.

He groaned. 'I could be quick—'

She gazed up at him. 'You don't need to be if I'm moving in with you. That is what you just suggested, isn't it?'

He nodded slowly, his need for her woven in with a relief that she seemed on board with that.

'It makes sense,' he said casually, his hand moving to caress her face.

Her eyes stayed steady on his but there was something vulnerable about her mouth. 'What do you mean?'

What did he mean? In truth, he didn't have a clear explanation, just that it felt like the right decision.

He shrugged. 'Like you said back at the villa, we're a good team. We like each other and the sex is incredible. I think we work.'

'But I don't work for you anymore, Harris,' she said slowly.

He frowned. 'That's not what I said, or what I meant.'

She stared at him, her face unreadable, but he could see the tightness around her eyes. 'No, you said that we like each other and that the sex is incredible.'

'I did. It is,' he said, her coolness kicking up sparks inside him. 'Why is that a bad thing?'

'It's not, it's just that it's not really—'

Not really enough, Eden thought, her stomach tensing around something hard and cold and unyielding.

Harris was frowning, his handsome face defying logic and expectation to somehow look even more handsome. 'It's not what?'

'It's just not what I expected to happen,' she said at last.

His frown darkened. 'What did you expect? That you would just go back to your old life? We need to make this work. For our child's sake. That's what's important, and I know you agree.'

She did. She knew what it felt like to grow up conscious always of the absence of her father but cohabiting with someone who only 'liked' you would be a different kind of absence.

An absence of love.

Back on the island, it had been easy to tell herself that love was not a word to be used lightly. Better to let Harris give a name to what he was feeling than force it on him, because she was certain that his feelings matched hers. He was simply a few steps behind, but he would catch up eventually, take her hand and pull her close just as he always did.

She wanted to ask him if that was true, but she also wasn't quite ready for him to answer.

She cleared her throat. 'I do want to make this work. But we can't just go into this blind—'

'We're not,' he said calmly. 'We worked together for weeks.'

'Worked, not lived together.'

'We just spent a week doing that.'

'That wasn't real.' She shook her head because she wanted, no, needed him to protest, and he did.

'Not real. How wasn't it real? We ate together. We slept together. We talked, we laughed, we had fun…'

It was fun, the most fun she'd ever had in her life and yet with anyone else it would have felt mundane. But it had felt miraculous and extraordinary and beautiful when she'd caught Harris watching her as she put on her make-up or when he reached out to brush sand off her ankle or as he stole a kiss when the security detail had glanced away to glower at a yacht that was too close to the shoreline and she'd forgotten where she was, and how to breathe, and even her own name.

And yet, it also wasn't real, she realised, the chill in her stomach spreading.

'Yes, because we were on vacation.'

His face shifted, and she felt a pang of guilt. She was being unfair, but something had shifted between them; there was an awkward pragmatism that hadn't been there at the villa.

'I didn't realise that's how you felt.' He was staring past her, his grey eyes impenetrable. 'But yes, I suppose that is what it was. Only we're not on vacation anymore. You are still pregnant though. And if that is my baby you're carrying then I don't want to be cut out of his or her life.'

'You won't be. But living together—'

'Will mean that doesn't happen,' he cut across her, his voice not the voice of the man who'd whispered her name as he'd lifted her onto his big body or the man who had wrapped her in his arms and comforted her. Instead, he sounded like the impatient, autocratic CEO who had turned up unannounced at her apartment and steamrollered her into coming with him to St Barth's. Her wishes, her needs had been secondary to his.

Subservient, in fact. And now?

She shivered. Maybe they still were.

'So, you want us to act like a couple. That's your solution. To lie to our child. You want to pretend that we love each other.' And it would be a lie on his part, she realised as his expression shuttered. Whatever it had felt like at the time, that closeness, that feeling of being connected was just a hoax, a shimmering mirage beneath the Caribbean sun.

'I think it's unhelpful to frame it in those terms.' He sounded as if he were reading from a script. 'What we'll be doing is finding common ground and using it to act for the greater good.'

The greater good.

In other words, she was just a cog in a machine. Her moving in had nothing to do with her needs. It was about creating or simulating a family dynamic. She would be his partner but not really, just like with Liam, only then she had been ignorant of the deceit. This time she would be complicit.

'And what about me? Where do I fit into this?' Her voice trailed off as he met her gaze.

'You're the baby's mother.'

Her throat tightened so that it was hard to speak, but she had to know, had to ask, 'And if I wasn't pregnant?'

In the heavy silence that followed her question she felt her heart, her stupid hope-filled heart, split in two and she stared at him, staggered by how much silence could hurt.

There was a bump as the plane's wheels hit the runway and she was glad because it gave her an excuse to grip the armrest as she tried to breathe through the crushing pain in her chest.

'We can—'

She shook her head. 'There is no we, Harris. And I won't be moving into your apartment. I need my own space.'

'I don't understand. I'm offering you security and stability. A life that most people dream of.'

'And that's very generous but I don't just want those things.'

'What else is there?'

Love, she thought. Reciprocal, equal, eternal.

But love wasn't on offer here. It never had been.

'There's love,' she said, lifting her eyes to meet his. 'You see, I like you as much as you like me, Harris. You know I do, but what you don't know is that I also love you. And I know you're scared of loving someone. I know because I'm scared too, so scared that after Liam I made a promise never to let myself get that close to anyone. But I couldn't not get close to you because you're here…' she tapped her forehead '…and here.' Now she touched her stomach.

'But most of all, you're here.' She pressed her hand against her heart. 'At the villa, I thought there was a chance you might love me too—don't worry, I know you don't. But I want… I need to be loved, not just liked. And I don't want to be a team player or act for the greater good. I want to have a partner. Someone who wants me for who I am and not because I'm carrying their baby.'

She waited, hoping, yearning, but after an interminable moment he nodded slowly. 'I understand. And I'm sorry.'

Then he was reaching down and unbuckling his belt and he was on his feet and moving up the cabin to talk to the pilot. She stared after him, mute with misery, wondering how it was possible that in the space of a moment she had gone from talking about moving in together to falling into this deep and lightless abyss from which there was no escape.

Later she would wonder how she'd got off the plane. She had no memory of the car journey back to her apartment.

When the limo stopped, he got out of the car without a word, and she had no option but to stand beside him in an awkward silence that was almost as crushing as the sudden distance between them.

'Thank you for taking me to the villa. Could you text me the clinic's address and the appointment time for the test and I'll meet you there?' she added quickly because she'd had enough of this brutal, new version of their relationship.

'I can pick you up.'

'There's no need.' She turned quickly because it hurt too much to keep looking at him but as she began to walk away, she felt his fingers catch her wrist and she turned towards him, hope spiralling up inside her.

'Eden.' He was looking straight ahead but his hand tightened a fraction, and she heard the sudden hoarseness in his voice like a reprieve. It was going to be okay. He was going to admit that he'd spoken hastily, that he'd not understood what he was feeling. That he loved her and wanted her in his life because he couldn't live without her.

'I've got a conference call first thing, so I'll make my own way there, but I'll send a car for you. Please take it.'

His voice was calm and detached, as if their conversation on the plane had never taken place. As if nothing had ever happened between them. He leaned in and brushed her cheek lightly with his lips and then he let go of her wrist and walked over to the limo. She watched it drive away just as her mother had watched all those other cars back in San Antonio and as it disappeared round the corner, the wave of misery and despair that was rising inside her toppled over, swallowing her whole.

CHAPTER TEN

SIDESTEPPING SMOOTHLY PAST a group of people gazing at a young man and woman playing covers of eighties hits on their guitars, Harris took the incline at a run, closely followed by his security detail.

He was running on the loop around Central Park. Mostly he ran before breakfast. Sometimes he ran this late but not on the street and not when he'd just stepped off a plane.

Jonas, his head of Security, hadn't said a word when he'd appeared in running gear and told him that he wanted to head out for a jog, but no doubt he was thinking that his boss could just as easily have gone and pounded on the running machine in his gym. Except that would mean staying at the apartment and he couldn't do that right now. Couldn't be alone in those beautiful, cavernous rooms.

Their emptiness haunted him.

She haunted him.

Eden.

She had been his paradise, but now he was cast out in the darkness, and it was all his fault.

His foot slid on a stone, and he stumbled.

'I'm okay.' He held up his hand as his security men swarmed forward.

He didn't want to stop, not yet. If he stopped, he would start replaying that conversation on the plane and he didn't want to have to hear the stupid, insensitive and inaccurate words that had come out of his mouth. All that nonsense about finding common ground and using it to act for the greater good.

The greater good.

His jaw tightened. What a sanctimonious coward.

No wonder he was alone. Each time someone tried to get close to him, he pushed them away. Jessie. Tiger. Eden.

He had let her leave, no, he had driven her to her doorstep, even though she had opened herself up, made herself vulnerable. She had told him the truth and offered her love. She had been honest and brave, but he was too scared to go beyond offering her stability and the trappings of wealth.

As he passed another of the entrances to the park, his body turned as it had done each time he was given the chance to leave. It would be so easy to let his legs take him where he wanted to go. To Eden's apartment.

It was tempting to do just that, because he missed her so badly that his bones ached.

But there was no point. He had made her feel that she was unimportant to him when the opposite was true and anything he said now would sound forced and fabricated. He had messed up everything, again. Made as many mistakes as he had all those years ago, only this was worse because at some point Eden would find the love she was looking for, and then he would have to endure watching her raise their child with another man.

Only it wasn't just about that. It never had been, but he hadn't realised it until now.

It was about Eden. Her smile, her strength, her intelligence, her bravery. And how she made him feel. Strong and certain. And seen and heard.

If only he could prove that to her, but there was no combination of words that would offer such a simple solution.

Yet sometimes actions spoke louder than words, he thought, his legs slowing down to a steady jog.

'Is everything all right, Mr Carver?'

He turned towards where his head of Security was jogging alongside him. 'It will be, Jonas. Call Owen, tell him we'll be home in ten minutes. I need him ready and waiting.' He knew from the expression on Jonas' face that the panic punching him in the stomach must be audible in his voice, but he didn't care. All he cared about was seeing Eden again. And getting her to give him a second chance. To give them a chance.

After the open skies and glittering seas of the Caribbean, the city felt crowded and noisy, and Eden was glad that she was sitting in the limo Harris had sent. She had dithered about taking it, but despite having fallen into a coma-like sleep last night, she still felt exhausted this morning. Too exhausted to make a stand.

She gazed through the glass at the people walking to work. What exactly was she taking a stand against anyway? Not taking his limo wasn't going to make Harris love her.

Nothing was going to do that.

She hadn't allowed herself to think about that awful conversation on the plane. Maybe she never would. Her one consolation was that Harris would never bring it up. No doubt, he would keep everything polite and formal.

Thinking that made her want to cry and she must have made some kind of noise because she saw the driver glance up at his rear-view mirror.

'Don't worry, Ms Fennell, we won't have any more hold-ups. I'll get you there on time.'

She smiled stiffly. On the flight out to St Barth's, this appointment had felt like the moment she would get her life back, or at least her freedom. But now freedom just meant a lifetime of being the mother of his child. Not the woman he loved or wanted or needed.

The clinic looked more like a boutique hotel than a medical centre. Even the staff looked as if they'd stepped off a catwalk. She sat and waited in a lounge area with expensive leather armchairs and tried to brace herself for the moment when she saw him again. If only she had thought to practise her expression in the mirror.

But had she done so it would have been a waste of time because he didn't turn up.

The doctor called her into the office and offered her a seat. Smiling apologetically, she told her that Mr Harris's people had called to let her know that he was unable to attend.

'I see.' In other words, he had thought about it and decided to take her claim of wanting space literally. Or maybe he was proving a point.

Reaching down, she began pushing up the sleeve of her blouse. 'I assume I can still do the blood sample.'

Now the doctor frowned. 'That won't be necessary.'

'Do we have to do it together, then?' Eden stared at her in confusion. 'Surely that isn't necessary.'

'It isn't, but that's not why I'm not going to take your blood,' the doctor said gently. 'Mr Carver has cancelled the paternity test.'

She nodded. 'Because he was unable to make the appointment? Did he say when he wanted to rebook it?'

The doctor cleared her throat. 'He doesn't. Apparently, it's not necessary anymore.'

The room seemed to sway a little. Not necessary. Like her.

She had no idea how she left the clinic. The black limo was hovering by the kerb, and it took every ounce of strength she had to compose her face into a careless smile and get in.

Call him, she told herself. Confront him. Ask him why he doesn't want to do a test. But even thinking about hearing his voice made her feel queasy.

What was the point of asking him something when she already knew the answer? Which was that he had backed off. Probably she had scared him off with her talk of love. And she couldn't face another of those awful, lopsided conversations that made the floor feel as if it were undulating beneath her feet.

Either way, she had got her wish, she thought as she walked back into the apartment. She had all the space she wanted.

And time on her hands too.

What with the pregnancy and then going to St Barth's, she hadn't booked in another client but, right now, she didn't need the money.

She needed to think about this baby and the life she was going to give him or her. Harris might have backed off but that didn't mean her life had to end. She wasn't going to shut down as she had after Liam. She was a different person now. Not just older, and wiser. She knew who she was, and she was proud of herself and everything she had achieved.

And she was going to keep achieving, keep moving forward in her life. She would even include Harris if that was what he wanted. She wasn't going to cut him out of his child's life, but their interactions would be on her terms, not his.

For now, though, she was, if not happy, then content to potter around the apartment. She would buy a bunch of pregnancy books and get prepared and in the meantime she was going to watch every possible vampire drama she could stream. She had lunch, then went out to buy some plants, but that was all she did for the rest of the day except call her mom and grandma and her dad and tell them that she was pregnant. They were all so supportive, and knowing that she was loved and supported unconditionally in her choices helped slightly mitigate the sadness she felt about her baby's father disappearing off the face of the earth.

Was that why she had agreed to going on this stargazing walk? So that she could scan the night skies for the man who had first shown them to her?

It was her neighbour who had invited her when they'd met on the stairs. Professor Paige Geffen was an archetypal boffin, with her wild grey curls and open-toed sandals, who lectured on astrophysics at various universities around the world, including Columbia University. And when she was back in New York, she ran a monthly walk to Pier 45 on the Hudson River.

They were not a big crowd, but everyone was very friendly and excited, and she was pleased she had gone. With Liam, she had stopped doing things that reminded her of him, but she wasn't going to do that this time. Why should she limit her life like that? Anyway, it was something she and Harris had shared, and she wanted to be able to share that with the baby too.

She had been spoiled, she realised as she gazed up at the sky. It wasn't as clear here as it had been from Harris's office, and certainly not as clear as the sky in St Barth's. But she could still spot various constellations.

'Now, can anyone tell me which is the brightest light in the sky?' Paige was asking.

'Is it Orion's belt?' someone suggested.

'No, that's a good answer, but not the right one.'

'It's the space station.'

Eden felt her heart flip over. She spun round, her eyes seeking out the owner of the deep, husky voice.

Harris. Lounging against the wooden railings, looking just as he had when she'd walked into that bar. Dark jeans, leather jacket and that beautiful, sculpted face, grey eyes fixed on her face intently as if she were his Pole Star.

As the stargazers moved further down the pier, she stood frozen to the spot as he detached himself from the railing and walked over to her slowly. Even though it twisted her insides, she couldn't drag her gaze away and, stupid though it was, it was still a joy to see him, despite the pain.

He stopped in front of her, and she stared up at him feeling slightly delirious.

'Stubble,' she said hoarsely.

He frowned. 'What?' Then he touched his jaw. 'Yes, I haven't shaved today.'

It suited him, but so would a bin bag. She should have walked away as soon as she saw him, she realised. Even a couple of feet was too close for comfort. She could already feel her body responding to his...

She cleared her throat. 'Why not?'

'I guess I forgot.'

'Is that why you missed the paternity test? Did you forget that too?'

'No, that was for a different reason,' he said and there was an ache in his voice that made her want to step forward and comfort him, but he wasn't hers to comfort, she reminded herself.

'So why are you here now?' She took a step back. 'How did you know where I was? Are you having me followed?'

That hurt, more than it should. That he didn't love her was a blow, but that he didn't trust her was crushing.

'No, I went to your apartment, and you didn't answer when I rang so I buzzed the supervisor. He told me where you were.'

'You still haven't told me why you're here,' she said flatly, because she knew why. 'Let me guess, you want to rebook the paternity test.' She shook her head, remembering the shock of his absence, the carelessness of his second-hand apology. 'Do you know what it felt like being told by the doctor that you'd cancelled it? You didn't even have the manners to call me or leave a message.'

He took a step forward and she saw that, beneath the stubble, he looked pale and there were dark smudges under his eyes. Once again, she had the stupid, self-harming urge to put her arms around him. *Not mine to hold*, she told herself.

'I know.' He looked wretched, as wretched as when he'd told her about Jasmine. But Jasmine was his daughter, and she was just the mother of his child.

'And I'm sorry.' He breathed out unsteadily. 'I wanted to call you. I wanted to see you, not to tell you about the test but because I missed you so much. But I knew that I was being selfish, that I was only doing it for myself and that if I saw you or spoke to you, I'd hurt you.'

'You did hurt me.' Her voice cut across the silent pier, and she felt the stargazers' eyes move towards her in unison.

'I know,' he said again. 'And I hate that I did that. I hate that I was such a coward.'

'Well, I hate you.'

He ran a hand over his face. 'Is that true?' His voice shook a little as he spoke. 'I mean, I'd understand if you did.'

She was shaking her head. 'This isn't fair of you, Harris, turning up like this, making me feel things I don't want to feel—'

'But I want you to feel them, because I feel them too.'

Considering everything that had happened, she had thought she was doing well. Yes, she had thought about him. Worried about him. Wondered where he was and what he was doing, but she hadn't spent every second weeping or raging. But now she wanted to do both.

'Don't do that. Don't say things you don't mean.'

'I do mean them.' There were shadows as well as stubble on his face. He looked exhausted and heartbreakingly beautiful, but her heart didn't need to be broken any more.

'And why would I believe you?'

'Because I can't lie to you, Eden. I can lie to everyone else—I have lied. And I can even lie to myself, but I can't lie to you. It breaks me,' he said hoarsely.

'You said I was just the mother of your baby.'

'I did, but then I got back to the apartment, and I hated it. I hated you not being there, and I hated that I cared but I couldn't stop myself, so I went out for a run in Central Park. I kept wanting to run to your apartment and tell you that I was wrong, and that I loved you, but I was scared that you'd take me back. I kept thinking about all the people I'd pushed away and all the times I'd been pushed away and I got scared that I didn't know how to love and that I'd hurt you even more than I already had, and I never want to hurt you.'

His grey eyes were fierce and brighter than any star. 'And then I realised that there weren't any words that could prove that I love you. That I needed to show you instead, and that's why I didn't turn up for the paternity test. Because I don't need proof that I'm our baby's father. I love you and I will love our baby, and I want the three of us to be a family. So, can we do that, Eden? Can we be a family? Will you let me take care of you? Both of you?'

Eden stared at him, her pulse slowing to a heavy thud, her heart spilling over with a love that was equalled if not surpassed by the love in Harris's voice and in his eyes.

'I'd like that. I'd like that a lot,' she whispered. And finally she reached for him.

Sucking in a breath that was spiked with relief, Harris pulled her against his heaving chest, curving his body around hers so that their foreheads were touching. Moments earlier he had felt as though he had been fighting for his life. And he had been, because Eden was his sunlight and his oxygen.

Only now she was looking up at him with those beautiful soft green eyes that made him feel so seen and clutching at him as if she never wanted to let him go.

'I am still scared,' he said then, because he couldn't lie to her. But she didn't pull away. She just pulled him closer, close enough that he could feel her heart beating in time to his.

'I'm scared too, but we want to be with each other.'

'Yes. Yes.' He nodded, although it wasn't a question and she smiled.

'It's not going to be easy all the time, but we want to make it work, and we're a good team.' She reached up and took his hand and pressed it against her stomach.

'We're not a team, we're partners...' he brushed his lips against her mouth '...and lovers...' he kissed her softly '...and soulmates.' Then he deepened the kiss, parting her lips and kissing her hungrily, both lost and found in her embrace.

EPILOGUE

THE LIGHT WAS different this high up, Eden thought as she shifted her cheek against the pillow. In Harris' New York triplex, two hundred metres above the city, it was soft and miraculous. Like the way Harris was touching her.

He was beside her, his muscular body propped up on his forearm, his fingers travelling over her body as they always did with that same mix of reverence and compulsion. Tracing the swell of her breast. Caressing the curve of her hip and then moving to the slick heat between her thighs as she wanted him to.

The breath squeezed out of her body as his finger stilled against the pulse beating there. Always beating there, matching the pulse of her heart. Because he was here with her. The man she loved and who loved her, she thought, her stomach swooping as he pulled her towards him and kissed her greedily.

'Do we have time?' he mumbled against her mouth.

'Yes...'

It was just one word but it was loaded with longing and intent and as she watched his pupils widen, her need for him made it impossible to be still. She arched closer, the air punching out of her lungs as the blunt tip of his erection slid inside her and then he was pushing deeper until there was nowhere left to go, his hands shaping her to fit her around him as his breathing grew ragged. Just like the first time it was astonishing and incomparable and right, so very right, and she was nothing but heat and a shuddering, flickering pleasure that pulsed through her in wave after shattering wave.

Afterwards, he kissed her everywhere that he had touched, before pulling her close enough that she could feel his heartbeat overlapping hers.

He was hers now. Not just physically and emotionally but legally.

They had married a month after getting back from St Barth's. It was a small, quiet ceremony, because it suited them both. It was perfect in every detail from her simple white silk dress to the emotion in his voice as he'd made his vows in the presence of their parents. All four of them. In a room together. Plus her grandma, of course.

They had, all of them, looked a little stunned to be there. But happy too, and, as far as his parents went, grateful.

As they should be. Her fingers tightened around his shoulders, and she felt a fiercely protective rush of love and pride, remembering the shock of his beauty as he'd stood waiting for her at the front of the room.

He had looked as a bridegroom should. Tall, blond and so swooningly handsome in his dark suit that the registrar had kept getting distracted. It had felt like a dream as he'd taken her hand and squeezed it as if he, too, had needed to reassure himself that this was real, that she was real.

'What are you thinking about?'

She glanced up. Harris was gazing down at her, his eyes fixed on her face, but his hand was moving again, following the contours of her belly.

'I was thinking about our wedding day. About how handsome you looked and how lucky I felt. How lucky I feel.' She could do this now. Speak without being afraid that she was giving too much away because nothing was held back. Letting him see how much she wanted and needed him was still terrifying but also intoxicating and necessary.

Reaching out, he cupped her cheek. 'I'm the lucky one.'

She felt his words, the truth of them, resonating through her and suddenly it was hard to do anything more than nod because she had thought this was something that happened to other people, other women. That for her it would always stay as some unattainable goal dancing just out of reach.

But there was an honesty and a straightforwardness to how they spoke to one another that she knew was as rare as it was beautiful.

'I love you,' she said softly.

His eyes held hers for a long beat. 'I know.' He did, but it was still new to him, and he liked to hear it and she liked to say it. Liked to watch his eyes soften—

A cry. Tiny but imperative.

Harris turned, they both did, their eyes arrowing onto the state-of-the-art baby monitor on the bedside table.

On the screen, the baby was moving, kicking up her feet and reaching her hands over her head, wispy golden curls framing her face, her green eyes bright in the soft morning light. She made another experimental cry like a kitten mewing, testing the sound, flexing her power and then, as if she was pleased with the results, her face split into a gummy smile that matched the one pulling at the corners of Eden's mouth.

Carina.

The look on Harris's face, so fierce and paternal, almost undid her.

Their daughter had been born nearly three weeks ago. The birth had been a long and exhausting process made worse by the panic that had risen unbidden and unwelcome when her water had suddenly broken. Her birth plan had been scrapped.

The scented candles were left unlit. Her favourite songs stayed un-played. Nothing on her list made it to the hospital.

Except Harris, and that was all that mattered. He was all she'd needed.

And he had been there the entire time. Taking the baby from the midwife and laying her on Eden's stomach so that she could feel her daughter's heart beating, his tears mingling with hers as he'd murmured garbled words of love and joy into her ear.

A lot had happened in the run-up to their daughter's birth.

Aside from getting married, Harris had reached out to Tiger McIntyre and after talking on the phone they had met up with him and his wife, Sydney. It had been a nerve-racking encounter. Tiger was as toned and taut with nervous energy as Harris and for a moment, as they'd stared at each other warily, it had felt like a mistake. But then Sydney had grabbed Eden's hand and told her that they were going to be friends whatever happened between their husbands, and they had left them to it.

She had half expected to come back and find them lying bloodied and spent on the floor of Tiger's open-plan living area that matched Harris's in scale and style. But when the two women had returned from a morning of mocktails and massage, both men had been sprawled on the sofas drinking beer and playing a first-person shooter as if they were back at college.

As for the drill bit: it turned out that there was no IP theft. As had happened so many times in the past, they had simply had the same inspiration.

'You know we talked about Tiger and Sydney being Carina's godparents?' she said, shifting closer to touch the marvel of his jaw. 'How do you feel about asking them today at lunch?'

* * *

Harris turned away from the monitor to look at his wife.

Eden. Having her in his life was like being in an earthly paradise. The tension that had hummed inside him for so long had vanished. His mind was mellow with pleasure right now but this, the two of them, was about so much more than sex. There was a quiet there now and yet he knew that he was heard and seen by Eden. He knew too that even when they were apart she was thinking about him. Thinking about when she would see him again, and the things she would ask him and tell him.

For each of them, that knowledge was a comfort and a necessity, a magnetic North that centred them. A pole star that combined the pull of the moon and the warmth of the sun.

But that was just the beginning. Eden had given him so much more. She had helped him start to create something approximating a relationship with his parents. And then there was Tiger.

In that moment of reconciliation, he'd felt both relief and gratitude to Eden and Sydney. Tiger had felt the same way, and now their friendship was a full-on bromance, much to the amusement of their wives.

He had no idea how Eden had made that happen. Just thinking about the man he'd been, the man he would have remained if they had never met, made him pull her close and hold her tight. Because he *was* lucky to have found her and he knew that she could not be replicated.

She was his equal. A partner and a muse because being with her seemed to stimulate his brain as much as his body so that his business was accelerating like a solar probe.

And then there was Carina.

His beautiful daughter. He had seen her every day of her life. She was a miracle. A blessing. And he loved being a hands-on father.

'I was thinking that might be a good time to ask them too.'

Eden kissed him lightly on the lips and he felt her smile ripple through him. 'We might even let them do a little bit of babysitting. Give Tiger some practice before Sydney has the baby. You can give him some tips.'

'I'm still learning.'

'You are. But you're a natural.'

Surprisingly, he was. But he got a kick out of hearing her say it. From knowing that she said it because she cared, because she knew that he still needed that reassurance sometimes.

Eden rolled onto him then, her eyes moving to check the monitor. But this time his gaze stayed put because she was straddling him now, and her breasts were there, fuller from the milk, and he felt his body stir.

'Hi, Carina.' The monitor again. This time, a child's voice with an Australian twang, then a giggle.

Eden leaned forward, laughing, and he groaned softly then grinned, a big, stupid grin. Because that was something else that he had to thank his wife for.

Jasmine was in his life too, now.

Reaching out to her mother had been a big step, but Eden had been by his side. Jessie had been cautious at first, understandably, but on Eden's advice he had let her set the pace and five months ago, Jasmine had come to visit him in New York with Jessie and her husband, Eric.

It had burned at first, hearing his daughter calling Eric Dad.

But now she called him Dad too. Which was fine because, as Eden had reminded him, two things could be true at once. And each time he saw his eldest daughter, he felt the connection deepen, not just with him but with Eden too, so that by the time Carina was born it was Jasmine who had chosen her baby sister's name, picking her favourite constellation in the night sky.

'*Can I bring Carina in to you? Please. I'll be careful.*' Jasmine was squinting hopefully up at the camera.

'*Yes, just remember to support her head.*'

'*I know, Daddy.*'

Watching Harris's face soften, Eden felt a deep, almost painful tug of happiness. Her love for him was so sharp, so compelling.

'I better put some clothes on,' she said softly, reaching for her robe.

'I guess you should.' He touched her cheek. 'I love you. I love this.'

'I love it too.' She pulled him closer and kissed him fiercely and for a moment there was just the warm touch of their lips and the press of their bodies and then Jasmine came into the room, carrying her baby sister, and just like that they were the family they had both longed to be for so long.

* * * * *

BILLION-DOLLAR SECRET BETWEEN THEM

CLARE CONNELLY

MILLS & BOON

CHAPTER ONE

EVEN WITHOUT TURNING AROUND, Luca Romano knew what he'd see. He would recognise her voice anywhere—despite not having heard it for almost exactly three years. There was something in her tone—husky, sultry without trying to be, honest and emotional—that evoked an instant, visceral reaction.

Just like the first night they met.

He clutched the Scotch and, in an exercise in restraint, continued to stare straight ahead, his eyes focused on the bottles of liquor that lined the back wall of the bar. All the while, Imogen crooned a slow ballad, the simple acoustic strains of her guitar an easy match for the din of the crowd. Even above the noise, there was a purity to her music that made it impossible not to listen, not to hear.

The hairs on the back of his neck stood on end, just as they had the first time he'd seen her, and out of nowhere, a thousand unwelcome memories rushed through him. That night, when he'd come to this very bar, in a foul mood, wanting to drown out the thoughts that persistently dogged him—of his failings and his guilt—and had seen Imogen for the very first time. She'd been singing, just like this, and her voice had done more than a succession of whiskies could: she'd been all he could focus on, a balm unlike any he'd ever known. She'd been the birthday present he'd allowed himself, a moment of weakness in which he'd surrendered to an animalistic need and passion, telling himself it would only be for one night.

Only he'd been wrong. The balm Imogen offered had been addictive. Another night had followed, and another, then many more, all tempestuous, overwhelmingly hot, the kind of passion that had made him want more and more, until he'd wondered if he'd ever get enough of Imogen Grant.

He'd had the knowledge in the back of his mind that it had gone on too long, that he was wanting her too much, almost coming to need her. As if she was some kind of sorceress, making him think he deserved that sort of happiness when he knew that to be the last thing he could ever enjoy, after what he'd done—or what he'd failed to do.

Luca had long carried the responsibility of his family's deaths, and the guilt of that was something he would carry for the rest of his life. So too his need for penance. Many times, he'd wished he hadn't lived. He'd wished he'd died alongside them and been spared from the fate of remembering his failures. But he hadn't, and so he'd committed to the only path he considered viable: a life of sacrifice. A life in which he went through the motions but astutely denied himself any of the pleasures other people took for granted.

The morning she'd told him she loved him, he'd wanted to stop the world spinning.

No, he'd wanted to scream. *You don't love me. You can't. No one can.*

But instead, he'd broken up with her, ending it in such a way to ensure she'd never want to see him again, because at that point, he'd known that was for the best—for him, and for her. Not only did Luca refuse to allow himself happiness, he knew he couldn't be trusted—not with another person's life. Not after what had happened to his parents and younger sister. He'd been responsible for their deaths—how could he ever trust himself not to make another fatal mistake, just like he had on that god-awful night? It was a risk too big to take—even if he thought he was worthy of her love.

Oh, he didn't doubt she'd loved him; Imogen was just that kind of person. Good and open, honest and emotionally available. A virgin when he'd met her, in more ways than one. While she'd been sexually inexperienced, he realised now she'd also been totally inexperienced with the world, and that had been part of the appeal. She was so different to the women he'd been with in the past, so unjaded, so uncynical. So easy and happy.

So warm.

Because he'd always gone for a certain type of woman before Imogen. Knowing the limitations of what he could offer, Luca had been careful to sleep with women who were as disinterested in a relationship as he was. Casual sex, very occasionally, was the most he was willing to allow for.

He dipped his head forward, staring at the amber liquid in his glass, willing it to flood his body with steel, to make him strong. He threw it back then turned slowly, bracing for the sight of Imogen, wondering if she would be very different. It had been almost three years—not long, really, but at the same time, going from twenty-two—which she'd been then—to twenty-five could bring about several changes in a woman's life.

She might be married now, for all he knew.

Even the turn towards the stage he executed with a mechanical slowness, as if to prove to himself every step of the way that he was in control.

And then he saw her, and he knew: he wanted her still.

Three years hadn't changed that.

Her honey-brown hair was in some kind of braid, pulled over one shoulder and loose enough that tendrils had escaped on either side of her love-heart-shaped face, framing it like a piece of art. Her eyes were almond-shaped and wide-set, a caramel brown in colour. Her skin was tanned, covered in a dozen or so tiny freckles across the bridge of her nose and the top of her cheeks. Her lips, usually pale pink but painted a deep red tonight, were naturally a Cupid's bow shape. She closed her eyes as she sang, tapping one boot-clad foot against the bar of her stool, her fingers moving as if they were in a ballet, glancing across strings and somehow producing the kind of music that had the capacity to reach inside a person and fundamentally change them.

He stood perfectly still, hating her.

Hating her for the fact he still wanted her.

Hating her for the fact she'd ruined what they'd had by claiming to love him.

Hating her for reasons he couldn't even fathom.

And then he began to walk, his gait long and slow. He wore an immaculate jet-black suit and a crisp white shirt, his black hair combed back from his brow. He walked with the sort of energy that made people turn and look, even when they didn't realise he was one of the wealthiest men in the world. He stopped just short of the stage, his eyes holding to her with a steadiness that he couldn't fight.

She continued to sing, her eyes swept shut, her mouth moving in a way that was making his body tighten just watching her. More memories—her mouth, tentative at first, on his body, and by the end, so skilled at pressing his buttons, at knowing exactly what he liked, wanted, needed.

He suppressed a groan. She finished the song and smiled when the crowd applauded. Her eyes swept across the audience, briefly passing over him without showing even a hint of recognition and then, with a look of sheer terror, returning. He felt the emotions flooding through her even as he displayed none himself, even when he felt none.

Shock. Surprise. Anger. Resentment. Fury. Pain.

He had thought of her from time to time, had wondered if

she'd forgiven him, then presumed not. He'd spoken to her in a way that was unforgivable. That had been his intention—and weirdly, at the time, it had been his pleasure. She had offered him something beautiful, something he'd known he didn't deserve, and so he'd taken a warped kind of pleasure in destroying it. He hadn't wanted to destroy Imogen, though; she'd been collateral damage. But if she'd created a fantasy of a life together, of being in a loving relationship with Luca, of loving him, then he had needed to annihilate that fantasy.

And so he had.

He saw now that she hadn't forgiven him.

Her fingers trembled almost imperceptibly as she reached for a glass of water, took a sip, then strummed the guitar. The crowd continued to buzz around them.

'Okay, guys,' she said, her speaking voice even more familiar than her singing. It was soft and husky, her accent British courtesy of having lived her whole life here in London. 'Just one more song to finish off. You'll probably recognise this one.'

She began to strum her guitar, the strains immediately familiar—it had been a hit a couple years ago, a number one song by an American pop star you couldn't go anywhere without hearing.

But in Imogen's hands, with her eyes practically cutting through Luca, the words could almost have been written for him. His lips twisted in a wry, mocking smile as she crooned the chorus,

And when the dawn light came
And the world started to glow golden
I saw you for what you really are
A man I'm not beholden
I saw you in all your glory
But glory's nothing to you

You're no one I want in my story.
I walked out, I stood tall
Next time I'll check before I fall.

Good. She should have checked before she'd fallen. And she was right about the glory thing too. Glory was nothing to him.

He'd presumed she'd known that about him, presumed she'd understood.

When he looked back, he wondered how the hell she'd ever thought she loved him. It was a testament to her goodness and nothing else. He'd made a point of restricting their time together to bed. Conversation had been kept to a minimum. She'd been a month-long booty call, nothing more—and he'd been the same to her.

Or so he'd stupidly thought.

His hand formed a fist at his side as memories he went out of his way to suppress seemed to strangle him now. Her smile when she'd arrived at his place, the small gifts she'd brought. Things she'd noticed he didn't have but needed, foods she'd wanted him to try, the guitar she'd bought at a flea market and left there, because she often picked it up and played, simply because the spirit moved her. Weirdly, he still had it somewhere. The back of his wardrobe perhaps?

She sang the chorus again, and her eyes didn't leave his face. It hadn't been written for him, but it might as well have been, at least the way she was singing it.

She finished to rapturous applause, stood, bowed and went to walk off stage. He moved without thinking about it, his steps echoing her own, so that when she stepped into the crowd, he was there, his powerful body so much larger than her slim, petite frame.

Imogen was more than just beautiful; she was interesting. Her face had all the mystique of the Mona Lisa's. Her expressions were often hard to pin down; there was the sense that her brain was working all the time. It had kept him on his toes and had been part of her appeal. She dressed as she had then—like a musician—in a pair of skinny jeans, a loose singlet top with a silky wrap over her shoulders and a series of long chains around her slender neck, giving her an unmistakably bohemian vibe. He noticed without meaning to that she wore a selection of chunky rings on her fingers, but none bore a diamond and none were on her wedding finger.

'Excuse me,' she muttered, as if she didn't know him. As if they hadn't spent thirty nights in his bed, tangled in sheets and each other. As if he hadn't been her first lover. His body tightened at the memory.

He hadn't known.

He hadn't expected it.

If he'd known, he would have walked—no, run—away from her. But she'd made a joke about it afterwards, as if it hadn't mattered, so he'd clung to that.

'A twenty-two-year-old virgin? Who woulda thunk it?'

'Imogen.' His voice emerged deep and raw. 'Let me buy you a drink.'

Her eyes widened and her lips parted. Hell, he was about three seconds away from pushing her against the wall and claiming that mouth with his own. He cursed inwardly, his whole body on fire.

'I can buy my own drink. I don't want anything from you.' She tilted her chin with defiance; he ached to reach out and stroke it with his thumb.

'Are you sure about that?'

She gasped again, glanced away.

'I'm meeting some friends,' she said after a beat.

'You sure you wouldn't rather meet me?'

And then, because he couldn't help himself, he shifted his hand, ever so slightly, so their fingers brushed and the familiar spark of awareness burst through him. As it did her. He saw it in the flush of her cheeks and the golden of her eyes.

She swallowed hard, her throat shifting visibly.

'I hope I *never* meet you again,' she said, with brutal honesty.

'I'm not so sure about that. I think you wish you felt that way, but in reality...'

'You don't know a damned thing about reality,' she volleyed back. Her eyes moved beyond him, and she smiled at someone over his shoulder. A tight smile, but it nonetheless changed her face in a way that made his gut roll, and for the briefest moment he was transported back to a time when she'd smiled for him. Not a tight, forced smile but a smile that radiated excitement and anticipation.

'I know that three years hasn't changed things between us,' he growled, dropping his head so he could whisper the words against her ear, his breath warm in the crook of her neck. He knew it drove her crazy and he felt her shiver in response. Power flooded his veins.

'Three years?' she managed to respond, but her voice trembled. 'Is that all it's been?'

He made a soft sound, a mocking half-laugh. 'You haven't missed me?'

'Like a hole in the head.'

She lifted her hand, perhaps intending to push him away, but instead, her fingers just stayed there, pressed to the crisp white of his shirt. Their bodies were so close, and as the pre-recorded music flooded the venue, the crowd grew louder and seemed to swarm around them, offering a level of anonymity he preferred.

'So you're not tempted to come home with me?'

Another gasp. 'Never.'

Still her hand was on his chest. He moved his hand to her

hip, separating her singlet from her jeans so his fingers could brush the bare flesh at her side.

'It could be our secret. No one would need to know.'

'I would know.' She groaned though, as his hand moved around to her back and pushed her forward, so there was not even a whisper of space between his body and hers. He felt the moment she became aware of his arousal. Her eyes flew to his, her lips parted, her cheeks flushed pink.

'Or we could find somewhere here,' he suggested, lifting one brow, no longer on the fence about this at all. He wanted her. He needed her. Clearly he wasn't thinking straight, but it had always been this way with Imogen. She was a sorceress, but now that he knew that, he could control it. One night, one little misstep, and then he'd forget her again.

'Charming,' she ground out, but didn't move away from him. 'You're such a pig.'

'Something I thought you always understood about me.'

'Yeah, well, I didn't.'

'But now you do.' He dropped his lips to her jaw, kissing the flesh to the side of it, flicking her with his tongue so she trembled against his body. 'Don't we both deserve this?'

'I deserve so much better than this,' she responded, and he couldn't help but agree. She did—he didn't.

Let her go.

It would be the right thing to do. He couldn't toy with her. Couldn't destroy her again. He knew how badly he'd hurt her the first time, and while he'd been glad to get her out of his life, glad to remove her from his, to permanently remove the pleasure she'd given him, hurting her had been anathema to him. He didn't want to do that again.

But she was an enchantress—or perhaps it was just the chemistry they shared. There was something between them that was akin to a drug. He was like a recovering pseudo junkie, and now she was right in front of him, he needed a hit.

'Come home with me.'

Another soft groan. Of surrender?

'I'm meeting friends.'

It only strengthened his resolve. 'I'll wait.'

'I can't.'

'Of course you can.' He moved the hand at her back lower to cup her buttocks, holding her hard against his arousal. 'You know I'll make it worth your while.'

A small sob. A sound that he recognised as one of desperation—and surrender.

Power throbbed through him.

'Luca—'

Cristo. He loved it, how she said his name. He'd made millions of pounds before he turned twenty-one and had been a billionaire many times over before thirty, but it was the capitulation in Imogen's tone that truly made him feel as though he had won the lottery.

'Come home with me and let me hear you scream that,' he demanded.

'I hate you,' she whispered back, eyes huge when they met his.

'Good. I like hearing you say that much better than "I love you."'

She gasped. 'You are such a bastard.'

'This time, don't forget it.'

And with every last bit of willpower he possessed, he pulled away from her, waited a few seconds, then walked back to the bar, his long, easy stride concealing how much he wished he was still pressed hard against her beautiful body.

She was aware of him the whole time. As she went through the motions of catching up with friends, talking, laughing, she felt his eyes on her. He had stopped drinking alcohol. She noticed he held a bottle of mineral water in his hand as he watched her. Imogen sat on her single glass of wine all night. For hours.

She would usually have excused herself sooner, but she liked making him wait. She liked punishing him in some small way, even though she recognised that even *thinking* about going home with him was the stupidest thing she could ever do.

For so, so many reasons.

Her pulse fired as she replayed their relationship like a time capsule in her mind. The whirlwind nature of it all, how overwhelming it had been, how unprepared she'd been for someone like Luca, how naturally she'd viewed him through the prism of her own parents' long, happy marriage, how easily she'd believed they were falling in love with one another. How foolish she'd been! How rapidly she'd given him her heart, with no doubt that he'd welcome her proclamation of love and even return it. How devastating it had been when she'd told him she loved him and he'd laughed in her face.

The things he'd said that morning were a part of her now. They'd calcified inside her heart, forming lumps that were embedded in her psyche.

'You are a silly, naïve girl if you think this is love. We're sleeping together, not dating. You are not my girlfriend, and I am not your boyfriend. You're just someone I'm having sex with when I want to have sex. I could replace you in a heartbeat. No, I will *replace you in a heartbeat. Get out of my house.'*

She had felt physically sick. She had, in fact, vomited as soon as she'd walked out of his mansion. And then she'd vomited again the next morning. His words were still ringing in her ears, going around and around and around a week later, when she did a pregnancy test and realised she'd conceived their baby.

She paled now to think of Aurora, their beautiful daughter, at home with Imogen's twin sister, who looked after Aurora while Imogen worked. She thought of Aurora, the baby he most definitely wouldn't have wanted and didn't deserve, and knew she was playing with the kind of fire that would burn her badly if she wasn't careful. She couldn't let him find out about Aurora. The smart thing to do was run a mile from this man. He had broken her heart; hell, he'd broken *her*. For a very long time, all the light in her life had been extinguished. If it hadn't been for Aurora, she had no idea how she would have coped.

Yet his words were spinning through her mind, the things he'd said that awful morning like the laying down of a gauntlet she ached to pick up now. He'd been needlessly callous and utterly cruel, his cutting dismissal of her a wound she would never fully recover from. How could she not make him eat those words? He'd spoken to her as though nothing they'd shared had been special—yet here he was, three years later, clearly still attracted to her. She despised herself for needing that validation, and yet somehow, it mattered. Back then, Luca had been the one who'd called the shots, and she'd loved him too much to question it. But now? What if they could have this one night, and all on her terms? What if they could sleep together, only now, it would be Imogen who walked away—who made him feel worthless and easily replaceable?

Adrenaline sparked in her blood as she slid her empty glass across the table, stood up and excused herself from her friends. She glanced at Luca and then, without waiting to see if he followed, she walked out, aware that in a moment he would join her, and the juggernaut would start all over again.

Not really, though. This was not a juggernaut but rather an indulgence. A single step back in time for the one thing that had been good about them. Sex.

It had been almost three years for Imogen, and there was a fire in her blood that Luca had lit. She'd let him stoke it and extinguish it and then she'd have the satisfaction of walking away all over again. Because not only was he a selfish son of a bitch whom she hated with all her heart, he was also the father of a daughter he knew nothing about, and Imogen damn well intended for it to stay that way.

CHAPTER TWO

THEY HAD ONLY just got into his car when he reached for her, his mouth seeking hers, tasting her, as if he had been waiting for this moment his whole life. And she responded in kind, her body seeming to take on a life of its own as she climbed onto his lap, straddling him and kissing him until she could hardly breathe. His hands pushed through her hair, pulling it from the braid, and despite the jeans they both wore, his arousal pressed hard to her sex, making her moan as she rolled her hips with eager, desperate hunger for him.

He swore and she felt it in her soul, the same desperate, aching desire that was strangling her.

Three years. Had it really been so long? Kissing him now, it all felt so normal, so natural, as if they did this every night. Then again, he probably did. It wasn't like he was tucking a toddler into bed and reading them stories.

She had not a single doubt that she had done the right thing for her daughter by concealing her from Luca. Until she'd met Luca, she'd seen the world through rose-tinted glasses. At one point in time, the idea of keeping a father from his own child would have been anathema to her. But then she'd met Luca and she'd come face to face with a heart of darkness; she knew it had no place in Aurora's life.

She didn't want to think about that now. She couldn't help but feel conflicted even when she knew she'd done the best thing for everybody.

Fortunately, Luca made it very, very hard to think about anything, as his hand pushed at her singlet and found the lace of her bra, his thumb brushing over the fabric, teasing her nipple so she arched her back with a cry.

He made a guttural noise of agreement, and seconds later his head was under her singlet, his mouth on her breast, his tongue rolling her nipple through the bra so she was whimpering with a kind of euphoria that was all the more intense for how long it had been since she'd known anything like this.

Heaven help me, she thought, as he moved to the other breast and jerked his hips to drive his arousal harder against her sex. She dug down into the seat, needing to feel him, needing to be with him.

'How long until we're there?' she groaned, glancing at the window, not recognising where they were.

'Too long,' he snapped back, the words imbued with as much desperation as she felt. Then he swore, pulled his head out of her shirt and sought her mouth once more, kissing her like his survival hung in the balance, kissing her hard and hungrily—angrily too. It was an anger she totally understood.

She was furious with herself for doing this, for wanting him. Furious with herself for being weak.

This man was lava, or quicksand. Dangerous. Bad for her. She knew that, and she knew she should avoid him like the plague, and yet it had taken Luca a mere three minutes to convince her to go home with him. Where was her sanity? Where was her self-preservation?

But this wouldn't be like last time. She was stronger now. She understood better.

Her childish idealism had been trampled, replaced with a lens of gritty reality. At least when it came to Luca Romano.

After what felt like an eternity, the car turned into the alleyway behind his mansion and the garage gate drew up. The driver manoeuvred the SUV in and cut the engine.

Luca moved quickly, easing Imogen off his lap as he opened the door and stepped out, his arousal obvious courtesy of the fit of his suit. The lights were fluorescent—a metaphorical bucket of water—but such a thing had no power to lessen her need for him.

Imogen half stepped out of the car and he half lifted her, throwing her over his shoulder and carrying her from the garage in the most expedient way possible.

'I can walk, you know,' she said gruffly, but his hand had curved around her bottom and her whole body was trembling with need, so she wasn't even sure if her statement was accurate.

'Do you want to?'

She hated him. She hated him for knowing her weakness, for knowing the depth of her need; she hated him so much and for so many reasons.

The house was instantly familiar, bringing back a thousand different memories, memories she wished to avoid.

But it also brought with it realisations. Time had elapsed. She'd grown older and a hell of a lot wiser. She'd never been here in the daylight. Not for longer than it took her to evacuate in the mornings. He'd never offered for her to stay when he was leaving for work, and he left early. In the evenings, they'd spend the night in some kind of wonderful thrall and then it would be over again.

How had she missed the fact it had just been sex for him?

She'd been so naïve.

They were just inside the lounge room when he eased her to the floor and started kissing her again. This time his powerful, strong hands stripped her clothes as he went, one by one, removing her shawl, her singlet, her bra. While she kicked out of her boots, he unfastened her jeans and pushed them down, his hands brushing her bare thighs as she stepped out of the fabric. Her hands pushed at his jacket as he removed her underwear, and then he was drawing a condom from his wallet as he unfastened his belt and trousers, then slid them down just enough to sheath himself. He lifted her with a deep, rough groan, the kind of sound she could never emulate because it was so masculine and so uniquely *Luca*. He thrust into her as he held her around his waist, the groan exploding into the room as he filled her more completely than he ever had before.

Or perhaps it was just his absence that had made her feel that way. Maybe it had always been like this, but she'd been in such a fog of fantasy land, thinking it would last for ever, that she hadn't completely appreciated how mind-blowing it was to be with him.

He stepped forward so her back was against a wall, and with each thrust she felt her sanity spiralling, her need growing, her passion exploding, so when she came it was like all the molecules in the universe were being rearranged, rebuilt, overbright and overlarge.

'Luca.' She cried his name, just as he'd said she would, and she didn't stop there. She called it over and over again, as he drove into her until her eyes were filled with a firestorm of lights and her whole body was singing. She dropped her head onto his shoulder in a sign of total and utter surrender, her body wrapped around his like a vine. Sweat sheened her body, and his. She was no longer conscious of where he began and she ended.

Heat licked the soles of her feet.

He began to move, carrying her deeper into the house, to his room, where he placed her on the bed.

Ghosts lingered here.

Ghosts of the kind of pleasure that was impossible to define. And the kind of pain that could almost kill a person. She ignored the latter. She didn't want to think of that now. Not when he was moving inside of her again, his powerful, strong body over hers. She realised, belatedly, that he was still dressed, and her hands moved impatiently to shove his shirt off his body, but the buttons were hard and her fingers hardly co-operated.

But somehow it felt important to be naked with him, a levelling experience of intimacy, a need to see that he had surrendered as much as she had. She grunted as she pushed at his shirt, breaking several buttons from the stitching, earning a gruff sound of amusement.

'I would have helped, if you'd asked.'

'I don't feel like asking,' she responded, shoving at his pants next. But this time, he helped, pulling away from her just long enough to push his own clothes off before returning to her.

'What do you feel like?'

'Isn't it obvious?'

'Tell me what you want.' His commanding tone sent shivers down her spine, shivers of need and desire.

'This.'

'No. Be specific.'

Heat flushed her cheeks. He was taunting her. He knew she was shy. He knew she was innocent and inexperienced.

'You are not a twenty-two-year-old virgin any more. You've been with other men, learned things. So? What do you like? What's changed?'

She was suddenly completely still.

She *hadn't* been with other men, as a point of fact. She'd been a little busy growing their baby then caring for her, but his easy supposition that her life had been a whirlwind string of affairs highlighted what his own had been like.

'I could replace you in a heartbeat.'

How many women had been in this bed since her?

Ice flooded her veins and she was momentarily stiff, cold, aching all over, just like she had back then.

'Imogen.' Only, his voice was a warm caress, bringing her back to the moment, to pleasure and passion. She closed her eyes, refusing to think about the past, his other women, about anything but this. Because she knew one thing for damned sure: when the morning came and dawn light broke, she would walk away from him, and this time it would be for good. Her small slice of payback. Childish, perhaps, but important to Imogen.

'I want this. One night of meaningless, amazing sex, and then I want to forget you even exist, you bastard.'

His smile almost looked to be one of relief. 'Excellent. That I can do.'

He was glad the next morning when he woke to find her gone. Glad that there was no need for a conversation about the past, for a conversation of any sort. He was glad that she hadn't stayed, even when his body still yearned for her, and he knew he would have liked one more chance to be with her before she'd left.

Had she left in the early hours of the morning, or once he'd fallen asleep? He had no recollection beyond their multiple comings together. He remembered making love to her until her voice was hoarse and her body spent. He remembered kissing her all over, pinning her arms above her head, delighting in the way his body could so easily master hers, even when the flipside was an uneasy dominance she held over him too. How one simple touch from her could drive him wild. He remembered her taking his length in her mouth as though she'd been fantasising about it for years, her eyes lifting to his as she took him deep, his hands curving around her head, touching her without driving her motions, needing some air of control though because his body was being shredded by what she could do to him.

It had been a perfect, sublime night. An excellent birthday present to himself, on his thirty-third birthday. And this from a man who never celebrated the passage of time. For each year he grew older was another year further from when his family had been alive. Each year he lived was a marked reminder that they had not. And that he had been to blame.

His fingers ran over his scarred side distractedly, the marks he bore a welcome, constant reminder of how he'd failed his mother, father and little sister, Angelica.

There was a new mark above his hip bone. A purple bruise. A hickey, he realised, recalling Imogen's lips pressed there, while her hands worked the rest of his body, his arousal, until he was calling her name, reaching for her hips, positioning her on his length and taking her from underneath, staring up at her breasts as she rolled her hips and tormented him with the perfection of her tightness.

He swore loudly into the bathroom, his gaze meeting its reflection in the mirror, as he acknowledged to himself, and only for a moment, what a liar he was.

He was *not* glad she was gone.

He would have endured any number of conversations if it meant he could screw her one last time.

'I want to have meaningless, amazing sex, and then I want to forget you even exist.'

He closed his eyes.

'You bastard.'

Fair enough. He was better to take her approach to this, and let sleeping dogs lie. He knew what would happen if he saw her again.

They'd fall back into bed together.

Again.

And again.

And again.

But to what end?

Imogen hated him now, but she'd loved him once and he

couldn't risk that she might do so again. He didn't want anything like that kind of complication. He shuddered at the thought. Imogen Grant was now firmly, well and truly, a part of his past life, and that was that.

At least, it should have been, but evidently, this was not the case. Not even three nights after his birthday, he found himself at the same bar, listening to Imogen once more, his whole body on fire with a need for her he couldn't ignore, even when he knew he really should.

She wore a long floaty dress and a heap of bangles that jangled prettily as she strummed the guitar. She sang as though the words had been dug from her soul, the ballad not one he knew but one he found instantly catchy. The crowd was mesmerised; such was her appeal. When she stood up to walk off stage, he left his place at the bar and strode towards her. She stepped down, not seeing him, walking towards another man instead.

He stopped walking, his gut twisting at the sight of her natural, full smile, at the way she pulled her hair over one shoulder before wrapping her arms around the man's waist and laughing at something he said. She punched his shoulder playfully—flirtingly—and Luca's body turned to stone.

The man leaned closer, whispered something. She looked up at him, nodded. He put a hand in the small of her back, guided her away, towards a table. Unlike the other night, there was no group of friends waiting for her. This was more intimate. A date.

His body went from ice-cold to red-hot.

So, what did he expect?

Obviously, she'd been with other guys since him. Obviously, she had no reason to not be seeing someone tonight. Never mind that it had only been a few nights since they'd slept together. What did that matter?

She was a free agent, and the sex had been meaningless. Right?

He stalked back to the bar, threw down some notes, grabbed his jacket and left, determined not to think of her again.

'It's not a recording contract or anything,' Imogen said with a shake of her head, trying to contain Gen's excitement. 'It's just an invitation to send a demo.'

'From the head of a label,' Gen exclaimed. 'Hel-*lo*. That's amazing. Why are you downplaying this?'

Because Imogen had learned not to count her chickens before they hatched. Because she'd learned to keep both feet firmly planted in reality, to not trust how things appeared. 'Until there's a signed contract, I'm just seeing this for what it is—an opportunity.'

'Come on, Immi. After that song, everyone wants a piece of you.'

'That's so not true. I've had some songwriting offers, but you know that's not my dream.'

'Right. *This* is your dream. And you're there, baby. They want you.'

Imogen rolled her eyes.

'Higher. More high!'

She turned back to Aurora who was on a swing, buckled in place, and had been enjoying the sensation of jettisoning through the air until her mummy and aunt had become so locked in conversation they'd stopped swinging her altogether.

Imogen gave the back of the swing a push, smiling as Aurora's chubby legs, encased in hot pink leggings, swung wildly through the air.

'They want me to submit a demo. Along with, probably, hundreds of other aspiring singers.'

'No one is as talented as you.'

'I'm not saying I'm not happy,' she conceded after a beat. 'I'm just being pragmatic. There's a heap of things that need to line up before I get a recording contract. This is just one step in a very long path.'

'But it is a step,' Gen said, batting her lashes with the kind of optimism Imogen had once had in spades.

'Yeah,' she conceded after a beat. 'It's a step.'

'Right.' Gen nodded approvingly. 'I have to love and leave you beautiful people. I've got a date.'

Imogen wrinkled her nose. 'Who is it today? Da Vinci or van Gogh?'

'Both, if there's time. You know I don't play favourites.'

Imogen hugged her sister, watching as she walked away from the playground and towards the tube, which would take her to the National Gallery. Where Imogen was fluent in all forms of music and had been for almost as long as she could walk, Genevieve adored art and spent every spare moment she had studying paints and portraits. It didn't matter how many times she looked at the same pieces, she swore that they conveyed different things to her each time. Her obsession would have been hard to understand were it not for the fact Imogen was someone who read scores as if they were novels.

'See you tonight. I'll make butter chicken.'

'Baba chimiken!' Aurora repeated, clapping her little hands together and tilting her head back. 'Buh-bye, Gen-Gen!'

Genevieve blew several kisses, waved and continued to walk away.

Despite the approach of winter, the day was clear and, in the sun, warm enough to enjoy, so they stayed at the park longer than Imogen had intended. After a while, though, Aurora began to flag. Imogen scooped her up and placed her in

the stroller, walking towards a nearby café to grab a fortify-
ing coffee for the tube ride home.

While there were several playgrounds closer to their home,
this particular place had become a favourite. Not only was it
huge, it was also fenced, close to Gen's work, and more often
than not, there were several other children playing there,
meaning Aurora could busy herself making toddler talk with
them. Besides, they quite enjoyed the tube trip there and
back—Aurora loved to ride the 'fast trainies.'

Stifling a yawn, Imogen pushed into a busy café, stroking the soft brown hair on Aurora's head as she joined the
queue to order her coffee. She was about five people deep
and while she waited, she thought about the songs she'd play
at the bar next time, the students she was teaching piano, the
pieces she was working on. She thought about anything, in
fact, besides Luca.

His touch had been a betrayal of everything she'd sworn
to herself. She was furious with herself, not least of all because it truly had exposed her to weakness.

She'd been doing *fine*. She'd been *over him*. She barely
thought of him any more, except when Aurora pulled a certain face or looked at her with those intelligent brown eyes
and she'd see right through their daughter to the soul of her
father. But other than that, Luca had been out of her life and
mind. And now he wasn't. Now he was the last thing she
thought of at night and the first thing she thought of in the
morning. Now he was back to being a source of torment and
torture and she was so damned mad at herself. How could
she have been so stupid as to think she could sleep with him
and walk away, as though he meant nothing to her? No matter how much she wished that were true, it would never be
the case. She might hate him, but she simply couldn't forget
him—it was a curse she had to live with.

At the front of the line, she ordered her drink, then moved

to the side to wait for it. Aurora was babbling, a sign that she was close to sleep. Imogen crouched down and spoke to her instead. She used Aurora's nap time—in the middle of the day—to work, and if Aurora fell asleep now, she wouldn't nap later. So, Imogen engaged the toddler with little sing-songs and nursery rhymes until the coffee was ready and her name was called.

'Imogen? Double shot oat cap with vanilla syrup for Imogen?'

It wasn't an uncommon name. There were undoubtedly many women who shared it. But for some reason, Luca glanced up when he heard the call, his own double shot espresso sitting on the edge of his papers.

And then, he saw her.

Unmistakably Imogen, but as he'd never seen her before. This was Daytime Imogen, not dressed to perform, but casually, comfortably, in leggings, an oversized T-shirt and a puffer jacket that did nothing to hide her fragile beauty. He couldn't stop staring. She reached for her coffee on the edge of the bar, her face lighting up as she smiled at the barista then turned her attention lower.

To something.

A pram.

A stroller.

And someone.

His gut twisted; he stood without realising it.

Was she babysitting? Or was she a mother now?

He hadn't expected that, but why not? What did he really know about her life, then or now? Hadn't he gone out of his way *not* to know about her?

He watched as she pushed out of the café, coffee in hand, talking to the occupant of the stroller the whole way, and he followed behind, as if drawn by some invisible thread. She turned in the direction of the tube station, then she was almost level with his own car, double parked on the sidewalk while he took a quick meeting.

But Imogen was not as fast as Luca. He walked quickly and, when he was at her back, said her name. Softly, but that didn't matter. She turned around, the guilt in her face impossible to miss.

'*You!*' she cried accusingly, her face pale. 'What the hell are you doing here? Are you *following* me?'

It was a ridiculous assertion. 'Like I have nothing better to do with my time,' he responded gruffly. 'I just finished a meeting around the corner, grabbed a coffee, and then I saw you.'

'Oh, right.' She pressed a hand to her forehead, drawing in a quick breath. 'Of course.'

But there was a stroller in front of her with a little high-pitched voice emerging from it endlessly.

'Anyway, I have to get going.'

'Where to?'

'Um, that's none of your business.'

Her usual bravado was gone, though—robbed by the surprise of seeing him, he suspected.

'Imogen, what's going on?'

'Nothing, I'm just— I have to go.' She turned away from him, began to walk again, faster now. Something was shifting inside of him. He should have just let her go—Imogen's life was her business, and not his, but there was the strangest sense inside of him, an instinct he had always trusted, that there was more going on than he realised.

'Mummy, dog! Dog! Stop, dog!' the occupant of the stroller called as a woman walked past with a little West Highland terrier.

Luca's footing faltered. He stopped walking, his lungs burning as he drew in a breath. He was very, very rarely surprised, but that made twice in his life Imogen had managed to pull the rug out from under him. Once, when she'd claimed to love him. And now, discovering she'd had a child. With whom? And when? And why did it matter? She was just some woman he'd slept with a million years ago. She was nothing to him. *Niente.*

'Imogen, stop.'

'Why?' She kept walking. In fact, she sped up, so she was almost running. He increased his own pace, then caught her arm.

'Is it some great secret?' he demanded. 'You don't want me to meet your child?'

She stared at him with such wide eyes and such *fear* that his instincts kicked into overdrive again. There was something going on here. Something he had to understand.

With a last glance at her pinched, pale face, he moved around the stroller so he could see the child for himself.

He almost passed out. Sitting there, beaming out at the world, with dark, dark eyes and soft brown ringlets, was a toddler who was the spitting image of his little baby sister, Angelica, a child he hadn't seen in twenty-one long years.

And he knew.

He knew in that way one simply knows the incontrovertible facts of life that the little girl sitting in the stroller smiling up at him was his daughter.

He had a child.

He was a father.

And he wished, with all his heart and every fibre of his soul, that it was not the case.

CHAPTER THREE

'YOU'RE SURE YOU can't at least eat before you go?' Gen's voice showed clear concern.

Eat? As if. Imogen felt as if her stomach was tied in so many knots it would never be able to accommodate food again.

'I'll grab something while I'm out,' she lied, amazed that her voice emerged mostly normal sounding. She cleared her throat to conceal the slight tremor. Inwardly, she couldn't stop shaking.

'We will discuss this tonight, Imogen, and that is non-negotiable.'

He'd spoken in a tone she'd never heard, reminding her forcefully of how much she didn't know about Luca. For all they'd spent a month together, three years ago, she had re-alised subsequently how much of himself he'd kept from her. She'd spoken freely about her life, her aspirations, her thoughts, her dreams and hopes, but he had revealed so very little, and what he had shared had been like pulling teeth.

She knew that he worked tirelessly, that he played to win, was super successful, and yes, she knew that he was ruthless. Even without the way he'd treated her, she'd understood that.

'But you went to so much trouble and it smells *so* good,' Gen said, eyeing the butter chicken, naan bread and pilaf.

'So good.' Aurora smacked her hand to the tray of her high chair. Genevieve smiled indulgently.

'If I'm hungry, I'll eat when I get home.'

'I doubt Missy here will leave any leftovers,' Gen quipped, and Imogen smiled, but it felt forced. She could hardly think straight.

'Okay, call if you need anything. I won't be late.'

'Don't rush back. We've got a scintillating marathon of *Bluey* awaiting us after dinner, and then an early night.'

'You're the best.' She pressed a kiss to her sister's cheek and then to Aurora's head, breathing in the little girl with a strange feeling in her chest. She knew what caused the sensation. As she pulled the front door of their flat closed, she admitted that she was hovering on a precipice. Behind her was the old world, the one with which she was familiar and comfortable, and which she'd made work for her. But with each step she took away from their flat, their home, from her sister and daughter, with each step she took closer to Luca's, she acknowledged she was travelling further into something new and terrifying.

He knew about Aurora.

He knew that she'd had his baby, and that she hadn't told him. He knew that they were parents. He knew the bare minimum at this stage, because he'd peppered her with questions once he'd realised, and she'd answered in a state of total shock.

What was her name? How old was she? Was she healthy? What was she like?

She had no clue what he'd do with that information, but at the very least, he wanted more answers than she could have given him standing on the footpath outside a busy café.

Her mind was every bit as knotted as her stomach. She rode the tube to Sloane Square, then walked the short distance to his house, her heart steadily palpitating its way to her throat with each step she took.

At the door, she could barely bring herself to press the

buzzer. It would bring about the crossing of a line from which there was no return.

But she had to do it. There was no escaping this and she wasn't a coward. She couldn't hide from him indefinitely. Not now he knew. Not when he had all the resources he did at his disposal. There was nowhere she could go that he wouldn't find her.

Fidgeting her fingers, she forced herself to ring his door-bell then took a sharp step backwards, as if to immediately put space between herself and the conversation that had to take place. She heard his footsteps, felt the whooshing in-wards of the door, then saw him on the other side and wanted to throttle herself and her traitorous body for responding to him on a physical level. Just one sight of him and her pulse went thready for a whole other reason.

This was *not* the time to think about that.

She swallowed hard, forcing herself to focus.

He gestured silently for her to enter. She did so, careful not to brush close to him as she crossed the threshold. He noticed and gave her a mocking arch of his brow.

She wanted to punch him.

'So?' She shrugged out of her coat, hanging it on a hook by the door, turning back to him in time to catch the last flicker of his gaze travelling the length of her body. She shivered. She'd worn a black blouse that was buttoned up to the throat with a frilly collar in a sort of turn-of-the-century bohemian vibe, tucked into tailored jeans, and ballet flats. Hardly se-ductive, but the way she caught him looking at her sent her pulse rate skyrocketing.

'We need to talk,' he muttered, gesturing towards the lounge room.

She eyed it suspiciously before stepping through the wide doors, remembering the last time she'd been here and they'd made love against the wall, unable to wait until his bedroom.

She studiously avoided that area of the room, choosing instead to focus on the plush leather armchairs. He moved past her, towards a sleek cabinet that housed a liquor cabinet and inbuilt fridge, opening it and removing the bottle of wine that she'd always loved.

Was that a thoughtful gesture or just a coincidence? Definitely the latter. He poured her a glass then walked back to her.

'Drink this before you pass out.'

'I'm fine.'

'You don't look fine.'

Her heart dropped to her toes. Had he been looking at her with sympathy rather than admiration?

'Well, whose fault is that?'

'Do you really want to start talking about blame, Imogen?' he demanded, so she felt the full force of his emotions rioting towards her. 'I have a daughter I knew nothing about until today. A daughter I never would have found out about were it not for pure chance.'

She swallowed hard, fidgeting her spare hand and then taking a gulp of wine. Suddenly her nerves were in disarray and it was the only way she could think of to calm them.

'I'm more than happy to talk about blame,' she responded tautly. 'What could I do, Luca? After the way things ended between us, when I found out I was pregnant, I didn't even think of coming to you. You'd made it abundantly clear what I meant to you, and what you wanted from me. It definitely wasn't to become parents together.'

A muscle jerked in his jaw; his eyes bore into hers. 'That was about you and me,' he said, slashing his hand through the air. 'The moment you found out you were pregnant, I should have found out too.'

'Why?'

'Decency? Courtesy? Respect?'

'All of which you showed me so much of, right?'

'So, was this some sick kind of revenge? This is a child's life, a parent's place in their life. You toyed with both of us.'

'How dare you?' she shouted, quickly taking another gulp of wine and rejoicing in the fire it lit on its way down her throat. 'You have no right to say that to me. I am a damned good mother. I give her *everything*. You stand there and act all holier-than-thou, when perhaps you should be asking yourself how many other kids you have out there.'

He put a hand on his hip. 'I am *always* careful.'

'Yeah? What's your point? We were always careful, and I still got pregnant.'

'You weren't on the pill.'

'So, you're blaming me?'

He closed his eyes in a wave of visible frustration. 'It's an extra precaution I'd presumed was in place.'

'Given that I'd never had sex, I'd had no need for contraception.'

His nostrils flared. 'There's no point discussing the "why" of this. It happened. You got pregnant. I'm more interested in how you justified your decision. Why keep it a secret from me?'

'I didn't keep it a secret from you,' she hissed. 'You weren't in my life. You were nowhere.' Her voice broke a little. She hated that. She hated the emotion he could still bring to the fore, even when she despised him. 'But I knew you wouldn't want her. I did you a favour, Luca.'

'Do not—' he spoke quietly, calmly, yet she could feel his anger pulsing towards her '—presume to tell me how I would have felt.'

'Oh, come on,' she said with a humourless laugh. 'We were both there. You made it abundantly clear what your priorities were in life. As if you would have wanted to be a father.'

'Whether I wished it or not, you were pregnant. I should

have known that, and I should have known our daughter before today.'

Her stomach rolled. Was he right? Had she made the wrong decision?

Not when she considered the way he'd spoken to her. It hadn't been about them as a couple; it hadn't been about revenge, or wanting to hurt him or withhold their child from him. It had been about wanting to protect their daughter as much as anything.

'I didn't trust you,' she admitted slowly. 'I *don't* trust you.'

'What does that mean?'

'You're cruel, Luca.'

He flinched a little, but concealed it quickly.

'I was so caught up in you at first, I didn't understand. I didn't see it. I was overwhelmed by the whole sex thing. But you're a bastard, cold and unfeeling and capable of using people for your own ends. Honestly, we were just…better off without you.'

She threw the words at him but didn't feel any pleasure in saying them. They hurt to say, in fact. She blinked quickly, to clear the sting of tears.

His only reaction was to take a step closer, reach for her wine glass and take a sip before returning it to her.

'I don't disagree.'

Her eyes widened and she tamped down on an immediate reflexive response of contradiction.

'Unfortunately, we're stuck with one another now.'

She closed her eyes in a wave of uncertainty. A bad moon was rising, and she didn't know how to deal with it.

'What does that mean?' It was her turn to sip.

He pressed a finger to her chin, tilting her face, and when she opened her eyes, she was staring right at him.

'If I could choose, I would choose not to have children. I have never wanted that.' His voice was cold, emotionless.

'But she is here—a real person, my daughter.' A hint of feeling darkened his words, but he smothered it quickly. 'I have no choice but to be a part of her life.'

Imogen flinched.

It was her very worst nightmare. How could Luca be a part of Aurora's life without being a part of *her* life too?

She groaned, shaking her head a little. 'It's not possible. It would be too confusing to her. She has no idea who you are.'

'And why is that?'

Imogen's knees felt wobbly. She gripped the wine glass harder.

'You have one option here, though perhaps you cannot see that.'

Wariness crept along her spine.

'I will tell you what I want, and you will agree. It would not be wise to fight me on this.'

Imogen blinked up at Luca, seeing the steel in his features, and she baulked. She knew he was cold, and she knew what he was capable of, but in her heart of hearts, she had still clung to the notion that there was some goodness in him, somewhere.

She had to believe that—he was a part of their daughter's DNA, and darling Aurora was all sunshine and light.

'Is that a threat?'

His eyes bore into hers, almost seeing through her. 'Threats tend to be idle. What I am saying is not.'

She shivered. 'And what exactly are you saying?'

He was so close she could feel his warm breath against her temple as he exhaled. 'I want custody of her.'

Imogen gasped. 'You can't be serious.'

'Not sole custody,' he said, as though that made any difference. 'But she is my daughter. I demand legal recognition of that fact.'

'You *demand*?' she repeated, incensed. 'You just said you don't want to be a father—'

'But I am.'

Imogen swallowed, shaking her head a little. Not because she was rejecting his demand, but because she couldn't process it.

'I have a daughter I knew nothing about,' he said, the words flooded with a strange, almost far-away emotion.

'I know.' What more could she say?

'I want her here, under my roof.'

Imogen gasped, her headshake becoming more determined. 'She has a home, with me...'

'And I recognise that it would be cruel to separate the two of you—at this stage, at least. Unfortunately, that means you will have to be a part of this.'

Her stomach clenched at the obvious displeasure he took in suggesting any such thing. He could not make it any clearer that having Imogen was the last thing he wanted. Why did that hurt so much, even now? She had to take back control of this conversation, to reassert her independence.

'No.' She shook her head quickly, dislodging his finger from her chin. 'No *way.*'

'You're not listening to me,' he interrupted. 'She is *our* daughter, and *we* will raise her.'

'If you want to be a part of her life, you can be, but I'm sure as hell not living with you.' Her whole body felt as if it were filled with an electrical current at the very idea.

'Let me say this more clearly. I would like us to come to an agreement, but if you will not be reasonable, I have a meeting with a lawyer tomorrow morning and you had better believe I'll get access to our daughter through the courts. It will not be in her best interests, but I will fight you for what should always have been mine, Imogen.'

She was trembling so much she thought she might fall. She stepped backwards and backwards again, collapsing into one of the armchairs and clasping the wine glass in her lap.

She stared straight ahead, her whole life flashing before her eyes, everything wonky and aching.

She couldn't fight him.

She didn't have the resources. While she and Gen were doing okay, and her parents were comfortable, no one was in a position to bankroll the kind of legal fight she had no doubt Luca would launch.

'She's my daughter,' Imogen whispered.

She wasn't even aware of the tears that were falling down her cheeks until Luca appeared at her side, holding a tissue. Instead of passing it to her, he wiped her cheeks with surprising gentleness.

'Yes. I'm aware of that, and I have no interest in taking her away from you, even when I can see that would probably be fair retribution for the fact you took her away from me.'

Imogen tried to suck in air but struggled.

'I am asking you to live here, with her, for a while. I am asking you to be reasonable and see this from my perspective. I have a daughter I just found out about. Don't I deserve a chance to get to know her? And wouldn't that be easier for her if you were a part of it?'

Luca stared at the wall without seeing. Their conversation was replaying in his mind like a film, every word, every sentence.

Every threat.

He dropped his head forward, staring at the floor, breath burning in his lungs.

Yes, he'd threatened her. He'd been so damned angry, so utterly shocked—at Imogen, as well as himself. Why hadn't it occurred to him that she might be pregnant? They'd slept together for a month, and before that, she'd been innocent. Hadn't it been foreseeable that there were consequences of their time together?

He clenched his teeth, trying to put himself back into the mind-set he'd had then. He'd been furious with her for loving him, furious with himself for letting it go so far, and he'd been missing her.

Missing her more than he'd allowed himself to admit...

Now, though, this wasn't about Imogen. It wasn't about his need for her, or her desire for him. None of that mattered any more. He was a father.

His gut rolled, and images of his own father populated his brain, almost driving him to despair. His own father had been the very best of men. He'd been a behemoth, a pillar of morality, intelligence, strength and good humour. He had stood like a beacon to Luca, a guide, always, as to how he should act—and Luca had failed him.

He couldn't fail his daughter—if only because Luca could finally do something which might, in some small part, atone for the mistakes of his past.

But what if he *did* fail her? What if he made a mistake again? What if he hurt her?

Panic stole through him, a familiar heat flooding through his veins so he couldn't think straight, and his breathing grew rushed.

He was not a twelve-year-old boy any more, though. The mistake of that night had been borne of his immaturity, his selfishness. Now Luca was a grown man, and he would give his life for Aurora's, in a heartbeat. He would move heaven and earth to keep her safe, to protect her. Though he'd never wanted to be a father, now that he was, he had no choice but to be the best damned father that little girl could have. Even if it meant having Imogen in the mix as well...

A scowl marred his face as he imagined what that might look like. Imogen was the one woman who'd ever weakened his resolve and got under his skin; she was the one woman who'd made him stray from his commitment to a lonely life of constant self-flagellation to atone for his guilt. In the past, he'd been weak, but he couldn't let that happen again.

He would keep her at arm's length this time around, even if the effort nearly killed him.

'You're *moving out*?' Genevieve whispered over a steaming cup of tea later that night.

Imogen grimaced, nodding. 'I can't see an alternative.'

'Run away,' Genevieve muttered, only half joking. 'Immi, listen. You didn't tell me the gory details, but you didn't need to. I know what this guy did to you. I *saw* what he did to you. I heard the goddamned songs you wrote. He *broke* you.'

Imogen closed her eyes on a wave of remembering. It had been bad. Very, very bad.

'He's her father. He has rights.'

'To see her, sure. But not to make you move in with him. What kind of sick control move is that?'

'Believe it or not, he's trying to do what's best for her. He wants to make up for lost time...'

Genevieve snorted, then placed her tea on the counter, her features rearranging themselves into a mask of serious contemplation. 'Listen, Im. You cannot do that with this guy.'

'Do what?'

'See the best in him.' Genevieve cupped Imogen's hands and lifted them to her chest. 'I know that's your default position, but not with him. Don't you dare let your guard down around this guy, or I'll never forgive you.'

'If I let my guard around him, I'll never forgive myself.' She squeezed Genevieve's hands. 'Try not to worry. We'll see you all the time; I'm just a few tube stops away.'

When Luca arrived the next day to collect Imogen and Aurora, she realised he'd worked fast. Somehow he'd had a car seat installed in his Range Rover, and the back pockets were stuffed with nappies, kids' books and rattles.

She tried not to let that endear him to her.

She was conscious, as she carried her suitcase to the door, of Genevieve's disapproving, arctic scowl.

'Im? Call me when you get there.'

'I'll be fine,' Imogen assured her sister. Then, belatedly, as Luca went to retrieve her luggage, she said, 'Genevieve, this is Luca. Luca, my twin sister.'

Luca went to extend his hand to shake but Genevieve glared at it as though he was holding a slither of snakes.

'Listen to me,' she muttered, moving close enough that a nearby Aurora wouldn't hear. 'You had better be nice, or so help me God, I will...do something. You don't deserve this,' she gestured to Imogen and then Aurora.

His eyes darkened and Imogen felt his surprise, but it just made her love her sister all the more. She reached across and squeezed Genevieve's arm. 'I'll be fine. I've got this.' She could only pray that was true.

Genevieve nodded once, smiled at her sister, hugged her, then scooped Aurora off the ground. She kissed the toddler's head, Genevieve's eyes a little misty as she passed the girl to Imogen.

'I can see my reputation precedes me,' Luca drawled, as Imogen clipped Aurora into the car seat then took her own seat beside him.

'What did you expect? A bed of roses?'

'I didn't expect anything,' he returned, pulling the car into traffic. She sat back in her seat, staring moodily through her own window without really seeing. He drove the busy London streets expertly, as she suspected he did all things in his life—except for relationships.

'Do you have any friends?'

He shifted a sidelong glance at her. 'Why do you ask?'

Deflection. She hadn't recognised his techniques three years ago—she'd been too mired in the fog of their chemistry to analyse anything very deeply—but she saw them now. He was nudging the conversation away, not answering her question but disguising that with interest in her. It had worked in the past. Now it frustrated her, but she didn't show it.

'Because you're such a charmer, of course,' she responded with a lift of one shoulder. Before turning back to her window, she saw the way his knuckles morphed into a shade of white, as if gripping the steering wheel very tightly.

They travelled the rest of the way in silence, except for Aurora's occasional babbling sounds from the back seat. Happy babbling, because Aurora was almost always smiling and shining. Imogen hoped that would continue to be the case. She gnawed on her lower lip as they travelled, until he pulled into the familiar alley that provided rear access to his home, pressing a button so the garage door opened seamlessly, and the car slipped in. Briefly she was reminded of the other night, when they'd come to his home and passion had been thick in the air between them. Now it was tension, so awful that it could be cut with a knife.

He went to the rear door, to lift out Aurora, but Aurora glanced at him then Imogen. 'Mama.' She pointed at Imogen. 'Want Mama.'

Imogen saw the accusing look in his eyes, but he took a step back, saying nothing to Aurora or Imogen. She felt what he would have said, though. She felt the blame and recriminations, and the certainty she'd once felt, that she had done the right thing by keeping Aurora from him, took a slight tumble.

With a reassuring smile at Aurora, she unclipped her and put their daughter on her hip, walking around the car towards the door. Luca had grabbed some luggage and was holding it, staring straight ahead, his shoulders tense. His whole body radiated stress. Anger?

Probably a whole host of emotions. This time yesterday, he'd had no idea about Aurora, and now he was moving her—and Imogen—in to live with him.

The moment they crossed the threshold from the garage to his home, she recognised just how busy he—or an army of minions—had been. The changes were subtle but noticeable to Imogen. All of the breakable artsy pieces had been moved from the coffee tables and low-lying shelves. Small plastic shapes had been added to coffee tables and sharp corners, in the event of a head bump from Aurora. A stylish wide basket was now in the living room, filled with brightly coloured toys and a tub of interlocking building blocks.

She glanced at him, not sure what to say now they were here.

Apparently, that was mutual. Imogen sighed softly, popping Aurora down on the floor and setting her free. The two parents stood back, a couple of feet apart, watching as Aurora went off, exploring her new environment. Toddlers learned by touching, and Aurora touched *everything*—his white sofas, his glass-topped coffee table—so she was sure Luca appreciated the wisdom of having moved anything fragile out of Aurora's way. She cruised the lounge room for several minutes before discovering the basket, but when she saw it, she squealed delightedly and ran on those deliciously chubby little legs towards it, plonking herself down at the edge and half diving in to examine the contents.

She heard Luca's sharp intake of breath and slanted a look at him.

Emotion.

She saw it on his face and felt it cut through her heart.

He was looking at Aurora as though she were the most incredible, fascinating, amazing thing in the world. He was looking at her with...*love.* A lump formed in Imogen's throat, and she blinked quickly.

'Mind if I make a cup of tea?'

He glanced across at her with obvious reluctance. Like he'd forgotten she was there. Imogen's heart thumped in pain. 'Make yourself at home.'

'Would you like anything?'

'Better not ask what I would like right now.'

She closed her eyes in a wave of desperation. 'You're never going to forgive me for this, are you?' She asked the question quietly, but with an intensity that was drawn from deep in her chest.

'Would you, if our situations were reversed?'

She glanced at Aurora and felt the reality of that sink inside of her like a stone. He was right, but he was also wrong. What he was missing was the very logical place Imogen had operated from: a certainty that a baby was the last thing Luca had wanted, or would be equipped to deal with.

'Watch her a moment?' Imogen asked, and Luca stared directly at her.

'She's my daughter,' he said with palpable, raw emotion. 'Of course I'll watch her.' And he turned his back on Imogen to do exactly that.

She was so like Angelica. Heartbreakingly similar, right down to their little voices. He watched Aurora and felt the slippage of time and place, of space and self, so he was a boy again, doting on the little sister who'd surprised them all with her arrival. Angelica had loved to be tickled, to have raspberries blown on her belly. She'd worshipped Luca and followed him like a puppy, but it had never occurred to him to mind. She had been the light in all their lives.

She'd shone, like Aurora shone.

He couldn't take his eyes off his daughter, and he knew he would never let anything happen to her. This time, if he had to give his own life to save hers, he would, in a heartbeat, and heaven help anyone who got in his way.

CHAPTER FOUR

'WE SHOULD PROBABLY talk about the practicalities of this,' Imogen said tentatively, when Aurora was settled for her nap.

Luca tilted her a glance, saying nothing. He was intimidating when he was like this.

Imogen forced herself to continue. 'I work three nights a week, and I teach a couple of kids piano some afternoons. I do lessons online, but generally schedule them for when Genevieve is around to help out. I've checked and she can come here, when I'm working, to look after Aurora.'

He swore softly. 'Because you do not trust me with our daughter?'

'Correct me if I'm wrong, but you don't have any experience with kids. Wouldn't you rather have some help, at least in the beginning?'

Something in his eyes shifted, an emotion she couldn't comprehend. 'I'm a quick study.'

'I…admire your confidence.' She sat down on the edge of an armchair, pulling her hair over one shoulder. 'But this is our daughter. I can't go to work unless I know she's safe.'

His features tightened perceptibly now. 'You don't think I can protect her?'

'That's a little dramatic. I'm not talking about some big bad wolf storming through the door. I just mean in case she falls over, or makes a run for the stairs.' She gestured around the apartment. 'Toddlers are non-stop. You have to be vigilant the whole time.'

'I intend to be.'

Imogen nodded slowly.

'You don't look reassured.'

Imogen's eyes widened. 'It's just—'

'She doesn't know me,' he said, crossing his arms over his chest.

And whose fault is that?

He didn't say it, but he might as well have. Imogen's cheeks flushed pink. 'What would you have done, if I'd told you back then?'

He hadn't been expecting the question; she could tell by the way his head jerked a little. 'I don't know.'

'Would you have made me move in with you then? What would you have said?'

'What I might have done doesn't really matter, as I never got the chance. I'm more interested in what you thought I'd do. That, after all, is the reason I was denied knowing her.'

Imogen flinched, but it was a fair question. 'I thought you'd completely flip out.'

Despite the seriousness of the conversation, the smallest ghost of a smile tilted his lips for a fraction of time before the thunder-clouds took over again.

'Difficult conversations still have to be had.'

'Our last difficult conversation was kind of hard for me to get over. I wasn't in the headspace for another.'

She toyed with her fingers, standing and moving towards the side table. It still had some interesting objects atop it, because it was too high for Aurora's curious little fingers. She picked up a glossy shell, running her fingers over its crenellations.

The truth was, she'd been depressed. After that morning, she'd gone into a dark, dark place and hadn't known how she'd ever get out of it. She'd barely existed. It was Aurora who had pulled her out of that funk, slowly but surely.

'Maybe I wasn't thinking clearly,' she said with a lift of one shoulder. 'At the time, I was sure it was the best decision for everyone.'

'You claimed to love me,' he said, and she shivered, hearing that word in his mouth, remembering how badly she'd wanted him to say it back to her. How *sure* she'd been that he would, because every moment they'd shared had *felt* like love to Imogen.

How stupid she'd been!

'And yet you really thought withholding a child from me was the best decision? How could you deny a child the presence of a man you claimed to love?'

'I didn't love you.'

Imogen had fantasised about saying those words for so long, and she'd thought it would be a heady delirium to throw them at his feet if ever she got the chance, but saying them now, she just felt very hollow.

Nonetheless, she spun around to face him, still clutching the shell, and she caught the shadow of surprise on his face and was glad. 'You were right. It was just sex. I loved sleeping with you, that's all.' She sucked in a breath, wondering why she didn't feel more victorious. 'Was it any wonder? I was a virgin, of course I got swept up in the excitement of it all.' She waited for the hit to land, then moved on, her voice soft and sadly reflective. 'I did like you, though. I thought you liked me. But the way you spoke to me made me realise I didn't even know you, and I sure as hell didn't think you had the emotional maturity to be a parent.'

He flinched and silence fell. She waited, breath held, for him to respond. To say something. To fight with her, to push her to admit that she had in fact loved him. Because she had, of course. Utterly and completely. But for pride, she'd lied to him now and she was glad.

Silence stretched, static and painful.

'If it makes you feel better, and you think it's best for Aurora, your sister can come over when you work.'

Tears threatened to fill Imogen's eyes. Not because he'd conceded the point but because he'd let her assertion stand, and she wanted to correct the record now and tell him she'd loved him with all her stupid, stupid heart.

She spun away, replacing the shell before swiftly leaving the room.

He stared at the wall for a long time after she left. Stared, replayed their conversation, pulling it apart, answering her questions to himself, now that he could explore them properly.

What *would* he have done if she'd told him back then?

Married her? Been secretly thrilled because he was actually missing her in his life?

He hadn't expected to. He'd truly believed he'd get over Imogen quickly, but she was a uniquely fascinating woman and a month with her had changed his parameters. He hadn't found her easy to forget, and months later, in the time frame of her pregnancy discovery, he'd been yearning for her in a way that might have weakened his resolve.

Marriage would have been wrong for her, because she would always want more than he could offer. She wouldn't be happy with a simple marriage for the sake of a baby. She would want it to be real, and he could never give her that.

He would never let himself have that, more to the point. Not after his family. Not after his failure to save them. He was going through the motions of this life, but he wasn't really living. He didn't *want* to live.

And there he found the problem, as he hadn't fully un-

derstood it then. Imogen had made him feel so alive. She'd
made him feel so *happy*, in a way he hadn't deserved. She'd
made him feel as though nothing in his past mattered. She'd
almost made him want to forgive and forget, but he couldn't.
His tribute to his family, the family he could not save, was
to exist in a kind of purgatory. Imogen had threatened that
with every single part of her.

She still did, he realised with a groan, dropping his head
forward and transferring his intense stare to the carpet.

'I didn't love you.'

Cristo, it had felt like she was plunging a knife right
through his gut, even when he recognised the sense of what
she was professing. Of course she hadn't loved him. It had
been a childish infatuation, nothing more, and he'd put an
end to it.

But for three years, he'd had the knowledge locked in the
back of his mind that if someone like Imogen Grant could
love him, he wasn't all bad. It wasn't as though he'd forgiven
himself for the loss of his family, and for what he'd failed
to do to save them, but in his darkest moments, the fact that
Imogen had loved him had been like a little touchstone of
warmth deep in his cold, black heart.

And now, even that was gone; all the light had gone out.

In the few seconds it took for Imogen to properly wake up,
she had the strangest sense of discombobulation. She reached
for her phone to check the time only to feel air—no bedside
table where hers usually was. She sat up, looking around
blearily, and with another deep, dark cry, she remembered.

She was at Luca's.

He knew about Aurora.

'I didn't love you.'

'I need to get there. Stop. Let me go.'

His voice was loud, angry, raw with emotion. She pushed

the sheet off herself, half worried he'd wake Aurora, half worried about him, and ran the short distance down the corridor, from her bedroom to his. She flung open the door without hesitation.

Luca was asleep, eyes shut, body naked—from the waist up at least—and sheened in perspiration. He thrashed as she watched, hitting the mattress. 'Stop! No! I have to get there, she's crying for me!' He slipped into Italian, and she recognised a dark curse in the midst of a string of other words.

Imogen had no idea what his nightmare was about, but it was terrifying to see Luca like this. Luca who was always in control, Luca who had a cool strength inherent to him.

'Luca.' She said his name loudly, sharply, but her voice shook.

He made a sound, barely human, and when she moved to him, it was partly because she was still worried he'd wake Aurora, but mostly, it was because she couldn't bear to see him like this. She told herself she would have done the same for *anyone*. Her humanity required her to offer help and comfort when needed.

She moved quickly to his bed and put her hands on his shoulders, steadying him. His skin was warm to touch, almost feverish, and his brow was covered in a light sheen of perspiration. Pity twisted her gut.

'Luca, Luca.' She shook him.

'Let me go,' he cried, louder. But he wasn't talking to her; he was in his dream. His nightmare. She'd never seen him like this—couldn't have imagined it was possible for him to feel such pain. 'I have to go!'

'It's me. It's Imogen.'

His eyes burst open and stared at her without really seeing. His face was lined with panic, his body prone with alertness. She kept her hands on his shoulders, holding him to the

mattress. Not that she was any match for him physically—
she just hoped he wouldn't lash out in his dreamlike state.

'You're okay,' she said, voice husky now, reassuring him.
'You're home. Everything's okay. Everything's okay.'

He frowned, as if still not comprehending. His body was
so tense, his face so unfamiliar to her. He shifted a little,
frowning and her heart turned over.

Her need to comfort and reassure him, to draw him back
into the present, was her guiding light. Instincts were at the
helm—instincts, she kept telling herself, she would have felt
if it were any other person. But that wasn't completely true.
There was no one else on earth she would have attempted to
soothe in the following manner. For a moment later, without
forethought, she leaned down, her lips finding his on autopilot, tasting the salt of his perspiration as she kissed him,
swallowing the rapid husk of his breathing, hoping to draw
him back into the reality of this life, and away from whatever had been torturing his sleep.

Stop! a voice in her head commanded her, shrieking at her
to remember who he was and what he'd done to her, how he'd
forced her to move into his home. To remember how capable
he was of wounding her. And yet he was also a man, tortured by a dream, and this was just a kiss, after all—something they'd done plenty of times in the past without it ever
meaning anything.

Until the threads of Luca's nightmare frayed and broke,
returning him to his usual self, and he was not responding
in a state of fear, but rather something else. Something more
urgent and primal, an animalistic need that ran through them
both.

His hands moved to her hips, lifting her easily and bringing her over him, and then he was kissing her back, his body
shifting to free the sheet that was between them.

'You had a nightmare,' she said into his mouth, as he rolled them, so she was on her back, his powerful body atop.

'Yes,' he agreed—which was more than she'd expected—and then he was kissing her so hard it was impossible to talk, much less think. She arched her back, her hunger for him catching her completely off guard. And yet why should it have? Wasn't this the way it was with them? Wasn't this their normal? No matter what she thought intellectually or knew to be true and right, this was an undeniable reality with them, and she couldn't fight it.

Not then.

Not when he needed her.

When he needed her, she would be there for him. Not because she cared about him—she wouldn't be that stupid ever again—but because he was a human being, in pain, and she was right there, and knew how to fix it.

Only it wasn't selfless.

Imogen needed fixing too.

Imogen needed the sense of wholeness and euphoria that came from being with Luca. When they were together, everything was right in the world, and she didn't need to think beyond that. How could she feel that way, after everything that had happened with them? She hated him, and yet she hated seeing him hurt. She hated him, and yet she needed him too. She needed *him* to need *her*. Proof that those awful words he'd thrown at her three long years ago had been a lie—it was something to cling to, a small power she held over him that was somehow mollifying and reassuring.

But that was almost too academic. When it came down to it, Imogen sometimes felt that being with Luca went beyond a choice: it was something that was almost predestined with the two of them, something that she could fight tooth and nail but never fully control.

Except it didn't change anything between them. Tomorrow,

the sun would dawn, and they'd be in the exact same pre-dicament, the trap created by Aurora's birth, but they would have had this—at least it was something, in the chaos of their lives, a small silver lining to this whole damned mess.

She remembered where he kept his condoms and reached across towards the bedside table, but her arms weren't long enough. Not when she was pinned beneath him on the bed.

'Please,' she groaned, lifting her hips.

He grunted his agreement, stretching out to open the drawer and remove a string of contraceptives. She didn't think about how well stocked he was. She didn't think about the fact he'd undoubtedly replaced her again and again in the three years since she'd left him.

Not now.

Not when he was sheathing himself and taking her, push-ing deep inside so Imogen cried out and writhed beneath him, waves of pleasure washing over her until she couldn't think straight.

Thinking was overrated anyway.

He had sworn this wouldn't happen. Hell, he'd wanted to keep her at arm's length, but in the tumult of his nightmare, in the torture of those memories, he'd woken to see Imogen, and she'd been like a beacon, a light in the abject darkness of his grief and failings, looking at him with her sweet, kind face, with all the goodness that glowed from her like starlight.

He'd wanted to shout at her, because her kindness and concern were the last things he wanted. His nightmare had been awful; his stomach was churning, just like it had that night, and he'd been relishing that pain, because he deserved it. How long had it been since he'd had a nightmare? In the beginning, they'd been frequent, but then he'd managed to control even his dreams. It must have been seeing Aurora. She was so like Angelica, so like his little sister, the memories had been stirred up and brought to life once more. And he'd been glad! Glad to exist in that pain and torture. But then Imogen had leaned down and kissed him, and any intention to control the spark that flared between them had been lost in the sheer urgency of their coming together.

He glanced across at her sleeping face, so innocent and beautiful, so achingly familiar, and regret slammed into him hard. Regret for his weakness, her kindness, for the passion that seemed determined to rule their interactions, even when they both clearly wished they didn't feel it.

There was nothing for it; Luca would simply have to try harder to control this. Imogen had offered herself to him once before, on a silver platter, and he'd known it to be impossible. Her love had been the last thing he'd wanted, the last thing he could accept, and nothing had changed. She wasn't offering love now, but she was still offering more than he would ever let himself have. She was still offering him a balm to his past, a way to forget, maybe even to forgive, and for that reason alone, Luca would hold firm. Imogen was not, and never could be, his, in any way.

She must have fallen asleep because it was dawn when she woke in his bed, then rolled to her side so she could look at him.

And her stomach churned because this was so familiar. Waking early, seeing his face, knowing she wouldn't have long before he stirred and started preparing for his day. Showering—always alone—dressing into one of those immaculate suits, gradually putting up all his barriers and pushing her away.

She hadn't realised it at the time, but Imogen had had three years to reflect and consider, and now she saw his morning rituals as a form of excising her from his life. Of showing her he didn't want her to be there more than she had been.

Why hadn't she understood that at the time?

She contemplated leaving his room, creeping out to avoid having to be pushed away again, but Imogen was older and wiser now, and more determined to do things on her terms. Whatever that might mean.

As if her being awake had somehow communicated itself to him, he blinked his eyes open and they landed straight on her, so her skin fizzed with a strange awareness, and her body trembled.

She didn't say good morning, and nor did he. It was almost too banal for them, after what had happened last night.

'You had a nightmare,' she said, as she had the night before, only this time, a question was couched in her words.

His jaw tightened.

'What was it about?'

His eyes darkened. 'I don't remember.'

Imogen's heart panged as if screws were being tightened on both sides. 'Don't you?' Scepticism tinged her words.

'It was just a dream.'

'No, it was a nightmare,' she insisted, as frustration whipped at her spine. 'You must have thought I was so stupid,' she said softly, pitying her twenty-two-year-old self.

Luca's frown showed he didn't understand.

'You did that *all the time* back then and I didn't even realise.'

'Did what?'

'Deflect. Not answer. I'd ask you a question and you'd deftly sidestep it, or turn it into a question about me instead. I hardly knew you, Luca, and all the while I was an open book to you.'

A muscle jerked in his jaw, but he didn't deny it.

'You're doing it now. If you don't want to talk about your nightmare, then just say that. You don't have to lie to me. I know what I saw.'

'And what did you see?'

She frowned slowly, searching for words. 'You were terrified. No, you were haunted.' She shuddered. 'It was awful.'

He pushed back the sheet and stepped out of bed, gloriously naked and uncaring, striding towards the en suite. It was all so familiar, she felt as though she'd been sucked back in time. He'd pushed her away so often then, but she'd been living in a fantasy land, failing to recognise what he was doing. She saw it now and it hurt like hell. She hurt for this moment, but also for all the moments that had gone before. For the younger woman she'd been, who'd loved so unquestioningly, so trustingly, and had been blind to what he'd been showing her all along.

He'd been using her. Using her for sex, for pleasure, because she was easy. Just like he'd been using her last night, to forget his nightmare. Nothing with Luca was real, and nothing with Luca was ever about Imogen. This was what Luca needed, what Luca wanted.

And damn it if she didn't keep letting him do it to her. She kept throwing herself at him, no matter what happened between them. She kept making it easy for him to make love to her,

But she was different now, she reminded herself once more. She was older, wiser and refused to soften towards him. She knew what he was now, when she hadn't then. As she had promised Genevieve, she refused to let her guard down with him.

'Then you have your answer,' he said, when he reached the door to the bathroom, surprising her, because she presumed his departure had signalled the end of their conversation. 'And yes,' he admitted, uneasily. 'It was more awful than I care to explain.'

Imogen would have said there weren't many things about Luca that could surprise her now. She knew he was callous, cold, selfish, unfeeling. But she hadn't expected *this* version of him. The Luca who was sitting opposite their daughter, lifting fingers of toast and aeroplaning them towards Aurora in a way that made the little toddler giggle with total abandon before stuffing the toast into her mouth and munching it with classic Aurora enthusiasm.

The contrast with the dark, tortured man she'd made love to the night before and *this* version of him was giving her whiplash.

'She's a good eater,' Luca said, with genuine admiration, turning to Imogen.

Her breath hitched in her throat because in that moment, he was just a dad, discovering things about his daughter, and loving it. Loving her.

Imogen's heart felt heavy and detached from her body. So, he was capable of loving after all. Just not of loving Imogen.

She nodded quickly, trying not to let that realisation hurt. 'She's adored food from the moment we introduced solids.'

'We?'

'Gen and me. Gen's been invaluable.' Luca turned back to Aurora, but not before Imogen caught the look of anger in his eyes.

'What else?' he asked, though, continuing the conversation.

'What else?' She took a seat at the table, a little way down. Observing but not intruding. Luca was right: he'd missed so much. This was his chance to make up for lost time, and Imogen had no need to get in the way.

'What else does she like, besides toast?'

'Oh, right.'

'Baba chimiken,' Aurora said, showing she didn't miss a beat.

'Butter chicken,' Imogen translated.

Luca raised a brow.

'Pasta. Rice. She's really good with vegetables. I make a broccoli soup that she can't get enough of. Cheese sticks, cucumber.' Imogen wracked her brain. 'I took her for sushi a couple of weeks ago and that was fun. Messy but fun.'

'Sushi.' He nodded slowly, as if cataloguing the list in his brain.

'She's very adventurous,' Imogen continued, because he wanted the gaps filled in and she possessed the information necessary. 'Not just with food, but with anything. She loves to go down slides—the higher the better. And to be pushed in the swings—same thing. I can never push her high enough. She loves see-saws but that makes me nervous so we don't do that too often.'

She watched as Luca took another piece of toast, flying it through the air with a buzzing engine noise. Her heart had gone way past painful and throbbed into no-longer-capable-of-beating territory. Years ago, she'd dreamed of this—of their happily-ever-after. She'd believed they were falling in love, that they would marry and have children, a family of their own. Those dreams were childish, not based in reality. She'd accepted that. So living, now, in a version of those dreams—one that was lined with darkness and enmity—was almost impossible to bear.

'Does she go to nursery?'

Imogen shook her head, trying to dislodge her painful thoughts. 'She's too young. She's made friends with some kids who go, though. She watches them scooter off in the mornings and can't wait to join them.' Imogen swallowed quickly. 'Sometimes I feel like she's the most independent toddler that's ever existed.'

'Independence is not a bad thing.'

'No, it's not. But it can be hard,' Imogen admitted with a wistful smile.

'Hard how?'

'I don't know. I guess I can already imagine the day she packs up and moves out.'

Luca turned to Imogen, scanning her face thoughtfully. 'There are worse things to imagine.'

Imogen frowned at the cryptic remark. He was right, but that didn't invalidate her feelings.

'It's just all going so fast. I feel like she was a new-born three seconds ago, and now look at her.'

Aurora finished the last piece of toast then started to pull at the restraint of her high chair.

'Breakfast is over,' Imogen said with a smile, as Luca went to clear Aurora's plate.

'I'll do that,' Imogen murmured. 'Why don't you play with her?' And then she added, 'I'll be in the kitchen, if you need me.'

Need her?

Of course he didn't need her.

Not only was Luca Romano apparently a Wunderkind in the business world, when it came to looking after their daughter, he had the skills of Mary Poppins. Of course.

Because he was just frustratingly good at everything. Except peopling, she reminded herself.

She should have been glad that he was adapting so well to the role of fatherhood, but she wasn't, because every time she saw him with Aurora, she was hit right in between her eyes with doubt as to her decision to keep them apart. It had seemed so obvious at the time, she hadn't once questioned her choice. But now?

How could she not?

She kept busy in the kitchen. Hiding, she admitted to herself. Initially, she cleaned up the breakfast dishes but then, she made a brownie with the ingredients she found in Luca's walk-in pantry, before cleaning up those dishes, so when he strode in almost two hours after breakfast was finished, the air was heavy with the smell of sweets.

'There have been four yawns in the last ten minutes. I take it it's nap time?' he prompted, looking at Aurora, who was snuggled into his hip.

'Yeah,' Imogen said, her voice throaty, her eyes suspiciously stinging. Aurora just looked so *right* on Luca's hip. She was so comfortable with him already. They were father and daughter, and Aurora seemed to somehow just understand that.

Imogen spun away quickly, busying herself with washing her hands and making a meal of it to buy for time.

'I'll take her up,' she said, when she could trust herself to speak.

But Luca waved her away. 'I can do it. At least, I think I can.'

'I have to change her diaper.' Imogen shook her head.

'I can do that too.'

'Really? Have you had much practice with changing a toddler's diaper?'

'More than you know,' he said, before turning on his heel and leaving.

What? What toddler? she wanted to call after him, but with Aurora on his hip, it wasn't the time to interrogate him, and so she stayed downstairs, one ear trained for calls for help while she set about making some sandwiches for their lunch. She wasn't really hungry, but it was something to do with her hands, something to help distract her, and God knew she needed that.

He was surprised by how much of caring for Aurora was, in fact, muscle memory. From feeding her to carrying her to placing her down for her nap, it all brought back so many memories of Angelica. And more than his little sister, it brought back memories of his late mother's voice, as she'd gently instructed him on the way to hold a baby, then a toddler; on the best methods for settling a little one into bed.

He knew he didn't need to stay with Aurora as she fell asleep, but he did so anyway, driven to watch her drift off for very selfish reasons. Firstly, he had missed so much of his daughter's life that he was now gripped by a visceral need to absorb absolutely everything. To watch as her lashes fluttered over her velvet-soft cheeks and her breathing grew slumberous.

But he was also avoiding Imogen.

Avoiding her intense stare, her perceptive eyes, her always kind questions. Avoiding her because she confused him, and made him forget everything he had sworn to himself.

Avoiding her because when he was with her, he wanted her.

She helped him forget, yes, but she also made him feel something other than this heart-rending grief and guilt, the gift that Imogen had always bestowed upon him. A gift he had no place accepting, let alone craving.

Imogen was off-limits. She should have been so three years ago, and she sure as hell was now—he just had to remember that.

CHAPTER FIVE

'LUCA, WHAT DID you mean before?'

She asked the question as soon as he returned to the kitchen, sometime after leaving to settle Aurora for her nap. And she asked the question with the full expectation that he would deflect, as always. Frustration champed at the edges of her belly; she braced for his defensive technique, but still she waited in silence.

'When?'

Sure enough, there was a cautious caginess to his voice, as though he knew she was buying time to work out his best obfuscation technique.

'When you said you had more experience with toddlers than I realised.'

His eyes met hers, carefully blanked of expression. Yet his jaw clenched visibly, and she felt his reluctance. 'It means you can count on me.'

'No,' she persisted, once again marvelling at how stupid she'd been three years earlier to have let him put her off so easily. 'That's not what I'm asking.'

'I know what you're asking.' He jammed his hands into his pockets, his jaw set in a mutinous line.

'So?' she prompted, refusing to let this go.

'What do you want me to say?'

'It's a simple question.' She stood firm. 'You made a statement. I'm asking what it meant.'

He opened his mouth to speak, then closed it, looking away sharply before removing one hand from his pocket and dragging a hand over his stubbled jaw. 'Aurora isn't the first toddler I've spent time with.' His voice was clipped, as if each word was resented.

He didn't want to talk about this, but Imogen wasn't prepared to let it go—not until she understood. Luca had indeed been a closed book to her, but that was no longer an acceptable proposition to Imogen. 'Who else?'

His eyes flicked to hers, then away again. 'That's not important.'

She sighed heavily. He wanted to keep hold of this particular barrier, hard and impenetrable. He wanted to make it impossible for her to understand him. Why? What was he hiding? And why had he referred to his experience with kids in the first place, then? Or had his admission simply slipped out?

'You can't have it both ways, Luca. If you don't want to talk about something, don't drop cryptic little hints.'

His brows shot up, his face angling back to hers. 'That wasn't my intention.'

She rolled her eyes, frustrated beyond belief with the man. Frustrated with how their relationship had been then, and how it was now. 'Fine,' she grunted with a hint of anger. 'Have it your way.' She pushed away from the bench and began to stalk towards the kitchen door, but right before she reached it, his hand snaked out and curled around her wrist, arresting her, so she turned to face him, scanning his features. His grip wasn't hard. The touch, if anything, was gentle, but every cell in her body sprung to life in response, which seemed to sear her skin.

'I had a little sister.' His voice was cool, his eyes locked to hers but revealing nothing. His features were bland. It was as if he were speaking from a part of him to which he had no access, reciting lines by rote, refusing to allow himself to feel them. 'She died when she was two and a half.'

Imogen reached behind her, needing to hold something for support.

'Her name was Angelica.' He paused, the silence heavy with Luca's pained confession and Imogen's questions. 'Aurora looks just like her.'

Imogen stared at him, utterly and totally shocked into silence for several long beats.

'I had— I didn't— You never mentioned her. I had no idea.'

'I know that.'

'Why didn't you tell me?'

'Why would I?'

'We were dating for a month, Luca. It seems like something that would have come up.'

'We weren't dating.' The words were almost a curse in his mouth. She pulled away from him, stepping back, her temper and hurt in conflict with her empathy.

'What happened to her?' she whispered, desperately sad to think of anything happening to a dear little toddler.

'That's not—something I care to discuss. She died. It was sudden.'

'Your nightmare,' Imogen murmured, and now empathy won out, for she stepped back towards him, putting her hands on his cheeks, holding his face. 'You were dreaming about her.'

Despite her grasp, he angled his face away, glaring at the window as if he were about to punch it.

'You asked about my experience with children and I told you. I don't want to discuss it any further.'

She dropped her hands to her sides, suppressing a sigh. She had to respect his choice. More than that, she supposed she should have been somewhat grateful that he'd confided in her, even to some small degree. She could see how hard it had been for him.

'How old were you, when she died?'

His Adam's apple shifted as he swallowed. 'It was the night of my twelfth birthday.'

Imogen closed her eyes on a wave of comprehension. The night they'd met had been his thirtieth birthday; he'd been in a terrible mood, determined to get blind drunk until they'd met and his plans had taken a detour. Then the other night had been his thirty-third birthday, and he'd come to the same bar, for the same purpose.

She bit into her lip. Despite the way he'd treated her, and how angry she was with him, she couldn't help but feel sorry for him too.

'That must have been so hard, Luca.'

He visibly clenched his teeth. 'I didn't tell you for sympathy. I told you to explain. I know what I'm doing with our daughter—to some extent.'

Imogen had so many questions she wanted to ask, like what had his sister been like and how much did he do with the baby, and did he have a photograph of her? But she could see he'd stepped out of his comfort zone and was already withdrawing from Imogen, pushing her away, boxing himself into a lonely little corner.

And she couldn't care. She couldn't.

For all that she might feel sorry for him, it didn't change the fact that he had broken her heart three years ago. He had spoken to her in a way that had been designed to wound; he had discarded her as if she were nobody. He had half destroyed her, and if it hadn't been for her music, and then her pregnancy, she had no idea how she would have got through it.

'Okay.' Her voice was a little unsteady. She stepped back from him quickly. 'Well, I'm here if you need help. With Aurora,' she added, stepping further away. She disappeared into the bathroom, needing space, and the freedom to let her tears roll without Luca seeing them.

It wasn't a big deal.

It wasn't like he could have kept it from her for ever.

Like it or not, Imogen had become someone who would be in his life for good. She was Aurora's mother; he was Aurora's father. They had to work together in some capacity, and it was only natural that she should know about his life. Some of it.

When he was comfortable enough to discuss it.

It didn't mean anything that she now knew. It wasn't like it changed anything between them, nor with his guilt and grief. That was the point. There was no going back. No do-overs.

He hadn't been able to save his family and they'd all died. That was the defining moment in his life. At twelve, he'd learned what it was like to betray everyone you loved, and he'd never forgive himself for it.

Imogen didn't need to know nor understand that, but as to the facts, who cared? His family had died in a house fire on the night of his twelfth birthday. It wasn't something he could hide from her now. Not for ever. Apart from anything, Aurora would have questions, one day. Was he going to lie to her about it?

He ignored the stitching pain in his chest, the awful, awful feeling he experienced whenever he thought of his parents. Not his guilt at how they'd died, but his world-shattering pain when he remembered their lives. How great they'd been. How much he'd loved them. How strong and powerful and capable of anything they'd made him feel. How his life had been great and perfect, until it wasn't.

He boxed those feelings away, tightened his tie then strode

out of the kitchen, needing space from this new domestic situation. And needing space from Imogen's intelligent, sympathetic eyes in particular.

'I'm heading to work.'

Imogen, dressed in a pair of jeans and a loose sweater, barely glanced up from the notebook she was writing in. 'Yeah, okay.' Her eyes had a dreamy, far-away look, so he wondered if she even saw him, much less heard him.

'Earth to Imogen.' He waved a hand in front of her face.

She frowned. 'I heard you.' She pulled the notebook closer without appearing to see him still. 'Have fun.'

He frowned, stalking away from her towards the back door, easing himself out of it and climbing into his car. What was she working on? What was she doing?

A frown etched itself across his face as he drove towards the City. Three years ago, she'd been like an open book, just as she'd said, talking freely about whatever he'd asked. And he *had* asked. Mainly to deflect her interest in him, just as she'd accused him of doing. But that didn't mean he hadn't enjoyed hearing her talk about herself. Her life. Her family. Her passion for music. He'd never met anyone quite like her—such a free spirit, but so dedicated to one area as well. It hadn't been about financial success for Imogen, but rather a drive to create music.

What was she doing now, besides playing in the bar and teaching kids to play piano? He pulled a face. It seemed like a waste of her talent.

Then again, it wasn't his place to get involved. They were co-parents, nothing more. Her life was none of his business; he couldn't allow himself to forget that.

Imogen and Aurora ate alone that night and Imogen tried not to think about Luca. She tried not to wonder where he was, nor to contemplate who he was with.

'I will replace you.'

She tried not to imagine his life outside the house, tried not to imagine the world she'd interrupted, albeit unwittingly. And unwillingly, come to think of it. She tried not to think about how many women he'd slept with since her, while she'd been busy raising Aurora.

But as the minutes ticked by and she went about the business of settling Aurora to bed, her temper built in waves, and she found it almost impossible to keep at bay.

She settled their daughter to sleep for the night, carefully disguising any hint of her irritation, and then went into the kitchen to make a cup of tea. The kettle had just boiled when she heard the back door close.

Her temper sparked.

She tried to tamp it down, without success. She knew it wasn't just about tonight. His being gone brought back too many memories. Too much of that same sense of frustration, at how hidden he was from her, at how he called all the shots. When he wanted Imogen, she'd been there. She'd never stopped to wonder if the same would be true in reverse.

'Why exactly did you insist on us moving in here?' she asked, whirling around to face him. Luca's face was without emotion, his eyes landing on her and giving nothing away.

'Excuse me?'

'It's eight o'clock. I've spent the last hour and a half feeding, bathing and putting Aurora to bed, and you were what? Where?'

'I told you I was going to work.'

She rolled her eyes. 'Whatever. I don't care. Just let me know in future so I can make plans.'

'What is going on here?' he demanded, crossing his arms. 'You know I work late.'

'No, I know you *used to* work late, but you've just discovered you're a father and your daughter is here. I would have thought you'd make that a priority, at least for a while. God, this is so stupid. I have been *so* stupid, yet again, to move in here with you and actually think you were capable of putting someone else first.'

His nostrils flared. 'You have been doing this on your own for more than two years. Are you telling me you couldn't cope without me?'

'No, I'm saying—' She floundered, because this wasn't really about Aurora, but rather the images she'd been conjuring all night of him making love to some other woman in some fancy hotel room or some gorgeous luxe penthouse. Some supermodel, or actress, or heiress. 'Don't worry. It doesn't matter,' she responded, her voice clipped. Their past was a visage from which she couldn't escape. Three years of imagining him moving on from her swirled like shark-infested waters all around Imogen.

She went to walk past him, cup of tea forgotten, but he caught her wrist and held her still.

'You're jealous.'

Her eyes flew to his. Anger was a dark, suffocating torrent, rising inside of her. She couldn't be jealous—at least she couldn't admit it—because it was so far outside of what she'd promised to herself, and Genevieve, when she'd come to live with Luca. She was hurt; there was a difference.

'Go to hell.'

'You think I was with another woman.'

Damn him for being able to see through her so easily. 'I don't care,' she responded quickly, coldly, but her heart was burning up and her body was trembling. 'It's none of my business.'

'Be that as it may,' he conceded with a nod, 'you are jealous.'

She looked away from him, angry because he was *right*.

Danger sirens blared. She wasn't doing a good job of keeping him at arm's length. She wasn't doing a good job with any of this.

'What do you want me to say, Imogen? Do you want me to say that I was alone in my office? Do you need to hear me say I was not with someone else? Why is that?'

She sucked in a breath, furious with him and with herself. 'I don't care who you're screwing,' she muttered.

'Liar.'

'But I don't intend to be someone you use to keep your bed warm on a quiet night. Keep your hands off me.'

And she pulled away from him with at least some sense of pride restored, stalking away from him with a spine that was ramrod straight.

He caught up to her little more than a few paces away but he didn't touch her. 'Need I remind you, you came into *my* room and kissed me...'

'Oh, just—just—go to hell!'

His brows launched towards his hairline. 'Were you always this dramatic?'

She spun around, fire in her eyes. 'I doubt it.'

'I am not using you to keep my bed warm. This is an evolving situation, and I am as unsure about it as you are. Clearly sleeping together is a terrible idea, given what happened last time. I would like to say it wouldn't happen again. I would like to *think* I was capable of behaving with a modicum of restraint, but the thing is...' His words trailed off, and he shook his head. 'I can't make that promise, and I don't think you can either.'

She shivered, because he was being so honest, and he was right. He was fighting the same battle she was, trying not to give in to temptation, when it was like a drug...

'Why would you jump to the conclusion that I'd gone off to sleep with some other woman?'

She stared up at him, her expression mutinous. 'Because

I'm replaceable, remember?' She spat the words at him, the taste of them in her mouth like acid. 'I've never forgotten, and thank God for that. It's probably the only thing stopping me from being a total fool again this time around. I'm replaceable, and you can replace me whenever you want. But please have the courtesy to give me a heads up when it happens, so I don't make dinner for you.' She tilted her chin and stalked away; this time, he didn't follow.

Once he started to remember that morning, he couldn't stop. He sat with a glass of red wine, staring at a blank wall, and heard himself. *Really* heard himself. The things he'd said to her, cold and assured, the way her face had crumpled and then dropped into her hands, so he didn't have to look at her as he berated her with all the reasons she'd been imagining anything between them.

He'd been *so* angry with her for falling in love with him. So angry with her, but he'd been even angrier with himself for being so careless. For telling himself that it was fine, that they were obviously just sleeping together and that surely she understood it meant nothing. He'd said things along the way in an attempt to convey that, to keep it light. But damn it, Imogen was too full of sunshine and warmth, too willing to see the best in anyone and everyone and she'd fallen hard for the wrong guy.

He'd told himself he'd been doing her a favour by ending it as harshly as possible, so she could forget about him and move on. But the way she'd thrown the word *replaceable* at him that night showed him how deeply he'd cut her.

He took a drink, a familiar feeling twisting low in his gut. Guilt.

Guilt at having hurt her like that. Guilt at having led her on in the first place, just because he liked being with her. Guilt at taking the break-up too far, rather than letting her down gently. He'd panicked and he'd just needed her to go, because being loved by anyone had seemed like a total rejection of the state he deserved to live in for the rest of his life. Unknowingly, she'd stepped right over one of his most fundamental lines, a boundary he'd established as a twelve-year-old and never intended to allow to be eroded.

He hadn't wanted to hurt her, though.

He'd spent three years confident that she'd have moved on, and easily. But what if she hadn't? What if he'd cut her too deeply for that?

He dropped his head forward, the thought one he didn't even dare contemplate.

'I hate you.'

She'd said that to him that night at the bar, and he'd been glad. He was still glad. He just needed for her not to forget it.

It didn't matter that it was late. When the soft knock sounded at her door, Imogen was still wide awake, reading a book without paying any attention to the words.

'Yes?'

He pushed the door in, his features strained. 'We need to talk.'

She didn't want to talk. She wanted to do something far more physical; she just couldn't decide if it involved punching him in the gut or dragging him to her.

'Do we?' she muttered, closing the book and placing it beside her.

He strode to the edge of her bed but stayed standing. Out of reach. Probably best, for both of them.

'Three years ago, you fell in love with a fantasy of your own creation. You saw something that wasn't there. It's not your fault. Like I said—far less gently than I should have—at the time, you were young and inexperienced, and the physical nature of our relationship overwhelmed you. I should have done a better job of making sure you understood what I wanted.'

Imogen was frozen still. This conversation was her worst nightmare. She had relived the past, replayed that awful morning, enough times in her mind. She didn't want to do it again now. Not with the instrument of all that pain right in front of her.

'I told you,' she said a little unevenly. 'I wasn't in love with you. I get that now.'

'Great,' he responded, a little tightly. 'But that's not my point.'

'Well, what is then?'

'I don't want history to repeat itself.'

'Believe me, I'm not going to fall in love with you. Or think I've fallen in love with you. Never gonna happen, buddy.'

'Because the sex is still overwhelming,' he admitted gruffly, 'it's easy to confuse that with something else, but I feel the same way I did then. I am not interested in a relationship.'

Her cheeks flushed with heat.

'We're parents. And I want us to live together, at least until we find out how to do this properly. But living together is bound to lead to sleeping together and I just need to know that I've been honest with you. Honest like I should have been back then.'

She shook her head, frustration making her lips pinch. 'You seriously think I'd be stupid enough to fall for you?'

'Probably not,' he responded with a tight smile. 'I'm just trying to avoid what happened last time.'

'Last time,' she hissed, 'I had no idea what you were like. Now I do, and believe me when I tell you I'm not interested.'

He lifted one thick, dark brow.

'Okay, sex has the potential to be a complication. We just… can't let it.'

'No?' He moved closer and even just that single action, his body brushing the edge of the bed, made her skin lift in goose bumps.

'No,' she said, but her voice was hoarse. 'We're stronger than this.'

He nodded once, his eyes heavy on hers. 'I hope you are right, Imogen. There's too much at stake now for us to mess this up.'

CHAPTER SIX

THREE YEARS AGO, he'd kept her at a distance using his work as an excuse. Now it was by mutual understanding, and a healthy sense of self-preservation. Imogen didn't try to get close to him. Not like she had then. She didn't try because she didn't want to.

Three years ago, he'd smashed her heart into oblivion, and it didn't matter how great he was with Aurora—he was still that same cruel-hearted man. He was still someone who was capable of blowing hot and cold, of making her feel things that seemed so much like love, and then coldly dismissing her from his life.

She would never trust him again, and without trust, there could be no true relationship. They were parents, and somehow, despite their past, they'd found a way to interact that was respectful and courteous. But neither pushed the other for personal information. Neither tried to have deep and meaningful conversations.

They were like strangers in many ways, despite the intimacy they'd once shared.

On Imogen's first night back in the bar, she felt a churning of butterflies in her belly.

She and Luca had formed a sort of arrangement that worked for them, but having Genevieve in the house was like the cracking open of the past, a reminder of her wounds, and Imogen didn't particularly want to think about that.

Gen could not have made her own feelings about Luca more apparent.

'Genevieve, welcome,' he'd said.

'Thanks,' she'd responded, as though she'd have preferred to be just about anywhere else.

Imogen grimaced, but she didn't have a chance to speak to Genevieve before leaving. She squeezed her hand though, leaned in for a kiss and whispered, 'Be nice. For Aurora's sake.'

Genevieve rolled her eyes in response.

Luca had organised for his driver to take her to the bar—it made a nice change from public transport—and she nestled back in the comfort of the four-wheel drive, watching London pass by in a streak of lights and autumnal beauty.

The bar was packed, and she lost herself to the music of her set, singing some of her own songs, some covers, playing whatever she wanted, aware that the crowd was in the palm of her hand and loving the feeling.

She wanted to do this for a living. To make music, to sing it, to offer it to the world as her contribution to the creative landscape. It had been her calling for longer than she could remember.

But there was also Aurora, and until she'd been born, Imogen hadn't realised that being a mother could also be a passion. She loved being with her daughter. She loved having the flexibility to spend time with her, to play with her, to teach her to play piano. And with Luca in the picture, she had even more flexibility to pursue both. If he wanted to be an engaged father, she could rely on him for so much more than she ever could Genevieve. While her sister had been an amazing support, Imogen had often felt bad for leaning on her so much, even though Gen had insisted she didn't mind.

Luca was Aurora's father and if he was willing to play that role, to help take care of her, then Imogen would conceivably have more freedom to pursue her career. All the dreams she'd put on hold when she'd discovered she was pregnant were suddenly viable again.

She finished her set, took a bow, waved at the crowd then made her way off stage, towards the bar.

'Great set, Im. What'll it be?'

She couldn't say why she was delaying going back to Luca's, only that it was the first time she'd been out of the place in a week, and with it came a sense of relief. She was glad to be away from him, glad to prove to herself that she could stay away. Because everything was so complicated, and she needed to make sure she didn't lose herself again. No matter what she said to him, she wasn't an idiot. She knew there was risk here.

She knew there *could* be risk, anyway, unless she was very, very careful. She could be with him. She could spend time with him, she just couldn't ever forgive him.

If she didn't forgive him, she wouldn't fall for him again.

'Glass of white.'

'Pinot Gris?'

'Perfect.'

She watched as Leon, who was always behind the bar, poured the drink and slid it across to her. 'No charge, superstar.'

She frowned. 'That's not fair.'

'No way. The nights you play are always our busiest. I owe you.'

'You pay me to play,' she reminded him.

'Nowhere near enough.' He winked, then moved off to serve someone else.

She sat at the bar, listening to the next act, forcing herself to stay right where she was. There was no better way to prove to herself, and Luca, that she was totally her own woman than by staying out just a little later and enjoying another musician. Even when her nerves were stretching taut, and she was itching to get back to his place.

She finished the glass and stood up, weaving through the crowd and out the side door, where Luca's car was waiting, the driver reading a book behind the wheel. She tapped lightly on the window, clearly startling him, for which she apologised.

He moved quickly but she waved him away. 'I can open my own door,' she said with a smile.

'All part of the service,' he quipped, opening it for her regardless.

She slipped in and sighed, pleased that she'd passed this milestone, pleased that she was being mature enough to make this work. Pleased all round, that what had seemed like a disaster a week ago wasn't actually turning out to be so bad.

'Your sister hates me too.'

'Too?'

'In addition to you, remember?' he reminded her, when she walked back into the room, having farewelled Genevieve— who did indeed despise Luca, more than words could say.

'Oh, right.' She lifted one shoulder. 'She's protective of me.'

His eyes lingered on Imogen's face a moment, long enough for her heart to thump and her skin to prickle with goose bumps, then walked towards an armchair and took a seat opposite.

'How was it?'

She smiled. 'Great.'

His eyes roamed her face. 'You're an excellent performer.'

Heat flushed her cheeks. 'I love it.'

'How many nights do you play at the bar?'

'Just three per week at the moment.'

'And you teach piano, you said?'

She nodded.

'Is that what you aspired to, Imogen?'

Her eyes widened.

'This. Your work. Is it what you dreamed of?'

'To make a living from music? Absolutely.'

He frowned though, a quick quirk of his lips.

'You don't approve?'

'It's not my place to approve or not.'

'Nonetheless, you're clearly thinking something. What?'

'I seem to remember you wanting to move to America, to get a recording deal with one of the big labels.'

Her heart thudded against her ribs. He remembered that?

Of course he remembered. He was smart and switched on, and she'd opened her soul to him, including her professional aspirations.

'I got pregnant,' she reminded him. Then, realising that might sound like a criticism, she softened her tone a little. 'And it was a blessing. It didn't feel like it at the time, but Aurora turned everything around for me. I still have aspirations, but they're not the only thing I focus on now. Maybe when she's older,' Imogen said with a lift of one shoulder.

His frown deepened. 'I didn't know about her,' he said, needlessly. Imogen was well aware of the facts. They'd discussed them ad nauseam, after all. 'I wasn't there to help you, but I am now.'

Imogen's eyes widened. It was exactly what she'd been thinking in the bar. Everything was different now that Luca was in the picture. Seeing how great he was with Aurora had opened up a door for her she'd been reluctant to look for earlier. While Genevieve was an amazing help, Imogen was reluctant to impose too much. With Luca, she didn't have the same concerns. Aurora was his child, and he'd made it abundantly clear he wanted to help.

'There is kind of an opportunity,' she said, her lips pulling to the side. 'A label that's interested in me. They want me to submit a demo.' She waved a hand through the air, tamping down on the instant rush of excitement, keeping her feet firmly planted in reality. 'It's not a big deal. It probably won't come to anything, but it's an opportunity at least. It would mean a bit of time in a studio. A few days, probably...'

He didn't smile. He didn't congratulate her. But he leaned forward, his elbows on his thighs, and said, 'I have a recording studio you could use.'

Her heart kerthunked. 'You do?'

'Sure.'

'Um, where?'

'It's at my place in Tuscany—I bought the villa from a musician—the recording studio is state of the art, though obviously I've never used it.'

'You have a place in Tuscany?'

'Does that surprise you? I'm Italian.'

'But you live here.'

'My businesses are headquartered here. My home is in Italy.'

She stared at him, surprised by that. Surprised that it had never occurred to her. Surprised, most of all, by his willingness to help her. Then again, it was easy for him to do. He had a home with a recording studio, and the means to travel the world at the drop of a hat. Still, she couldn't help but feel a flood of warmth at how quickly he'd extended his support to her. Like he cared about her life, and her career.

'Let me do this for you,' he said, intensely, as though mistaking her silence for hesitation. 'I owe you this.'

'You owe me?'

'Who knows what your life would be like if I'd been a part of Aurora's from birth?'

She shook her head, dispelling that sentiment. 'I didn't tell you about her, remember?'

'I remember,' he replied, but without the sting of their prior arguments on the matter. This was almost conversational. 'I do not believe our daughter should ever be a reason that you have not succeeded in your career.'

She shook her head. 'I don't see it that way. I love what I do—'

'You have a gift.' His words slammed into her. They were emphatic and insistent, as though he *needed* her to see it his way. 'You should share it with as many people as you are able. Of course you should record a demo, and the recording label would be stupid not to snap you up.'

His blind faith in her almost brought tears to her eyes. She hadn't expected such passionate support from Luca, of all people.

'For years, your voice has been in my mind,' he muttered. And now, a hint of his resentment was back, a rush of darkness that he hadn't been strong enough to blot her from his memory. 'Your songs, your sound, the way you can sing as though yours is the only voice to ever find a melody. It is… mesmerising.'

'Mesmerising,' she whispered, thinking that, if anything, it was *his* words that were addictive, his voice that had cycled around and around in her mind until she'd almost lost touch with reality.

'Addictive,' he added, his eyes boring into hers, like he was as bound by the power of this stare as Imogen was. She couldn't look away; she was powerless in the face of his offer, and his admission. 'I woke up hearing you.'

The hairs on the back of her neck stood on end.

'Come to Italy with me, Imogen,' he implored again, throatily, raw, and her heart palpitated against her ribs.

How could she say no? Setting aside the fact he was taking away any practical barrier to her recording this album, there was something else tightening inside her chest, making her yearn to agree with him. If Imogen were honest with herself, she'd admit that it wasn't just about recording the demo.

Here was Luca, a man who had fiercely guarded every aspect of his private life from her, even as they'd been as intimate as any two people could ever be, offering her a glimpse behind the curtain. His home in Italy must mean something to him, as it was where he was from.

Something like hope surged inside Imogen, but she tamped it down, just as she did when she thought of her music.

'Aurora…' she said thoughtfully.

'Will come with us, naturally,' he interrupted, misunderstanding.

Imogen swallowed. 'She doesn't have a passport.'

'Leave that to me,' he said with easy authority.

Imogen bit down on her lip. 'Luca—'

'We can go to Italy as soon as that's organised.'

Imogen toyed with her fingers, nervous suddenly. But there was nothing for it; he'd find out for himself soon enough. 'There's something you should know about Aurora.'

He waited with the appearance of patience.

'She has my last name. You're not… I couldn't put you on her birth certificate.'

His eyes briefly closed. She could feel the tension emanating from him. 'Okay,' he said after a moment, and there was no sign of anger in his tone. 'We can fix that.'

Fix it.

Because she'd messed up. It hadn't felt like it at the time, and she couldn't have put his name down, anyway, without having Luca there. She'd made her peace with that situation, but having seen the two of them together now, she felt that lapse deep in her heart. 'You have a high profile. I thought…'

'You wanted to hide her from me.' The words lacked emotion, but Imogen had an abundance of them.

'I—didn't want you to be blindsided.'

'How did that work out?' he responded, then shook his head, as if to dismiss the subject. 'You made a decision. We've dealt with that.'

She nodded slowly, knotting her fingers together, glad he was apparently so accepting of that, finally. 'Do you have any other homes, Luca?'

'*Sì.*'

Her lips twisted into a smile without her consent. She'd always loved it when he slipped into Italian. Usually it was in bed, in the heat of passion, when a string of foreign words would curl around her, warm and delicious.

'Where?' She settled back into the sofa, strangely relaxed now.

'New York, Paris, Sydney, Singapore.'

'So, just the usual then?'

His grin surprised her. It warmed her. She tamped down on the feeling, sat up straighter, let the feeling of relaxation go, to be replaced by wariness. She couldn't do this again. She wouldn't let herself soften towards him, to see things that weren't there. Wishful thinking had no place in their relationship; Luca was being kind to her, but that didn't mean he was a changed man. As far as she was concerned, the man opposite her, who was now bending over backwards to help her career, was the same bastard who'd broken her heart, utterly and completely, three years earlier.

'Anyway, I'm beat,' she lied, standing then, brushing her hands over the front of her jeans. She needed a break from the emotional juggernaut that was careening her from one emotion to the next, but mostly, she needed to escape the temptation of spending any more time with this man she'd once loved… 'I'll see you in the morning.'

She slipped away, her heart pounding, trying not to think how good it had felt to just sit and talk with Luca. That was most certainly not a safe path to travel.

* * *

She knew he was wealthy. Obviously. His house in London was huge and in one of the most exclusive areas, he had a fancy car and a full-time driver, he wore suits that were made for his frame—hand stitched and clearly expensive—and there was an air about him that spoke of money and luxury. But it wasn't until the trip to Tuscany that she really comprehended the sheer scale of his wealth.

They boarded his private jet at City Airport. It was as big as a commercial plane, shiny white with a jet-black tail and a bold white 'R' there, denoting it as his. Inside was like the lobby of a five-star hotel. Elegant armchairs, coffee tables, lamps. Walls partitioning the front section of the plane from the middle, which boasted two bedrooms, either side of the aisle. Beyond that, there were bathrooms, but unlike the usual airline offerings, these had proper showers, space to get changed, lovely lighting and décor. Right in the back there were seats more akin to a commercial airline's business class seating section—wide and with full recline abilities.

'For staff,' he said. 'Or if I need to convey multiple guests.'

'Do you do that often?'

'I use the plane for business,' he said with a lift of his shoulders. 'Meetings around the world. That involves taking members of my team with me sometimes.'

Imogen settled Aurora on one of the plush seats and buckled her in. 'You know, I have no idea what you do, Luca.'

'I invest.'

She glanced at him, scanning his face. 'What does that mean?'

'Putting money behind something I believe in.'

Imogen rolled her eyes. 'I know what it means, as a dictionary definition. I mean, what do you personally invest in?'

'A number of things. Property, commercial interests, the tech sector.'

She sat beside Aurora and clipped her seat belt together. Luca took the seat opposite them, his long legs permanently at risk of invading Imogen's space, of brushing against her own legs, if he wasn't careful. Aurora made a gabbling noise, and tried to reach for the lamp. Imogen distractedly reached into her handbag, pulled out an old, much-favoured picture book and passed it to the little girl.

'Do you enjoy it?'

He looked at her as though she'd asked if he spoke Martian. 'It's what I do. I'm good at it.'

It was Imogen's turn to look confused. 'Is it what you wanted to do as a kid?'

His eyes darkened momentarily and he glanced towards the window. It was a lovely autumnal day, clear blue skies, crisp and cool. 'I don't remember.'

Liar.

'We're ready for take-off, sir.' A pretty woman in her twenties clipped efficiently into the cabin. She wore a business suit, and her bright blond hair was secured into a fiercely tight bun. Imogen's stomach popped with unwelcome jealousy.

'I will replace you.'

She flipped the page on Aurora's book, pointing at a picture of a witch with big warts on her nose and enormous pink shoes. Aurora laughed, as she always did, at the absurdity of the image.

'Would you care for any refreshments?' The woman glanced from Imogen to Luca, her cherry-red lips curving into a full smile when she glanced at him.

'Imogen?' He looked at her though, and her stomach popped for a different reason.

She bit into her lip, shook her head once.

'Some champagne,' he said. 'And strawberries for Aurora.'

Imogen's heart turned over. She pointed at another picture and pulled a face that made Aurora giggle once more, then turned the page again. Aurora said the words that were on the page, not because she could read them but because she'd been read the book so many times it was rote for her now.

When Imogen glanced at Luca, he was staring at them with an intensity that made her pulse go haywire.

'Do you just travel with a buffet of fruit on board?' she asked, simply for something to say.

'There's a selection, yes.'

Imogen glanced around. 'This plane is incredible.'

The crew member returned with a glass of champagne, a coffee and some strawberries.

'You're not having one?' Imogen asked, curling her feet up beneath her on the plush armchair.

'You seemed nervous.'

She tried not to care that he'd noticed. 'I'm...overawed, I guess. This is incredibly opulent.'

'You get used to it.'

She shook her head, marvelling at the sheer volume of things she didn't know about Luca. 'Did you grow up like this?' she asked, gesturing around the plane.

'No.'

Imogen tried not to be shocked by the fact he'd actually answered her question instead of hedging around it. When they'd first started dating—or, rather, sleeping together—she'd searched his name on the internet and found a heap of dry biographical information to do with his company, but even that hadn't really told her what he did on a day-to-day basis. It was all corporate speak and for Imogen, who existed in a musician's bubble most of the time, it had just bored her. But there'd been nothing more personal about Luca anywhere, and she'd looked. Oh, there'd been some photos of him at events—fundraising dinners and the like—and yes, she'd noticed that he was always with a beautiful woman. Back then, she'd felt a hint of pique that he hadn't invited her to any of those events, but because she'd had her rose-coloured glasses on, she'd invented a narrative that it was because he didn't want to share her.

What a fool she'd been.

'Your parents aren't wealthy like this?'

A slight pause. 'No.'

'So you just invested your way to this lifestyle?'

'*Sì.*' The engines began to whirl, and the plane pushed back from the hangar. Aurora looked around, slightly alarmed, but with a reassuring smile from Imogen, she relaxed.

'You'll like it, I promise,' Imogen said. 'We're going to climb all the way up into the clouds. Look out the window, little one. Watch and see.' Aurora craned towards the window, her sweet little fingers pressing to the glass.

'Do your parents see her often?' Luca asked, and Imogen recognised what he was doing. Driving the conversation in a parallel direction, subtly shifting it from his family to hers. Irritation barbed beneath her skin but she didn't show it.

'They've been great. Very supportive. But mainly it's Gen who helps out on a day-to-day basis.'

He made a gruff noise.

'Don't be annoyed at her for not liking you.'

He arched a brow. 'Did I say I'm annoyed?'

'You look unimpressed.'

'If I'm unimpressed, Imogen, it's because you had to rely on anyone to help you, rather than turning to me, her father.'

'Oh.' Chastened, she focused all her attention on Aurora, not brave enough to look at him for the anger and disapproval she might see in his eyes. She couldn't bear it. Just like that, the conversation was dead in the water, Imogen's attempts to draw him out flattened by the immutable reality that would always exist between them, no matter what he said to the contrary. He would never really forgive her for keeping Aurora a secret.

And so what?

She'd never forgive him for how he'd treated her, so they were even.

Except they weren't, because no matter how badly he'd hurt Imogen, she knew she was comparing apples and oranges. To keep a baby from a parent seemed, now, like a terrible decision.

But at the time, it had all made sense. She'd weighed up her options and had known Luca wouldn't want to be a father.

Or was it just that she couldn't risk that he might?

That despite all the horribly cruel things he'd said to her, she might have to raise their baby with him at her side anyway? Had she pretended the decision was based on what was best for Luca and Aurora but, in actuality, she'd chosen the path that most suited her?

Her skin was pale as they lifted into the skies, and Imogen only hoped that if Luca noticed, he'd put it down to a slight aversion to air travel and not the ice-cold sensation in her veins, a conviction that she'd made a terrible mistake three years ago—a mistake she could never truly fix.

CHAPTER SEVEN

HIS VILLA IN Tuscany was like something out of a film. Having landed at Pisa Airport, they had been met by a car straight off the plane and driven for about twenty minutes, through stunning vistas of rolling green hills on either side, towards the Ligurian Sea. Eventually, the car had turned off the main road onto a smaller, dusty track lined on one side by enormous pine trees, before turning once more, this time to pass between wide wrought-iron gates. The drive was sweeping and long, showing more of the mesmerising countryside views on one side and an incomparable outlook over where the River Arno met the sea on the other.

From what she could see, the house was surrounded by a large parcel of land, bounded on all sides by those magnificent pine trees. As for the house, it was old and classically Tuscan, with earthy rendered walls, red terra-cotta tiles and curved architectural features. It was single story and sprawling, and when the car pulled up, an older Italian woman, slim and neatly dressed with her hair in a low ponytail, strode out to meet them.

'My housekeeper,' he explained.

'You have a housekeeper?'

'The villa is well-staffed,' he said. 'It has to be. I don't spend much time here. They take care of things.'

Right on cue, two more staff members appeared, younger

men, moving to the trunk to remove their suitcases, so Imogen could focus on lifting Aurora out of her car seat. After the flight and the drive, her little legs were itching to run, and Imogen put her down on the ground.

'Is there anything on the property I need to be aware of?' she asked, turning back to Luca, who was looking at their daughter with that same expression she'd now seen multiple times—as though he'd seen a ghost.

He glanced back at her. 'There's a lake, but it's all the way down there. She'd have to run pretty fast to make it without us realising.'

'Okay, good to know, though. Nothing else?'

He looked around. 'Not that I can think of.'

She watched as Aurora crouched down and ran her hands over the grass then picked a flower—bright pink with lush green leaves—then ran back to Imogen and held it out to her. 'For you, Mama.'

Imogen's heart turned over. 'Thank you, my darling. I love it.' She took the flower and tucked it neatly into the band of her plait.

Luca's voice was gruff. 'I'll show you around.' He strode towards the house, not pausing to see that they were following. Imogen took Aurora's hand rather than lifting her, to give their daughter time to use her legs and also to explore at her own pace, but it meant they lagged behind Luca, and he had to stop and wait for them inside the foyer.

Imogen was glad he'd waited, but not so glad when he began to walk again because she wanted to stop and take everything in.

'This place is incredible,' she said, shaking her head. 'I was about to say it's not what I would have expected for you, but that's not entirely accurate. It's actually... You're perfect here.'

He frowned, his non-comprehension clear.

'You look completely at home. It's as if you were carved from these hills and valleys.' She gestured to the expansive view shown from the living room windows, of the rolling, verdant hills.

'I grew up on the other side of Siena,' he said, and then turned away from her. He clearly regretted giving her that information, that tiny kernel, as if it told her anything fundamental about him! Frustration swirled in her gut, but she didn't push him further.

They walked through the house, which was every bit as charming inside as the outside had indicated. From the large terracotta floor tiles to huge glass windows and furniture that seemed to blend into the surrounds, it was a quintessentially Tuscan home, and Imogen couldn't help but fall a little in love with it.

He left the recording studio until last. They descended a set of stairs, into a basement. 'The wine cellar is that side.' He nodded towards a timber door. 'The recording studio this one.'

'So, if recording is going badly I can wander across and grab a bottle?' she joked.

His smile was tight. Irritation shifted inside her but she opened the door to the recording studio and looked around, then pivoted back to Luca. 'You weren't kidding. This is state of the art.'

'As I've been told.'

They'd arranged for a producer from Florence to join them for a couple of days, while she was recording, and Imogen was glad she wouldn't have to get to grips with the technical equipment.

The housekeeper—Anna—had made a platter and set it up on one of the terraces that overlooked the ocean side of the property. It was all so beautiful, and, in her heart, Imogen felt a small pang to imagine—for the briefest moment—what it would be like if there were more substance to their relationship.

If they were a real family.

The thought was like acid in her throat. Midway through reaching for an olive, she sat upright, her chest hurting. Growing up, her parents had been blissfully happy, and Imogen had always presumed her life would be like theirs. That she'd meet someone, fall in love, get engaged and married, have babies and live happily ever after. It hadn't seemed like a fairy-tale to her; it had seemed like reality. A bona fide fact of life, in fact. Perhaps that had made her particularly susceptible to the fantasy of Luca. She'd been attracted to him, so it had been easy to tell herself she was falling in love with him, that she loved him—even when she could see now that she didn't really know him. And love couldn't exist when it was one-sided. Not real love. It had to be mutual and shared, and theirs certainly hadn't been.

He had given her a wake-up call that morning, and not just in terms of them as a couple, but in terms of how she viewed life. Her parents' happy relationship, far from being a given, was a gift: a rare, special form of connection and respect that had always made marriage look easy. Imogen knew, now, that wasn't the case.

Life wasn't easy either. It was messy and complex, and Luca had taught her that.

This wasn't real, this wasn't romantic, this wasn't a family vacation. It was a gesture, from Luca, to help her with her career. She kept that at the front of her mind as they ate, refusing to be seduced by the beauty of the setting or the man sitting opposite her, even when one look at him had the tendency of turning her insides to lava.

* * *

He shouldn't have brought her here. He shouldn't have offered up his studio to her. Or, if he had, he should have sent Imogen alone.

Because seeing Imogen and Aurora in Italy was tugging at a part of him he'd had no idea existed. A yearning to come back to Italy, to be *home*.

The same country he'd run hundreds of miles from as soon as he was able, because every glance had reminded him of his parents and sister. How painful those memories had been, how awful his recollections of those happier times, because of their absence.

Every day after the accident had been torturous. All he'd been able to focus on was how badly he'd wanted to escape. How badly he'd *needed* to escape.

And then he'd bought this villa, as yet another form of torture. He'd come here sparingly, when he'd needed a touchstone to his grief, a reminder of why he didn't deserve happiness.

He'd come here after Imogen.

He'd come here when he'd wanted to recommit to his intention.

He was not worthy of love. He could not be trusted with it. He did not deserve happiness.

And yet…seeing Imogen and Aurora here, set against the landscape of his youth, he wasn't sure he knew how to fight this any longer. Not his guilt—that was an incontrovertible part of him.

But so was Aurora.

And even Imogen, because they shared a daughter.

Italy was his home, and in no small part, he wanted it to be Aurora's home too. He wanted to claim this part of her, to make sure it existed.

Because his parents would have wanted that, he realised,

a lump forming in his throat unbidden. Nothing would have made them happier than Aurora.

Becoming a father might have been the last thing Luca had ever wanted, but this would have been something his parents desperately longed for.

Didn't he owe it to them—as much as he did his sacrifices and misery—to raise Aurora in line with her heritage?

He closed his eyes as the reality of that twisted and shaped inside of him, altering his understanding of things, and how he must now live. While Luca could never forgive himself for the past, he was no longer an island, able to exist without others, isolated and alone. And he certainly couldn't punish Aurora for his mistakes, nor keep Imogen at a distance because she'd acted out of what she'd mistakenly believed were the best interests of their child.

Could he blame her, given how he'd been at the time? Given what he'd knowingly subjected her to?

A dark groan escaped Luca's throat and he closed his eyes against a rush of realisation. The past had been a noose around his neck for a long time; Luca had no choice but to set it aside, at least partially, to give Aurora the life she deserved. As for Imogen…he had no idea how to navigate their relationship, but he had no choice. He had to try.

The next morning, the sun broke over the Tuscan hillside, bathing Imogen's bedroom in gold and peach, and she pushed back the covers with genuine excitement. She felt like a child on Christmas day. Outside, the valley was every bit as beautiful as it had been the day before, but even more so now because of the dusky light and the clarity of morning. She dressed quickly, checking the time—it was still early—and then moving to Aurora's bedroom. She was still asleep.

Excitement fizzed inside Imogen's belly as she crept into

the kitchen and made a cup of tea then moved out onto the terrace, energised by the brush of the crisp morning against her skin, the simple act of sucking air deep into her lungs somehow calming and restorative.

'You're still an early riser.'

His voice was gruff, and close.

She spun around guiltily, cheeks flushed, to see Luca was seated at a round table only a meter or so away, a single shot of very dark coffee before him.

'And you still drink coffee like mud.'

One half of his mouth lifted in a wry smile.

'It's just so beautiful out here. I love the early morning.'

'I remember.'

She looked away, pain in her chest as though she'd been speared with something hot and sharp. She hated that he remembered. She hated that she'd been so unguarded with him, so open and honest. She needed to say something to bring it back to the reality of what had happened, how he'd used her and discarded her when it had suited him.

'Was I unusual?'

She kept her gaze pinned to the valley beyond them.

'In what way?' His voice was casual, easy, but she wasn't fooled. Everything with Luca was a calculation. Reading her before responding.

'In terms of waking early. I guess your usual lovers were more…sophisticated.' She turned to face him, scanning his face. He sipped his coffee, replaced the cup.

'I don't have a "usual."'

Not *didn't*, she noted, but the present tense. *I don't*.

She wanted to say something acerbic, to pick this fight with him. Despite the beauty of the morning, old pain had surfaced fast and she felt a pull to flex it. But before she could speak, movement caught her eye. He stood, walking towards her with his easy, confident gait. She held her breath, wondering what he would say, how he would continue the conversation. If he might touch her—kiss her. If she might weaken and do so first.

'You're recording today?'

She glanced up at him, frowning. It was a total conversation swerve. She sipped her tea. 'After lunch.'

'Then you're free this morning?'

Her heart stammered. 'Why?'

'I was thinking of taking Aurora to the beach.' He paused. To read her reaction? Or out of uncertainty? 'Join us.'

Imogen ignored the strange sensation of pain, the feeling of being on the other side of that 'us.' She ignored the sense of being excluded, because that was the exact opposite of what he was doing.

Besides, she was here to work. He was trying to facilitate her recording of this demo—by offering her his recording studio, by minding Aurora while she worked. For all his faults, she could hardly charge him with anything new in the present circumstances.

She looked towards the rolling hills, wondering at the stitching sensation in the centre of her chest.

'It's not far. You'll be back in plenty of time.'

It almost sounded like he *wanted* her to go with them. 'You'd be fine without me,' she said, wondering if a fear of being alone with Aurora was at the heart of it. 'I've seen you with her. You're great.'

'This is one of the most beautiful coves in the world—though having grown up near here, I might be a little biased. Even at this time of year, it's worth the trip, though I wouldn't recommend swimming.' He was quiet, thoughtful. 'I thought you might like to see it. But of course, the choice is yours.'

Well, now she felt a little silly. She sipped her tea, torn between going with her heart, which was telling her, *Heck, yes! Explore and enjoy!* and her mind, which was shouting at her, *Steer clear, you can't trust him!*

She angled a glance at him, wariness in the lines of her face.

'I'll come. But only to see the beach.'

He nodded once. No smile, but something warmed her in the middle of her chest, and she realised, after he'd left, that it was the *way* he'd looked at her. The same way he'd looked at her back then that had made her feel like she was the very centre of his world, his eyes laced with such admiration she could hardly blink away. He was like a solar eclipse—impossible to look back at without getting burned. Only, back then, that very same look had made her believe they were in love. It had been a lie—something she would remember this time around.

They left the villa as soon as Aurora woke, which was not long after their conversation on the terrace. Imogen only had time to pack a beach bag with some towels, hats, spare clothes and some snacks for Aurora before Luca was propelling them out the door towards his garage. When he opened it, she realised he had not just the four-wheel drive that had driven them yesterday, but a fleet of cars secured in here, including a sleek sports car with a soft top. And naturally, he'd had car seats installed in several.

She glanced across at him, a teasing expression on her features, but he simply shrugged and set about securing Aurora into the back of the sports car, leaving Imogen to settle herself in the front passenger seat.

Halfway to the beach, he pulled off the road, turning into a sleepy-looking town that was so wonderfully Tuscan.

Imogen took at least a hundred photos with her phone as they drove through it. Cobbled streets, higgledy-piggledy rendered houses, flowerpots overflowing with rosemary and lavender, window baskets with geraniums spilling down towards the ground, laundry strung from one window to another, and little shops set up with artful displays of fruit and vegetables. He pulled over near one of these shops, turned to Imogen and asked, 'Hungry?'

She was. They hadn't had time for breakfast, and besides the snacks she'd packed for Aurora, food hadn't occurred to her.

He disappeared into a bar and returned a few minutes later with some paper bags and a couple of take-away coffees. She salivated as the aroma hit her nostrils and peeked into the bags to see a couple of flatbreads that were overwhelmingly garlicky, with red tomato sauce oozing into the melted cheese.

At the beach, she spread out some towels and they sat side by side, eating their *piadina* and watching as Aurora delightedly played in the sand. She ran it through her fingers, pressed it to her cheeks, pushed it around to make different shapes.

'She's never been to the seaside before,' Imogen admitted, halfway through her flatbread.

Luca tilted a glance at her. She felt the heat of his inspection, his curiosity, and found herself letting down barriers she'd sworn she'd keep in place. Because he was here, and he'd bought her the most delicious breakfast ever. Because he'd suggested this outing. Or maybe because she felt relaxed, for the first time in a long time? Wasn't that a problem, though? To relax around Luca was the first step towards forgetting, and she couldn't forget.

'Why not?'

She'd been silent for long enough that he'd been led to probe further. 'No time or opportunity,' she said after a pause. 'We've travelled to my parents', for Christmases, birthdays, that kind of thing. They live in the Cotswolds, so that's kind of become our go-to holiday destination. It's beautiful, and free, so it ticks all the boxes.'

He nodded thoughtfully, but said nothing.

'Did you come here, growing up?'

The air crackled. Imogen could have sworn she saw a spark. She'd asked him about something she knew he didn't want to discuss, but so what? Why shouldn't she get to return volley?

'From time to time.'

It was classic Luca: evasive and dismissive, all at once. But Imogen remembered. She remembered how angry she'd been after he'd dumped her, for not pushing him harder. For not making him open up to her. Maybe if she had, she'd have understood him better sooner. Been able to save herself.

'What does that mean?'

'It means occasionally.'

'With your parents? Friends?'

'My parents, and my aunt and uncle. My cousins occasionally. Friends.'

She had to concentrate on not rolling her eyes. He'd listed just about everyone under the sun, which had given her no real impression of what his life had been like in Italy.

'Did you like to swim, as a boy?'

He had only a small piece of *piadina* left. 'What boy doesn't?' He finished his flatbread then scrunched up the paper bag, holding it in the palm of one hand. Nearby, Aurora had stopped playing with sand and was now staring at a pair of seagulls squawking towards the shore, their beaks doing frequent inspections of the wet sand, hoping to strike gold.

'What else did you do?'

He was quiet, moving the scrunched-up paper from one hand to another.

'At the beach?'

'As a boy.'

'Typical stuff. Football. Hikes. Skiing in winter.'

Her smile was wry, but in the back of her mind, she felt a slight tremor, a thrill, because he'd told her *something* that was real, something biographical. Not that it was particularly interesting or important, but it was a start.

And why do you care? a voice challenged.

She was supposed to be keeping him at a distance, not trying to drill down into his past. And yet…he was the father of her child. There was some common sense in getting to know him more deeply: a necessity now, more than it ever was before.

'Not so typical for someone like me,' she said.

'No? You hiked, as a child.' There it was again. The imbalance. His memory of her, his knowledge, because she'd shared so openly and willingly in that month they'd spent together.

'Yes. I still do, when I can.'

He nodded slowly. 'My father taught me to hike. Not in parks, but rather in the wild. He showed me how to read the weather, look for predators' tracks, find food if necessary.'

'He sounds like a natural outdoorsman.'

Luca was saved from replying by Aurora, who wandered over to them with a look of such excitement it was as if she'd won some kind of lottery. She held in her tiny hand a shell that was picture book perfect, curved and a deep silvery brown in colour. 'Look!' she squealed. 'Mama, look!'

Imogen smiled indulgently, taking the shell in one hand and examining it. 'That's very pretty, Aurora.'

She handed it to Luca to inspect. He took it, looked inside, then gestured for Aurora to come closer. 'Let me show you something,' he said, and the little girl trustingly settled herself into Luca's lap, pulling at every single one of Imogen's heartstrings. He held the shell towards her ear, but she spun to look at it.

'No, no,' he said, gently though, and with a smile that made Imogen's eyes sting, because he'd never smiled at her with that look of simple pleasure. Her heart hurt. She glanced away quickly, pulling hair behind her ears and blinking rapidly, before turning back in time to see him press the shell to Aurora's ear.

'Do you hear it?' he asked, watching the little girl's face flicker with emotions.

'Ocean!' She pointed towards the water.

'Yes.' He smiled again. Imogen too, but her own was wistful. Despite the simplistic beauty of that moment, she couldn't help but feel sad. Sad at what Luca had missed out on—and what Aurora had likewise. Because she'd made a decision based on her experiences of him. She'd judged him by how he'd treated her, as though that defined him. As though that meant he was only capable of cruelty, when in fact, towards his daughter, he was capable of...love.

Yes, love. She saw it on his face now and almost gasped. She had the strangest sense that Aurora and Luca had formed a bubble, and for the first time since Aurora's birth, Imogen felt like an outsider with her own daughter. She stuffed the rest of her *piadina* into her mouth, but could no longer enjoy the complex, savoury flavours.

'Mama, listen. Mama!'

Imogen turned back to Aurora and took the shell, held it to her ears and listened.

'My mother used to say it was a way of bringing the beach home. She always hated leaving, and so I would collect these shells for her, so she could listen no matter where she was.'

Imogen's heart twisted. Before she could answer, Luca was standing, dislodging Aurora, whose little hand he clasped in his. 'Come on, *bella*. Let's go feel the water in our toes.'

* * *

Luca had found himself dreading Aurora's bedtime that night. When their daughter was with them, it was easy to focus on her, to distract himself and stay busy with the child they shared. It was easy to watch her and laugh at her and focus all his energy on her needs. But when Aurora was dispensed with for the night, it left him and Imogen here, in a place he now recognised was incredibly beautiful and...romantic.

Romantic.

God, he'd never thought of it that way before. This had always just been a good investment. A place he'd got cheap because the rock star who'd owned it had lost their fortune, come on hard times and needed to sell. Luca had paid above the asking and still got it for a steal. He'd bought it because it made solid financial sense, and he'd always viewed it through that lens.

But Imogen being here gave the place a different kind of life. It gave it a whole new light and air, a vibe that he'd never noticed before. Even the sunlight had hit the house differently from the moment they'd arrived.

It was Aurora, too, he admitted, pouring himself a glass of local red wine and cradling it in his hand, stepping out onto the terrace and looking towards the now ink-black sea. He had known she was his daughter from the moment he'd seen her. She was instantly familiar to him. But seeing her here, in Tuscany, he'd had the sense of bringing her home. Where she belonged.

Where he belonged.

Something cracked in the centre of his chest.

A pain. A comprehension. A sense of dread.

He'd left Italy on his eighteenth birthday, turning his back completely on the uncle and aunt who'd cared for him after his parents' deaths, ignoring them to the point of callousness; turning his back on everything that reminded him of how much he'd lost, and who he'd been before. He came here sparingly, as a form of punishment. When he wanted to be most pained by the past, he visited Tuscany and he wallowed in his memories, in reflections of how perfect his life had once been.

But seeing Aurora here, dangerous promises were whispering to him. Seductive, tantalising temptations, like: *What if it could be perfect again?*

He knew it couldn't be, though. It never would be. Even if, somehow, he could find happiness with Imogen and Aurora, he would never let himself enjoy it.

Being here with them was an added form of torture—that was all. Seeing Imogen smile, hearing her joke and laugh and watching her cuddle Aurora, who was as Italian as the day was long, made him want to forget his past. But Luca never would. Nor would he forget his failures and his grief. A mistake had defined him as a twelve-year-old; nothing would ever change that.

And yet, even knowing he didn't deserve happiness in life, there were other things he had started to realise. Such as the vulnerable position he was currently in. Imogen had moved in with him, for Aurora, to ease this transition, and because Luca had insisted upon it.

They weren't a family, but at the same time, they were. For Aurora's sake, shouldn't they strive to be? Shouldn't they try to give her something like he'd known as a child? Like Imogen had known? This wasn't about them, their attraction, nor their history. Everything now hinged on the present, and the future they wanted to create for Aurora.

They'd made the outing to the beach work.

It had been pleasant.

More than pleasant, it had been… He searched for a word and found he couldn't come up with one to describe it. The trip had been spontaneous but also…perfect. Cathartic, perhaps. He'd loved seeing Aurora discover the things he'd discovered and adored as a child. He'd felt a heavy connection to his parents, being there with his own child, feeling things they must have felt. He wasn't just walking in their footsteps; he was being shepherded by them. Never had he felt their presence so keenly.

He'd loved seeing Imogen there as well. He'd loved watching her watch Aurora, seeing the adoration on her face, knowing that despite everything that had happened between them, Aurora was a gift. A gift he hadn't asked for, but one he wasn't stupid enough to take for granted.

If anything, he'd been bowled over by how much Aurora had flooded his heart—a heart he'd sworn was cut off from the world, and would be for all time. The total, possessive love he felt for her, because she was *his* child, to love and protect. He was her father, a role that he knew to be sacred and important, because of how his own father had been. Atoning for the past by denying his own happiness had always been a driving force for Luca, but now there was an equally important goal in his mind: to be everything Aurora needed him to be. He would be a real father to her—not just a temporary dad, but someone who was there, day and night, whenever she wanted his advice or presence.

Yet an uneasiness crept through him as he acknowledged how temporary this situation might prove to be. He had no idea what Imogen's life had been like in the last few years, but he'd seen her that night at the bar with another man, had seen her hug him and smile at him, and he'd felt everything slipping with the realisation that other men saw her as he did, wanted her as he did.

That had been *before* he'd known about Aurora. What would happen if Imogen met someone now—if she started dating, fell in love and married, and Aurora then had a stepdad? On the one hand, Luca recognised that the pain of that would serve him right—an excellent punishment for having let his family die.

Even he couldn't go that far, though. Though punishing himself was a long-held habit, too much was at stake now to lean into those patterns. He had to protect this world they were building, this mirage of a family. He had to make sure this lasted, for Aurora's sake alone…

CHAPTER EIGHT

AFTER A LONG and immensely satisfying session in the studio, Imogen wanted company. No, she wanted Luca's company, she admitted to herself, in a way that she knew she should resist. And yet, she approached the terrace, where Luca stood, but she hesitated before stepping out onto it.

In London, they'd established a rhythm that worked for them. A sort of truce that made it possible to juggle the complexity of their arrangement. But here, in Tuscany, it was different. He was different and she was different; even Aurora was different.

It was a special place, the kind of home that invited magic to dance in the air around them, so a sense of awe and awkwardness swirled through Imogen as she stood just inside the villa, looking out at Luca's back. But he was still the same Luca. Even when she glimpsed something vulnerable in him, even when he said something that made her wonder about him on a deeply human level, she knew what he was capable of. And it didn't much matter what had caused him to be the way he was. He'd always be capable of repeating the callous way he'd treated her before. He'd always be capable of hurting her. She'd be stupid to let her guard down, even somewhere like this that invited true, heartfelt intimacy.

That wasn't what she wanted from him. It wasn't something they could ever achieve—not after their past.

So when she stepped onto the terrace, it was with a grim

expression and a certainty that despite the beauty of their surroundings, the relationship between them was rotten at its core.

Perhaps to remind them both of that, she asked him something she'd wondered for a long time, though hadn't ever really planned to bring up. 'How soon after I left did you replace me anyway, Luca?'

It certainly set the tone for their conversation. Just like that, she'd wiped away the pleasant day and evening they'd spent and had plunged them back into the sparkling animosity of three years, or even two weeks, ago.

He turned to face her, his expression giving nothing away. The moon was high and full, shining and white, and it cast his symmetrical face into a shadow.

'It's not a tough question,' she said when he didn't respond.

'No, it's not. And yet I doubt you want the answer.'

Her stomach dropped to her toes. She turned towards the view, sucking in a sharp breath. He hadn't answered, and yet he had. He'd basically confirmed what she'd feared and hated most at the time. He'd moved on straightaway. He'd replaced her straightaway. She had been dispensable to him. *Replaceable.*

Her heart hurt.

Not because she still cared for him, but because she had then. She'd cared for him, loved him in an open and innocent way, and he'd discarded her like a nobody. She forced herself to be strong, to keep her back straight when she felt like slumping, to keep her features expressionless when she halfway wanted to cry.

'I'm interested as to why you would ask.'

'I've wondered about it over the years, that's all.'

Silence fell, staticky and sharp. Imogen curled her hands around the railing, her throat hurting with the emotions she was containing.

'Did you truly not realise that I thought I was falling in love with you?'

More silence. 'I saw what I wanted to see,' he admitted.

'Which was?'

'Us being on the same page.'

'We weren't.'

'I know that now.'

She swallowed. 'I can't be the first woman who's claimed to love you.'

She glanced at him to see him frown thoughtfully. 'You were.'

'But not the first woman to feel it. Or to think she felt it,' she corrected quickly, the distinction an important one for her pride.

'Believe me, Imogen, what happened between us was a one off. I don't sleep with virgins. I don't sleep with anyone for weeks on end.'

'Then why me?' she pushed, his revelation doing something funny to her stomach, making it twist and loop.

'You know the answer to that,' he responded, a tone in his voice that spoke of repressed anger and impatience.

'Spell it out for me,' she demanded.

He glared at her and then moved quickly, his mouth seeking hers, taking it, crushing it, demanding her submission. A submission she gave all too willingly, her body pliant against his, the emotions of the last few days, of the last few weeks, building up to an enormous fountain of need that was erupting between them both.

'This is your answer,' he groaned, moving his hand to her back and pushing her towards him. 'I don't know why, but from the first moment we met, I haven't been able to resist you. I had to have you then, and God, I want to have you now. I want to have you always, Imogen. Do you understand that? You are a fire in my blood, a need that overtakes all of my senses. You are a drug to which I am addicted, and I hate you for that, even when I know I would give my life for yours.'

She was breathless from passion and confusion. His words almost sounded like a declaration of love, but they weren't. There was a darkness to them, an anger, a resentment and bitterness, as though wanting her was the worst thing that had ever happened to him.

She pulled back to look at him, needing to see, to understand, but he kissed her again, and this time, he lifted her, bringing her with him back inside the villa, to the rug by the unlit fire, laying her down and kissing her while his knee wedged between her legs and his body lay heavily on hers, moving just enough to awaken every single one of her senses. Except common sense, which had deserted her the moment their lips connected.

'Do you understand what you do to me?' he ground out, pushing her shirt up to reveal her bra and then lifting her breast over the cup, exposing her nipple to his hungry gaze and then his desperate mouth, which ravaged her until she was moaning and arching her back on spasm after spasm of pleasure—pleasure so intense it was a form of torture in and of itself.

His hand curved around her bottom, lifting her to meet his arousal, and she whimpered, fully convinced that if he didn't take her now she might crumble and die. 'Please,' she moaned, over and over, her hands pushing at his clothes impatiently while he reached for protection and unfurled it over his length. She wore a skirt, and he reached underneath it to find her underwear, sliding them down her legs and pushing the skirt up, entering her without even undressing her; such was their need, mutual and hungry.

She whimpered with gladness as he filled her and her muscles squeezed around him, her whole body trembling with the gift of her first release. She curled her legs around his waist as he began to move once more, and again and again she rode a wave of ecstasy, until finally he joined her, his voice thick and dark in the room, his convulsions echoing her own tidal euphoria.

He pressed his head into the curve of her neck and then pushed up onto his elbows so he could see her properly.

'Listen, Imogen.' His voice was hoarse, his breath still coming in fits from their exertions. 'I need to talk to you.'

Her heart stammered; dread filled her veins with ice. 'What about?'

'This.'

Her lips parted. She didn't pretend to misunderstand. 'Us?'

His brows knit together. If he denied there was an 'us,' she was scared she might slap him. He was still atop her, inside her, filling her senses and body with his presence; she wouldn't let him sideline her again.

'I like you.'

Her heart stammered. It was an underwhelming declaration, especially after the need he'd professed to feel for her moments earlier, and yet it was doing something strange to her insides, churning them up and making them unrecognisable.

'I respect you.'

Her pulse rushed.

'And I think you are a very good mother.'

Warmth slid through her. She bit into her lip, fighting a strange urge to cry. Her hand lifted up and pressed to his chest, connecting with the solid wall of his pectoral muscles and the heavy thudding of his heart.

'I do not want to hurt you again, Imogen.'

Her eyes fluttered shut. It was an admission that came close to being an apology. It was an acceptance of what he'd done to her that she'd badly needed to hear.

'You won't. I'm different now.'

'I can see that.' There was a strange heaviness to his tone. Guilt? Well, that would make sense. Imogen had become cautious because of him. It was his treatment of her that had driven her to view people with mistrust, to overcome her natural instincts and be wary wherever possible.

'I don't love you.'

She gasped. It was one of the most hurtful things she'd ever been told, and that was saying something. They'd just made love, after all.

'I am not saying that to be cruel—I am, in fact, trying to protect you.'

'To protect me from what?' she demanded with hauteur.

'From misunderstanding me.'

'You're being pretty damned clear,' she muttered.

'I would like us to get married.'

It was the very last thing she'd expected him to say. Her whole body trembled and her skin lifted in goose bumps. It was a proposal she'd dreamed of, over countless nights, because her sleeping thoughts were well beyond her control. Everything stopped. The ticking clock above the mantel, the shimmering moon, the rolling waves of the ocean, the rustling grape vines, the night birds flapping their wings, the earth spinning in its place. Everything stopped and fell silent.

'What did you say?'

'Aurora deserves that from us. She deserves the certainty of a real family.'

'I can't... I—'

But he pressed a finger to her lips, silencing her with the intensity of his stare. 'Our marriage would be for Aurora, but that's not to say we would not find a silver lining to it,' he promised. And he moved his hips a little, reminding her that he was still a part of her, and damn it, her body flushed with ready, all-encompassing heat. 'Be my wife, Imogen. Sleep in my bed, night after night. Be mine.' And he kissed her in a way that almost made her think he meant it, that he wanted her to be his wife, even when he'd just told her, in no uncertain terms, that none of this was about her. Not really.

'Stop. Just stop.'

Now she found the strength to push him away, or maybe he simply accepted her need in that moment for space, and acquiesced to it. Luca pulled back, standing, disappearing briefly before returning while still in the process of straightening his clothes.

Imogen sat where she was on the floor, her nerves rioting. 'Did you actually just suggest we get married, after everything we've been through?'

He put his hands into his pockets, looking down at her with a face that was carefully wiped of expression. And she hated that! How easily he could conceal his feelings—if he even had any.

'It makes sense.'

'About as much sense as a polar bear in the Sahara,' she disputed passionately. 'You can't be serious.'

'Why not?'

'Because—because—look at us!' she spat. 'Besides sex, tell me one good thing about our relationship.'

'Aurora.'

Imogen rolled her eyes. 'I'm her mum, you're her dad. We don't have to get married to keep performing those functions.'

'You grew up with the security of two parents who loved one another very much, who doted on you and left you no room for doubt about your place in the world. Tell me that didn't help shape who you are as a person.'

'But it was also their love for one another. Their obvious respect and openness. Seeing their relationship made me want, for myself, a fraction of their happiness.' Her chin jutted defiantly. 'I will never have that with you, and I'm not marrying for anything less.'

For just a flash, she saw his reaction. A visible expression of some dark emotion she couldn't fathom and then he was Luca again, impenetrable, confident, assured. 'We are her parents, and we should be with her. Both of us.'

Imogen pressed her fingers to her temples, shaking her head a little. 'That's crazy. It makes literally no sense.'

'On the contrary, it's the only sensible option.' He moved across to Imogen and crouched down, so their eyes were level. 'I want to make this work, for both of us. Tell me what you would need to consider this.'

Her gut twisted. The answer to that was oh-so-simple and oh-so-terrifying: love. But she didn't love Luca and never would, so why would she want him to love her? Because she wanted her parents' happiness? Or because it was how she'd been raised—to believe that marriage was the ultimate expression of romantic love? It didn't have to be, though. It could be an expression of a parent's love for their child—such as in this instance. Marrying to give the baby stability and the permanence of a family home.

'Lots of people raise children in shared homes,' she said, fighting herself now. 'It's old-fashioned to think we need to be married to do this right.'

'Lots of people do, and I commend them,' he agreed. 'But you and I both want the same version of a family for our daughter. I know that is true.'

She scanned his face. 'Why do you want it, Luca?'

'I've told you—'

'No,' she interrupted quickly, shaking her head with impatience. 'I know what you're *saying*, but that's not the whole answer. It's not the complete truth. What makes you think marriage is such a worthy institution?'

He was silent.

'You never speak about your parents,' she insisted. 'And yet you know all about mine. You know how happy they are, how much that influenced me, because I told you, years ago. But I don't know anything about your parents' relationship and how that shaped you. If I had to go off your reaction to me, though, I would guess something happened to turn you off the whole idea of love and romance at some point in your life. So why this about-face?'

'Our marriage isn't about either of those things.'

'Then it's not a marriage,' she responded, pulling away a little and moving to stand, glad to stretch her legs and gain some space. 'Were they unhappy, Luca? Is that why you were so cruel to me three years ago?'

'That had nothing to do with them,' he responded, but his hand slashed through the air in a way that made her think she was getting to the heart of something. Some truth he wanted, desperately, to keep from her.

'Did they fight?'

'I was a thirty-year-old man when we met, more than old enough to have had my own experiences to take into account.'

'So, it was a woman then? Someone who broke your heart and made you swear off relationships?'

A muscle jerked in his jaw. 'I am not here to be psycho-analysed. We're discussing the prospect of our marriage.'

'There is no prospect of our marriage,' she replied instantly. 'Not when you're so intractable. You can't even tell me the most basic information about yourself. You keep everything locked up, hidden away. If I agreed to your proposal, I'd wake up one day and find that I had married a stranger. I'm not going to be surprised by you twice, Luca.'

Silence arced between them. He strode towards her and she held her ground, staring up into his face, daring him to keep arguing with her. He stopped short a few inches away, his eyes holding hers, his features a tight mask of control.

When he spoke, it was with a voice she barely recognised. Low and throaty, his accent thicker than usual. 'My mother and father were, like your parents, very happy. They laughed and loved with total abandon. I knew myself to be their ultimate pride. When I was nine, my mother discovered she was pregnant—it had not been planned, but was a welcome surprise. To all of us. We adored Angelica. Our angel. She was the most beautiful little girl.' His lips twisted into a ghost-like smile. 'So like Aurora.'

He shook his head, the memory clearly painful. She resisted the temptation to reach out and console him by touching his arm. It was a strange barrier after the intimacy they'd just shared, but something held her immobile.

'For my twelfth birthday, we went away together, as a family, to a cabin in the Italian Alps. My parents felt they'd been neglecting me, since Angelica's arrival. They wanted to make a fuss. My father took me out one on one; we hiked, played cards.'

Imogen blinked up at Luca, struggling to reconcile this image of him with the man she knew. The man who'd cut her heart into a thousand little pieces as though it were nothing.

'On the night of my birthday, we had dinner together. I went to my room afterwards—I'd been given some new football trading cards and wanted to sort them.' Another smile, less grim this time. Nostalgic and sad. Her fingers itched to touch him. 'I fell asleep, but awoke sometime later to a loud crash.'

Even if she spoke, she suspected he wouldn't hear. He wasn't really talking to her now, but rather replaying events like a film in his mind, recounting things exactly as they'd happened. And Imogen braced, because it was abundantly clear this wasn't going anywhere happy.

'It was a beam in the lounge room. The fire had not been fully extinguished, and a spark leapt from it to the rug and quickly caught fire. It didn't take long for the whole cabin to be alight. I was down the other end to my parents and Angelica—she was not a good sleeper. They wanted to spare me from that. I tried to get to them, but a beam fell on me.' He ran his fingers over his side distractedly.

Even with his shirt on, she could see the scars there. The delicate bunching of his otherwise perfect skin, the ripples that had always fascinated her. She'd asked about them once; he'd demurred, and she'd let it be.

'I passed out. The next thing I knew, I was being dragged from the cabin by neighbours. They saved me. I was hurt but alive. I wanted to go back in, to save my parents and sister. I could see how badly their section of the house was burning. I needed to get to them. I cried out, I pushed, but the neighbours held me back.'

Tears slipped down Imogen's cheeks.

'I was weak.'

'Weak,' she whispered, askance. 'How?'

His eyes lanced hers. 'I should have been able to reach them. Do you have any idea how many times I have replayed that moment in my mind? There is no force on earth that should have held me where I was. My father had spent the whole trip teaching me to be a man, talking to me about responsibilities and courage, and yet, in that moment of truth, I failed him. I failed them all.'

She gasped, her heart hurting for him now, and not herself. 'No, Luca, no. How can you say that? You were a boy of twelve, you'd been injured, there was a raging fire, and you were being physically restrained.'

'I was afraid,' he muttered, clearly disgusted with himself. 'I fought to go to them, but I was simultaneously terrified. Maybe that's why I let them restrain me? Maybe if I hadn't been afraid, I would have been able to free myself and run back in?'

'And then what? Do you think there's any possibility you would have survived?' A muscle jerked in his cheek. 'Do you think your parents would have wanted you to die trying to save them?'

'I should have saved them.' His eyes showed such awful torment. Imogen acted then, putting a hand on his chest, where his heart thumped hard against her palm.

'You couldn't have. You were pinned by a beam. The fire had reached their bedrooms. What happened was a terrible tragedy, but it was not your fault.'

'Do you know what else my father did on that trip, to encourage me to become a man? A man he could be proud of?' Luca said, the words ice-cold.

Imogen shook her head a little.

'He gave me tasks. Responsibilities. "Every person in a family carries their weight, my boy."'

A shiver of presentiment ran the length of Imogen's spine.

'One of my *duties*—' he almost spat the word '—was to extinguish the fire each night. But I was too excited by my football cards to do it properly. I rushed. I didn't check. I just wanted to sort through the damned things.'

Imogen's face scrunched up. 'That's not your fault.'

'Are you kidding? It's the definition of "my fault."'

'Listen to me, Luca. Listen to me properly a moment. If your father was anything like mine, he was always there, a shadow, like training wheels, guiding you when I needed it, but always, always checking on you. There is no way, absolutely none, that your father would have given you a task as important as that and not checked you had done it. Particularly not on your birthday, when it's entirely predictable that you would be distracted by your gifts.'

Luca's eyes closed. It was clear that while he'd heard her words, he didn't want to take them on.

'You knew him. Am I wrong?'

A muscle jerked in his jaw. 'There is no defence for what I did, and then failed to do. None.'

She felt as though she were being handed the keys to something important—she just couldn't quite work out what. It didn't matter, though. This was about him, not her understanding of him.

She stroked his chest gently, letting her fingers move to his sides. 'You were just a boy.'

His Adam's apple shifted as he swallowed, visibly regrouping. 'After that night, the lights went out for me. But before that, my life was... I saw what you saw. My parents were in love, yes, and more than that, Angelica and I were their reasons for being. Nothing made them prouder or happier than when we simply walked into the room.'

Her heart was thumping into her ribs.

'I would like our daughter to know that feeling.'

Imogen groaned softly.

She wanted that too. She wanted them to raise Aurora together, to be able to make this work. She was far from believing marriage to be a prerequisite for raising a child together. She'd been doing it alone for more than two years, and she'd met heaps of single mum and dads, and couples of all sorts of configurations—married, engaged, never planning to marry, gay, straight. She had no preconceptions about what a modern family looked like. All that mattered to Imogen was what was right for *them*—for their family, and for them as individuals.

For the briefest fraction of time, she was tempted to simply say *yes* and work out the details later. The old Imogen would have. The Imogen he'd first met, three years ago, who'd taken everyone on faith, who'd loved without boundaries, who'd believed the best about people and life. But she'd learned her lesson, she'd taken it to heart, and it was wrapped around her now, protecting her even when her old nature wanted to reassert itself.

'I understand why you've suggested this, and I'm not going to lie and say I'm not open to considering it.' His eyes probed hers, his face back to a blank mask of control. 'But I need to think about it, about everything.' She lowered her hand further, to catch his with hers. 'Just give me some time.'

CHAPTER NINE

EVERYTHING WAS DIFFERENT NOW. She still hated him—at least, she hated what he'd done to her, how he'd treated her—but she pitied him too, and she ached for him. She now *knew* him in the way she'd been wanting to know him all this time. More than knowing small details about him, she *understood* him.

His pain was such that one could not easily recover from it. His pain was a burden he'd carried since he was twelve, and it had shaped him, formed him, formed his beliefs and opinions, his thoughts about himself.

'Oh, Luca,' she sighed wistfully, because it was all so very sad. She went to bed thinking about him, and woke the next morning in the same headspace, but Luca was back to being Luca—closed off, acting as though they were polite acquaintances. Acting as though he hadn't asked her to marry him the night before.

It drove her wild, but a new level of sensitivity had entered her thoughts, and so she let it go, treating him with the same cool reserve as she made a cup of tea. Aurora woke, and they spent the morning exploring the grounds of the villa, but the vibe was completely different from the day before. Imogen hung back, allowing father and daughter to bond, to spend time together, to get to know one another.

The same sense that she was an outsider to their bubble permeated Imogen. His marriage proposal twisted in her mind. At first, she'd dismissed it as impossible. It was an idea so totally out of left field that she'd been blindsided. Yet it wasn't totally unrealistic.

'Tell me what you need to make this work.'

That was a good question. What did she need? He was obviously an excellent father, but would he continue to have this kind of time for Aurora when life resumed a more normal routine? It was still a novelty. What if she agreed to marry him and found that he became as unavailable to Aurora as he had been to Imogen during their relationship? Somehow, back then, he'd subtly created the expectation that his days were his own, and she hadn't even noticed, far less minded. She'd come to care for him, to rely on him being a part of her life, and he'd let her down. What if he let Aurora down too?

Did she want to be married to someone who was capable of partitioning her and Aurora so completely from his life?

But why did she think he'd do that with Aurora? How he'd treated Imogen had nothing to do with his decisions as a father. It was, nonetheless, something to discuss with him—what did he imagine his role would be? What would this possible marriage even look like? Who would have what responsibilities?

Out of nowhere, she saw Genevieve's face and shivered, because her twin sister had been her guiding light for so much of her life. Genevieve's judgement was flawless—and she would not condone even the discussion of a marriage to Luca. She'd tell Imogen to scoop Aurora up and run a mile.

Only, Genevieve hadn't really seen Luca with Aurora. Not for more than a few hours when she'd come to help out, and Imogen was pretty sure that just by her presence, she would have changed the dynamic. She also didn't know Luca, outside of how he'd made Imogen feel three years earlier. That wasn't unimportant, but it also wasn't everything.

Wasn't it?

Imogen stopped walking, frowning. Was she actually starting to let that pain go? To admit that it wasn't the be-all and end-all of the lens through which she should see Luca?

She couldn't. Self-preservation made her cling to it, to remember the hurt, his coldness, his awful dismissal of her.

But it was overlaid by his confession the night before. His throaty, raw voice as he'd talked about his parents, and losing them, and how he felt he'd failed his whole family. Had he got professional help back then, to deal with his grief? Had he spoken to anyone about it since?

A breeze rustled past, cold enough to make her shiver and wrap her denim jacket more tightly around her frame, her fingers lingering over her flat stomach.

Aurora had grown in there. New life, Luca and Imogen's child, and Imogen had felt their baby inside of her, swirling and swishing around. She had known and loved Aurora for almost as long as her heart had been shattered by Luca. Every decision she'd made in life from the moment she discovered she was pregnant, had been in Aurora's best interests.

For their daughter, she would do anything—even step back into the lion's den.

Only, he didn't seem like such a lion now—or at least, she couldn't see the lion without also recognising the cub he'd once been, badly hurt by events in his life, and unable to escape their long, dark shadows.

Shadows, though, were not impenetrable. She watched as Aurora said something, pointed and clapped and Luca crouched down to lift her up, holding her higher, so she could see the fruit on the tree. She touched it, and Luca nodded and smiled, so his eyes creased at the corners. Imogen's pulse ratchetted up.

Aurora had been named with care, for the Roman goddess of dawn, because Imogen had known she would be just that: a new dawn after so much bleak sadness and grief. And she had been.

Aurora had been her dawn, her morning light, her sunshine and warmth, and as she watched father and daughter together, she had no doubt she would be for Luca as well. And Imogen smiled at the exact same moment he turned to look for her, so their eyes met, and her heart flooded with warmth, as a new hope crested inside of her once more. Genevieve's warning was forgotten—for now at least.

After two days of recording, Imogen had laid down enough tracks for a decent demo, and the producer had promised to get the finished files to her the following week. Luca insisted on dinner on the terrace to celebrate, and Imogen found she couldn't refuse. The sky was dark with hints of mauve lingering like streaks, whispers of dusk and the day that had passed. The stars were shining, and the trees formed perfect silhouettes, reminding Imogen of the picture books she'd read as a child.

It was nothing to the terrace itself though, as ancient as it was beautiful, with the hip-height columns forming a railing over which ivy had begun to scramble many years earlier, covering it now with verdant green tendrils. The table had been set with white linen and a candle sat in the middle, only just lit, so it was still tall and proud, casting them in a flickering golden light, and an ice bucket held a bottle of expensive champagne, the cork already removed.

'It's really not worth celebrating yet,' she said, shaking her head a little. 'Not until the demo's been sent in and they like it.'

He poured her a glass of champagne regardless, then lifted his own to salute it. 'Have you done this before?'

She shook her head a little. 'Not specifically. I recorded a couple of demos when Aurora was much younger.'

'And?'

She flushed pink, remembering the day she'd got the call from the major label. 'I sold one of the songs.'

'You sold a song?'

'It was the sound they'd been looking for, for one of their artists. I was in a fog of looking after Aurora, I was exhausted, and then this call came through—I couldn't believe it.'

He was quiet, watchful.

'It all happened so fast. One minute, I'm signing a contract, and the next, the song was on the airwaves. It was the strangest feeling, to hear my words, my music, being sung by someone else.'

'That's an incredible achievement. You must have been so proud.'

She tilted her head a little. 'I was a thousand things. Proud, excited, shocked, overwhelmed.'

'Have you sold anything since?'

'I haven't wanted to. I was flattered and excited—to have a bona fide pop star singing my song was such a rush. But it's *my* song, and I want to be the one to sing my songs. If I can.' She gestured towards the house, where the recording studio was situated. 'This is my dream. I know it's a long shot, but I have to at least try.'

'It's not a long shot,' he denied, shifting his gaze thoughtfully to his champagne flute, as if transfixed by the bubbles rioting inside the fine glass. 'The first night I heard you sing, I was transported. Your voice is ethereal and at the same time completely grounding. I didn't know, until I heard you sing, that music could make you *feel*, deep in your soul.'

She stared at him, a thousand feelings exploding through her. He'd praised her singing before, but now she understood why he almost seemed to resent the impact her voice had on him. So much of Luca was an act—an effort to keep himself from showing pleasure, so that he couldn't feel it. To keep himself walled off. Sympathy softened her.

'You have a beautiful voice,' he said, without expanding further.

She stifled a small sigh, but wrapped his praise in her memories. 'If I can't get a deal, I'll just keep doing what I'm doing. Teaching and singing gigs. I love that too, you know. Connecting with an audience, watching them sing along and dance, it's very rewarding.' She sipped her champagne. 'Anyway, we'll see what comes of this.'

'What's the label?'

She named a big American-based company. 'One of their executives has been coming to watch me sing for a few months now. We've become friends, I guess. He's really supportive and thinks I have a good chance.'

Luca was still, his eyes probing hers, as if remembering something, or thinking it. 'Tall guy? Dark hair, beard?'

She frowned. 'How did you know?'

His laugh was without humour. 'Let's just say I've been having persistent fantasies about punching the guy in the face.'

Imogen blinked across at him. 'What are you talking about?'

He gripped his glass, then released it. 'I came to see you, a few nights after we were together. You came off stage and I saw you go to some other man. Hug him, smile at him.'

'That's just Brock,' she said, lifting one shoulder. 'But why would you want to punch him, Luca? You can't seriously have been jealous?'

His smile was cynical. 'Can't I?'

She told herself it meant nothing. A person could absolutely be possessive of another without it suggesting that emotions were involved.

'Of what? You and I hadn't seen each other for three years before that night. We were nothing to each other.'

His frown was contemplative. 'I don't know if that's true.'

She sipped her champagne simply so she had something to do with her hands. 'Then what is true?'

He looked at her without responding, a frown continuing to etch across his face.

'Why did you come to see me?' she persisted, a little breathily.

He arched a brow, as if to imply the answer was obvious.

'Sex?' It flashed in her gut like a flame. She glanced away from him, towards the inky black void where the ocean would be, so she missed the expression that very briefly crossed his face—one of uncertainty. 'Of course, how stupid of me.'

She felt hollowed out and exposed. She was raw and hurt, all over again. She felt that the person she wanted to be with him—strong and unemotional—was far from who she really was. She ground her teeth, trying not to think about her weakness with this man, and how stupid it made her.

'Like I told you, you're a fire in my blood. I didn't think about it. I just knew I had to see you again. Like a moth…'

Her heart raced. Her body trembled. She felt the power of his admission, what it had cost him; she knew how hard that had been. And how much it meant? Could it really mean *anything* when he wasn't prepared to dig deeper and analyse *why* she was a fire in his blood?

'We need to talk,' she said thoughtfully, pausing as his housekeeper brought out a tray of food. Italian delicacies, fresh seafood, *crostini toscani*, *panzanella*. Once she'd left, Imogen leaned a little closer. 'If, and that's a *huge* if, we were to get married, I would need to understand what it would look like.'

He was very still. 'Okay. What would you like to know?'

Heat suffused her cheeks, but she knew she had to get past

her embarrassment and be brave. 'Well, where we'd live, and how we'd live—would we share a bedroom or each have our own? Who would get to make the decisions in Aurora's life? For example, who chooses where she goes to school, and who takes her to swimming lessons? Are you going to be hands on with her, or will it go back to being like it was before—with you working from dawn 'til late and us relegated to just the briefest moments in your evening?'

His features tightened and he looked towards the ocean, but when he spoke, his voice was level.

'I presume you'll want to live in London, to be near your family.'

She toyed with the corner of her napkin before reaching for her fork and pressing it into a perfectly seared scampi.

'We're very close,' she admitted.

'That's fine by me. I rarely come to Italy. Though I must admit, seeing Aurora here—'

Imogen's breath caught in her throat. 'I've felt it too.'

Their eyes met and the air between them sparkled.

'It's like she's of this place in some way,' Imogen continued unevenly. 'Seeing her at the beach the other day, it was the strangest sensation of her having come home.'

Luca's jaw shifted, and he made a grunting noise.

'When did you leave Italy?'

'When I was eighteen. As for bedrooms—' he quickly pirouetted the conversation back to their potential marriage '—is there any point in not sharing? We both know how things are between us. Do you want to keep fighting it? Because I sure as hell don't.'

She bit her lip. The problem for Imogen was her inability to separate sex from love. She'd fallen victim to that weakness in the past, and despite everything that lesson had taught her, everything *he'd* taught her, she wasn't sure history wouldn't repeat itself.

'I'll have to think about it,' she responded with caution. 'Why did you leave Italy?'

He looked at her and it was as though she were torturing him, asking him to walk across a bed of nails towards her or something, but he answered, even though the words seemed to have been dredged from his soul against his wishes.

'There was an opportunity in London.'

'No.' She'd had enough of his obfuscation. 'Why did you really leave?'

Again that look of torture. Or terror. 'You know why.'

Yes, she realised, she did. 'You wanted to get away.'

His eyes swept shut.

'Everything here reminds you of your parents, and you were running away from that. You're still running.'

He opened his eyes and lanced her with the directness of his gaze. It was agreement. An admission.

'Luca.' She leaned forward a little, scanning his face, her heart twisting in a way that made her wary, for it indicated in a way that was deeply problematic that his pains were in some way hers. 'I searched you up on the internet, you know. Back then, I mean. There was nothing about your parents, your sister. It was all very bland.'

He nodded once. 'I'm glad.'

'But why isn't there something online? I mean, just a news article, or a mention of you having been orphaned?'

'For the simple reason that I didn't want there to be.'

'That's not really how the internet works.'

His lip quirked in mocking acknowledgement of that. 'After the fire, I went home, and everyone knew about it. Everyone wanted to talk about it, to make sure I was okay. I got tired of pretending I was. My aunt and uncle moved me to a different school, and I began to use their surname. My mother's brother is my uncle, so I didn't see it as a betrayal. Romano is my mother's maiden name.'

'Oh.'

'I couldn't face the constant inquiries. Everywhere I went, someone brought it up. I wanted to be someone else, someone different. And so, Luca Romano was born.'

'But your aunt and uncle must have wanted to talk to you about it.'

'They wanted to do whatever they could to help me. I just wanted to be left alone.'

Imogen frowned. 'Did you see a therapist, Luca?'

He pulled a face. 'Once. It wasn't helpful.'

A lump formed in her throat. She saw him again as a little boy, a twelve-year-old on the cusp of manhood, grappling with huge emotions and trying to shape them around his ideals of manhood, maturity, masculinity and responsibility.

'Oh, Luca,' she sighed.

'Don't pity me. I don't want it.'

'How can I not pity you? What you went through was awful.'

'It was a long time ago.'

She shook her head. 'But look at how it still affects you.'

'Is there a statute of limitations on grieving your parents, your sister?'

'That's not what I meant.'

'Then what do you mean?'

She bit into her lower lip, food forgotten. 'Grief left unexplored metastasises and forms a hard, hard lump. That lump gets bigger and bigger as time goes on.'

'Speaking from experience?'

She glanced down at her plate, her heart thumping. She couldn't compare her grief to his. She'd been heartbroken, it was true, but that was nothing compared to having lost your parents and sister.

She shook her head slowly. 'I don't know.'

'What is it, *cara*?'

The term of endearment slipped through her, landing dangerously close to her heart. She pushed it aside, assuring herself it was just the way he spoke. Just the way he was sometimes. It didn't mean anything; none of this did. But when she tried to reassure herself that she still hated him, because of how he'd treated her, she found it harder to believe than she had even a week ago.

'Nothing. I'm just saying you need to process what happened, to let yourself off the hook.'

'Why?'

'So you can live without guilt. So you can live at all.'

'I don't want to live.'

She took in a sharp breath.

'Not in the way you mean it. I don't deserve to.'

Her heart trembled. 'How can you say that?' She was aghast, pained.

'Easily. If it weren't for me, they'd still be here. I should have died with them that night. I didn't, but that gives me no pleasure.'

'You really wish you'd died?'

'Of course.'

'No,' she denied hotly, food forgotten as she stood and crossed to him, sitting on his lap and grabbing his cheeks in both hands. 'Don't you dare say that. Your parents would be devastated to know you felt that way.'

A muscle jerked in his jaw. 'It's how I deserve to feel.'

'Luca, stop. You deserve to be here, you deserve to live— and not just to live but to live well.'

'I deserve *niente*. This is not self-pity. I am certainly not looking for your pity. I'm simply stating the facts.'

'As you perceive them, yes,' she agreed quickly, because she could tell there was no artifice to this, no bravado. He felt as he said he did—he felt it to his core—and that dreadful belief had guided his each and every move from when he was a boy. She pressed a kiss to his forehead.

'You survived, and if your parents could tell you anything, it would be that they are glad for that. You said it yourself— you lit up their lives, just by walking in the room. That you are here would mean everything to them.'

He didn't respond. All she could hope was that on some level he'd heard her words, and that he might even let them filter through to his mind, to begin changing his perception of things.

CHAPTER TEN

SHE WAS WRONG. Not about his parents, but about his deserving to let go and live. He couldn't. He had killed his parents, and while he appreciated Imogen's inherently good and kind nature—that she could care about him enough to offer such advice after what he'd done to her—his whole life was, and had been for a long time, predicated on the fact that he had done something so heinous and unforgivable that he would always, always be alone.

The more he wanted someone or something, the more he fought it. The more he thought a path might lead to happiness, the harder he drew back from that path.

Imogen was a perfect case in point.

He wasn't a fool.

He knew that sex had been a cornerstone of what they'd shared, but only because he'd kept it that way. He'd known what the potential had been. He'd known how dangerous it was to be with someone like her, who had obsessed him to the point of distraction.

Every morning, he'd woken up and sworn that would be the last time he saw her, but then he'd always weakened. It had been a never-ending cycle of dependency, until she'd done the one thing that had convinced him it had to end, then and there.

She'd fallen in love with him. Or she'd believed she had, anyway. She'd offered him the one thing he'd known he'd never accept: love. Because to let someone love you was to imply you thought yourself worthy of that love, and for Luca, that would mean forgiving himself on some level. As though his parents' and sister's deaths hadn't meant anything.

And now he had to walk an even finer tightrope. Marriage to Imogen was essential for many reasons. She'd asked what the marriage would look like, and he hadn't been able to give a clear-cut answer. He knew only that he would still need boundaries. Barriers. Roadblocks. Defences.

She had to keep hating him, or at least to never love him again. She needed to stop looking at him with those gentle, perceptive eyes, as if understanding way too much about him.

Because the moment this thing started to feel real, he would need to put distance between them again. He would never let her love him, or even care for him. He would never weaken. He wasn't worthy; he just had to make sure she remembered that.

It was an almost impossible scenario to manage. To marry a woman who was more alluring than any he'd ever known, and to keep her at arm's length, all the while knowing their chemistry would make it impossible not to fall into bed together?

He clenched his teeth, his spine infusing with iron.

It would be difficult, but it had to be done. Not marrying her wasn't an option. It made him too vulnerable, too exposed to the possibility that she'd meet someone else and he'd lose her altogether. That he'd lose Aurora as well. He had to find a way to make it work. Determination flooded his veins; he would do this. He had to.

'Do you see them often?' Imogen curled her legs beneath her on the sofa, a cup of tea clasped in her hands.

He glanced across to her, a frown on his face. 'Who?'

'Your aunt and uncle. Your cousins.'

He was quiet a beat, then shook his head. 'I have only seen them once or twice since I left.'

Imogen's face softened with sympathy. 'You don't get on?'

'I get on with them fine.'

'Then why don't you see them? They're family, Luca.'

Because they loved him. They forgave him. They acted as if it hadn't happened.

'I've been busy.'

She sighed—a soft, husky sound that curled around his chest. 'No one's too busy to see family. Even just for a weekend.'

His grip tightened on his coffee cup. 'We email.'

He practically heard her rolling her eyes. 'That's the same thing.'

'Why does it matter?'

'I don't know yet, but I'm convinced it does. You push people away as a matter of course, even your own flesh and blood.'

'More psychoanalysing?'

'You're the father of my child,' she said softly. 'You're trying to get me to marry you, for her sake. You want to give her a family and I want that too—I do.' She paused, as if weighing her words. 'But what if you decide to push her away, like you did with me? I have to protect her.'

A muscle jerked in his jaw. Imogen was right. He'd given her no reason to believe he was trustworthy. In fact, he'd demonstrated he wasn't. The fact she was even giving him a chance was, again, a testament to her goodness rather than an indication of him deserving it.

'I won't let her down.'

She sipped her tea.

How could he make her understand?

'I never wanted to have children. I've known that for a long time. That, however, was a theoretical viewpoint. From the moment I realised I was already a dad, that Aurora was here, my child, my daughter—' his voice cracked a little '—I have known the role I would want to play in her life. With Aurora, it's not about me. It's about her. I will spend the rest of my life being whatever she needs me to be.'

Imogen nodded once, blinking away from him. He still wasn't sure if he'd convinced her.

'My aunt and uncle don't need me. They have children. They raised me because they felt they had to, after my parents died. There was no one else to take me in.'

'Luca, how can you say that? They're your family; they love you.'

'No.' He said the word like a curse. 'They don't. Or if they do, they're wrong to.'

Imogen closed her eyes; he had no way of knowing what he was thinking. 'You have to forgive yourself.'

He dismissed her words. She didn't understand. She couldn't. Imogen was too good to properly grasp the depths of his guilt. Silence sparked between them, and when she opened her eyes and pinned him with her gaze, there was a sadness in her expression that washed over him, leaving his chest heavy and sore.

'Poor Luca,' she sighed, reaching across and putting a hand on his, briefly. He refused to allow the gesture to comfort him, even when her touch pulled at something in his gut, as it always did. When he didn't say anything in response, she stood, removing her hand. Coldness settled around him.

'I think I'll go for a walk.' She gestured towards the garden. 'I...want to soak all this in, before we leave.'

She walked away and he expelled a long, slow breath of relief. For reasons beyond his comprehension, he was telling Imogen things that he had never contemplated sharing with another soul. He was opening up to her in a way that was anathema to him. Because of the stakes now? Because he had to convince her he could be trusted in marriage? Of course. She was smart and she was cautious, with good reason. Showing her his mentality would serve two purposes: she would understand that when it came to his daughter, he would do everything he could to live up to his father's example; and it would also serve as an insurance policy against her ever believing herself in love with him again.

Imogen walked, and she thought, and the more she did so, the more confused and sad she became. The more she wanted to make excuses for him and the more she ached for him, the more she realised that they were in a very difficult situation.

And protecting her heart seemed at once both vitally important and impossible.

It was strange to miss a place having only spent a few days there, but arriving back in London, Imogen had to admit that she had a hankering to be in the sunlit Tuscan countryside, or at the delightful white sand cove, rather than in the city that was gradually turning grey and cool as autumn took a real hold.

The impulse to run away was natural, Imogen knew. She'd felt it herself, after Luca had dumped her, and when she'd discovered she was pregnant. But she had strong, deep-rooted connections to a supportive and loving family.

And in time, the feelings had lessened, the sting of hurt had faded—even when it'd left in its wake a certainty that she'd never be the same again.

Six years had elapsed between Luca's tragedy and his leaving Italy. Six years in which she imagined that poor young boy had been running from his grief the whole time. Even before he'd left the country, he'd changed his name and school, changed everything that had linked him to his immediate family and that accident.

He'd been running for longer than he hadn't been. It was a habit now, as worn into him as was breathing and walking.

He'd never stop running and she needed to accept that, or she'd get hurt all over again.

The idea of keeping a distance from him was becoming harder and harder. She was a human being, not an automaton, and there was something about Luca that just got under her skin.

But as he'd said, this wasn't about them. It wasn't about him; it wasn't about her. They were parents, and they both wanted to give Aurora the same kind of loving childhood they'd benefited from. Perhaps that was even more important to Luca, because of how his world had been so drastically and awfully shattered. Aurora deserved the best of them; she always would. And Imogen was starting to realise that Luca was right: they could give that to her, so long as they worked together.

She found him in his bedroom, tightening a tie around his neck, and for a moment it was impossible to speak because he was so strikingly handsome, her whole world tilted on its edge.

'This won't be easy, and it won't be simple, but okay,' she said, slowly, giving herself every chance to back out even then.

He turned to face her, and it was obvious he understood what she was referring to despite the lack of preamble. 'You're sure?'

She laughed softly, shaking her head. 'Not really. But I know we won't regret trying this. For Aurora's sake.'

He stalked across the carpet to her, taking her hands in his and lifting them to his lips. 'For Aurora,' he agreed, but when he kissed her, it definitely didn't feel that it was about anyone but them, Imogen and Luca, with a fever in both their bloods and a need time seemed unable to extinguish.

He pulled away though, looking down at her, his face so close she could see every fleck of gold in his eyes, each dark, clearly defined lash that circled them. She could see the turmoil there, the thoughts.

'You're not happy,' she murmured, then could have kicked herself. Of course he wasn't happy. This wasn't a normal engagement. She wasn't making all his dreams come true by agreeing to become his wife.

'I'm relieved,' he admitted, and her chest panged a little. 'But, Imogen—' He broke off, frowning deeply. 'You were hurt by me in the past. I don't want to hurt you again. It's important that we both go into this with our eyes open.'

'My eyes are open,' she said quietly.

'If I was a different man—' his voice was gruff '—you would be all my dreams come true.'

Her heart churned.

'But I'm not. This is who I am, who I'll always be. I don't want marrying me to be a ticket to misery for you.'

'Three years ago, I didn't understand. I thought we were something we weren't. I thought you wanted the same thing as me.'

'That was my fault.'

She bit into her lip. She couldn't deny that. 'I didn't have enough experience to see what you were clearly trying to show me. I took everything about you at face value—I presumed your having to go to the office early to be about your workload, rather than you putting a ring-fence around the time we would spend together.'

His skin paled slightly, and his lips tightened. 'I should never have been with you.' He wiped a thumb over her lower lip, and his voice was rich with earnest pain. 'You trusted me, but I was never worthy of that trust.'

For three years she'd been desperate for him to apologise.

To hear him say how wrong he'd been, to say he regretted it. But those words gave her little satisfaction now.

'I should have walked away after that first night, but you were so—'

'So?'

He shook his head slowly. 'I don't know.' The answer was honest, if frustrating. 'There was something about you, about how I felt when I was with you.'

Her stomach churned.

'I should have known better then, and I want to do better now.'

'We will.'

He squeezed her hands. 'I wish I could offer you more.'

Something like grief washed over her.

'You deserve more.'

She shook her head, denying it without understanding. 'Are you trying to talk me out of marrying you now?' she half joked.

'No. I still want this. I just need to know you're sure.'

She sucked in a deep breath. 'I'm not sure about everything,' she said after a beat. 'I'm not sure how it will work, I'm not sure that it's not a mistake, but I'm sure I want to try. I'm sure we both have the stubbornness and determination to make it work. So, let's do it.'

His face relaxed a little, and he nodded. 'Okay then. Let's get married.'

Her heart popped in a way that made Imogen realise it didn't understand. This was just an arrangement. It wasn't real at all.

Telling Genevieve was not something Imogen was looking forward to, and it was certainly not something she wanted to do with Luca in the house. So, she waited until he was at work, then invited Genevieve over for lunch. She made a simple soup and fed Aurora early, so she was ready for a nap by the time Genevieve arrived.

Aurora's aunt gave her a cuddle and insisted on settling her to bed, then came into the kitchen, where Imogen was spooning lunch into two bowls and removing crusty garlic bread from the oven.

'God, I miss her,' Genevieve murmured as she walked into the state-of-the-art kitchen. 'Please tell me you're coming home soon? It's so depressing without you guys.'

Imogen's stomach was in knots. This was the moment of truth. 'Actually, Gen, I need to tell you something.' She passed one bowl of soup towards her sister before taking a seat at the kitchen bench. She made no attempt to reach for her own bowl. She was far too anxious.

'What?' But Genevieve's hesitation was telling. She knew something was going on. 'Im?'

'Luca asked me to marry him.'

Genevieve closed her eyes. 'And you told him to go to hell, right?'

Imogen bit down on her lip. 'At first.'

'Oh, God.'

'Hear me out.'

Genevieve blinked across at her sister, shaking her head. 'I've heard you out, though. I heard you crying, Im. Every night, for months on end. I watched you grow thin and pale, even though you were pregnant. I watched you stare into space, your face tormented by memories you wouldn't share. I saw you fall apart at the seams because of that bastard, and now you're going back to him?'

'It's not like that,' Imogen whispered, her voice cracking a little. 'This isn't the same as before.'

'Really? Because it sounds a bit the same.'

'I know him so much better now. I understand him.'

'If that were true, you'd be running a mile.'

'Gen, I love you to bits, and I know you're trying to be supportive of me. But you *don't* know him.'

'I've known men like him, and I know what he did to you before. Leopards don't change their spots.'

'He's not changing his spots—I just see them better now.'

'What does that even mean?'

'We're not in love. This isn't about us. It's about giving Aurora the kind of family that matters to both of us.'

Genevieve stared at Imogen as though she'd gone mad. 'Are you hearing yourself?'

'I know, I know. It's not...like me,' she said with a lift of one shoulder. 'But some things matter more than romance and being swept off your feet. I want to do this for Aurora. I want her to have what we had growing up.'

'But you guys aren't Mum and Dad. You just said it yourself—you don't love each other. Kids are perceptive. She's going to see that her parents hate each other—'

'We don't hate each other either.'

'You have hated him for three years. I've heard the songs.'

Imogen winced a little, thinking of the enormous catalogue of songs she'd written, most of them inspired by the feelings he'd caused her to have.

'That was then.'

'But what's functionally changed? You always knew he was Aurora's father.'

'I've seen another side to him.'

Genevieve pulled a sceptical face.

'Gen, I'm going into this with my eyes wide open.'

'That's no guarantee your heart won't get broken.'

'But my heart has nothing to do with this. We're getting married for Aurora.'

'So there's nothing going on between the two of you? You're not sleeping with him?'

Imogen glanced down at her soup, her cheeks flushing pink.

'You're not going to bed together and waking up finding it hard to clutch at the threads of reality because in that moment, you're side by side and he's everything you want in life?'

Imogen gasped.

'I'm your twin,' Genevieve muttered.

'Yeah, well, you're not psychic. I don't feel like that,' Imogen denied hotly.

'You can lie to me, but please don't lie to yourself.'

'I'm not.'

'You're not capable of being in a relationship with someone and not loving them.'

Imogen gasped. 'Why do I feel like that's an insult?'

'It's not, believe me. It's one of the things that's different about you and me. You give with all of yourself. You can't help it. You're the same with friends, family, Aurora. You put all of your heart into the people you're with, and if that's him, then you're going to do the same. Except he will chew you up and spit you out for breakfast.'

'Don't say that,' Imogen whispered, her heart dropping to her toes. Was Genevieve right? She'd spent so much time with Luca since coming to live with him. Was it possible he'd brainwashed her, and she just wasn't seeing the forest for the trees?

'Listen, Imogen. I want you to be happy. You're my sister, and I love you. But I'll have no part in this sham of a wedding. Get married or don't, but whatever you do, don't expect me to be there on the day. I have no interest in watching you make the biggest mistake of your life, and I'm pretty sure Mum and Dad will feel the same way.'

She stood up, pressed a kiss to Imogen's cheek and then walked towards the kitchen door, soup totally abandoned. 'Oh, and get a damned good prenup, because after he screws you and breaks your heart all over again, you should at least get some of this.' She waved her hand around his expensive town house before blowing a kiss and stalking towards the front door.

Imogen stared at the empty space her twin had previously occupied, her heart thumping hard against her ribs, acid rising in her throat.

Was Genevieve right? Was Imogen about to make the biggest mistake of her life?

Uncertainty settled around her and refused to budge, so by the time Luca returned, she almost couldn't bear to see him.

Unlike in the past, he came home around four, so he was available to spend time with Aurora before she went to bed. He'd become a very involved father, and loved reading to her and running her bath, supervising her dinner, cleaning up afterwards. If Imogen had expected him to want to hire a team of nannies and wash his hands of any actual parenting, she'd been completely mistaken.

When he walked in the door that particular afternoon, Imogen was dressed in her exercise gear. 'I thought I'd go for a run,' she said, not quite meeting his eyes.

He opened his mouth to say something, then closed it and nodded instead. 'Good day?'

'Sure, great day. See you.' She waved in his general direction, opened the door and stepped outside, exhaling into the cool air, grateful to have avoided being face to face to him.

She turned the music up loud on her phone and plugged her ears with earbuds, running hard and fast, doing everything she could to drown out her thoughts. They had been swirling around and around in her mind all day and she needed to escape them.

But she couldn't. Each step made her body tired, but her mind wouldn't stop.

She remembered the time they'd spent together in the past. Each night, each morning, each small little thing. She remembered how easily she'd fallen for him, and how little he'd cared. She remembered their madness in coming together again; she remembered the nights now, the way he was with Aurora, and panic rose inside of her, because they had to get this right, and she had no idea if this was going to be a huge mistake that she'd always regret. What if she was messing everything up for their daughter?

What if she wasn't being honest with herself and she did actually love him? What if, what if, what if?

Frustration was a beast inside of her, uncertainty a wave she couldn't escape.

It was dark by the time she came home, and Aurora was dressed in her pyjamas, reading a book with Luca. Imogen smiled tightly at them both.

'All good?' she asked, moving past them without waiting for an answer.

'*Sì. Perfetto.* And you?'

She nodded quickly. 'I'm going to shower.'

She took her time there, too, hiding out, avoiding him, her brain ticking over, looking at this from every angle. But it didn't matter how many times she pulled at the threads of this—she always came back to the same answer.

They were different now. They were doing this for Aurora, walking into the marriage with their eyes open to the kind of marriage it would be. Imogen wasn't the same girl she'd been back then. It was natural for Genevieve to worry: she'd seen Imogen at her very rock bottom. But so much had changed since then.

They could do this, and it would be fine. It had to be.

CHAPTER ELEVEN

'I'VE BEEN THINKING about the wedding,' she said later that night, as he stacked their plates in the dishwasher.

He turned to face her, giving her his full attention. 'Yes?'

She made a throaty sound of agreement. 'I don't want a big fuss. Why don't we just elope?'

A frown pulled at his lips. 'What about your family? You're close to them. Won't they want to be there?'

She glanced down, hoping he didn't see the hurt in her eyes. The thought of getting married without Genevieve or her parents was awful, but Gen had been right: she couldn't ask them to be a part of something that was so outside the bounds of the kind of marriage they'd want for her. They'd proudly come and watch her get married for love, but not for these reasons.

Though wasn't this a little about love? Love for the child they'd made, love for the little girl who was their whole world? What wouldn't they do, as parents, to secure Aurora's future, to give her everything she deserved in life?

'Imogen? Did something happen today?'

She glanced at him quickly, then away again. 'Why do you ask?'

'You're avoiding me.'

'We just had dinner together.'

'And you were somewhere else the whole time.'

Her stomach squished. He knew her so well; he always had. He could read her like a book.

She blinked quickly. 'I told my sister today. It didn't go well.'

He nodded slowly. 'I see. And that's important to you.'

'She's my sister,' Imogen said, as though that explained it. 'My *twin* sister. We have done everything together for as long as I can remember. She's my biggest cheerleader, my best friend—as I am hers.'

'And she doesn't support the idea of this marriage.'

Imogen shook her head.

'Okay.' He didn't sound deterred. 'Then what would you like to do?'

'I told you, elope.'

'This doesn't make you question what we're doing?'

She shook her head. 'It did. I have been questioning it all afternoon, but I keep coming back to the same conclusion. This is what's right for us. That's not up to anyone else to decide.' She sighed softly. 'What does it matter? This isn't a normal marriage, we don't need anything big. We're just getting married for Aurora, right? So let's elope and be done with it.'

He studied her for a long time, his eyes narrowing, his brow furrowing. 'We can elope, *cara*. Whatever you want is fine by me.'

The next morning, he left as if going to the office, careful to act as though everything was normal. Instead of heading to the City, however, he had his driver take him to a little apartment in Putney. He pressed the doorbell, waited, and when Genevieve opened the door, he braced himself for this conversation.

He'd convinced Imogen this was the right thing to do, but he suspected it was going to be a lot harder winning her sister over. However, having seen the crestfallen look on Imogen's face, the tightness around her eyes, he knew it wasn't optional. Having her twin sister's support really mattered to Imogen, and if he could fix it, then he would.

If not, they'd elope, just the three of them, but he knew that wasn't what Imogen wanted. What she deserved. He was better not thinking about what she deserved, because the second he pulled at that thread, this whole preposterous house of cards fell over.

'You.' Genevieve's voice was a growl.

'Can we talk?'

It was obvious that she wanted to refuse, but at the same time, she loved her sister, and her invitation for him to come into the apartment was clearly motivated by that. 'I've got an appointment, but I can spare five minutes. What do you want?'

'To talk about the wedding.'

Genevieve made a scoffing noise. 'You mean your idea of the century?'

'With respect, your sister is an intelligent woman who's made her own mind up about marrying me.'

'Yeah, she also made her mind up about falling into bed with you three years ago, and again now, and neither of those were particularly strong decisions.'

'You presume to know a lot about our relationship, given you've met me twice.'

'I don't need to know you to know what you're capable of.'

He bristled. Her anger was grating but it was also gratifying. She was speaking to him as he believed he deserved to be spoken to. She viewed him as the worst of the worst and in this way, they were in agreement.

'I'm not going to hurt her.'

She made a noise of disbelief. 'Of course you are.'

'Why do you say that?'

'It's what you do.'

He flinched. Had Imogen told her about his family?

'You hurt her back then, and you're going to hurt her again. I don't know when and I don't know how, but you don't have what it takes to be a decent human and take care of her.'

He flinched again. Every single one of his worst fears was in her words.

'You're not a decent human being.'

'What happened between us in the past was regrettable—'

'Regrettable? You almost killed her. Do you have any idea what it was like for her?'

He blanched. He knew he'd hurt her, but at the same time, she'd downplayed that. She'd told him she'd been fine, that she'd moved on. Or had he simply presumed that, because of the air she projected. She'd told him she hadn't actually loved him.

'If she hadn't been pregnant, I have no idea what would have happened. You *destroyed* my beautiful, loving, free-spirited, kind sister once and I'll be damned if I'm going to let you do it again.'

'Imogen is fine,' he said again, because he needed to believe that was true. 'She was fine—'

'You didn't just break her heart—you broke her soul, her spirit, her everything. You are a monster and I will always hate you.'

Just like Imogen had promised. Did a part of her still hate him?

'She told me it wasn't a big deal,' he said, searching for something to grab hold of.

'She lied. Probably to protect her pride or maybe even to protect you, because she's just that much of a good-hearted fool, apparently.'

He shook his head. 'She's not a fool.' But hadn't she been the definition of that three years ago? She'd kept coming to him, wanting him, needing him, when he hadn't deserved her. Anyone could have seen that, but Imogen had been his regardless.

He dropped his head forward, stars in his eyes as the full impact of his carelessness three years ago came home to roost.

'We both know what she was back then,' Genevieve ground out. 'Imogen was innocent, totally inexperienced. And do you know why?'

'No.' He'd never bothered to ask. He hadn't understood it, but she'd acted like it was no big deal, and he'd accepted that at face value. Because he hadn't wanted to dig deeper? He hadn't been willing to hear that it had been something she'd been saving?

'She didn't fool around in college like the rest of us. She went on a couple of dates, here and there, but she always kept a level head because she was waiting to meet "the one."'

His skin paled beneath his tan.

'The first night she met you, she came home on cloud nine. She was in love even then.'

'That's not true.'

Genevieve rolled her eyes. 'If you're going to marry her, you need to know the full story. You think she's strong and brave? Well, she is, but not where you're concerned. You have to be strong and brave for her, and save her from making the same mistake all over again.'

Hadn't he been trying to do that? He'd been honest with her all along, making sure she understood his boundaries this time. Hell, he'd even explained why he was this way.

But hadn't he also been selfish? If he really cared about protecting her, he wouldn't be sleeping with her every chance he got. He'd be working out a way to co-parent that was respectful, amicable, and had zero risk to Imogen.

There was also the possibility, though, of her meeting someone else, and when he thought of that, it was like the air had been sucked from his lungs. He couldn't breathe; he could barely stand. That wasn't a good enough reason to tie her up in this marriage, though.

Only, Imogen had assured him, again and again, that she wanted this. That she was okay. That she understood his boundaries. What right did he or Genevieve have to question that?

'This isn't your decision.'

'But it is yours.'

'No, it's Imogen's.'

'And you're really happy to let her make this mistake again?'

'What mistake? We are marrying to give our daughter a family. This matters to us both.'

'That might be why you're marrying her, but I can guarantee it's more than that for Imogen. She probably doesn't even realise that yet, but if you think she doesn't love you, you're an idiot.'

He stared at her. 'She does not love me.' She couldn't. No one could. Memories of that morning, with the sunlight shifting through the bedroom window, as Imogen had rolled over and told him she loved him, slammed into him, unwanted and awful—memories he rarely examined because the feelings had been too extreme to navigate.

'I'm as shocked as you are,' Genevieve muttered.

'Three years ago, we misunderstood one another—'

Genevieve made a noise and rolled her eyes. 'Whatever.'

He frowned. 'She has told me she didn't love me. That she only thought she did, because of her inexperience. We've both moved on.'

Genevieve looked at him, aghast, then shook her head. 'Wait here a second.'

She returned a moment later with a CD.

'Listen to her music. She might have told you something,

just like she might have told me something, but in her music, she's always honest. Go, listen to the songs, then tell me this is a risk you're happy to take. Tell me you're not going to mess her up all over again.'

He played the CD on the drive to his office, but even when the car pulled into the secure car park, he continued to sit where he was, listening to each and every lyric, his heart pounding so hard and fast it formed a new backing track to the songs.

These were incredible songs. Songs of desperation. Of love. Of yearning and need. Of hurt and anger and hatred. In these eight songs, he ran the full gamut of her feelings, from realising she loved him, to her breaking heart, to her utter dejection and misery, the feeling of betrayal and then angry hatred. He recognised the last song. It had been a huge hit, played everywhere in the world when it was first released and for months afterwards. It must have been the song she'd told him of, the song that had been purchased off this demo.

He groaned, dropping his head into his hands. She'd sung this song at the bar, and looked at him—how good that must have felt for her, to be able to serenade him with a hate song she'd written just for him.

He dragged his hands through his hair, the world tipping wildly onto its side. Because Genevieve was right, and he'd known it all along. The album gave him more of an understanding and insight, but it was just clarifying something he'd been feeling, instincts he'd been having, since she'd first come back into his life.

He was playing with fire, and didn't he know the reality of that? Fire always burned. Fire killed.

No way would he put Imogen through this again. No way on earth, no way in hell. He cared for her. Recognising that was like the slipping into place of a foundational brick. He *cared* for her. He'd cared for her then too. That was why he'd reacted so harshly, needed to break things off swiftly, to make her hate him. And he cared for her now, too much to let her be hurt. He cared for her enough to set her free.

With Aurora settled in bed for the night, Imogen pulled a lasagne from the oven and began to serve their dinner, but Luca forestalled her. 'Do you mind if we talk a minute?'

She frowned. 'Can we talk over dinner? I'm starving.'

He frowned. 'Sure, okay.'

She glanced at him. 'Is everything all right?'

'Fine.' His smile was forced though, and a sense of uncertainty spread through her. Nonetheless, she served up their lasagne, handing a plate to him. But he collected both and carried them through to the dining table, which she'd set earlier with placemats and cutlery.

'What did you want to talk about?'

He looked down at her lasagne. 'Eat first.'

She took a scoop of the food to her mouth, enjoyed the flavours, but was impatient to know what was on his mind. He was adamant, though, and waited until she'd almost finished before leaning back in his chair a little, his own meal untouched.

'I made a mistake, Imogen.' His words were wooden. She glanced at him, not sure what he meant.

'What with?'

'Us. This.'

She was very still. 'I beg your pardon?'

'The marriage. It's a mistake. I didn't think it through.'

She pressed her cutlery to the table, appetite completely gone. 'What?'

'We can be in Aurora's life without marrying. We can even live together. But I think it's imperative that the lines not be blurred between us—as a man and woman, and as parents.'

The blood in her veins turned to ice. 'What does that mean?'

His lips compressed. 'We're attracted to each other. We always have been. But the moment I knew about Aurora, that should have been the end of it. Sex between us is a mistake. Getting married is a mistake. We will do better by Aurora if we find a way to work together that doesn't have the potential to blow up in our faces.'

'I thought that's what we were doing.'

A muscle throbbed in his jaw. 'Three years ago, I ruined your life. I'm not going to do it again.'

'You didn't ruin my life,' she denied, clinging to that falsehood. 'I was fine.'

'You were not fine.' His back was ramrod straight. 'I heard the songs.'

She blinked quickly. 'You what?'

'I heard the songs.'

'How could you—' She closed her eyes as comprehension dawned. 'Genevieve.'

He dipped his head once. 'She was looking out for your best interests—as I should have done.'

'Damn it.' Imogen slammed her palm against the table. 'Did it occur to either of you that I'm a big girl who can look after my *own* interests?'

'Like you did three years ago?'

'I'm not the same person any more.'

'And why not?'

She went silent.

'You're not that same beautiful, innocent, trusting woman because I broke you.' His voice was rent with self-directed anger. 'I destroyed you. I heard the lyrics. Every single word was written for me, about me, about us, about what I did to you. I will not take that risk again.'

'I was fine,' she repeated, aware they both knew it was a lie.

He shook his head once, seeing through it. 'This was a mistake.'

'How come I don't get to decide that?'

'Because you're too damned good,' he muttered. 'You're not the same as you were three years ago, but you're still too fair-minded, too kind. You would marry me because of Aurora, and you'll look past any of my faults because of what I've been through. You put everyone ahead of yourself and it has to stop.'

She gawped, his words etching lines in her soul. 'What if this marriage is what I want?'

He ground his teeth. 'We both know it's not.'

Imogen jammed her lips together, on the brink of saying something she knew she'd regret. Because he was wrong. This marriage had come to mean so much more to her. It wasn't just about Aurora, or the past. It was the slotting into place of a piece of her that she hadn't realised she'd been missing.

She toyed with her fork, trying not to react as her mind spun faster and faster.

The truth was, Luca was a part of her.

He always had been.

Not all of him—he would never give all of himself to anyone. But that didn't matter. Imogen would take the bread crumbs. Just as she had back then.

Because she loved him.

She sucked in a soft breath, the thought almost knocking her sideways.

She loved him now, just as much as she had then. No—more. She loved him because she knew him so much better now. She understood his faults and flaws and the reason for them. She understood the trauma he'd survived but found it impossible to live through, a trauma that had trapped him in an awful, awful web of misery and self-loathing. A trauma that had made him sabotage any relationship, push everyone away, even his aunt and uncle and especially Imogen.

He was doing it again now. He was making it seem as if it was about protecting her, but that wasn't true. At least, it wasn't the whole truth. He was protecting himself. Because he loved her? The suspicion popped into her mind unbidden and, at first, she yearned to dismiss it. Why would she be stupid enough to believe he loved her? What kind of glutton for punishment was she?

And yet, didn't it make sense?

He had been a lone wolf for so long, and completely by choice, because he wouldn't let himself be loved; he didn't think he was worthy of it. Could it be true? Her heart hurt at the very idea.

'What do *you* want, Luca?'

'That's not important.'

'Says who?'

'Me.' His lips curved into a mocking smile. 'Your sister.'

'Ignore Gen, for now.'

'I can't. She knows you better than anyone.'

'Does she?' Imogen challenged. 'You don't think you know me pretty well by now, too?'

'I didn't know about this.'

Imogen's cheeks flushed pink. 'I'm a musician,' she muttered dismissively. 'Writing about my feelings is a part of what I do. Sometimes it sounds worse than it is.'

'I don't believe you.'

She didn't contradict him. Her songs were an accurate reflection of how she'd felt at the time. 'Okay,' she said unevenly. 'You broke me. You did. I fell in love with you—I don't mean I thought I loved you. I fell in actual, hard, all-consuming love with you and then you talked to me as if I was nothing. Nobody. Like I could walk out of your house, and you wouldn't ever think of me again. Do you have any idea how tortured I was by the idea of you and other women? You said you'd replace me straightaway, and all I could think about, night after night after night, was you doing exactly that.'

He sat completely still, his face a mask of impenetrable cool, but she could see the emotions in his eyes and knew he was feeling this. She knew he was hurting too.

'I should never have said that. I just needed you to leave.'

'You were honest with me.' She tilted her chin. 'And even though it hurt, I'm glad. You were honest with me that day and you've been honest with me ever since. No matter what happens, you have never promised me something you couldn't give me.'

'That's not true.' His voice was gravelled. 'I promised I wouldn't hurt you, but I'm not so sure about that now.'

'Again, that's not up to you.'

He shook his head. 'You're misunderstanding me. This isn't a debate. I'm not marrying you, Imogen. I won't do it to either of us.'

Her lips parted on a soft breath, surprise contorting her features. 'I can't believe this.' She pushed back from the table and stood, her whole body shaking. 'So what do you want, Luca?'

He stared at her for several seconds. 'I want to work out how to do this without messing everything up. We're Aurora's parents, but that's where it has to end. We can parent together, be civil to one another, but we can no longer sleep together, or eat meals together as if something more is going to come of this. I know it won't, and going through the motions feels a hell of a lot like leading you on.'

She stared at him, her heart pounding against her ribs. He was right. He hadn't led her on, but everything they'd been doing had become real to her, despite his warnings, his insistence on maintaining boundaries. Even in spite of her own certainty that she would be able to keep this in a box this time around. She hadn't. She couldn't.

She dropped her head, the reality spilling over into her soul. 'I need to think,' she muttered, stalking towards the door, slipping her feet into shoes and leaving the house before she screamed. She was so damned angry, so frustrated, she wanted to punch something. Instead, she slammed the door behind her, then slumped her shoulders and let a single tear roll down her cheek.

How could she be here again?

CHAPTER TWELVE

HE'D DONE THE right thing. He'd hated every minute of it, but wasn't that the point? He was back in his comfort zone, back where he thrived.

Alone.

Angry at the world.

Angry with himself.

He paced the living room like a caged beast, each stride a commitment to this path. Imogen couldn't become collateral damage in his quest for misery. Imogen had to be set free.

He had done the right thing.

He repeated it, as a mantra, because in saying it, the words became something solid to cling to, a reassurance in a sea of uncertainty, an unravelling of all that he'd held fast to all his adult life.

'I thought I'd see you,' Genevieve said, opening the door to their flat and waving Imogen inside.

Imogen shook her head at her sister, angry, sad, bereft. 'You had no business getting involved, Gen.'

'You think? Who picked up the pieces last time? Literally held the baby while you were coping with what he did to you?'

'All he did to me was not love me back. That's not a crime, and it's not something you need to punish him for.'

'No,' she agreed. 'But you're planning to marry the guy,

so of course he should fully comprehend what that means for you.'

'Don't you think that's my decision?'

'When it comes to Luca Romano, you make terrible decisions.'

Imogen ground her teeth together. 'Luca is—' She shook her head. 'You don't know him.'

'I know that he's going to marry you, even though I've told him how disastrous it will be for you. I know that he's a selfish son of—'

'No,' Imogen spat, shaking her head as tears stung her lashes. 'He's not.'

Silence crackled between the sisters.

'He's called it off.'

Genevieve let out a low whistle, moving towards Imogen and wrapping her in a hug. The floodgates opened then, and Imogen sobbed against her.

'Oh, honey,' Genevieve murmured. 'I know it doesn't feel like it right now, but it's for the best.'

'It feels like the opposite of that,' she whispered. 'I understand why you're worried, but Gen, I'm telling you, Luca is… There's something about him. He's…'

'He's Aurora's father,' Genevieve said. 'Of course you feel something for him. You'll always share her, and—'

'No, this is about him and me. We're like magnets. No—' She pulled back as realisation dawned. 'We're like soulmates,' she corrected. 'My soul seeks his soul and nothing else matters.'

'Do you hear yourself?' Genevieve groaned. 'How can you say that after what he did to you?'

'You don't understand. He is on a path of self-sabotage. He refuses to get close to anyone. He's been fighting me this whole time, but that doesn't mean he doesn't want this.

In fact, the harder he fights, the more he wants. I know it sounds ridiculous—'

'Yeah. It really does. If someone loves you, they say that. They put it out in the open because nothing is simpler or more important than love. Luca doesn't love you.'

'Then why call off the wedding?' Imogen challenged. 'If he doesn't care about me, why not just marry me, to hell with the consequences for me?'

'Because he's not a total jerk,' Genevieve conceded. 'He must have some scruples, somewhere in that big, dumb head of his.'

Imogen stiffened, pulled back from her sister. 'I know you think I'm doing the wrong thing—'

'I *know* it, with all my heart.'

'Okay.' Imogen blinked slowly. She loved her sister; they were closer than the best of friends. But Imogen still had to live her life and make her choices. 'I'm sorry you feel that way, I really am.'

'But you're going to marry him anyway.'

'If I can change his mind, yes. I'm going to marry him.'

And for the first time in days, she felt the certainty of that decision like a blade in her spine, a strengthening force that had her standing tall, staring right into her future. Every single piece of her was pushing her towards this, and him.

For the smallest window of time, he'd let this feel real. He'd let it feel real even when that broke every rule he'd set for himself. And he'd been telling himself it was all in his control, that they were on the same page. He'd told himself she wouldn't get hurt because he kept laying out the ground rules, but he hadn't really understood just how explosive things were between them. Trying to control this situation was like trying to tame the ocean.

He should have ended things between them the moment he'd found out about Aurora.

He paced the lounge room, listening to small noises from upstairs—Imogen singing to their daughter, speaking softly. Reading, perhaps. When she came down, they'd finish the conversation he'd started the night before and begin drawing up a future that didn't involve a personal relationship.

It would serve him right. Not just for what he did to his own family, but for how he'd treated Imogen. He would be a spectator in her life for ever, watching her go from strength to strength—as surely she must. He no longer feared her meeting someone else. He almost relished the prospect. Let him stand by and watch her be swept off her feet, as she deserved. Let him watch her be joyously happy with a man who wasn't broken and damaged, who was capable of loving her as she deserved. Let that man form the family Imogen wanted and Aurora deserved.

His gut twisted and seemed to drop to his toes; the pain of that spectre almost weakened his resolve, so he ran his palm across his scarred chest, the ridges palpable through the cotton of his shirt, reminding him of the core beliefs that had defined his life.

He'd given up so much in the name of punishment; this was just one more sacrifice.

'She's asleep.' Imogen's voice was soft, tentative. As if she knew they had a messy conversation ahead of them and was bracing herself for it.

'Good.' He turned to face her, felt his stomach tighten at the sight of her, the way her long hair was loose and wavy around her face, tousled like it became after they made love. He looked away quickly, jaw clenched. 'Are you hungry?'

'No.'

When he glanced back at her, Imogen had wrapped her hands around her waist, as if to offer herself comfort. He cursed inwardly; he had to stop hurting her. He had to get her out of his orbit, in which everything he touched turned to dust.

'I spoke to a lawyer today.'

Imogen's sharp intake of breath shouldn't have surprised him. She was afraid he was going to take away their daughter, even now? One look at her face confirmed that—she was paler than a ghost.

'To discuss how to set up a shared custody arrangement,' he continued, his voice eerily calm given the maelstrom of his emotions. 'Since learning about Aurora, I have made a mistake at almost every opportunity. It's time to start getting things right.'

Imogen's lips parted, but a little colour returned to her face. 'You acted out of love—'

He opened his mouth to deny it, but as if she couldn't bear to hear that denial, Imogen quickly continued.

'For our daughter. Every decision you made was borne of a love for her, right?'

He ground his teeth. 'Please, don't do that.'

'Don't do what?'

'Make excuses for me.'

'Is that what I'm doing?'

'It stops you from seeing me as I really am.'

'I've been seeing you this whole time, Luca. Way better than you see yourself.'

'No.' The word was rich with finality, a sharp denial. 'I'm not going to get into this with you. We're not discussing me, or my merits. There's no point. Let's keep things relevant to Aurora.'

She opened her mouth and then sighed, shaking her head a little before moving with innate grace towards one of the armchairs. She didn't sit down, though; instead, Imogen pressed her hands to the back of it, using it almost as a shield.

'What did the lawyer say?'

'There are several options, depending on what we think will work best. One solution is nest parenting,' he said, voice gruff. 'We have a shared home, which is for Aurora, and we move in and out. I stay with her, then you do, and vice versa, so she continues to have a stable residence. The lawyer said this may be particularly helpful to school-aged children, who have busy schedules and would prefer not to be lugging things from one parent's house to another.'

Imogen's eyes were wet with unshed tears; she didn't bother to blink them away.

Seeing them only hardened his resolve.

This was what he did. *This* was what he was good at, and why he had to let her go. If she stayed with him, he would keep hurting her, even when he didn't want to.

'Alternatively, we can stick to a more standard custody arrangement, where I have Aurora here some of the time and you have her the rest.' He frowned, a deep groove. 'However, I would insist on buying you a home, ideally somewhere near mine. Naturally, your sister could live with you there.'

Imogen blinked rapidly. 'I have a home.'

'You have a flat,' he responded sharply, then softened his tone. He hated everything about this conversation, though, and it was impossible to keep that from his voice and manner. 'Aurora will need more space as she gets older, she'll need more things. And vitally, I would like her to know that I am looking after her mother.'

Imogen bristled. 'I don't need you to look after me.'

He felt the hint of combat in her voice and tried to calm his own rioting emotions. 'I mean to financially support you, as I would have been doing all along, had I known about her.'

Imogen dropped her head forward, staring at the back of the armchair as though it was endlessly fascinating to her.

'The lawyer said that given our relative financial positions, a support arrangement would form part of a shared parenting agreement.'

'Please, stop.' She whispered the words, but they seemed to reverberate around the house as if she'd yelled them. 'Don't say another word.'

Per her request, he compressed his lips, crossing his arms over her chest. Silence now rebounded against the walls, bouncing in a way that he felt in the core of his being.

Imogen lifted her head slowly, and for a moment, accusation glittered in her eyes before it was replaced by something else. Determination? Impatience?

'You and I agreed to get married because we wanted to give Aurora the kind of family life that we both enjoyed, a family life that matters to us. We wanted her mother and father living together, under one roof, supporting her, loving her, building her up before she goes out into the world on her own. *You're* the one who has been pushing that all along, and I don't think it's fair that you get to just pull that away from me when you decide to.'

Waves of emotion rolled through him. Fair? *Fair?* What about this was fair? What about *anything* in life was?

He slashed a frustrated hand through the air. 'We cannot separate us as people from us as parents.'

Imogen made a scoffing noise. 'Isn't that normal?'

'Not for us. Not for what we are.'

'You keep trying to define us. Why can't you just let us be, and see where this goes?'

'We've done that,' he responded sharply. 'And you got destroyed. Annihilated. Remember, I heard the songs. You trusted me, you loved me, and I twisted that love into something dark and furious. I twisted you.'

She blanched. 'Yes, you did. I loved you with all my heart, but you couldn't handle that. You pushed me away then and you're pushing me away now. Anytime I get close to you,

you panic. You're terrified of letting me love you, aren't you, Luca? That's just about the worst thing you can imagine.'

Hadn't he said as much? She wasn't wrong; he knew that, but he didn't want to admit it, because he knew what the logical progression of that was. He knew the conclusion she might leap to, but it didn't change anything about what he wanted. About what he'd let come of this.

'And why is that? Why are you so damned afraid to just let yourself be loved?'

'You know the answer to that,' he muttered. 'And we're not talking about me right now. This is about Aurora, and how we're going to both be in her life without…'

'No, we're talking about you. Three years ago, I let you push me away because my feelings were hurt, my heart was broken, and it stopped me from seeing that your heart was broken too. It stopped me from seeing *you*. But I see you now—I see you so well, Luca. I see all the parts of you, and guess what?'

He braced. He held himself still. Fear was a throttle at his throat.

'I love you anyway.'

His body reverberated on a tide of terror. Of disgust and anger. And of something else, something that was warm and addictive, something that was urging him to look towards the golden light of what she was saying, rather than into the dark torment of his past.

'I don't want you to love me,' he said, voice harsh, even when he knew the words weren't completely true. He hated himself for being so selfish, but her love…it meant something. It was a validation and a reassurance. It was a balm. But Luca didn't *want* a balm to his pain; he wanted to feel it, deep and hard, for the rest of his life.

'You can control a lot of things in this life, but not who loves you.'

'You'll get over it.'

'Well, it's been three years, and I haven't got over you yet, so why do you think that's going to change any time soon?'

He glared at her, shaking his head. It was preposterous to suggest he'd occupied a place in her heart and mind in these intervening years.

'I'm serious,' she reiterated. 'There hasn't been anyone else for me, Luca. I used to think it was because I've been busy with Aurora, but that's just a lie I told myself to feel better about still loving someone who didn't want me. I had the chance to date. I've been asked out by guys, and Genevieve would always have minded Aurora, but I couldn't bring myself to so much as look at anyone else. Because of you, and what you still meant to me.'

'Stop it,' he said, dragging a hand through his hair. He couldn't hear this. He couldn't hear any of it. Knowing he was the only man to have been with her, the only man who'd worshipped her body, made her cry out with sensual heat— how could that fail to pull at him?

He groaned inwardly, needing to put a stop to this conversation.

'You can't keep fighting me, Luca. I'm here and I want to be here for the rest of our lives. Three years ago, I let you push me away, but that was a profound mistake, and it's not a mistake I intend to make this time around. I can't lose you again, and I don't think you want to lose me.'

'You can't lose something you never had.'

She flinched—as he'd intended. He'd said he didn't want to hurt her, but if that was the only way to get her to accept that he'd never be the Prince Charming she was imagining…

'You're sabotaging your life,' she said softly, surprising him with the strength in her features though, and the fact she was willing to continue this conversation. 'You told me you'd never met anyone like me, that spending a month with me was something you'd never done with another woman. You didn't treat me like some disposable woman you were taking to bed—you treated me like your lifeblood. You treated me like oxygen. *That's* what I should have said to you that morning.'

He closed his eyes on a sinking feeling of fatigue and despair. Imogen had been right; she had changed. Three years ago, he'd been able to control their break-up, even when it had almost destroyed him. Now she was fighting him, tooth and nail. Fighting for them.

'It wouldn't have made any difference.'

'Wouldn't it?'

'No. I needed you out of my life.'

'Because you were scared of what I meant to you.'

His eyes met hers. He should deny it. He knew he should keep shutting down her statements, keep holding to the truth he'd built in his mind. But he was suddenly weary—the kind of weariness that came from carrying a deep, possessive grief for a lifetime. So, he stayed silent, staring at her and beseeching with his eyes for her to understand and relent. To stop pushing him to admit things he couldn't, or didn't want to.

'You were scared of loving me back, even when I think you already did.'

His hands formed fists at his sides; he tried to take strength and command from the physicality of controlling his muscles, to build himself back up cell by cell, but Imogen was pulsing inside of him, weakening him just as he'd always feared she would.

'And you're still scared. You're still running.'

He didn't move to touch his side but instead reached for another wound, mentally. He closed his eyes and remembered the fire. The smell of smoke and burning flesh, the contrast with the cold beneath his feet, the neighbours' strong arms holding him back, the grief and anger and self-recriminations. He reminded himself that he was the worst person in the world, that he'd denied himself her love, and the ability to love her back, because he deserved that, because he owed as much as payment for the crime he'd committed.

'I killed them,' he said quietly, as though that were an answer.

Sympathy washed over Imogen's face.

'You did *not* kill them,' she said, so firmly, with such determination, he almost believed her.

'You weren't there.'

'You were twelve years old and you formed an opinion that you haven't let yourself grow out of. You were not at fault, Luca. You were just a boy—there is nothing more you could have done.'

'The fire—'

'Not your fault. I have no doubt your parents checked it before they went to bed. What happened was an *accident*. A terrible, terrible accident that you will always grieve and regret, but it was not your fault. It's time to stop punishing yourself. It's time to start living.'

'No.' The word was torn from him, so loud that he clamped his jaw and spun away from her, his chest moving with his ragged inhalations. He didn't want to wake Aurora; he didn't want to yell at Imogen either.

'You have to confront this head-on and see how futile your self-loathing is.'

'Why?' He angled his head back in her direction, raking her with his obsidian eyes. 'Why does it matter?'

Her smile was one of torment. 'Because it's not just your life you're ruining, but mine too. Our fates are bound, Luca. They were from the first night we met, from the moment we made love, and they always will be. Not just because of Aurora, but because of us.'

He closed his eyes on a wave of guilt—bigger than he'd ever known. 'I never should have let this happen.'

'I don't think either of us could have stopped it.'

Silence fell, crackling with the pain of the past and the sheer impossibility of any kind of shared future.

'Listen to me.' Imogen's voice emerged husky and raw. 'I believe in my soul that you love me. I don't need to hear you say it to know that it's true. And I think you've been trying to work out a way to have me in your life without betraying this idea you developed as a twelve-year-old that you'd have to spend the rest of your days miserable and alone because of the accident. So you've been putting up electric fences and barriers and holding me at a distance. But then you started to let me in anyway, and you asked me to marry you, and you told me that I am in your blood. I am telling you that this is enough for me.' She tilted her chin with defiance. 'I am saying that I can live my life without you saying that you love me; I can live my life with the understanding that there are parts of you you'll never share with me. I can live my life with those limitations, but I want you in it. I don't want to turn my back on this, or you, again.'

How easy it would have been to take her at face value and accept what she was offering. Wasn't that his dream? To have her without needing to give her more than he wanted to?

But it wouldn't work.

Not because she would make him the happiest man on earth when he'd sworn he would be miserable always, but because the limitations she was willing to accept were an insult to Imogen, and she was worthy of so much better.

'That's not good enough,' he muttered. 'It won't work.'

'Of course it will. It's been working, hasn't it?'

'No. We've been sitting on a ticking time bomb and it's exploding all around us.'

She flinched again.

'I will stay here with you, for the rest of our lives, as your wife, or your lover, or whatever, and I will never tell you I love you again, I will never ask you to love me, if that's what you want.' She sucked in a deep, shuddering breath. 'Or I will leave, in the morning, and that will be the end of us, once and for all. The decision is yours.'

A muscle throbbed at the base of his jaw as he stared back at her and felt the tearing of his being. There she was—the person he wanted, the woman he loved—but she was across an impossible divide, a barrier he couldn't straddle.

He had to let her go, but it couldn't be like this. He couldn't let her doubt what she meant to him; there was no way he would allow her to go without fully understanding how damned difficult this was for him. He was being torn apart and she should understand that—if only to save her from existing in the same hell space he occupied.

'I love you,' he said, so simply, and bizarrely, it didn't hurt to say the words. It didn't even feel strange, because loving Imogen was such a part of him now. He didn't know when that had happened, but she was stitched deep into his soul and probably always would be. 'But I can't be with you. I love you, but I refuse to let myself love you. And if you really love me, you'd understand that, and you'd accept it.' He closed his eyes on a wave of disgust. 'It's just the way I am, *cara*. It's just who I am.'

CHAPTER THIRTEEN

AT FIRST SHE barely cried. She was in shock. A deep, mind-altering state of confusion and despair, because she was besieged by the kind of grief that made everything unrecognisable. She showered, staring at the tiled wall for so long the lines of the grout began to blur, and then, when she flicked off the water, she sobbed. Her tears fell freely, mingling with the water from the shower, and as she patted her body and face dry, the tears kept falling, silently slipping down her cheeks, as her chest moved with each sob and her body shook on wave after wave of sadness.

Because she'd fought for Luca, and it hadn't been enough.

She'd argued for them. For their relationship, their family, their future—and yes, their love—and he'd pushed her away, just like he had before.

What more could she do?

He'd been so emphatic at first, so clear, so determined, but the more she'd pushed, the more she'd felt his resolve weakening, felt him getting closer and closer to admitting the truth, until he had. And it had been the hardest thing she'd ever have to listen to.

Going into their conversation, she'd had a theory about how he felt about her, but it had been just that—a theory. A hope. A belief that she couldn't love someone and be so wrong about them.

But when he'd said those words she'd been so desperate

to hear, then quickly followed them up with 'but I refuse to let myself love you,' it had broken her heart all over again, and this time, it had broken her heart on his behalf too. She felt so desperate for both of them, for this awful mess they were in. She was still reeling.

She pulled back the cover and curled up in bed, hugging her knees to her chest protectively, squeezing her eyes shut and praying for the relief of sleep; but it didn't come, not for a long, long time. Before it did, Imogen replayed every word, every look, and the tears kept falling.

It was unnaturally silent. So silent he could hear the beating of his heart, its accusatory thumping like a drumbeat of blame. Of recrimination.

He'd told her he didn't want to hurt her again, and that had been true. Regardless, that was exactly what he'd done.

He'd seen it on her face, and he'd never hated himself more.

He cursed the day they'd ever met. For Imogen's sake, he would take it all back, if he could. He would take back every kiss, every touch, every moment that now seemed to shimmer with gold dust because of how special it had been. He would undo it all if it meant he could spare Imogen the pain he'd inflicted upon her again and again.

Darkness wrapped around him, silent and accusatory, and then, somewhere in the small hours of the morning, he heard the worst noise he could possibly imagine: Imogen's sob.

He dropped his head and groaned on a wave of self-disgust.

She must have slept eventually, because Imogen woke just after six, her face pale and eyes puffy. She was not even granted a few scant moments of forgetting—there was no relief in the liminal seconds between sleep and waking, no reprieve from pain. When she woke, it was with the ache of their confrontation at the forefront of her mind, his every word imprinted on her soul.

Acid filled her mouth as she stood and dressed quickly, scraping her hair back into a ponytail before pushing out of her room and moving silently towards Aurora's.

She had to get out of his home. She had to leave.

It was impossible to remain here, feeling as she did, knowing how determined he was to ice her out of his life.

She wanted to silence her brain, to shut down the hateful memories, but if anything, they were growing stronger and louder as she packed Aurora's things. Almost as if the simple act of wrapping up their life here was filling that argument with greater imperative.

Imogen had told Luca that she would fight for him, and she'd done that. She'd fought. She'd been reasonable and calm even when her insides were quivering with sadness and want. He'd rejected her, but not because he didn't want her.

Because he didn't know how to make this work.

Because he was wedded to this idea of guilt, and his answer—the answer of a child, really—was an eye for an eye. He felt he'd taken his parents' and sister's lives, and so his answer was to offer his own in penance.

But what about her life? If he really loved her, surely that counted for something? Surely that could be the beginning of him letting go of this awful pledge of sorrow?

For the briefest moment, hope pierced her heart, like sunshine determinedly finding its way through a thick storm cloud. He loved her. He *loved* her. That had to mean something; she just had to get him to understand that…

After glancing at their still-sleeping daughter, she strode out of Aurora's room in search of Luca, her heart palpitating because if this didn't work, it really would be over. And she desperately didn't want that to be the case.

* * *

'What about me?' she asked, when she found him in his study, seated as his desk and staring at the laptop screen. He glanced at her, his expression giving little away.

She noted the glass of Scotch to his left and wondered if he'd poured it because he wanted to take the edge off their conversation.

He lifted a dark brow in silent enquiry, looking to all the world calm and unaffected. But she saw his eyes; she saw through him. She understood him now.

'You're determined to punish yourself for the accident, but what about me?'

His lips compressed as he stared back at her. 'I've told you, I don't want to hurt you.'

'But you are, and you'll keep hurting me, every day that you refuse to let me love you, to let me be loved by you. Are you really okay with that?'

He reached for the Scotch and curled his hands around the glass, gripping it without drinking. 'I've told you—'

'You've told me nothing,' she said with a slash of her hand through the air. 'Nothing that makes sense, anyway.'

'You know why I am this way.'

'You know what you haven't told me, Luca? You know what you never say?'

He was silent.

'What would your parents want?'

He stood up as though she'd electrocuted him, Scotch still clutched in one hand. 'Don't.'

'You speak of them with love. Admiration. You describe a childhood that was happy and filled with the certainty that you were adored. Would they have wanted you to be alone and miserable for the rest of your life?'

'It's not about what they would have wanted, it's what I deserve.'

She expelled an angry breath. 'I don't believe that. I don't believe that for even a second, but even if I did—what about me? What about what I deserve? Can't you just try, try a little, to put this aside for my sake?'

He closed his eyes, so she had no way of knowing if she was getting through to him, no way of knowing if he was starting to understand how his path of self-loathing was affecting her.

'I'm letting you go because of what you deserve. I recognise that you should have so much more than this.'

'I don't want more than this; I just want you.'

He shook his head. 'It's impossible.'

'No, it's not. You could fight for this. You could fight for me, for us.'

He stared at her, as though her words were torture, but also, vitally, he was listening.

'For your aunt and uncle,' she continued, hope stretching in her heart. 'Your cousins. For Aurora. You've built an enormous fortress, and a crocodile-infested moat around yourself, and yet here we all are: people who love you, who will *always* love you, no matter how hard you push us away. Maybe *that's* what you deserve? To know that there is nothing that you can do that would make us stop loving you?'

'Don't,' he groaned. 'I don't want to hear it.'

'But you need to hear it, you need to feel it.' She closed the distance between them and caught his hand, pressed it to her chest. 'You have my heart, Luca. You hold it in your hands, as much now as you did three years ago. Please, I'm begging you—don't throw this away as though it means nothing.'

'It means *everything*. I told you that. This isn't a question of love. It's not about whether or not I love you, or believe you love me.' His voice was thick with emotion. 'I am choosing a different path, something other than this—'

'I can't let you do that,' she whispered. 'I just can't.'

'It's not your decision.'

* * *

He needed her to understand that. Damn it, why wouldn't she hear him?

He'd never seen Imogen like this. She was acting as though her whole life depended on his acceptance of her argument—didn't she understand? He couldn't give her that!

Only Imogen reached up and grabbed his jaw with her fingers, holding his face steady so their eyes had to meet and stick, and something inside of him shifted and gave way, something important and vital. Something he'd always relied on, to hold people at bay. His whole world seemed to be shifting—in fact, tipping off its axis—so nothing was recognisable now.

'Listen to me, Luca Romano.' He *was* listening. Intently. 'I love you. I love you because you are good and decent.' Her eyes bore into his, long and hard. 'You are good, and you deserve to be happy.' His first instinct was to fight that—or rather, it would have been. But now, her words washed over him, and he actually let them. Not just wash over him, but seep in, deep into his soul. 'Let me spend the rest of our lives enjoying that happiness with you. Just let me love you—and when you're ready, love me back.' Her voice was husky, and yet somehow reassuring. 'It's that simple.'

He shook his head, but not hard enough to dislodge her grip. She stood up onto the tips of her toes and brushed her lips over his. His heart jolted. 'I love you,' she repeated, and the words continued to seep into him. 'And you are worthy of that love.'

His breath shuddered and it was another release, of the old hatreds and blame, the guilt, the determination to destroy his life because of the past.

'I love you,' she said again, like an incantation. 'I'm not going anywhere. I can't.'

He closed his eyes in a wave of relief. Imogen leaving was

the last thing he wanted; he'd grappled with that all night and now knew it to be true. He wanted her to stay. He *needed* her.

She was his family.

He lifted a hand to her cheek, touching her as if to reassure himself that she was real. 'I don't know what to say,' he admitted, then shook his head, because that was only part of it. He placed his Scotch glass down on his desk, then put one hand behind her back, drawing her to him. 'Even if you stay, I can't promise this will be easy. I don't want to hurt you, it's just… I don't know how to do this…any of it. I'm…lost.'

The honesty of that admission pulled at Imogen's heartstrings as nothing else could. Here was big, tough, lone wolf Luca Romano, the man who could do *anything*, admitting that this was new to him. She leaned forward and pressed a kiss to his chest.

'I know that. I get it. I'm not expecting you to change overnight. You've spent decades hating yourself, blaming yourself for that awful accident, and walling yourself away from anyone who got close to you. I know there are some instincts you're going to have to work to unlearn. But I love you, I'm not going anywhere…and I have faith in you. I know you can do this; I know you can let me in, Luca.'

He dropped his forehead to hers, inhaling deeply. 'I can't let you again,' he admitted on a groan. 'But *Cristo*, nor can I live with hurting you, with messing this up…'

'So don't mess it up,' she said with a lift of one shoulder. 'You're a really smart guy. You've got this.'

He furrowed his brow as if trying to make sense of the world he was stepping into, of the world she was showing him.

'Are you saying…you really want to marry me?'

Imogen laughed softly. 'I'm saying I love you, but no. I'm not going to marry you. Not yet.'

His frown deepened.

'Let's walk before we can run. I love you, and you love me, so let's wait and get married down the track, when we're used to this situation, when you've met my parents and I've met your aunt and uncle, when you're able to love me without feeling as though it's some kind of a betrayal,' she added gently. 'Let's wait and do it all slowly, let's do it properly.'

'Yes,' he exhaled with a breath of relief. 'I want that for you.'

'Oh, Luca. I want it for both of us.'

Genevieve was, in the end, not such an enormous stumbling block. Whether it was seeing the pair of them together, or Luca's determination to win her over, it didn't take long before Genevieve was disavowing any possible reason to hate Luca and instead singing his praises. He was 'such a good dad' and 'wonderfully supportive of Imogen,' and when Luca and Imogen drove out to the Cotswolds to meet Imogen's parents, Genevieve went with them.

She continued to help with Aurora, having the little girl some weekends so Luca and Imogen could escape for quick romantic trips. They always felt that they were making up for lost time, and Genevieve seemed to understand that.

Reuniting with Luca's aunt and uncle was an emotional and heart-wrenching experience—but also one of joy. They were overwhelmed with love for Aurora, and when Imogen finally saw pictures of baby Angelica, she could see for herself that the two girls were indeed like twins. Luca's aunt and uncle doted on Aurora, and they couldn't stop staring at Luca, at how much he'd changed, at how grown-up he was, how successful. They'd kept a folder of newspaper clippings, showing his various successes; their pride was so obvious.

They loved him. They understood why he'd pushed them away, but they'd missed him, and they were eternally grateful to Imogen for helping him find his way back to them.

And so it was, on one such trip back to see Luca's family, when they returned to his villa in Tuscany for the night, and lay on a blanket beneath the stars and among the vines, Imogen was reflecting on how glad she was to have fought for this, on how much had been at stake, and Luca's thoughts were apparently of a similar bent. He lifted up onto one elbow and smiled across at her, a smile that radiated true happiness and inner peace, and reached for her hand, intertwining their fingers.

'I love you.'

Three little words that meant so much, and all the more because she knew Luca had never intended to say them to another soul.

'And I've been thinking about something.'

Her eyes scanned his face. 'Oh?'

'What I said to you that morning—that you would be easy to replace.'

'Luca, it doesn't matter.'

But his lips quirked downwards. 'You brought it up, the first time we came here.' He nodded towards the villa. 'You said those words had tortured you for a long time.'

'It all seems like so long ago.' She furrowed her brow. 'It feels like something that happened to someone else, not us.'

'I agree. But I need to tell you something I didn't dare admit back then.'

She held her breath, no idea what would come next, yet somehow secure enough in their love to know the bubble wouldn't burst.

'I didn't replace you. I couldn't.' He brushed a thumb over her lips, staring at her as if mesmerised.

'I don't understand.'

'I met women. I thought about asking them home with me. Something always held me back. At the time, I told myself it was further punishment of my sins—not just towards my parents and sister but also towards you. I told myself I didn't deserve even the pleasure of sex any more. But really, I just didn't want to be with anyone but you.'

Imogen's jaw dropped. 'You're saying there was no one else after me?'

'I'm saying that, yes.'

She shook her head a little, and tears flooded her eyes. 'Oh, Luca.' She bit into her lip. 'You have no idea how much it hurt, to imagine you with other women.'

'Actually, I have a fair idea. You are not the only one who played out those scenarios. I was a glutton for punishment, quite literally, and the knowledge that you had undoubtedly moved on was a frequent source of self-flagellation for me.'

She closed her eyes on a wave of pity and sadness. 'We wasted so much time.'

'I didn't admit to myself that I loved you, but I knew you were irreplaceable, that it would be impossible to even try.'

She wriggled forward so their bodies connected. 'I'm glad you came to your senses finally.'

His lips quirked. 'You and me both.'

'When you came to the bar that night, was it because you were looking for me?'

He scanned her face thoughtfully. 'Undoubtedly. There was so much I didn't admit to myself—so much I didn't understand. But the second I heard your voice and then turned around and saw you, it was like the stars were aligning for me. I felt a burst of life and adrenaline, a need that rocked me to my core. I just needed you,' he said with a lift of his shoulder. 'I'll always need you.'

'And I'll always be here.' She kissed him beneath the blanket of stars, knowing that truer words had never been spoken.

The next morning, she received the email from the record label executive; they wanted to meet the following week. It was an email that began a juggernaut—of meetings and recordings and, eventually, a career that would defy all of Imogen's wildest dreams. A career that Luca was immensely proud of her for, as he watched from the sidelines with love and admiration for the woman he loved and the talent she possessed.

After she'd recorded her first studio album, and before things became too wild and fast-paced, Luca arranged a night out with Imogen—to celebrate her success. Only it was a night like no other. With Genevieve ensconced at their home on Aurora duty, Imogen and Luca were conveyed to the closest airport and his private jet, which traversed the short distance to Paris, touching down in the late afternoon. They were whisked to the Eiffel Tower, and straight to the top of it, where they stood and sipped champagne as the sun went down and the sky filled with gold and mauve and everything was glorious. Imogen was utterly transfixed by the view, so she didn't notice at first that Luca had crouched to the ground, until she spun around to point something out to him and found him on one knee.

'Luca.' She lifted a hand to her mouth, fingers trembling.

'*Cara mia*, you know how I feel about you. You know how much I love and adore you, how much I worship you. I am indebted to you for bringing me back to life, out of the fog of a grief I thought I would never escape. You are responsible for every single piece of happiness I will ever feel in my life. You have already given me one of the greatest gifts with our beautiful Aurora, yet here I am, asking you for another gift. Would you do me the honour of being my wife?'

Imogen had forestalled the idea of marriage in the past, because she had known the most important part of their journey—at that point in time—revolved around Luca's recovery. Luca accepting that he was worthy of love, of happiness, of a future untinged by the grief of his past. He had recovered, though. Not fully, but day by day, step by step, smile by smile, he was finally moving on, and she no longer believed his past had any ability to hurt them.

She curved her hand around his cheek, smiling and nodding, tears in her eyes. 'Yes,' she said, her voice high in pitch. 'Of course I'll marry you.'

Her eyes dropped then to the ring box he held, and the stunning, enormous solitaire diamond at its centre. He removed it and slid it onto her finger, and at that exact moment, the sun gave a last fiery burst before dipping behind the buildings on the horizon, casting rays of gold from her finger—a metaphor for their future if ever she'd seen one.

They didn't wait to marry. Six weeks was more than enough time to plan a simple ceremony saturated in love and affection. They chose his villa as the location, and Luca's assistant organised every last detail perfectly. There were marquees in case it rained, bohemian rugs on the ground so guests could take off their shoes and relax, exquisite food, prosecco in abundance, and a wonderful local band played music late into the night. They even played the song Imogen had written, that had been such a global success, and Luca sang along to it, grinning at Imogen, because those words were a part of the fabric of their past. They were a lesson, for both of them, about feelings, and love, and not wasting opportunities.

They would never waste their second chance; it was a pledge they'd made in their wedding vows, and intended to make to one another always.

When news broke that Imogen's first single had hit number one on the charts in several countries around the world, including the UK and America, one might have thought it was the most exciting news she'd received that day. And it was certainly wonderful, but nothing compared to the two bright lines that stared back at her from a little white pregnancy test.

It hadn't been planned, and yet they hadn't exactly been careful. There'd been slip-ups from time to time, when passion had moved them. Their honeymoon in Egypt had been so romantic, and when Imogen counted back the dates on her calendar, she suspected it had indeed been the night after their wedding that had placed new life inside of her.

She pressed a hand to her stomach, her heart fluttering in her chest, because the suspicion that had been growing for the last few weeks had finally been confirmed.

Only, they had a house full of people! Imogen's parents and sister had come to celebrate her success, as well as some friends from the bar, and Brock, the executive who'd discovered her. The house was full and brimming with excitement, Imogen's album playing in the background as they all talked excitedly about what the number one news might mean for her. 'Magazine covers, definitely.' Genevieve grinned, and Imogen's head swirled.

'Are you okay?' Luca caught her in the kitchen, making a cup of tea. 'You seem distracted.'

'Oh, I—guess I am.'

'It's overwhelming?' he said, lifting her chin.

She bit into her lip. 'It is, it is. It's just… I've hardly been able to think about the album, to be honest.'

His brows drew together. 'Really? Something more exciting on your mind?'

He'd said it as a joke, teasing her, but Imogen nodded, then quickly scanned the room to make sure they were still alone. She lifted up onto her tiptoes and whispered the news in his ear, then pulled back to see his reaction.

It was impossible to interpret all the feelings that flitted across his face, but her heart lifted to see him smile. 'For real?'

She nodded. 'You're happy?'

'Happy? I'm ecstatic. Oh, Imogen, it's the best news I've

ever heard. Aurora is the meaning of our lives, I know that, but there is so much I missed. So much I didn't get to support you through. I want to be there with you this time, through the pregnancy, the birth, the early days. I want to see Aurora become a big sister, to watch her beam with pride when she holds her little brother or sister. I'm beyond happy. Thank you.'

'I didn't do anything.'

'Oh, yes, you did. You brought me back to life—you stood by me and made me wake up, and now I am living some kind of fantasy. You are everything to me, my darling.'

She kissed him, her heart soaring, her happiness impossible to contain.

They were blessed with three more children, and Imogen had more than ten number one singles during her career. She became famous the world over, but none of that mattered to her. It was a by-product of doing what she loved, that was all. The people that really mattered to her were the people she'd loved and been loved by before her success; she never lost her grounding. From time to time, she went back to the bar that held such a special place in her heart, to sing for unsuspecting crowds. It always garnered an enormous response, and each time, as the night wore on, and social media lit up with the knowledge she was there, the place would get packed, but Imogen barely noticed. When she played at that place, it was like stepping back in time, and memories of her and Luca, meeting in the bar, beginning their story together there, were what she felt most of all.

When the bar went on the market, they bought it in an instant, and Imogen put her energy into turning it into a place for fledgling musicians to come and perform. She saw it as her duty to support those attempting to break into the industry, and her connections ensured record label executives and social media music influencers were always in attendance.

Ten years after their wedding, in a sign that the past was still very much a part of them, even when it could no longer hurt them, Luca and Imogen stood side by side as they opened a burns unit at a top hospital, in his family's name. With state-of-the-art technology and some of the best specialists in the world, the unit would become a beacon to those who needed it. His parents were gone, but never forgotten; his sister was someone they spoke of often. Indeed, a family photograph of Luca, his parents and sister now had pride of place in their home, and Imogen smiled at them whenever she walked by. She hoped that somehow they knew just how happy Luca was, how well he was doing, and that he'd found his way to a family that truly loved him, and always would.

* * * * *

If you couldn't get enough of
Billion-Dollar Secret Between Them
*then don't miss these other passion-fuelled stories
by Clare Connelly!*

The Sicilian's Deal for "I Do"
Contracted and Claimed by the Boss
His Runaway Royal
Pregnant Before the Proposal
Unwanted Royal Wife

Available now!

MILLS & BOON®

Coming next month

RUSH TO THE ALTAR
Abby Green

As if being prompted by a rogue devil inside herself, she blurted out, 'I couldn't help overhearing your conversation with your solicitor earlier.'

Corti's mouth tipped up on one side, and that tiny sign of humour added about another 1,000 percent to his appeal. For a second Lili felt dizzy.

'What was it you heard exactly?' He folded his arms now, but that only drew attention to the corded muscles of his forearms.

Lili swallowed. 'About how you have to marry and have an heir if you want to keep this villa.'

'And this is interesting enough for you to bring it up...why?'

The night breeze skated over Lili's bare skin, making it prickle into goose bumps. She was very aware that she was wearing just a swimsuit and a tiny towelling robe, her wet hair streaming down her back. The sense of daring fizzled away. She was being ridiculous.

She shook her head. 'It was nothing. I shouldn't have mentioned it.'

'But you did.'

There was a charge between them now. Something that felt almost tangible. 'Yes, I did.'

Continue reading

RUSH TO THE ALTAR
Abby Green

Available next month
millsandboon.co.uk

COMING
SOON!

We really hope you enjoyed reading this book.
If you're looking for more romance
be sure to head to the shops when
new books are available on

Thursday 22nd
May

To see which titles are coming soon, please visit
millsandboon.co.uk/nextmonth

MILLS & BOON

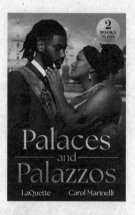
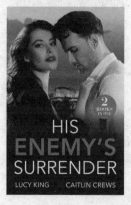
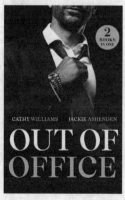

Afterglow Books is a trend-led, trope-filled list of books with diverse, authentic and relatable characters, a wide array of voices and representations, plus real world trials and tribulations. Featuring all the tropes you could possibly want (think small-town settings, fake relationships, grumpy vs sunshine, enemies to lovers) and all with a generous dose of spice in every story.

♪ @millsandboonuk

◎ @millsandboonuk

afterglowbooks.co.uk

#AfterglowBooks

For all the latest book news, exclusive content and giveaways scan the QR code below to sign up to the Afterglow newsletter:

SCAN ME

afterglow BOOKS

✈ International　　📖 Workplace romance

☯ Opposites attract　　🚫 Forbidden love

🌶 Spicy　　🌶 Spicy

OUT NOW

Two stories published every month. Discover more at:
Afterglowbooks.co.uk

LET'S TALK
Romance

For exclusive extracts, competitions
and special offers, find us online:

- 🄵 MillsandBoon
- 𝕏 @MillsandBoon
- 🄾 @MillsandBoonUK
- ♪ @MillsandBoonUK

Get in touch on 01413 063 232

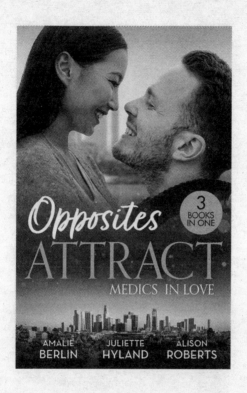

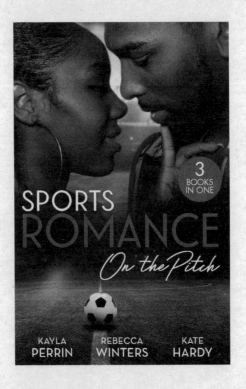